Ægir's Curse

Ægir's Curse

by

Leah Devlin

Penmorepress.com

Ægir's Curse by Leah Devlin

Copyright © 2013 Leah Devlin

All rights reserved. No part of this book may be used or reproduced by any means without the written permission of the publisher except in the case of brief quotation embodied in critical articles and reviews.

ISBN-13: 978-1-942756-44-6(Paperback)
ISBN -978-1-942756-45-3(e-book)

BISAC Subject Headings:
FIC014000 Fiction / Historical
FIC008000 Fiction / General
FIC031010 Fiction/ Thrillers / Crime

Cover work by Christine Horner
Editor: Chris Wozney

Address all correspondence to:

Penmore Press LLC
920 N Javelina Pl
Tucson. AZ 85748

Or visit our website at:
www.penmorepress.com

Dedication

For Pete

Author's Note

Woods Hole is a real village on the southwest corner of Cape Cod. However, all characters in this novel are purely fictional. Their resemblance to persons alive or dead is coincidental.

Woods Hole Women Swim with Mermaids was graffiti spray-painted under the bascule bridge in Woods Hole, Massachusetts, circa 2000.

Ægir's Curse

Prologue
Vinland, 1149

Thorsen mustered the last of his strength to heave Einar over the prow of the longboat. The dead man hit the dark water on his back, the heavy leather boots and air pocket in his tunic tilting him upright as if he were treading water and cajoling Thorsen to join him for a swim. As a boy, Einar had loved to swim, Thorsen remembered, even when other children were too timid to venture into the chill of the fjord. Now his cousin's corpse stared dull-eyed toward a muted orange sky. What past sin deserved such a punishment, a death of abdomen stabs, bloody coughs, and a fire in the head? Thorsen prayed that the tide would be swift and drag the body of his cousin from the inlet and out to rest in the sea realm of the god Ægir.

Einar had been the most skilled of navigators, measuring with his notched stick positions of the North Star and the sun, observing changes in bird flights, seaweeds, and water color to determine the location of the timber ships. Never with Einar on the steerboard did the Greenlanders sail by the inlet of their summer encampment. And it was he who had first found this camp with arrow-straight trees and forests of wild grapes. Now Einar, like the rest of the mariners, was gone, his body ravaged by a cruel plague.

When the first two mariners had collapsed in sickness, the men had cast torches into their dwellings to rid themselves of the contagion, as the red men, the Skraelings, watched the Greenlanders in bafflement from the shadows of the leaves. The Mainlanders' grain, for which they had traded furs of the white bear, must have been infected with plague, the men had agreed. So the Greenlanders had scrambled onto the longboats anchored in the inlet, leaving the grain stores and huts aflame. But the retreat came too late; another dead mariner, then another, had broken the still waters.

Thorsen struggled to prop himself against the single mast, his body wracked by convulsions. All was silent, except for a hushed scurry of rats below in the ballast stones and the chirp of insects in the marsh grass. Thorsen lamented. The timbers lashed to the deck would never be masts or wagons or beams of long houses in Greenland or Iceland. Casks of berries below deck would never be wine. His journey had been for naught. The blisters on his hands yesterday had begun to ooze blood. His hands, so horrible now, would never touch his beautiful Jorun again.

The pain in his head surged like storm waves, the same agony that had caused Didrik, who could not swim, to throw himself overboard, and Kjell to slice open his own throat. The new land must be cleansed of this sickness forever! Thorsen dragged himself toward the shards of jasper to light the longboat on fire.

Six days' sail from Vinland in eastern Greenland, Jorun had a premonition: the timber ships would not be returning over the western horizon. The unease was strong in her belly; this time, Thorsen was not returning. The plague that ravaged the coastal villages was not carried by birds, waves, or wind, but had been transported on the trading ships from the continent to

Ægir's Curse

Greenland. She was sure of it. That meant that the timber ships of the Greenlanders could have spread the sickness westward to Helluland, Markland, and possibly as far south as Vinland. Mercifully, a few outlying farms like hers and the monastery had been spared the agonizing death by their remoteness from the ports.

Jorun remembered the map and shuddered.

The summer before, after much convincing, Brother Vegar had shown Thorsen and Einar how to create maps, as the two mariners were intrigued by the priest's drawings of the Greenland and Iceland coastlines. That one night ... Thorsen and Einar leaning over her table, conjuring memories from their Vinland voyages, Thorsen drawing a large peninsula with bays, rivers, and inlets. The mead that Einar brought from the village was strong, and she drank too much of it. She wished that Einar would find a woman in the village, but he only wanted the woman who had been won from him by a gambler. Now he worked on the farm beside Thorsen and slept on a fur mat by the fire pit, when not navigating some ship across the northern seas.

"It is done!" Thorsen finally announced.

Jorun rose from where she had been lying by the fire and peered over the men's shoulders. The place looked to her like a bent arm. The sailors' camp, marked by a black circle of dye, was situated in the armpit. Tiny islands trailed off to the southwest, while two larger ones lay southeast in deeper waters. Thorsen pulled her onto his lap, remarking that he often dreamt of swimming with her off the sunny beaches of Vinland.

What would warm air and water feel like, surrounding her body? It was unimaginable, she concluded; her world had always been wet, windy, and cold. She dropped her face into Thorsen's neck, slid her hands inside his tunic, and drew in the scent of him: mead, fire smoke, and man. The winter winds howled fiercer. Her hands slid further beneath the leather.

Glaciers from the north were encroaching on once fertile pastures. The soil scarcely produced enough winter hay to feed the livestock. Even the richest plots that the Church had appropriated would not sprout wheat or barley. Trading vessels rarely came to their shores anymore, since walrus ivory and white bear furs were no longer valuable commodities to the Mainlanders.

And now the timber ships were not returning. Jorun told her oldest daughter to watch the young ones, then she wrapped a cape around her frail shoulders. She grabbed the hide map and pushed through the winds to the monastery on a barren promontory. At a door in the rampart, she asked for Brother Vegar. After some time, which she spent shivering against the stone wall, a wizened priest appeared.

She anxiously extended the map to him.

The old priest unrolled the hide and studied the fine workmanship. A singular black dot on the parchment was puzzling and he inquired as to its meaning.

"It is a place of forests, beaches, wineberries, and butternuts," Jorun answered. "A cache of coins is there to trade with the Skraelings, but they do not want coins; they only want swords. Take it, Brother. Hide it among your other maps, but no sailors should see it or return to Vinland. The place is cursed."

Chapter 1

Woods Hole

A tan woman waded into the still water and let her hands stroke the surface. She looked eastward. The sun was just peeking over the island of Nantucket. It felt primal to be alone on a beach just after dawn. Had she been an ancient Greek, she might have given thanks on that morning to the sea god, Poseidon. If she were Marquesan, like her assistant, Sara, she might have worshiped Tana'oa. If she were Norse, she might have made offerings to Ægir. But she was none of these, nor did she worship a pantheon of nature gods. She, Lindsey N., was simply a drunk, and so worshiped a singular deity called Higher Power.

For five summers on this anniversary, she had visited this same beach, regardless of weather, to reflect and offer thanks. She could not have wished for a more radiant morning. The day was Higher Power's gift, as the deity was generous and benevolent. She took a deep breath and dunked herself under the water. Emerging with a gasp, she warmed herself with a brisk swim out to Shark Rock, named for the ominous dorsal fin shape it displayed when viewed from the shore.

The tide was out and, once at the rock, she walked its perimeter, searching for the easiest path up. Shark Rock was a misnomer, she knew, as the black rock was actually an immense boulder deposited during the last Ice Age. The entire landmass of Cape Cod was a terminal moraine, the massive edge of a retreating ice sheet; the boulder, in comparison to the Cape, an insignificant speck of sand. And next to the boulder she was more insignificant still, a thought which was comforting.

The boulder was fringed by seaweed that moved like a dancer's skirt to a rhythm of the tides. There was only one way to the top where the slope was not too steep. She lifted her body over the seaweed border and climbed gingerly on all fours, avoiding the barnacles and mussels. For some time she stood, bewildered by the solitude of the ocean. A small patch of the rock was devoid of barnacles, so she sat for a while, gazing out toward the vast North Atlantic.

Five years ago, earlier on this day, she'd awoken from a blackout in a drug and alcohol rehabilitation center in Newport. She'd vaguely remembered heading from Woods Hole to a boat show in Rhode Island, but nothing else. How she arrived at the rehab was anyone's guess. For the entire thirty-day program, she was on edge from Glenlivet withdrawal. Her roommate had been a teenage prostitute named Maggie. Fearing incarceration for past crimes, Maggie escaped into the night, and Lindsey found herself overwhelmed by guilt and loss. To compound this, she, who had never once thought about children, found herself pregnant. At some time during the blackout, she'd had sex with a stranger.

Over time, some events of the blackout had emerged, and other pieces had later been filled in by her neighbor, Rob, who lived with his small son, Danny, on the houseboat next to hers. She'd found out that he'd driven her to the rehab hospital in Newport, but all the beds had been full, so they'd waited at a nearby hotel for a bed to open. There she'd seduced him; like most alcoholic women, she had a lot of experience in the bedroom. Rob was the father of her child.

Ægir's Curse

Thirty days later, she'd returned home to Woods Hole to find Maggie huddled fearfully on the deck of her houseboat. The girl had crossed paths with a violent john. That was Maggie's last trick.

Now five years sober, Higher Power had bestowed upon her and Maggie infinite gifts. She rose and perched on the highest precipice of Shark Rock, from which she had often watched her children, Maggie, Ava and Danny, leap joyfully into the waters below. She spoke her daily prayer aloud, though only seagulls and Higher Power would hear her—*Please keep me away from a drink just for this day, grant me serenity, and protect my family from harm. Amen.*

The muscles in her legs tightened and her knees bent. Her arms flung forward in triumph. She launched herself off the rock ledge and into the warm summer air. She hit the water with a resounding splash. That night at an AA meeting, Lindsey N. would be picking up a five-year chip.

Bergen, Norway

Adrian Arrano watched the old professor's fingers quiver, unsure if it was from the aftereffects of the stroke or from excitement. Professor Ragnar Ingvars slid his plate of boiled fish and potatoes aside, unzipped a flat leather satchel, and slid out an ancient parchment. Adrian quizzically raised an eyebrow, relieved that the stagnating dinner conversation might take a more interesting turn.

Earlier that afternoon, Professor Ingvars, Adrian's mentor for over a decade, had pushed his walker down a side aisle of a lecture hall to the podium where Adrian had just spoken, after two German graduate students had discussed the meaning of runic inscriptions. Adrian had only half-listened to the their interpretations, implausible and incorrect as they were, disconcerted by the expression on Ingvars's face, a look of suppressed excitement, the blue in his sagging eyes sparkling in a way that Adrian had never seen before.

Had a new rune stone been unearthed, perhaps while tearing up the ground for a condo development in the expanding suburbs of Oslo? A new bog man found in a Danish swamp? Another Viking hoard from the army of Guthrum been excavated in England? Adrian's imagination jumped to the various possibilities.

Ingvars commended Adrian on the informative lecture and then, after the graduate students departed, asked insistently, "Can you please come to dinner tonight at my apartment? It's quite important."

Adrian inwardly winced. He had planned to call that attractive Italian woman, a Norse art historian from Positano whom he had met at a poster session the night before, and have drinks with her. He hesitated.

Ingvars rested his hand on Adrian's shoulder. "I could have another stroke at any time. We really need to talk. Something I want you to handle, should I become incapacitated."

There was a certain urgency in the old man's voice. Yes, Adrian concluded, a new rune had been unearthed. And his own research of late was drying up. Four years into the tenure process, this was an opportunity that could not be passed up.

"Of course, sir," Adrian had responded. "Name the time."

The ancient parchment, hermetically sealed in plastic, was gently laid between glasses of aquavit, dinner plates, and a bowl of fruit. Adrian studied it intently as Ingvars explained. The map had been discovered in a monastery outbuilding in eastern Greenland by a local historian named Jens Tryggvesen. The parchment had been tucked into the binding of a larger book.

Ægir's Curse

Until its authenticity was verified, only Tryggvesen and Ingvars could know of the map's existence, the old man explained. The two scholars had promised one another not to announce it publicly until the laboratory results were confirmed and the manuscript was completed and reviewed by some trusted experts in the field. This was why Ingvars had turned to Adrian, his young American colleague, who was attending the Scandinavian Studies and Historical Society meeting, to serve as an objective referee.

With difficulty Adrian forced his attention from the parchment back to Ingvars. "Surely this has to be hoax, a forgery by someone familiar with maps from that period," he remarked with skepticism. "But this forger's very good."

A slight smile appeared on Ingvars's thin, cracked lips, and he shook his head.

"This can't be authentic," Adrian protested, confused. The Vinland map at Yale—which was obviously a forgery—and the Skálholt map that showed a Promontorium Winlandiae were the only ones; everyone in their field of research knew that.

Ingvars pointed to a corner of the map where a tiny bit of leather had been excised. "Two different labs have radiocarbon-dated it. One in Switzerland and one in Germany. I didn't tell them the source of the parchment, of course, but both labs corroborated the others' results. The material is reindeer hide that dates from 1150, plus or minus twenty years. The DNA from the reindeer is genetically identical to extant reindeer populations in Greenland and is genetically dissimilar to other reindeer subspecies from Canada, Scandinavia, or Russia. The dye was also made from ores found in Greenland. One thing is clear; this map was made in Greenland in the mid-1100s."

Adrian frowned dubiously. "Besides the Skálholt map and the bogus map at Yale, I've never read of a map pinpointing Vinland. All that I've read were speculations about New Brunswick, Maine, and every other place down the north

Atlantic seaboard, including New York City, as the alleged site of Vinland. Also, the sagas describing Vinland are vague and largely fictitious." His eyes returned to the map. "I know exactly where this is. I vacationed there as a kid."

"Yes, the detail is amazing for that period." Ingvars's knobby finger pointed toward the black dot. "Possibly this mark, this small inlet within the large bay, was a staging area for other expeditions, or a permanent settlement?"

"Possibly. But why was the map so obviously hidden up to this point in time?"

"Maybe someone didn't want Vinland to be found?"

Adrian squirmed in his chair, struggling for the right words. "Sir, couldn't I be involved in the writing of the manuscript? I could really use another paper right now. I go up for tenure in only two years. A find of this importance would seal the deal."

"I'm sorry, Adrian, Jens was quite frank with me," Ingvars stated in a firm, paternal tone. "We're to be the only two authors. He doesn't want the article diluted by multiple authors."

"Please! Perhaps I could write up a section comparing this map to the Skálholt map? Or visit the site of the black dot and send you photos of this place? It's not far from my home in New Hampshire. If there is anything I can do, sir...." Adrian was disgusted by the whining tone in his own voice.

"We could really use your help as an informal referee before it goes to the editorial board at *Antiquity*. As you know, that journal has a very rigorous process of peer review. We'd be glad to mention your role in the acknowledgements section."

Adrian nodded solemnly and sighed in resignation. "Okay, I'm happy to critique a draft of the manuscript when you're done with it."

"Thank you, Adrian. I'll look forward to your comments. I want this paper to be perfect. It is to be my opus!" Ingvars replied cheerfully, unaware of the dour expression on Adrian's face. Adrian took a last sip of aquavit and excused himself for the bathroom.

Leaning on the sink, he searched his face in the mirror. From his father of Spanish descent, he had inherited the man's large, expressive eyes, full lips, and soft brown hair. He watched himself take a few deep, slow breaths, which he hoped would stop the surges of blood in his head. The revelations of the map had caused a quick spike of adrenaline and a racing of his heart; but he reminded himself that this could be another Piltdown Man scenario, and buying into such hoaxes destroyed professional careers. Yet Ragnar Ingvars was the top Viking scholar in the world and would only test his samples at the most reputable, state-of-the art forensics labs. The fact that the labs in both Zurich and Bonn had confirmed one another's findings in a blind test was strong evidence for the map's authenticity. Nor was there a glimmer of jest in Ingvars's eyes; the old man was a believer.

Tryggvesen and Ingvars would coauthor the manuscript. And what a groundbreaking manuscript it would be! Adrian would merely serve as an informal referee before it went to the editorial board of the journal *Antiquity*. He would be mentioned in the acknowledgements, but who read the fucking acknowledgements section? Like the Promotion and Tenure Committee would really give a shit about a picayune acknowledgement! His last two manuscripts had been rejected. He had no clue which journals would accept them at this point. What if he had to stoop to publishing them in a local historical society newsletter? The P and T Committee would never regard newsletters as legitimate, refereed publications. To add insult to injury, his application for a travel grant to the archives at the University of Minnesota and a museum in Iceland had been denied. Instead, his dean had awarded travel grants to two ass-kissing professors, a political scientist and a mathematician, whose researches were esoteric bullshit. If he was not awarded tenure, he'd be teaching Introduction to Western Civilization to imbeciles at a community college for the next forty years!

Adrian continued to stare into the mirror. All he saw was the desperate face of a floundering academic. His groveling before the professor had been pathetic. True, he had inherited his father's outward appearance; but his inner fuel, his energy, and his ambition came from his Danish mother. Viking blood flowed in his veins, he reminded himself. And Vikings were ruthless opportunists. His confidence surged. Jens Tryggvesen had told Ingvars that he did not want the article "diluted by multiple authors." Adrian saw the logic in that. What if there were only ... one author?

Adrian fumbled in his blazer pocket and found the sleeping pills that he had reserved for his flight back to the States. In that instant he decided to return to the kitchen and make the professor a pot of tea to help him to sleep.

Chapter 2

The Woods Hole Passage

"Thirty-eight days," Jessie said to herself.

She sifted through a crumpled shoe box of shells on the galley table, bypassing the Scotch bonnets, Florida cones, slipper shells, and apple murexes. Finally she spotted it, a shell from *Busycon contrarium*, the lightning whelk. She tapped sand from the shell and inspected it again. The lightning whelk was perfect. A small hole in its whorl, made by some burrowing worm, was just the right size to thread with string. Her salty fingers nimbly tied the whelk to a longer necklace of shells. It would be the last one added to the chain. Jessie hung the shell necklace across the windshield of her small boat where it chimed quietly as the boat slid over the swells.

"Thirty-eight shells, thirty-eight days at sea."

Except for intermittent hops to the coast for fuel and provisions, Jessie had spoken to no one over that time. Bursts of wind, the splash of waves against the hull, and the chug of the engine were the only sounds. *Mermaid*'s single forty horsepower outboard had churned faithfully up the eastern coastline without as much as a cough or sputter. The sky had been unusually kind. Only once was *Mermaid* delayed, by the fringe of a hurricane that forced a retreat into a narrow creek draped with Spanish moss somewhere in South Carolina.

At the moment *Mermaid* cruised slowly alongside Naushon Island. Months earlier Jessie had found the sun-faded, forgotten boat on cinderblocks in a back corner of a boat yard in St. Augustine, just up the highway from the marine laboratory where she had lived and worked. To pay for the boat and a new engine, she'd sold her old clunker of a car, and she'd depleted most of her savings from her graduate student stipend. But it was well worth it. The boat had originally been called *Vagabond*, but over many weekends she'd scrapped off the old paint and with a stencil added the new name, *Mermaid*. She'd also installed racks for dive tanks, built a wood frame to house gasoline canisters, and bought two large plastic bins to serve as port and starboard dive lockers. On the same day that she'd defended her dissertation and collected the signatures from the faculty on her dissertation committee, her worldly possessions—clothes, laptop, sleeping bag, box of shells, dive equipment, as well as canned food and cases of water—were loaded onto *Mermaid*, the engine fired up, and the boat aimed northward.

The days and nights of the voyage had passed like a shuffling of playing cards. During the day she slumped down in the captain's chair, her hand moving in small arcs at the top of the wheel, a lukewarm water bottle clasped between her knees. To escape the heat of midday, she snorkeled around the hull, or clipped on her old BC—buoyancy compensator vest—and scuba tank, and followed the anchor chain downward. Occasionally she spotted a flounder or grouper, but for the most part she might have been hovering over the lifeless dunes of a desert. The dives had ended when she used up the last of the air near Cape May, New Jersey.

At night, Jessie slept outside on a rumpled sleeping bag when the cabin became too stuffy. If she was close to shore, a citronella candle glowed at her side to drive away the mosquitoes that showed no diminution in their ferocity as she moved up the coast. She knew nothing of northern bugs, animals, plants, or people. Prior to this, her most northerly excursion had been to see Civil War monuments in Atlanta on a high school field trip. On sleepless nights she stared skyward, questioning her motives for choosing such a distant place to take a job. After all, there were closer marine labs along the coasts of the Carolinas and Virginia. Still, throughout her voyage, the same constellations that she had seen during her youth, when she had fled the trailer park and slept in the dunes, lit up the black sky.

The Cape Cod village suddenly appeared like a hazy mirage, and Jessie let *Mermaid* drift in neutral. Countless times she had studied the website for the town on the peninsula, or zoomed in using Google Earth so that the buildings of the marine laboratory, oceanographic institution, aquarium, and central pond were now familiar beacons.

She was jittery about reentering the human world. Worse, she would have to dress. During the voyage her only attire had been two bathing suits that were scrubbed in a cooking pot to remove salt and sweat, then anchored down to dry with dive weights so as not to be lost in a sudden gust. They were now as frayed and transparent as seaweed. She stepped down into the cabin and pulled on a pair of shorts and a T-shirt, the fabric chaffing and unfamiliar against her skin.

Between *Mermaid* and the seaside village flowed treacherous rip currents, the swirling eddies reminiscent of the legendary maelstrom off the Lofoton Islands that had sucked whole Viking longships into the icy gyre. She was convinced that she had read, while waiting endless hours on the vinyl chairs of the hospital, every nautical book ever written. Dog-eared paperbacks of Melville, Verne, Stevenson, Cousteau, and Carson were packed into the bottom of her seabag. The idling boat, trapped in the current, drifted northeasterly. For an insane, fleeting moment an impulse to steer the boat into the

North Atlantic overtook her, but instead she turned the wheel toward her port of call.

She gripped the throttle and shoved it forward; the jolt of the engine pushed her deep into the captain's chair. For an instant the prow aimed skyward; the hull rose out of the water and careened with a loud shimmy across the Woods Hole Passage. The engine roared in exhilaration, pushing *Mermaid* through the spray. Buoys of a no-wake zone appeared to either side so she eased off on the throttle and allowed *Mermaid* to drift toward a bascule bridge. Her escape was nearly complete. Jessie McCabe prayed that the village of Woods Hole would be a place of sanctuary.

Bergen

It must have been the combination of aquavit and chamomile tea, Professor Ingvars thought, that so suddenly brought on such heavy drowsiness. Perhaps it was also the strain of leaving the apartment to attend the conference, which this year had finally been held at his proud university. Over the past years the overbearing Swedes on the conference organizing committee had insisted that the annual conference be held in Stockholm, but this year they had finally relented and permitted the conference to be located in Norway.

Since the stroke, Ingvars had spent his time in pajamas and robe, working on a laptop and convalescing in his small apartment. It had been a struggle to get on his suit and push the walker to the various classrooms in time to hear the lectures during the conference, but it had been well worth the effort. In every passageway he had been stopped by young scholars asking to him to autograph copies of his earlier books, in particular his best-selling volume, *The Vikings in the British Isles*. The interaction with the students had been energizing, and they had been eager to tell him of their research projects.

Ægir's Curse

Some moments earlier, Adrian had assisted Ingvars's slow shuffle into the bedroom, the young man's hand gently supporting his elbow and lifting his legs onto the bed. Ingvars fought to stay awake, for there was something else he needed to tell Adrian—something very important, but what was it? Muted clinks of glass and running water sounded from the kitchen as Adrian soaped up the dinner dishes quietly, so as not to disturb Ingvars's passage to sleep.

How long had he known Adrian? the old professor wondered. Forever it seemed. Yes, he remembered. He had received an email from teen-aged Adrian. On a vacation with his father, the boy had visited Dighton Rock in Massachusetts. A digital photo of the rock had been attached to the message. Adrian's email explained that he had read every book every written on the Vikings, including all of Ingvars's texts, and had been trying to teach himself to read runic and speak Danish using language tapes. Ingvars remembered trying to decipher the inscriptions on the rock, his magnifying glass hovering over the photo, but he'd finally had to report back with genuine regret that from the weathering of the rock, the inscriptions were unintelligible. To encourage the boy, he'd forwarded Adrian some additional readings and information on undergraduate programs in Scandinavian history, as well as summer language programs in Iceland and Norway. This initial communication had been followed by intermittent emails that revealed that the teenager was being raised by his father, a carpenter, in a rural town in Vermont, his mother having died of breast cancer.

Some years later, he'd received an email from Adrian, saying that he was doing his junior year abroad in Oslo and was traveling with a friend around Norway over the semester break. Could he visit Ingvars at the University of Bergen? Ingvars had envisioned Adrian as a brooding, bookish scholar; instead, the long-haired American undergraduate who'd excitedly shaken his hand in his office doorway was affable—and had a lovely traveling companion hanging on his arm.

The sound of running water stopped, and Ingvars heard the close of the dishwasher. His eyelids were too heavy to open. Suddenly he remembered. Jens Tryggvesen—he needed to give Adrian Tryggvesen's contact information in the event he had another stroke, especially as the mini-strokes were coming with greater frequency. Where was his cell phone? Tryggvesen's email and phone number were in his cell phone.

Footsteps approached. Sleep descended upon the old professor like a heavy black storm cloud.

Chapter 3

Woods Hole

Mermaid was small enough to pass under the bascule bridge, yet it idled in a narrow channel on the orders of a bridge attendant above. A huge yellow gate on the bridge shrilled as the attendant heaved it into a closed position, blocking the flow of car and pedestrian traffic. Ducking back into a control booth, the attendant pushed a series of buttons that activated a series of counterweights, and the bridge reared skyward like a gaping mouth.

In front of *Mermaid* lay the small circle of Eel Pond. The boat glided slowly through the channel, allowing Jessie time to read graffiti sprayed on the bridge's underbelly. Most were proclamations of teenage love and anarchical slogans. But one scrawl of red spray paint caught Jessie's eye: *Woods Hole Women Swim with Mermaids*. A portentous greeting. The bridge slammed down with a thundering clang behind *Mermaid*'s transom, the yellow gate opened, and tourists and cars resumed their slow crawl across the bridge.

Eel Pond was occupied by wooden dinghies, skiffs, and sailboats, and *Mermaid* eased along the backside of shops and restaurants toward the marine laboratory. Months before, when Jessie had decided to accept a job at the lab, she'd inquired about a boat slip. The prompt sending of a modest processing fee and copy of the boat's registration had guaranteed *Mermaid* a slip against the stone seawall enclosing the pond. She tied the vessel up at slip number sixteen as specified in the confirmation letter.

The first priority was finding an ATM somewhere in the village. Jessie's cash was gone and she badly needed a hot meal, as her last few had consisted of soggy pretzels and warm lemonade, the last of her provisions. For weeks she had subsisted on cans of tuna, beef stew, or soup heated over a propane grill. Her greatest fear had not been capsizing at sea, or running out of gas, but losing her can-opener, which she'd finally tied to a cabinet handle to give herself peace of mind. Besides a meal, her other craving was for a drink with ice cubes.

The second priority was a shower, as the sink in the cruiser was too shallow to adequately shampoo her hair, and it had not been washed in days. Her short, salty hair spiked upward like the spines of a lionfish.

Ice cubes, shower, and a hot meal, Jessie fantasized.

"That boat is longer than sixteen feet," a voice stated imperiously, startling Jessie.

A mixed race teenager, hands on her hips, stood on the seawall and suspiciously eyed the boat. "That boat is longer than sixteen feet," she repeated in her raspy voice.

Jessie answered cautiously, "Yeah, it's twenty-two feet."

"The maximum length allowed at the dock is sixteen feet," the teenager informed her.

"No one told me that when I registered it!"

The girl cocked an eyebrow at the woman's flustered tone. "Hey, don't sweat it. I don't give a shit." She pulled a plastic ziplock bag from her surfer shorts, removed cigarettes, and knocked one out of the pack. While flicking a lighter, the girl examined the boat. "I know everything in the world about boats. I'm the mayor of Woods Hole," she said with a smirk.

Ægir's Curse

Jessie relaxed a bit. The teenager was just a sarcastic local, eager to give a newcomer a hard time. "Okay, Mayor. Then where is a marina with public showers?"

The girl blew smoke rings into the air and finally responded, "Not in this town."

"I really need a shower!" Jessie said emphatically.

"Dave's Marina has a bath house, but it's about a quarter mile up the coast. I'm going there if you want to follow." The girl gestured toward a purple and yellow Jet Ski.

"There's not a marina here?" Jessie asked, her frustration growing. The last thing she wanted to do was untether her boat before getting some food. Still, she couldn't walk into her new place of employment and introduce herself to her new boss reeking of salt and sweat.

"Nope," the girl responded decisively.

Jessie weighed her limited options and sighed. "Okay. I'll follow."

The teenager climbed off the seawall and onto her Jet Ski. "Are you going to work here?"

"Yes." Jessie leaned to untie the lines.

"I used to work here." The girl zipped up a yellow float-coat while a cigarette dangled from her lips.

"So you're a budding scientist?"

"No, I hate fuckin science. It was just a job." She pushed an electric starter on the Jet Ski and let it quietly rumble while she untied herself from a cleat.

The tracks and scars on the girl's forearms gave Jessie pause.

"Are you coming or what?" the teenager asked impatiently.

Jessie reluctantly turned the key in the ignition. "Yeah, I'm coming," she answered uneasily.

The girl jerked down the throttle and the Jet Ski blasted away from the seawall and swerved wildly between the buoys and skiffs. Its wake bucked *Mermaid* and tugged the other boats at their tethers.

Bolting from the control booth, the bridge attendant lurched over the railing of the bridge and glared down. Jessie predicted that the girl would make a run for it and gun it all the way to the channel, but surprisingly the teenager slowed and coasted toward the bridge.

"Maggie, slow down!" the bridge attendant shrieked.

Jessie next expected some obscenity from the teenager, or perhaps a raised middle finger pointing upward at the attendant and pedestrians poised along the railing to watch the commotion. Instead with a bombastic sweep of her arm, Maggie cupped her hand behind her ear.

"What?" the teenager called.

"I've told you this a thousand times! This is a no-wake zone," yelled the bridge attendant.

"What?" Maggie repeated as if deaf. She grinned brashly at Jessie, floating behind in *Mermaid*.

"I know you can hear me, you smart-ass punk! I said slow down! I'm going to call the police! Or worse... Dr. Nolan!"

With another theatrical gesture, Maggie touched her fingers to her lips and extended her arm, blowing a defiant kiss upward at the bridge attendant. Then she yanked the throttle down, the Jet Ski shot under the bridge, into the no-wake-zone and currents of the Woods Hole Passage. In seconds, the Jet Ski was gone.

Jessie slumped with dread in the captain's chair. She had travelled thirty-eight days and God knows how many nautical miles only to follow a teenage drug addict to a dubious place called Dave's Marina.

Some minutes later, the Jet Ski appeared in the distance. Through the shimmering heat, Jessie spotted a town to the north which she knew from her GPS to be Falmouth. Maggie idled off a beach of sand and stone, waiting for *Mermaid* to catch up. She circled back to the starboard side of the boat.

"The marina is up that creek through the marsh," Maggie called over the rumble of the engines. She gestured toward a stone breakwater.

"How deep is the creek?" Jessie shouted back, concerned about scratching *Mermaid's* hull.

"Believe me, way bigger boats than yours cruise in and out of here all the time."

"*Mermaid* might get stuck in the mud when the tide changes!" Jessie started to argue, but Maggie didn't wait for a response. She gunned the throttle and swung around the tip of the breakwater and into the mouth of the creek. Over the breakwater only the girl's ash-blonde head with beaded dreadlocks was visible moving toward a green marsh. Again, the teenager was gone.

Maggie was right, Jessie realized. The creek was plenty deep. As *Mermaid* pushed further into the marsh, the scent of saltwater, mud, and sand stirred up memories of the mangrove swamps on her island home. High walls of *Spartina* grass rose along the sides of the boat, the green shafts beaded with small black snails, some species of periwinkle. The periwinkles were probably *Littorina*, but she'd check on it later. The holes in the mudbanks belonged to fiddler crabs, just as they did in the south. A quiet excitement arose at the thought of discovering the invertebrates of Cape Cod.

The meandering creek eventually opened into an inlet. Jessie squinted into harsh glints of sunlight bouncing off the water, searching for Maggie. A surprisingly large marina spread across the entire northern side of the water, comprised of a bait and tackle shop and an assortment of space metal buildings and storage sheds. A few sunburnt men were sharing a six-pack on the porch of the bait store. A pickup truck and trailer eased down a slippery boat ramp to retrieve a bass boat floating in the shallows. A low building across the parking lot near some dumpsters had the look of a bathhouse.

Most of the boat slips were occupied by some form of small speedboat, sailboat, or cruiser. At the far end of the dock, near a cluster of scrub pines, were two old houseboats similar to those that lined the canals of Florida. A magnificent white motor yacht floated next to the houseboats. A glittery cigar boat was tethered to the yacht.

Both arms moving in slow wide waves above her head, Maggie stood on one of the old houseboats, the one with a pirate flag attached to a lanyard. Next to Maggie stood a slender, handsome man, wearing a bathing suit and a straw cowboy hat.

"Tie up here," Maggie shouted, pointing to a cleat on the dock. "Next to *Annie*."

Jessie turned her wheel and guided *Mermaid* in.

Maggie turned to the man. "Rob, she's just driven her boat from... where are you from?"

"St. Augustine," Jessie answered, coiling a nylon line around a cleat.

"She needs a shower," Maggie explained to the man. "She's come to work at the lab."

"Okay then," Rob acquiesced. "Show her the shower on the *Anne Bonny*. There are too many spiders in the bathhouse." He spoke with a Boston accent.

"Thank you!" Jessie grabbed her seabag and approached Maggie. She paused to admire the transom of the houseboat. A ferocious female pirate wielding a saber was painted across it, and old-fashioned letters read *Anne Bonny*. "Very cool."

This prompted Maggie to describe the fate of the pirate queens, Anne Bonny and her companion, Mary Read. "In 1720 both lady pirates were acquitted and escaped the noose at Gallows Point, Jamaica, by 'pleading their bellies,'" Maggie

Ægir's Curse

expounded. "Mary died in prison during childbirth, but Anne eluded the hangman's noose and escaped into obscurity."

Jessie had read *A General History of the Pyrates*, allegedly written by Daniel Defoe under a pseudonym, and knew the legend of the two pirate queens. "And Calico Jack Rackham and all of the male pirates were hung at Gallows Point," she elaborated.

Maggie grinned widely, pleased to find a compatriot who knew pirate lore. "Yo ho!"

"Yo ho, Mayor." Jessie smiled in anticipation of a warm shower.

Dave's Marina

From the shadows of a boat repair shed, Lindsey squinted through the afternoon heat at Maggie and a stranger on the deck of the *Annie*. Her attention briefly returned to a jumble of wires in a radar system on the workbench. Exasperated, she wiped sweat from her face, leaving a swipe of motor oil across her forehead. If she had only remembered to screw the protective housing on the radar last night, she would not be fixing it for a second time! Sometime during the night, Tiger, a feral cat from the marsh, had hopped through the broken window of the shed, shattered a jar of metal screws, hacked a hairball onto the floor, and decided to chew and shred the exposed wires of the radar unit.

Lindsey's wary gaze returned to the houseboat. The stranger, in her mid-twenties, was slightly older than the other lost souls that Maggie occasionally brought home from her Narcotics Anonymous meetings. The stranger's age was worrisome, as she was old enough be a cop, a lawyer, or worse yet, an investigative reporter. It was a relief that high-definition security cameras had been installed around the boats some months ago. At her initial suggestion of purchasing them, Rob had dismissed the idea outright and accused her—yet again—of paranoia, but another pair of eyes, if only electronic, gave her peace of mind. Lindsey unclipped her leather tool belt, hung it on a hook over the workbench, and headed toward the dock.

Maggie noticed Lindsey approach and informed the stranger, "The *Anne Bonny* is Lindsey's. She won't mind if you use it. We don't live on it anymore."

"Jessie's a new biologist at the marine lab," Maggie explained to Lindsey as she stepped onto the houseboat. "She's going to use the shower in the *Annie* since she's been at sea for weeks."

For an uncomfortable stretch of time Lindsey eyed the young woman. It seemed unlikely now that Jessie was one of Maggie's NA acquaintances, as she was far too healthy, athletic, and alert. Nor was she likely a lawyer or reporter, as she was far too tanned for a person with a desk job. Lindsey scanned the boat. *Mermaid* had clearly logged some time at sea, was full of dive equipment, and had a Florida registration sticker on the bow, and the stranger had the impoverished look of a new academic. Yes, it was possible that the woman was actually a biologist.

"Alright," Lindsey finally agreed. She glanced down at her black, oily hands. "The door's locked. Open it, Maggie. My hands are too dirty."

Maggie grasped the doorknob on the *Anne Bonny* and held her hand motionless on it. After a second there was a whir and a click. She released her grip, and then the door swung open under its own power. Astonished, Jessie stared at the doorknob for a moment.

"There's no keyhole!" Jessie exclaimed, mystified.

Lindsey shrugged dismissively. "It's a simple thing, really. It just reads handprints."

Ægir's Curse

Soon after, Jessie stood in the doorway of the *Anne Bonny*, struck by the scent of dry teak, salt pond, and motor oil. In the salon, fishnets with plastic lobsters drooped from the ceiling like those found in cheap seafood restaurants. A faded futon bed leaned against one bulkhead. A disassembled outboard engine was spread across newspaper on the galley table, and a car stereo system was in pieces on the counter. Black pirate flags of Blackbeard, Calico Jack Rackham, and Captain Kidd hung from cabinets in the galley. Lining the dusty bookcases were pirate heads made of coconut shells, seashells from local waters, plastic blunderbusses, toy parrots, and skull candles. At any other time Jessie would have lingered over the tacky knickknacks, but she was simply too hungry and grungy to think rationally. Through the window, she noticed the mechanic woman pacing the dock, eyeing *Mermaid*. Jessie was unnerved. She dropped her seabag onto the bed in a cabin, peeled off her clothes, and stepped quickly into the head.

After a hurried shower, Jessie put on her last clean shirt and pair of shorts and stepped outside to find Maggie and Lindsey on *Mermaid*. *Mermaid* had been her home for so long, uninvited guests were an unwelcome prospect. Worse, Maggie was smoking a cigarette while standing next to the gas canisters! And Lindsey—with her filthy hands—was on all fours under the helm. Oil smudges covered the instrument panel!

"What are you looking at?" Jessie asked with a strained smile.

"The electronics," Lindsey answered frankly. "This is the best design of a twenty-two footer that I've ever seen." With a groan, she got off her hands and knees and stared thoughtfully at the instrument panel for a moment longer. "C'mon. Let's get you fed." She slung her leg over the gunwale of *Mermaid* and headed toward the white yacht in the next slip.

The *Mary Read* was a sixty-five-foot transoceanic motor yacht of the latest design. Constructed of white fiberglass, the sleek boat had two decks topped and a flybridge. Jessie was dazzled, for she had never been on a yacht before; her own experience was only with small dive boats. The interior was a deep mahogany and well lit by numerous portholes. The salon was full of feminine clutter; towels, sandals, sunscreen, dolls, and comic books were strewn across bulbous leather sofas. She followed Maggie to the galley, passing a tiny girl in a princess gown playing on an oriental carpet. The small princess looked up at Jessie, smiled demurely, and then returned to her fairy figurines and pink toy castle. Lindsey glanced wordlessly over her shoulder at her guest, then focused on the adjacent houseboat. Jessie followed Lindsey's gaze out the window. The mechanic seemed fixated on Rob in the cowboy hat, smoking a cigar on the bow of the *Green Monster*.

Without a knock, a tall, dark woman in a black karate uniform barged through the door and swept into the salon of the *Mary Read*. "Hey, Curly." The woman bent and ruffled her hand through the little girl's jet-black hair.

The girl grinned. "Hi, Sara."

"Is the file completed, Lin?" Sara asked.

Lindsey's eyes remained focused on the *Green Monster*. "Yes, but it's too large to send. You know I don't like sending certain types of stuff by email."

"I know that," Sara retorted. "That's why I had to drive all the way over way here."

Lindsey turned from the window. "All three point two miles."

Jessie suddenly felt Sara studying her. An awkward silence fell over the salon and galley.

Maggie shot a quick glance at Lindsey, who said apologetically, "Sara, this is…" but she had forgotten the new arrival's name.

Maggie interrupted, "Sara, this is Jessie. Jessie, this is Sara. Lin is a dimwit! She remembers nothing!"

Sara stepped threateningly toward Maggie. "And you owe her your life, so put a lid on it!"

Maggie flinched at the reprimand and retreated toward the refrigerator.

"Jessie's come to work at the marine lab," Lindsey said to defuse the tension.

Sara's glare faded and her attention returned to the young scientist. "Really? Which one?" she asked, genuinely interested.

"I'm starting a postdoc in a reef ecology lab," Jessie answered. "I work on wound repair cells in sponges and corals."

"That's cool." Sara nodded approvingly.

"Here, Jessie," Maggie offered, still subdued. She set two plates loaded with cold cuts and macaroni and cheese on the galley table.

Jessie was anxious to eat but found it impossible not to watch Sara, who moved with the dangerous grace of a panther. Geometric tattoos ran down the woman's arms to the back of her hands. Her sandaled feet were entwined with ink spirals, the Polynesian tattoos looking like lace socks. Sara glanced again at Jessie, and then sat down in front of a computer.

The small girl approached Jessie. "That's pretty," the child complimented. She rubbed her finger over Jessie's rope bracelet.

"What's your name?" Jessie asked the girl.

"Ava," she answered. "Where do you live?"

"On a boat."

"So do I. Where did you come from?"

"A small town called Toulossa. In Florida."

"Disney World's in Florida. I'm going there some day." Ava turned excitedly toward Lindsey. "Right, Mom?"

"Right, honey," Lindsey answered. "Someday."

"If your workaholic mother would ever take a day off," Sara quipped under her breath. She swiveled toward the center of the room. "The computer's not turning on."

"Some software's been changed," Lindsey explained.

"Can I show her, Mom?" Ava yanked on the belt loops of Lindsey's cutoffs. "Can I?"

"Sure."

"What's the computer called today?" Ava asked her mother.

"Antonio," answered Lindsey.

Ava squeezed herself in front of the computer and climbed onto Sara's knee. "Watch very carefully, Sara." She leaned toward the gray monitor, her lips slowly commanding, "Antonio, wake up."

The computer hummed on without a touch to any button. Ava grinned at Sara, her new teeth shining like tiny white pebbles.

"Good afternoon, ladies," the computer responded in a seductive Spanish accent.

Sara hooted with delight. "You're kidding me! It sounds just like him!"

Maggie muttered to Jessie, "Lin thinks that she has a chance with Antonio Banderas."

"I might meet him someday," Lindsey commented wistfully. "Sometimes I meet celebrities. Who knows?"

Maggie rolled her eyes. "Dream on."

The talking computer was intriguing, but Jessie remained in her seat, her nervousness growing. The food in her stomach was starting to congeal. The boat mechanic must have been hired by some millionaire to be the boat's caretaker. Clearly the man had some amazing software, or was perhaps a computer guru himself, and these women were messing about on his computer.

"No freaking way!" Sara blurted, laughing. "I don't believe this!"

Jessie craned her neck toward the computer.

Lindsey grinned. "Yes freaking way."

Ægir's Curse

Intrigued in spite of herself, Jessie moved next to the Polynesian at the computer. A cyber Antonio strolled across the same mahogany boat salon in which they were standing. Jessie turned to see if Maggie was watching this remarkable software program, but the teenager was preoccupied by loading another heap of macaroni onto her plate. Awaiting the next command, cyber Antonio sat on the leather sofa and started reading a comic. Jessie eyed the folders on the computer's desktop. NASDAQ, BioCorp Stock, TIAA-CREF, Vanguard, Neurotox Data, Epilepsy Data, Publications.

Ava stretched belly down across Sara's lap and reached for Jessie's ankle bracelets. "I like this one too, Jessie," the little girl said.

Sara's coal-black eyes watched Ava's fingers stroke the leather strips and beads encircling Jessie's ankle. Jessie became rigid; Sara's gaze slowly wandered up her leg, hip, waist, breasts, neck, and, just briefly, their eyes locked. Sara smiled pleasantly. Jessie quickly looked away and hurried back to the table.

Sara looked at the time on her smartphone. "Where's the file, Lin? I'm going to be late for karate."

"Antonio, open the PowerPoint epilepsy doc," Lindsey ordered.

"But of course, señora," Antonio answered.

A PowerPoint icon appeared on the monitor and Sara slid a flash drive into a USB port. While waiting to copy the file, Sara drew squiggles down Ava's back, causing the girl to giggle and squirm.

The folders on the computer triggered an unease flutter in Jessie's chest. Were these women stealing the boat owner's data? And what about the car stereo and boat engine parts in the *Anne Bonny*? Were they disassembled to etch away serial numbers? And why had the mechanic been examining the wiring of the navigation system on *Mermaid* so intently? To see how to unwire it... to steal it?

Everything about the marina was a tad off-kilter. Though these women were certainly friendly and generous, a quick escape from the marina was imperative. She'd return to the village of Woods Hole and search for apartment rentals. It was the peak of the summer season, so rents in the village would be high until they changed in September. Perhaps her income could be supplemented by chartering her dive boat?

West Hampshire College

Adrian entered his office and plugged in an electric teapot. His lecture that afternoon to the students in HIST 501: Graduate Seminar in Medieval History had been particularly animated. The class had just finished the reign of Charlemagne and the unification of Western Europe, which meant by the end of the week they'd begin his favorite topic, the Viking Age. Since his return from the conference in Bergen, his teaching was infused with a renewed zeal. And it was contagious—the students were responding to his lectures with energy and interest, which meant that his teaching evaluations on RateMyProfessor.com would be positive. Better yet, from the two lusty girls in the front row, who always laughed at his jokes, he'd probably receive a hot chili pepper. High teaching evaluations certainly would not hurt during his tenure review. Tenure was now a certainty. A huge weight had been lifted.

He bent down and unlocked the bottom drawer of a filing cabinet. His heart started to thump as always when he opened this singular drawer. The Vinland map was still there. His eyes fixed on the black dot until the steam and whistle from the teapot woke him from his trance. He gently slid the map back into its hiding place, between folders of makeup exams and old course syllabi.

Ægir's Curse

Adrian poured hot water into a coffee mug, dropped in a tea bag, and waited for the tea to seep. God, he loved this perfect job, and he loved this perfect office! The office was perfectly located at the very end of a long corridor in the history department. The old codgers in his department could never lumber such a distance to bother him. Along one wall was a floor-to-ceiling bookshelf that contained his books on Norse and medieval history, as well as a fleet of Viking ship models that he had built as a teenager. Best of all were his posters and paintings of his Viking heroes. Among them was an image of Guthrum the Dane and King Alfred at the Battle of Edington in 878. There was a poster of the comic book character the Mighty Thor. Another depicted the savage Norse raid on the monastery at Lindisfarne in 793 that initiated the Viking Age. The Oseberg burial ship of Queen Asa, built around 800, had the graceful curves of a woman. But his favorite painting was of Freydís Eiríksdóttir, the ruthless daughter of Eric the Red. Breast bared and sword in hand, she was sneering at a band of terrified and retreating Skraelings. What a woman! How many idle Freydís fantasies had he had over the years?

Adrian contentedly sipped his tea. Since returning from Bergen, he no longer felt a thrall, a slave, inferior to the Norse heroes surrounding him. He had the map! The name Arrano would be synonymous with the rewriting of North American history. He now sat amongst his gods and heroes as their equal.

A knock at his office door startled him. He opened it tentatively, glancing back once more to ensure that the filing cabinet drawer was locked. His graduate student pushed hotly through the door, shut it behind her, and slumped into a chair. She tore a paper from her backpack and flung it across his desk.

"A fucking B! I worked so hard on that paper, Adrian, and Dr. Peterson gives me a B. You got to be kidding me! Do you know what he marked me down for? Incorrect citations of online sources and an insufficient number of references from peer-reviewed journals. If I get a B in his course, my GPA is screwed. I hate this course, and this topic. Who cares about the Battle of fucking Stalingrad?"

Adrian looked sympathetically at his thesis student. He'd never had much interest in World War II history either, but he was in too good a mood to have it ruined by her complaints. He considered the time on his wall clock. There was half an hour until a departmental meeting to discuss fall teaching schedules.

"Then Dr. Peterson had the audacity to tell me that—"

"Shh," Adrian interrupted her. He grabbed her hand and pulled her to her feet. They crossed the office to his research room where books and charts were spread across a worktable. He grinned lasciviously. She knew the drill. She grinned back, term papers, GPAs, and Dr. Peterson no longer of import. The research room only meant one thing. Games. Bad Student/Stern Dean was one of her favorites, Adrian recalled.

Adrian positioned her in such a way that she was seated on the edge of his worktable, her ankles locked at his lower back. That way, when he thrust into her, he was able to look over her shoulder and concentrate on the map of Massachusetts and that singular place on the southwest corner of Cape Cod. That village called Woods Hole.

Chapter 4

Woods Hole

Jessie's research at the marine lab was off to a promising start. Another scuba diver in her lab was working on a related ecological project, and the two of them spent most of the summer mornings collecting sponges and measuring whelk populations off the reefs of the Elizabeth Islands. The New England species were variations on the same theme as those in Florida and occupied the same ecological niches. Usually by midday she and her dive buddy were tired and waterlogged, so they'd motor back in on *Mermaid* and deposit their specimens in salt water tanks in the aquarium building. The afternoon was devoted to conducting experiments in the laboratory.

But the apartment hunt was less successful. Jessie scoured the village of Woods Hole for days in order to find living quarters, but as she'd suspected apartments and room rentals of any sort during peak season were, even if available, wholly out of her price range.

Living on *Mermaid* at the seawall—which she did for a week—proved intolerable. The galley table was too small for her to spread out her work. All day there was car exhaust from continuous coming and going of cars in the adjacent parking lot, and there was no escaping that odd mechanic! Almost daily, Lindsey wandered the seawall, most certainly casing the engines and electronics on the other boats. Worse, she had stopped once to ask questions about *Mermaid*'s GPS! Jessie's heart had pounded; she'd answered politely but curtly, all the while hoping that Lindsey would stay far away from *Mermaid*.

Nor was there any privacy at night, when the cabin became too stifling and forced her to sleep outdoors. At ridiculous hours of the night, students stumbling from the Captain Kidd bar would laugh and carry on at the seawall, then peel off their clothes and splash around Eel Pond. There were no options left. Jessie motored reluctantly back to Dave's Marina, as it offered the only possibility of quiet sleep and access to warm showers.

It was dusk when *Mermaid* returned to the marina. Across the parking lot, Rob pitched Wiffle balls to kids lined up next to a green dumpster. Sport fishermen emptied bags of ice into coolers on the porch of the bait store. Maggie and a teenage boy with a Mohawk sat on the dock, smoking cigarettes and laughing at some video on a tablet.

Lindsey emerged from the repair shed. "Any luck?"

Jessie shook her head. "No. The rents in this town are a complete rip-off. I've been staying at the seawall, but it's too noisy to sleep there. Who can I talk to here to see if any slip is available?"

Lindsey seemed to ponder the question carefully. "Dave and Sheila own the marina, but forget about that. Use the *Anne Bonny* until the rates drop. I'd be glad to have someone occupying it."

Jessie hesitated. Such a generous offer was unexpected. Caution... the boat possibly belonged to a thief. Still, a shower, a large table in the galley, a futon sofa, and a full-sized refrigerator and kitchen were luxuries after the privations of the past few weeks. Plus, it would only be for a short amount of time until a cheap apartment became available. "Okay. How much do you want for rent?"

Ægir's Curse

Lindsey tilted her head curiously. "Rent? I have no clue. Whatever you can afford." She departed with a wave of her hand.

Jessie stepped onto the aft deck of the *Anne Bonny*, baffled at the keyless doorknob. "How do I get in?" she called.

"Oh, right," Lindsey replied absently, returning to the houseboat. She held her hand motionless on the doorknob, just as Maggie had. The same whir and click and the door opened automatically. "I'll need to get your handprint so you can open the door." Lindsey noticed the disarray of engine parts spread across oily newspapers on the table. "I'll also need to remove my... projects."

The comment filled Jessie with dread. *Christ, that's all I need!* she thought to herself, *to escape one group of criminals ... only to fall in with another!*

For days after, she cautiously monitored the activities around the marina. Some aspects of life there were ideal. There were hot meals, daily showers, dependable Wifi, an ATM, and a wide food selection—though no fresh produce—in the bait store. Sheila, Dave's wife, who ran the bait store, was helpful and pleasant, and so was Dave. Then there was the downside: the questionable couple next door. The carefree man in the cowboy hat—did he ever go to work?—seemed content to wander the dock and chat with the boaters all day. The two small children, Danny and Ava, were normal enough and played around the marina with Dave and Sheila's children, Brianna and Max. Maggie called neither adult Mom and Dad; she must have been adopted. She and her boyfriend chain-smoked cigarettes and groped each other on the bench by the dock every evening after work. And then there was Lindsey, who's sole interest seemed to be the repair shed and the enthralling tools and instruments therein. Every night as Jessie crawled into bed on the *Anne Bonny*, she said a prayer that *Mermaid*'s electronics and engine would be intact the next morning.

Leah Devlin

The Friday Night Lecture Series was a decades-old tradition at the marine lab, her lab mates assured Jessie, and they were buzzing with excitement over the upcoming speakers. At eight o'clock that evening, however, she was less than thrilled by the prospect of listening to bioengineers talk about some bio-imaging invention. It was a miracle that she had passed college calculus; as for physics, forget it. She'd had to retake it in summer school. Still, as the new postdoc in the lab, it was best to appear collegial; so, muting her irritation, she followed the others to the auditorium. Another postdoc in her lab suggested that they all go for pitchers of beer at the Captain Kidd after the lecture, but she was thinking that if she snuck back to the empty lab instead, she could scan her samples under the Zeiss microscope for an uninterrupted hour or two.

The seats were occupied and the press had blockaded the aisles with cameras, so Jessie and the others stood along a back wall. A palpable electricity crackled in the air. This was a big night at the marine lab. The two speakers were Woods Hole's own, local legends of a sort.

The lights dimmed and a wild-haired old man hobbled to the podium. Though his cane-shaped body was failing, his mind was alert. With affection and humor, he introduced the speakers. Preoccupied with her plan for skulking back to the microscope, Jessie missed the first part of the lengthy introduction. One speaker, a scientist from the Marquesas, had received an undergraduate engineering degree from Stanford and a PhD in bioengineering from Cornell. The other speaker, a native of Annapolis, had BS, MD, and PhD degrees from Johns Hopkins in Baltimore. Both scientists had impressive résumés, especially the second, who had innumerable patents and as an undergraduate had designed some electrode that was now standard equipment in US hospitals.

Ægir's Curse

Even on tiptoes, it was impossible to clearly see the two speakers who sat in a shadow along the side of the stage. The first speaker, introduced to wild applause as Dr. Kauni, rose from a chair and approached the podium. Jessie squinted, and gasped with shock. It was the Polynesian in the black karate uniform from the *Mary Read.* Her attire that evening was a sleeveless dress of gold, black, and red flowers with a high Asian collar. Sara's words stumbled a bit at first, but she calmed herself and hit a rhythm when images of an electronic device, used to train neurosurgeons, that simulated epileptic seizures appeared on the large screen. Having finished her portion of the talk, Sara moved from the podium and whispered something to the second speaker, who rose from the shadows.

Cameras from the press flashed, catching the second speaker in a nimbus of light. Jessie again disbelieved her eyes. Behind the glowing podium stood the grease monkey from the salt pond. *Doctor* Lindsey Nolan. Her long hair was massed haphazardly into something resembling a bun. She wore a string of pearls, white silk blouse, tan suede skirt, and low brown pumps. She fidgeted to remove her shoes, and then, flashing a red beam at the images on the screen, wandered around the stage in her stocking feet and spoke of a new electrode that could locate "hot spots," or epileptic foci, the diseased brain tissue that generates seizures. The new electrode could localize precisely the diseased areas. The days of a neurosurgeon's scalpel excising large chunks of cortex were gone. Abnormal clusters of cells could be removed with a microscopic laser, also of Nolan's design, with no damage to the surrounding brain tissue.

It was not a dry, technical lecture, but an exhilarating drama of speculation, problem solving, setbacks, tenacity, and eventual success. Jessie was mesmerized. At times it seemed as if the entire auditorium stopped breathing, awaiting the next revelation. It was the most logical and lucid lecture that Jessie had ever heard. Lindsey was funny, informative, and self-effacing. The lecture ended in uproarious applause.

Lindsey motioned Sara back to the podium and wrapped her arm around her assistant's waist. Sara gave a tentative curtsey, while Lindsey briefly nodded and seemed to want the whole business over and done with.

Upon the announcement of a wine and cheese reception in another building, columns of people streamed out into the summer night. Jessie begged off the beers at the Captain Kidd and remained, still stunned, against the back wall of the auditorium. Two old women in the aisle snickered over innuendos that one of the speakers was "a wild child." Jessie inched through the tide of bodies, groping mentally for something—anything—sensible to say to the famous inventors, but with no luck. Sara and Lindsey were surrounded by an impenetrable wall of science sycophants, reporters, and the silver-haired men of the upper science echelon. Jessie watched from the edge of the crowd.

Lindsey nudged Sara ahead to field the reporters' questions while she slowly backed away. Upon reaching the frail old man who had introduced them, Lindsey whispered a good night into his large ear, kissed him on the cheek, and vanished out a side door.

Sara noticed Jessie skirting the crowd, caught her eye, and smiled warmly at her, but a statuesque French woman positioned possessively at Sara's side glowered.

Jessie cowered reflexively and stepped back, nearly tripping over a chair.

Sara was immediately taken up by her companion, and a quick, heated conversation in French ensued.

There was no sign that the science groupies were dispersing anytime soon, so a "congratulations" to Sara would be impossible. Jessie left the auditorium, made her way to her boat, and motored out into the darkness.

Ægir's Curse

In the Vineyard Sound, she stopped the engine, left the captain's chair, and leaned over a gunwale. *Mermaid* drifted silently in the night like a ghost ship. Phosphorescent microorganisms shimmered an eerie green in the boat's wake. The stars above were unusually bright. The sea always calmed her, especially after difficult encounters—like the ones with her brother, Alan.

The flight from Alan and his friend, Clayton, had been an uncharacteristically bold move on her part. Her confidence, what little she had of it, momentarily swelled. She looked starward again and wondered about the constellations over the southern oceans, over the Marquesas.

Dave's Marina

The cabin of the *Anne Bonny* was too stuffy for sleep, so Jessie dragged her sleeping bag and a citronella candle up the ladder to the flybridge. With a sense of relief, she lay on top of the flannel and laced her fingers behind her head. Lindsey Nolan was not pirating engine parts, but tinkering compulsively with any mechanical or electrical gadget that she could get her hands on. This explained all of the peculiar inventions around the boats, like handprint-scanning doorknobs and talking computers. *Mermaid* was safe from pillage.

Yellow car headlights swerved into the marina's parking lot. Jessie rolled on her side to look. From under the awning on the *Green Monster*, Rob also spied the Jeep and closed his laptop. Lindsey crossed the parking lot. Early that evening she had managed to look somewhat scholarly in a blouse and skirt. Now her sleeves were rolled up, her shirttails were pulled out of her skirt, and her collar was opened wide across her chest. She stepped onto the *Green Monster* and flung her purse onto a deck chair, while Rob lit a slender cigar and asked her, "How'd it go?" She maneuvered a deck chair across from his and sat on its edge, hitching her skirt high and parting her knees. "Same old same old," she answered casually. Bending forward, she rolled a stocking down her leg while his eyes noted every flicker of her fingers. The other came off the same way. Wadding the stockings into a ball, she tossed them against his chest.

"You wear these," she suggested with a quiet laugh.

"That'll be the day," he replied, smiling.

The couple rose together, entered the boat, and stopped at the foot of a foldout berth in the salon. Jessie watched their movements through the window. The two children, Danny and Ava, were nestled into white pillows. Neither child resembled Lindsey, as they were both small replicas of Rob, their black-haired, blue-eyed father. Jessie was unsure if Danny was Lindsey's child at all, since he called her not Mom, but simply Lin. Lindsey bent and kissed the sleeping children and moved to a refrigerator in the galley. She squeezed a stream of juice from a plastic lemon into a water bottle and drank deeply, then wiped her mouth with the back of her hand and said something. Her remark, and the salacious look that went with it, arrested Rob's steps. He smiled and shook his head. She grabbed his hand and tugged him toward a cabin. He resisted. Shaking her off, he strolled to a shelf of CDs and took his time, considering the titles. She leaned against the counter and sipped slowly from the bottle, watching him with a self-possessed, pleased expression. Being toyed with clearly amused her. Finally he decided on a music selection and slid a CD into the player.

Low music emerged from a speaker on the aft deck. Without comment, he pulled her back outside. Under the shadow of the awning they moved together to a torchy ballad of destructive passion, a mix of tribal and jazz elements crooned by a female vocalist. As the tempo increased, their movements slowed. Their faces hovered inches apart, their lips silent or occasionally whispering.

Ægir's Curse

Jessie felt guilty at witnessing the private dance, but their moves were irresistible. Besides, her romantic experiences had been few: clumsy, unsatisfying fumbling around with Clayton in the woods behind the trailer park. Perhaps something could be learned from this tantalizing, mutual seduction. She pressed herself into a dark crease on the flybridge to ensure that she could not be seen. Lindsey leaned backward from the circle of Rob's arms and slowly unbuttoned her blouse. He gazed appreciatively at the lace revealed. The citronella candle flickered in a breeze, and Lindsey glanced toward the *Anne Bonny*. Jessie stopped breathing. The unbuttoning stopped. A second later, the couple resumed their dance.

A girl's sudden shriek burst from the black marsh. Two flashlight beams sprayed the grass and surface of the pond.

"They're being eaten by mosquitoes," Rob remarked humorously.

Lindsey untangled herself from Rob and re-buttoned her blouse with obvious consternation. Maggie and her boyfriend with the Mohawk slowed their dash when they hit the dock. Towels slung around their necks, the teenagers stopped, panting in front of the *Green Monster*, a trail of wet footprints following them down the dock.

"What's for dinner?" Maggie asked.

"Whatever you want to make yourself," Lindsey remarked flatly. "It's Friday night. I'm busy."

"Yeah, I see that," Maggie quipped, smirking.

"There's pizza in the fridge," Lindsey continued. "Toss it in the microwave. Brian, love you, honey, but you're gone by midnight."

"Midnight? Fuck!" Maggie shouted, whipping the towel off her neck.

"We go to the hospital tomorrow at ten. Remember?" Lindsey responded insistently.

Maggie furiously swatted her towel at a plastic owl on the dock. "But I was going Jet Skiing with Brian!"

"No choice, Maggie. One more series of shots and a check of your blood. That should be it for a while."

Maggie stormed into the *Mary Read,* while Brian followed timidly behind. Lindsey turned to Rob, whose cigar ember glowed in the darkness. She pulled the cigar from his fingers, took a drag, and blew a fast angry plume into the air. He leaned from his chair, his hand climbing her thigh. The gesture disarmed her momentarily. She walked to a gunwale and tilted her head upward to view the constellations.

"The new drug hasn't worked yet," she said in a sorrowful tone. "Maggie's white blood cells are still dangerously low."

"Give it time, baby," Rob replied consolingly.

Jessie lay on the flybridge, confounded by the events of the evening. This woman blowing cigar smoke at the stars, together with her beautiful Polynesian lab associate, Sara Kauni, had won a Nobel Prize for Physiology.

West Hampshire College

When Adrian Arrano entered the meeting, the committee chairman was well into a mind-numbing, droning presentation about the faculty senate policy regarding paper usage. This was the third year in a row that their committee had been charged by the dean to review how many reams of paper and toner cartridges should be allocated to each faculty member over the course of an academic year. If this year was like the others, they'd debate it once a month for twelve months, grudgingly find consensus, and pass the committee's recommendation on to the dean, only to have the man say that he'd "think about it."

This, like all other committee meetings, would be an exercise in futility, so Adrian decided to make the best of it. He deliberately chose a seat near a window and next to the perky new English professor in the short skirt. She greeted him with a roll of the eyes at the pontifications of the old goat at the front of the room. She too had chosen the back row. He glanced briefly at her desk and saw that she was correcting essays from a summer school course. The papers were slashed with red ink. He opened his white Mac laptop. The chairman interrupted himself to ask if Adrian had received an agenda.

"Yes, thank you," Adrian responded cheerfully. "In fact, I'm looking for it at this moment."

The English professor looked over at Adrian's computer screen and saw that he had instead opened MapQuest.

He shrugged sheepishly and whispered, "Vacation."

She whispered back, "I need one in the worst way. Our students are morons."

He nodded in agreement and returned to MapQuest. The driving instructions revealed that it would take him a few hours to reach Cape Cod. His father's car was available, since the old man had been moved to a nursing home. That would leave the new car for Adrian's wife to commute to her job in the city.

Adrian gazed out the window. The college green was dandelion-infested and crisscrossed by sidewalks. It was quiet at this time of the morning. Summer enrollments had declined over the years, since it was cheaper to take the same courses at a community college. Enrollments during the academic year had steadily dropped as well. Too late the administration had tried to rejuvenate the academic programs by hiring a new tier of young faculty, he and the English professor among them; but any creative initiatives were squelched by an intractable group of senior-level deadwood who produced nothing in the way of meaningful publications but wouldn't retire, as their retirement accounts had tanked during the economic downturn. The deadwood were happy to collect a full professor's salary for doing the bare minimum.

Adrian scrawled a message on a piece of paper and slid it over toward the English professor. "Death and Destruction to the Old... Rebirth of the Young!"

She sighed. "Ragnarök."

The English professor understood his allusion to Norse mythology immediately. He grinned at both her astuteness and her shapely legs. It was time to end the current world order and reign of the old gods, to incite a takeover by newer gods with a fresh world vision! He wished he could toss the full professors from a window right there and then and allow the assistant and associate professors, who had at least partially functional brains, to make the decisions. That way, hour-long meetings could be reduced to fifteen minutes. Better yet, the young faculty might do all their meetings by email or Skype, and then everyone would have time for more interesting things, like searching for Viking ruins.

Adrian checked out the English professor's legs again, then clicked out of MapQuest. He opened a folder called Maps. The Woods Hole area had such a convoluted coastline, it would take forever to walk the shoreline searching for the black dot on the Vinland map. It would be best to charter a boat.

Chapter 5

Woods Hole

From Adrian's home in the White Mountains, Woods Hole was just under three hours by car. It was smart not to have told his wife of his actual destination. As far as she knew, he was working at a university library in Boston for the day. Had she come with him, she would have begged him to take her to a beach, out for a seafood lunch, and to Christmas shops to buy ornaments for her assorted nieces and nephews. This one-day scouting expedition needed to be solo.

By midmorning the village was already bustling with tourists waiting for the ferries to Martha's Vineyard and Nantucket. Adrian drove around the village twice, until he found the last available parking space in town. His father's compact car fit snuggly into a space next to Waterfront Park. After stuffing quarters into a parking meter, he excitedly set off to explore.

He first walked behind the buildings of the marine lab toward Eel Pond, hoping to find a vast marina. To his disappointment, all he spotted were collecting trawlers owned by the lab and private watercraft ringing the pond. He walked onto a dock behind the Captain Kidd bar. There one captain said that he only chartered his boat for deep-sea fishing, and added gruffly that he didn't rent out his boat for scuba diving excursions. A second fishing boat captain said the same.

Frustrated, Adrian started up Water Street. He passed assorted gift shops and the oceanographic institution, then came upon a convenience store. He ducked inside. With growing desperation, Adrian asked a clerk behind the cash register if he knew of anyone in town who might be interested in renting out their boat to go scuba diving.

"Sure," the clerk said helpfully. "Check out Jessie McCabe's ad on the notice board outside."

On her run along Water Street, Jessie passed her ad for McCabe's Dive Adventures outside the convenience store. The dive business, like her research, was off to an encouraging start. Since she'd posted the ad, most weekends were taken up by guiding scientists out to local reefs where the sea life was abundant.

Maggie and Brian had driven her to a local dive shop to pick up supplies: anti-fogging spray for the masks, more weights, and extra straps for the fins. Her tanks and regulators were inspected and found to be in good condition, but both buoyancy compensator vests, or BCs, were showing their age. One BC had been her first big purchase when, as a teenager, she'd gotten a job at a dive shop; it and *Mermaid* were her two prized possessions. Her old BC was lucky; it protected her and ensured that all of her dives would be safe ones.

Jessie had acquired her second BC through the weirdest of circumstances. She'd gone diving with a particular graduate student more than a dozen times in the waters around St. Augustine; Phil was an experienced and reliable dive partner. During past dives an occasional sand shark, a barracuda, and even a few small hammerheads had swum by them, more curious than threatening.

One afternoon they set out in a small motorboat and turned into the Matanzas Inlet, the site of a terrible massacre of French

Ægir's Curse

Huguenots by Spanish soldiers in the 1500s. Phil climbed down the boat ladder and entered the water first. Jessie leaned against the gunwale and watched him adjust his mask and regulator. Suddenly a shape arose from the depths, moving toward their boat like a torpedo. She screamed his name. He splashed back to the ladder.

A tiger shark—no, worse—a bull!

Phil scrambled up the ladder rungs. The snout of the bull shark reared out of the water, its serrated teeth perforating his fin. Jessie grabbed her friend. Her nails embedded in the shoulders of his wet suit, she threw her body weight backward to pull him up and over the side, but he was immobilized by the unrelenting jaws. The dead black eyes of the shark stared into hers. Phil frantically thrashed his foot, and suddenly his fin strap snapped, releasing him from the shark's hold. Jessie and Phil spilled into the boat in a heaving tangle of rubber and quivering limbs.

"Christ!" She quickly righted herself and yanked the cable of the outboard engine for a rapid escape. She should've known better! Bull sharks love murky river water.

Phil was ashen and uncommunicative, sipping from a water bottle and staring fearfully at the water for the entire journey back to the marine lab. When they pulled up at the dock, he flung his dive equipment into a heap on the planks. "Jessie, it's all yours. I'm done." Within fifteen minutes he had cleared out his small dorm room, thrown his possessions in his car, and disappeared in a cloud of exhaust up Route 1.

Years later, the memory of the bull shark still rattled her.

That morning Jessie's diving services had not been hired out, and she was grateful for a run. Too much of her time she was sedentary: behind a microscope, at a computer, or in a captain's chair. The best runs were the bike trail between Dave's Marina and Falmouth, along the coastal road, to Quissett and back; but her favorite run was the loop around Eel Pond and across the bascule bridge. There was a welcoming, relaxed spirit to the village, unlike any place she had lived before. The trailer park of her youth had been squalid and sweltering; there time did not budge. After much pleading, she had finally been allowed to leave, but only after making that horrible promise to Alan and Clayton. At the university, time had spun wildly forward, as if to make up for eighteen years of slack and neglect. The science courses blurred as she rushed desperately to finish before scholarship monies ran out.

Here in Woods Hole all was different; time was measured in laps of water against the seawall and the pull of the moon on the sea. The natural rhythms and the runs through the village almost made her forget Florida.

On School Street Jessie ran past the Woods Hole Visitors Center and the Children's School of Science. She turned on to Millfield Street, where her run was interrupted by a "Hey you!" coming over a hedge. She stopped and looked around. On the porch of a clapboard house sat Sara Kauni, a mug of coffee clasped in her hands and her bare feet stretched across to another chair.

"In case you're wondering, it takes you three minutes to do a circle around Eel Pond. You're getting faster, though," Sara called. "Two weeks ago it took you three and a half minutes."

"Sometimes I run through the neighborhood, not just around the pond," Jessie replied, irked at her predictably.

"And you run staring at your sneakers. You should look up once in a while. The world's a rather beautiful place."

"Is this your house?" Jessie asked, hoping to change the subject.

"No, I'm a homeless person. I thought I'd just camp out on some random porch in my bathrobe." Sara smiled widely as an apology for the sarcasm. She rose out of the chair. "Have coffee with me."

Ægir's Curse

Jessie walked apprehensively along a slate pathway, past bright gold forsythia bushes and orange lilies, and up the porch steps.

"Shoes come off," Sara commanded.

Jessie bent to unlace her running shoes and added them to a row of shoes in the entryway. The house was old, similar to the other gray shingled houses in the village, though the interior had been newly renovated. Walls had been knocked out on the first floor to create an airy open space. The wide planked floors were new. A breeze off the pond fluttered large tropical plants in front of the windows. The furniture was oversized and colorful. The artwork consisted of wood carvings of South Pacific design and paintings and prints of coral reefs and jungles by various artists, including Paul Gaugin.

In the kitchen Sara lifted a mug from a line of hanging cups and stepped toward a coffee machine. Her long black hair had not yet been combed and fell wildly over her shoulders. The morning sun that shone through the French doors made her white bathrobe transparent, revealing a purple bikini underneath.

Jessie averted her eyes, climbed onto a stool at the kitchen island, and distracted herself by watching the activities on Eel Pond. A family in a small boat was motoring out, and a man was hoisting the mainsail of a daysailer; otherwise the boat activity was slow.

"Does the pond freeze?" Jessie wondered aloud. "I've never seen snow."

"Really? Then I'm going to take you sledding this winter." Sara slid a mug of coffee and containers of sugar and cream across the island. "Let me give you a tour of the place. I've only been here a year, so it's still a work in progress."

Jessie prepared her coffee, slid off the stool, and followed Sara up a staircase.

"Properties in the village almost never go up for sale because the families hold onto them forever," Sara explained over her shoulder. "As soon as I saw this house, I grabbed it. Zephyr, my son, and I lived as transients while I was in graduate school. We're glad to settle down. I'm going to live in this house forever and work with Lindsey forever. Our energy paths are in harmony."

They stopped in the hallway. Sara pointed to a closed door. "Zephyr's room." She moved down the hall and Jessie followed. "I'm not sure what I'm doing with this." This room was empty except for some paint cans and drop cloths crumpled in the corner.

"And here's my room."

The décor was a mix of Asian and Western features. Enclosing a sleeping mat on the floor was a bamboo framework strung with translucent curtains reminiscent of mosquito netting that Jessie had seen in jungle movies. Small votive candles lined the hardwood floor. Sara watched Jessie study her sleeping area and smiled.

"What?" Jessie asked defensively.

Sara didn't answer immediately. "Nothing. Let me show you my view." She walked to a wood dresser next to a computer workstation, pulled something from the top drawer, and stuck it in her pocket. Jessie followed her through a set of double doors onto a balcony and climbed up steep wooden stairs to a widow's walk. The two women stood against the railing.

Clouds seemed almost within reach from that height, while the boats in the pond seemed like bath toys. The lab building where Sara worked was in direct view, while Jessie's lab was off to the right. Beyond the shops in the village and the oceanographic buildings were the Woods Hole Passage and the Elizabeth Islands

"Amazing view," Jessie said in awe.

Ægir's Curse

"I am so blessed. Have a seat." Sara sat on the edge of a chaise lounge and pulled over a small table with an ashtray and coffee can holding pens and pencils. "Sometimes when things get chaotic in the lab, Lin and I come up here to brainstorm. Some of her cleverest ideas gelled here." She held up a pen. "Look. She only uses blue pens. The best of ideas are conceived with blue ink, Lin always says. Blue is the color of truth."

"Her husband has amazing blue eyes," Jessie confessed.

"Rob's her boyfriend. Her parasitic husband, Duncan, who won't divorce her, lives in Scotland. Men are flies on her. Flies on honey. That's the problem. Too many men want a piece of that action." Sara smiled devilishly. "And she's distractible, but not like she was before when she drank. Anyway, let's not talk about men. Sex with men is not a reciprocal act of giving and receiving pleasure. It's their mechanism to possess and control."

"Do you really believe that?" Jessie asked.

"Absolutely, so I don't date men. I've loved women since the moment I was born. It's just the result of my superior genetics," she stated matter-of-factly. She pulled a joint and a lighter from her robe pocket and lit the tapered end.

Jessie tensed. "That stuff is illegal."

Sara grinned. "Then don't tell on me. You could use some of this. It will help you relax."

"I am relaxed!" Jessie cried.

"Right," Sara remarked sardonically. "Haven't you smoked weed before? I hear that bales of it wash up on Florida beaches all the time."

"I smoked it once at a frat party. And I drank too much. I made such a colossal fool of myself that I never went to another frat after that," Jessie admitted. "And I've never seen any bales."

"That's too bad."

Jessie asked uneasily, "Where's Zephyr?"

"He's playing soccer. I'd love to watch his game, but moms are not cool to eleven-year-old boys."

Sara took a drag and moved to lean against the railing again.

"Do the tattoos hurt?" Jessie asked, studying the intricate designs on Sara's arm.

"No. They feel wonderful and sensual. I'd have my whole body covered if I had the time."

Jessie closely observed Sara's behavior. She appeared serene and rational, not at all deranged by the pot. The potheads that had lived in Jessie's college dorm, she recalled, were always pleasant and talkative.

"Okay, let me try that stuff," Jessie ventured, determined to disprove her priggishness. "But don't let me jump over the edge if I become crazy."

Sara laughed. "I'd never let that happen."

Jessie took a drag, coughed, and tried again. "This tastes pretty good," she conceded. She took a second drag. "This is way better than the weed I smoked at the party."

"Slow down, if you're not used to it," Sara warned.

The pot began to have an effect. Jessie's cautious mode was replaced by a fun one. "Sweet... I like this stuff!" She inhaled a few more puffs, then handed it back to Sara.

Sara stubbed it out in the ashtray. "I think we're good for now." She slid off her robe and reclined in the lounger.

"I feel great!" Jessie proclaimed. "Hey, have you ever noticed the grain in this wood?"

"No." Sara closed her eyes and let her skin absorb the morning heat.

Jessie bent her face toward the railing. "It's so gray and beautiful. It looks like little mountain ranges." Glints of light from the pond were sharp and bright and seemed to leap off the surface of the water. The sky was a brilliant blue. "I bet if my arm was elastic and I could reach up and grab a cloud, it would feel like a sponge and I could squeeze the rain out of it. Who's that comic book character with the elastic arms?"

Sara's eyes remained closed. "I don't remember. We can ask Zephyr. He'd know."

"I guess that planes have to swerve around all the clouds," Jessie giggled, still studying the sky.

Sara opened her eyes incredulously. "You're kidding, right? Planes fly through the clouds. Clouds are just condensed water vapor. You're a frigging PhD; you've got to know this. Haven't you been in a plane before?"

"No," Jessie responded simply.

"Shit, girl, what have you been doing with your life?" Sara asked, still stunned.

"I've been taking care of my sick mother. She died recently."

"I'm really sorry, Jessie," Sara said contritely. "I'm sure that you were a wonderful daughter. How about other family?"

"My father has Alzheimer's. He's in a home. He doesn't recognize me anymore. I have a brother and sister-in-law near Toulossa."

"What do they do?"

"Who's Zephyr's father?" Jessie blurted.

Sara decided to permit the evasion tactic, at least for the moment. "You're wondering if he was conceived by the turkey baster method."

"No. I mean ..."

"Most people naturally assume that a woman of my preferences conceives that way. Actually, Zephyr was conceived the old-fashioned way, with my legs spread and a man huffing and puffing on top of me."

"Waaaay too much information."

Sara shrugged. "You asked. He was a close friend all through school. After high school, he went to a university in Japan. I got a scholarship to go to Stanford. We hung out together over school breaks. He was distraught, lovesick over a girl in our village, but he had no experience with women and had no idea how to court her, much less make love to her. And I had no interest in men, but I wanted a child, so we made a mutually beneficial bargain. Sperm for practice time." She relit the joint, took a drag, and passed it Jessie's way. "So what's your story?"

"I have no story."

Sara sat pensively for a moment. She pulled the other chaise lounge closer to hers. "How about you sit down and relax?"

"My brain's really messed up. I'm drifty," Jessie muttered vacuously, still leaning against the railing.

"Drifty is not a word," Sara said.

"I'm absolutely sure that it is. I can't feel my legs. Do you think that I'll be able to walk again?" The green branches of the treetops swayed languidly next to the roof below, and Jessie was suddenly dizzy. Sweat broke out across her nose and forehead.

Sara sat upright. "Are you alright?"

"I feel sick. I think I need to sleep," Jessie murmured.

"Let's go downstairs. Very carefully." Sara rose and held Jessie's hand.

"Sara ..." Jessie whispered, her eyelids drooping.

"What?"

"Can I touch your tattoos?"

Jessie didn't remember Sara's response. Sometime around noon, she awoke on the sleeping mat, but the beautiful Polynesian was gone. Jessie crept quietly through the empty house, found her shoes, and promised herself never to jog down Millfield Street again.

The notice board outside of the convenience store was a patchwork of information: a call for tryouts for a summer theatrical production, sailboats for sale, therapeutic massages, beach house rentals, yoga classes, 5K runs, and the like. The colorful ad for McCabe's Dive Adventures was easy to spot. It had been created with clip art and had orange fish, a green starfish, and a pink mermaid in the corner. Adrian noted that there was no phone number listed, only an email address for Captain McCabe at McCabe@whml.edu. That was easy enough to remember. The captain was evidently affiliated with the marine lab.

A woman stepped next to him and held a smartphone over an ad for tennis lessons. She snapped a picture of the ad and turned to walk away.

"Excuse me," Adrian said loudly.

She removed her headphones. "Yeah?"

"Do you know anything about this dive charter?" he asked, pointing to McCabe's ad.

The tanned woman wore a tank top with Johns Hopkins Medicine written across the chest and baggy gym shorts with a logo for the Orioles. She was a walking billboard for the city of Baltimore. Her tank top was tight and fit her perfectly. She was a bit on the skinny side, but had curves in all the right places.

She read McCabe's ad and smiled. The woman clearly had fond memories of the captain, Adrian figured. "Captain McCabe is an excellent dive master," she stated, "and *Mermaid* is the best dive boat in Woods Hole."

A tourist would not know these details; she must be a local. Adrian decided to engage her further. "Where can I get the best cup of coffee?"

She pointed up Water Street. "The pastry shop has good coffee and baked goods." She pointed directly across the street. "And that coffee bar has a wide selection of coffees. It all depends on what you're looking for."

She was definitely a local, and befriending a local might be helpful in the upcoming weeks. Adrian decided to speak boldly.

"I'm looking for you to have coffee with me." He flashed his most charming smile.

"No," she responded immediately.

He was not going to be put off so easily. "Please? I'm just a lost tourist and don't know this area."

"Lost Tourist, you can get a map at the tourist center around the corner," she replied tonelessly.

"You know my name, The Lost Tourist," he said grinning. "At least tell me yours."

She stood silent and resolute.

"I guess your mother taught you not to talk to strangers," he added lightly. At the mention of a mother, he could see her visibly bristle. Storm clouds passed across her large green eyes and just as quickly passed.

"I have no mother. I was raised by sea nymphs, and yes, they told me not to talk to strangers. So good-bye." She started down Water Street.

"Good-bye, Dr. Nymph!" he called amicably.

The woman did not respond, but that did not mean Adrian was through with her. Self-assured and feisty, she was a turn-on. He walked up to the bascule bridge and slouched against the metal rail to watch her disappear down Water Street. She veered off to the right, toward the marine lab, not toward the oceanographic institution on the left. The marine lab was not that large a facility. She'd be easy to find. And she was a bit older than he was, which was also a turn-on. Perhaps she was looking for a young stud to tumble with this summer? There was no wedding ring on her finger, which was a slight turnoff. Single women always expected him to commit in some way. Married women were so much easier to deal with.

Adrian stopped for lunch and wandered back down Water Street. He stepped carefully along the edge of the seawall until he spotted the cruiser, *Mermaid*. The captain was an experienced dive master, the tan woman had said. His diving experience was very limited, so an expert dive partner would be a good idea.

The boat was by far the most seaworthy of the vessels parked along the seawall. It was tidy and clean, and when he peered through the cabin window, he saw a panel of navigational aids, plus a small worktable that would do for his laptop and charts.

Yes, *Mermaid* was perfect for his needs. He'd speak to Captain McCabe before he returned to New Hampshire that afternoon. He sat down on the seawall next to slip sixteen and dangled his feet over the water. As he leaned forward, his reflection stared back at him. Minnows swam under his rippling shadow. His long hair made him appear more youthful than his thirty years, and the goatee and droopy mustache gave him the look of a swashbuckler.

Should he solve the mystery of the black dot, within the year his face would be on the cover of *Time* and *Newsweek*, and definitely on *Archaeology* and *National Geographic*. This would be bigger than the Ingstads' discovery of a Viking settlement at L'Anse aux Meadows. Tenure was in the bag. Soon he'd be able to negotiate a promotion to full professor. And finally, he'd be able to leave his backwater college for the Ivy League. He glanced at his watch. Where was this guy McCabe?

A cell phone rang in his backpack and Adrian opened the zipper. He glanced at the screen. Hadn't he told his grad student never to call him on his cell phone? Hadn't he told her that his wife paid the phone bill and checked the phone records? His student was only to contact him on his personal email account! He promptly turned off his ringer.

Adrian turned his back to the pond. Scientists, mainly white-haired old men and grad students, moved across the parking lot toward a building with a cafeteria. Two chattering women exited from the back door of a laboratory building and headed his way. They were bent over a lab notebook. He stood abruptly. What luck! One was Dr. Nymph. He waved to her, pointed down to *Mermaid*, and gave her a thumbs up.

"Thanks. *Mermaid*'s perfect!" he called to her.

She nodded slightly and hurried past.

Adrian's eyes leapt to the woman next to her. Whoa! What position wouldn't he love to see that Polynesian babe in? When he made his amazing discovery, the babes would be all over him, including a hottie like that one.

Chapter 6

Woods Hole

The new charter was off to an inauspicious start. The client was a male tourist of about Jessie's own age, with a blond crew cut and dressed in a sports shirt and cargo shorts. He showed up at their specified meeting time at the seawall on Saturday morning, but already the skies were swollen with black clouds. His interest was in a cruise down the coastline rather than a dive, he explained in his pleasant manner, as photographs were required for *Quest* magazine, where he was employed as a photojournalist. His recent assignment was a story on the Woods Hole and Buzzards Bay area.

So he was not a tourist after all; Jessie was thrilled by the prospect of expanding her dive charter to local businesses such as travel magazines. Maybe later in the day, when the skies cleared, he'd be interested in diving, but for now shooting pictures of the coastline seemed fine with him. As his request was to follow the shoreline, Jessie turned on the depth finder to ensure that *Mermaid* wouldn't graze any submerged boulders. For a few hours he sat contently on a dive locker and snapped photographs while Jessie sat in the captain's chair and tried to stay awake.

Since the visit to Sara Kauni's house, her sleep had been light and sporadic. She reached into a small refrigerator for an energy drink, desperate for a jolt of sugar and caffeine. Should she go to Sara's house and apologize for getting stoned and passing out in her bedroom? Or avoid her altogether?

Avoid her altogether.

Why should she apologize? Sara was to blame for this. Sara invited her in for coffee. Sara got her high. Sara slid off her robe. Sara was trying to seduce her. She was, wasn't she? No, impossible. Sara was a brilliant engineer. Jessie was nothing, just an escapee from a nuthouse of crooks and arsonists. She was a chick and Sara was a chick. The whole thing was unnatural.

Avoid her altogether, most definitely.

A steady drizzle began around noontime and the photojournalist ducked inside the cabin. Jessie offered him a sandwich, which he ate seated in the passenger's seat at the helm. At the first crack of lightning across a blackening sky, *Mermaid* made a quick U-turn. The passenger had flinched at the lightning. Not an experienced boater, he admitted. His following questions revolved around the boat's navigational equipment. When Jessie showed him a high-definition view of the seafloor using the side scan sonar, he was intrigued and stared transfixed at the screen all the way back to Woods Hole.

The photojournalist, Craig Russell, arranged for another trip the following Saturday. That day the weather was glorious, in the mid-eighties with a gentle offshore breeze. Though he hadn't been scuba diving in some years, he said, he asked Jessie to take him for a dive. As they were passing under the bascule bridge and he was rummaging through the dive lockers, he pulled out her old BC.

The air hose that connected the regulator to the BC suddenly snapped.

"Jessie, I'm so sorry," Craig explained through the cabin door. "I just lifted it out and the hose broke off."

Ægir's Curse

She stared at the dangling black tube, struggling to hide her devastation. The lucky old BC! The air tanks had been filled the previous afternoon. Food and drinks were in the cube refrigerator. The gas canisters had been topped off. Why hadn't she checked the BCs last night? She knew better! But while dropping off a case of water bottles on the boat, she had spotted Sara across the pond having dinner with Zephyr on the back porch. What if Sara saw her, and signaled for her to join them? Jessie had panicked and refused look in their direction. Instead she'd turned on the ignition and quickly motored back to Dave's Marina. This was all Sara's fault!

Be professional and calm, Jessie told her herself. "No, I'm sorry," she replied to Craig, attempting to keep her voice even. "I should have inspected it. It was very old. We'll need to get another one."

But where? The postdoc that she dove with during the week was in Boston visiting his fiancée, so she couldn't borrow his. Jesus, how could she be so stupid! Lindsey Nolan had a shed full of every water toy and flotation device imaginable, but Lindsey, Danny, and Ava were in England for a few weeks. Maggie and Rob were around the marina. Maggie was a scuba diver. Maybe she had a spare BC?

Suppressing her agitation, Jessie motored rapidly up the coast to Dave's Marina. She hoped to borrow a BC from a neighbor, she explained Craig. Once at the marina, she tied up to a cleat on the *Anne Bonny*. "That's where I live," she explained to the man. "Pretty cool painting on the transom. Check it out. It's Anne Bonny," she added, forcing a pleasant tone into her shaking voice.

Jessie hurried down the dock to the *Mary Read*. While banging on the door, she glanced over her shoulder to notice Craig wandering about the deck of her houseboat. First he appeared to be stretching his legs and flexing his back. Next he pressed his hands and face against the window. He was probably scanning the pirate trinkets, she guessed. Maggie finally answered the door on the *Mary Read*; the teenager was completely disheveled.

"*What*, Jes?" Maggie asked testily.

"Are you okay?" Jessie asked.

"You woke me up."

"Sorry, Maggie. I'm really sorry."

"And Rob is a fuckin' asshole!"

"What happened?" Jessie asked cautiously.

"Fuckin' nothing! I don't want to talk about it. What's up?"

"Do you have a spare BC I can borrow? Mine broke! I'm in the middle of a job. I'm desperate!"

Maggie grabbed the broken BC from Jessie's hand, and inspected it. "What a piece of shit."

Jessie and Maggie headed toward the storage shed.

Jessie turned once again toward the *Anne Bonny* where the client was fumbling around with the doorknob. "It's locked," she called.

"I was wondering if I could use your bathroom," Craig inquired.

"Can you use the men's room in the bathhouse? My place is a wreck." She pointed. "It's right there."

"Sure, no problem."

Lindsey Nolan's array of dive equipment was impressive. Maggie offered Jessie the use of two new BCs, one pink and the other black, and new masks and fins. Jessie was thrilled. Hopefully the new, top-of-the-line equipment would make up for the delay in the charter.

Jessie scanned her houseboat once again, but Craig was nowhere to be seen. She finally located him on the porch of the baiting store, drinking a Coke and chatting with Sheila, the voluptuous redheaded clerk, who flirted with all of the male customers.

Ægir's Curse

A tropical depression loomed over the Cape for nearly a week and forced Jessie indoors to catch up on lab experiments. She and a biochemist experimented to find the correct mixture of enzymes to disperse cells from red beard sponges, and whenever she could get time on the Zeiss microscope she checked if the cells were healthy. Her laptop, however, distracted her at every turn, and she obsessively interrupted her experiments to check her email. Her account at the University of Florida was still active, and her brother Alan sent message after message imploring her to respond, echoed by Clayton. Their use of her uf.edu address meant that they still believed her to be working on her degree there; she had never told them that she was done. They insisted that she come home. To talk.

When the forecast reported that the storm was finally moving off the coast, Jessie received an email from the photojournalist asking about her availability for another dive, this time for a multi-day charter so they could stay at sea. His editor, Craig wrote, had given him permission to expand the length of his article. Craig's plan was to photograph and dive on a number of sites around Buzzards Bay, and then possibly conduct a side scan survey of one particular inlet.

This was an unusual request, as all of her previous charters had been day trips. She pondered the request for some time. The thought of being alone on a boat with the same person, especially a man, for an extended period of time was unnerving. But Craig had been wearing a wedding ring and had mentioned a wife, she was sure of it, so he should not be a threat in that way. Also, he was friendly and an interesting conversationalist, and helpful with cleaning equipment and setting anchors. Her mind switched to logistical issues. He could sleep in the v-berth while she slept outside in her sleeping bag. If it rained, the bimini top could be assembled to keep the deck dry. *Mermaid* had a small head, but no shower. Food was no problem, as *Mermaid* had a small propane stove and a refrigerator. As long as he was okay with canned food, and they could keep the meals simple and inexpensive, a multi-day cruise would be fine. She emailed him a price that included the cost of gasoline, air for the tanks, water, drinks and food, and a proposed date that spanned the weekend so that she wouldn't lose too much time at work. In his prompt response, he said that everything sounded ideal and he'd see her at Eel Pond in a few days. And no problem, he could bring his own sleeping bag.

Yes! After this charter there would be enough money saved up to purchase her own BCs, and she could return the pink and black ones to the storage shed. Those BCs were clearly part of one of Lindsey Nolan's oddball projects. A tiny electrical device that did god knows what had been stuffed into a pocket of each of the BCs but, as far as she could tell, the device did not impact the normal functioning of the vest, the flow air between the BC and regulator, or the inflation and deflation of the vest, and so she paid it no further mind.

The best part of the upcoming trip was that Craig always paid in cash. The money from the charter would be hidden with the rest of her stash under the futon on the *Anne Bonny*.

One drizzly morning, Sara approached her lab building with uncharacteristic trepidation; she would be running the lab meeting, for Lindsey was visiting colleagues at the Engineering Department at Cambridge University in the UK. Anything reeking of administration made Sara's head pound. She halted at the lab door, cursing herself. Shit! She'd forgotten to write a meeting agenda. At this point all she could do was wing it and encourage the postdocs to talk about their research and conference presentations. As feeble compensation for her ineptitude as an interim lab supervisor, she rushed up Water

Street to buy the group fresh blueberry muffins from a bakery. As she exited the shop, she collided with Jessie, who had ducked inside to get out of a brief downpour. They had not spoken since the morning of Jessie's run down Millfield Street, and Sara knew any conversation would be awkward.

"How's the head, party girl?" Sara jested to break the ice.

Jessie glanced around and asked in a nervous whisper, "Did I say... do anything ...?"

"No, you just went to sleep. Sorry to leave you there, but I had to run to the lab for a bit." Sara checked her watch. "I have to dash. There's a lab meeting in ten minutes. But let's talk for a second."

"We can talk later if you're in a hurry," Jessie suggested, anxious to avoid further conversation.

"Are you walking back to the lab?" Sara asked.

"Yes."

"I'll wait for you."

The expression on Jessie's face flashed like a lightning strike. Dread. Nevertheless she said, "Okay. I'll be right out." Jessie entered, ordered a coffee and donut, and returned to the doorway. They started down Water Street toward the marine lab.

"So, how's everything going with your experiments?" Sara asked.

"I'm not getting enough time on the Zeiss microscope, so I'm not getting as much done as I'd like. Too many summer scientists have invaded the lab."

"Lin and I have an excellent microscope. You're welcome to use it anytime."

"I'll think about it." Jessie paused. "Maybe I should just to stick with the one in my lab. The cells might get messed up crossing the street."

"Are they old enough to cross the street on their own?" Sara grinned.

Jessie groaned at the bad joke. "I'm signed up for the Zeiss on Tuesday and Thursday nights, but I'm going to tear up *Mermaid*'s hull on the shoals going to the marina in the dark."

"Sign up? Screw that. Our Zeiss is free all the time. Really, you're welcome to use it. And don't drive your boat in the dark. It's way too dangerous. Crash out in my spare room on those nights if you want to. That room's finally been painted and it has a comfy sofa bed."

"Okay, thanks. I'll think about it."

"Lucky for you I won't be around Tuesday and Thursday nights to scramble your thoughts with my killer weed, since those are my karate nights," Sara said with good humor.

Jessie grimaced and avoided Sara's eyes by veering around puddles in the sideway.

Sara continued, "By the way, drifty is not a word. I checked the Oxford dictionary, because I don't have better things to do." Sara noticed Jessie look longingly at the provisions store, her escape from the teasing.

"I need to pick up some things in here," Jessie said eagerly, darting toward the shop front. "I'll catch you later."

"Yeah, later," Sara replied blandly. "You're still welcome to the spare room if you're worried about your boat," she added.

There was no response from Jessie, as she had already fled into the store.

Whoa, was her gadar malfunctioning! How had she misread this? She was getting nowhere with Lindsey's cute tenant. Yet Jessie's eyes had been all over her on the *Mary Read*, and again after the Friday Evening Lecture. It had seemed as though Jessie had wanted to talk that night, but couldn't make her way through the crowd. Maybe that French bitch, Monique, who had been affixed to her like a leech that night, had intimidated Jessie.

No, Jessie was clearly not interested. There would be no further thoughts about her, Sara promised herself. No more checking through the French doors to see if *Mermaid* was at the slip or out to sea, or watching Jessie heave dive tanks around the boat in that tight blue wet suit.

Adrian checked his watch. He had twenty minutes until his dive charter on *Mermaid,* so he stepped into a laboratory building, searching for a bathroom. At an auditorium, he noticed a poster in a glass display case. He stopped to read most of the notice boards around the village, as it gave him ideas on how to spend his evenings. It was a hopping little village, with juggling, theater productions, concerts, and classic movies. At the oceanographic institution he had heard talks on the submersible *Alvin*, on the discovery of new hydrothermal vents, and the development of coral atolls. His graduate seminar in New Hampshire had ended, and he was having a wonderful time on the Cape, though sadly, the elusive Dr. Nymph could not be found.

The poster listed speakers for the summer's Friday Night Lecture series. There was a lecture by an embryologist, another by a neurophysiologist, then a marshland ecologist, another by... no way! A few weeks ago a lecture had been given by two bioengineers. Adrian couldn't believe his eyes, or his good luck. He stared at a photograph of the two women standing in front of a rack of electrical equipment. Dr. Nymph's actual name was Lindsey Nolan. The Polynesian babe was Sara Kauni. More amazing luck: their home institution was this very marine lab. He whipped out his smartphone and found the lab's directory. The Nolan-Kauni bioengineering lab was on the third floor. Just up the stairs!

He dashed to a men's room to check his appearance, chewed a breath mint, then excitedly headed toward the third floor. A metal statue of Confucius sat at the end of a hallway. In the prophet's cupped hands lay a few coins, the scientists' daily offering for meaningful experiments. He snatched the change for bus fare and started up a back staircase.

It took no time to locate the women's lab. The nameplate next to the door listed Lindsey Nolan, MD, PhD, as Director, Sara Kauni, PhD, as Chief Engineer. The lab door was open. The Polynesian stunner was seated at her desk, reviewing a document with a person the age of a graduate student or postdoc. The desk across the room was vacant. Nolan, he presumed, was making tons of cash on a summer lecture tour, as he would do when he announced the map, and whatever archeological ruin he might find at the black dot, to the world.

Though the world did not know this yet, he was now a historian of superstar status. Why shouldn't he have a Nobel laureate for a plaything? Either one of them would do. Both? The chase had just gotten so much more interesting ....

Lindsey Nolan could spot a cop from miles away. She had just unpacked from her trip to England and bought milk and bread from Sheila in the bait store when she'd noticed a blue sedan pull into the marina parking lot. Her heart raced, a vestigial response from her boozing days. The cop was not coming for her, she'd tried to convince herself, as there had been no trouble in quite some time. Not since that party in Provincetown that the cops crashed. She had been upstairs with those two guys... and that was nobody's business but hers! Nor had she had any knowledge that the host and some other guests were doing lines of coke in the boathouse. All charges against her had been dropped, but it had been a messy, highly publicized ordeal.

The blue sedan parked next to her Jeep. A tall man emerged, scanned the marina for a moment, and strolled with graceful confidence toward the *Mary Read,* where she stood with her arms folded across her chest. He seemed to be inspecting the *Anne Bonny* floating at the far end of the dock, but she wasn't sure, as he was wearing sunglasses. His white-blond hair was mixed with some gray, and when he introduced himself as Inspector Sven Halvorsen of Interpol, of the Arts and Antiquities Unit, she guessed him to be about fifteen years older than herself, in his late forties. He spoke with a Scandinavian accent. His identification card revealed that he was based out of an office in Oslo. He asked if they might talk on her boat, to which she quickly said no.

"Dr. Nolan, does anyone reside on the *Anne Bonny*?"

Lindsey's heart jolted. He knew her name and the name of the *Anne Bonny*, even though the name on the transom couldn't be seen from where they were standing. Clearly he had been to the marina before, in the weeks she had been abroad. "It's my boat. I reside on it," she answered tersely.

"And no one else?" he asked curiously.

"I reside on it," she repeated, turning away.

"Thank you for this very helpful information, Doctor," he replied in a tone heavy with sarcasm. "One more thing. May I have your autograph for my daughter?"

Was this a ploy to get on her boat while she searched for pen and paper? "No!"

The officer's gaze lingered on the *Anne Bonny*, and he departed, stating with certainty, "We'll talk another day, Dr. Nolan."

Lindsey stared after him. What bothered her most was that this Norwegian in the expensive tailored suit was completely unfazed by her noncooperation. She would have a conversation with Jessie, whom she doubted had recently stolen artwork in Norway and was lying low in Woods Hole, disguising herself as a marine biologist. She headed quickly to her office on the *Mary Read* to do some homework on Inspector Sven Halvorsen.

At 5:30 a.m. Sara awoke and pulled on sweatpants and a tank top. In bare feet she padded down the stairs silently, so as not to wake Zephyr. Derick Briggs, a friend from graduate school days at Cornell, lay asleep on her living room sofa. Sometime during the night he had arrived in Woods Hole, driving up from Atlanta. In the darkness he had groped around for the key hidden under a flowerpot, let himself in, folded his leather jacket into a pillow, and collapsed on the sofa, still wearing his black chaps.

Sara quietly pulled a water bottle from the refrigerator and a yoga mat from the corner by the French doors, then moved out to the back porch. In her driveway sat a Ducati touring motorcycle, laden with motorcycle luggage, that Derick had owned for as long as she could remember. He dreamed about purchasing a retro bike like an Indian, Royal Enfield, or Norton.

She turned her gaze to the pond. At that hour the only movement was a fish snapping at an insect on the water's surface; otherwise, the pond was silent. Her workout, a combination of tai chi, yoga, and Pilates, varied every day. She checked in with herself and decided that tai chi and yoga were what her body and soul needed that morning.

After an hour she arose from the yoga mat and entered the house. The aroma of Sumatran coffee dripping through an automatic coffee maker filled the kitchen. Derick momentarily lifted his head, flashed Sara a boyish smile from under his thick biker mustache, muttered something about a sore throttle hand and frozen lower back, and promptly dropped back into the cushions.

Sara returned to the porch with a coffee cup in her hand. Across the pond on Water Street delivery trucks were off-loading dairy products and fresh produce at the restaurants and stores before the street filled with tourists and scientists.

Ægir's Curse

Leaning against the railing, she glanced toward the marine lab to see that the windows of the Nolan-Kauni bioengineering lab were dark.

How was it that Lindsey was able to make spot-on decisions about potential business partners, Sara wondered. That company in Vermont that she had thought would be ideal to manufacture the Nolan-Kauni simulator, Lindsey had suddenly wanted to "wait on." Days later, Lindsey had casually said, "Oh, by the way, we're not going with the Vermont firm."

"Why?" Sara had asked in disbelief.

Lindsey hadn't answered immediately. "A bad gut feeling." To avoid further discussion on the matter, she'd pulled on a white lab coat and retreated to the electroplating room.

How could Lindsey walk away from such an enormous signing bonus and lucrative cut of the profits? This decision impacted her finances as well, Sara had wanted to argue! Instead, she'd said nothing and worked in moody silence over the next few days. Later that week she'd turned on the TV in the living room while preparing dinner for Zephyr. A news anchor on CNN was describing a breaking story on a corruption scandal between a senator from Vermont and the electronics firm.

Gut feeling ... bullshit.

Lindsey must have hired a private investigator to check on the management team and operations of the company. After Lindsey's BioCorp profits had been depleted by her ball-and-chain husband Duncan and his bloodsucking girlfriend, while she was drying out in rehab, her boss didn't mess around. Perhaps the same private investigator could tell Sara a little more about Jessie's elusive brother, Alan?

Only one handprint could access the doorknob of Lindsey Nolan's office on board the *Mary Read*. Hers. The risk of having one of the children inadvertently leave the office open, allowing a corporate spy or competitor to slip onto the boat and rummage around with a digital camera was too high; the information in the computers and notebooks was too valuable.

Lindsey's office was stripped down to the bare essentials. Worktables lined the perimeter of the cabin and were covered with assorted legal pads, pens, rulers, and calculators. A whiteboard on a bulkhead was covered with circuit diagrams and mathematical formulae. Three supercomputers sat along the tables furthest from a single porthole, which was covered over with cardboard and duct tape and too small for a thief to crawl through. Absent were photographs of family or children's artwork. It housed nothing personal; that room was all about business.

Lindsey turned on a computer and opened an instant messaging program. She expected her computer engineer in Boston, Dr. Sylvia Benson, to answer within minutes, as the woman only left her computer for the bathroom or to pay the pizza deliveryman. Lindsey had first met Benson in person to discuss a software development problem associated with one of her electrode designs. *Nirvana* music had blared from Benson's computer speakers throughout the entire conversation, but a professional bond had formed, and Lindsey had since supplied Benson with a steady stream of software jobs over the years.

Benson could also be hired for Other Business, and the Norwegian cop fell into the category of Other Business. Lindsey looked at her watch, waiting for a response. Seventeen seconds passed before Benson's IM name appeared on the computer screen.

    Cobainlust: things good?
    Scibabe: things weird u?
    Cobainlust: busy
    Scibabe: i have a job. a personnel profile.

Cobainlust: who?

Scibabe: a cop. sven halvorsen. interpol oslo. antiquities unit

Cobainlust: lol really?

Scibabe: really

Cobainlust: mmm. not so keen on this type of job. good cop or bad cop?

Scibabe: thats wht i wanna kno

Cobainlust: yikes!

Scibabe: can it b done?

Cobainlust: hey it's me. :) but im really busy right now. conf in canada next week

Scibabe: will pay the same as the other job

Cobainlust: thinking

Cobainlust: ok. need $ right now. im redoing my kitchen r u in trouble?

Scibabe: no 4 once. but maybe a friend

Cobainlust: 2 days at earliest.

Scibabe: thanks! make these IMs go forever

Cobainlust: what IMs? :)

"Good Cop, Bad Cop, Choir Boy," read the subject line. "File attached."

The brief message sent from Cobainlust to Scibabe's gmail account arrived, as promised, two days later. Lindsey clicked open the attachment. Sylvia Benson's Other Business services were not hired out frequently, only when researching new business partnerships, when it was essential to gauge the ethics of potential partners. It was one of life's ironies that the integrity of future collaborators was verified (or not) by Benson "penetration testing" the firewalls of their databases and personnel files.

Chapter 7

West Falmouth

It was only a matter of time before Inspector Halvorsen returned to the marina; Lindsey was sure of it. An Interpol agent was not going to turn around and go back to Norway simply because she rebuffed him. Next time she would speak with him and lay this whole business to rest. Past encounters with the police had gone badly, largely because of her unquestionable guilt in an array of drunken follies, but a sober mind had made for sound decision-making, so there was nothing to fear from this officer. Her problems as a drunk were with the police, but her problems as a sober woman were with lawyers representing her parasitic husband, Duncan, and other leeches who wanted to bite deeply into her profits.

Though her inventions had provided the means to purchase art, the art field held little interest for her. In fact, her interests were admittedly limited: family, the Baltimore Orioles, work, and sex. Art was definitely not among them. It was likely that Interpol wanted to question her about one of Duncan's get-rich-quick schemes, or his snail-brained Scottish girlfriend, what's-her-name. Duncan must have bought a forgery, or stolen some painting or artifact. But he was a jock and knew nothing about art. Perhaps Snail-brain was entangled in some art fraud, like that castle restoration debacle that had nearly drained her

BioCorp account. Before Lindsey spoke to the Interpol cop, she needed to have a conversation with Duncan. Unfortunately, for the past few days her emails had bounced back with an out-of-office message.

And she hadn't had a chance to speak with Jessie either. Where was she? Lindsey hadn't seen *Mermaid* in the marina since she'd returned from England, nor were there lights on in the *Anne Bonny* in the evenings. Why hadn't Halvorsen asked about the *Green Monster* or *Mary Read*? What was so intriguing about the *Anne Bonny*?

It had been a particularly tiresome Friday, as two postdocs in the lab had bickered about who should have first authorship on a manuscript. Then there was a dog and pony show for a CEO from an electronics firm, who was considering the purchase of the 5M imager. Some broken equipment and misdirected requisition orders had proved an annoyance for the remainder of the afternoon. When Lindsey returned home from work, the last thing she wanted to do was to drive to Fenway Park and sit among thirty-five thousand screaming, beer-sodden fans to see a ball game that did not involve the Baltimore Orioles. Maggie's boyfriend, Brian, was thrilled to take her ticket, so Rob and the children set forth up Route 3 toward Boston.

Lindsey pulled off her dress and changed into shorts, a bikini top, and flip flops, intending to savor a quiet evening on the empty boats. Earlier in the day the children had been riding their mountain bikes in the marsh, spackling them with sandy muck, so she stood for some time, mindlessly spraying down the bikes with a garden hose at the fish-cleaning table. Then the blue sedan crossed the parking lot, and her blood pressure spiked.

The inspector emerged from the car, his stiff suit replaced by khakis and a white dress shirt.

"I see that you've adopted the American tradition of dress-down Friday," Lindsey said wryly when he approached.

"What?" he asked, perplexed.

"Never mind. How can I help you, Inspector?"

"Doctor," he asked with a policeman's formality, "can you and I talk? This really is a matter of great importance." His face was grave but pleasant.

"Yes."

The houseboats floated serenely on the water; the only sounds were the chirp of crickets and the murmur of a pickup truck maneuvering a speedboat down the boat ramp. He glanced at his watch, then at her red belly button stud, and then at his watch again.

"Over a meal," he remarked.

A comment, not a question, she noted. "Alright. This is a good time. The family's at Fenway tonight."

"Right, the Red Sox," he replied.

"Let me go change." She turned the hose on herself, splashing water from her face to her toes. "Shower's done." On her way to turn off the spigot, she flung the hose down, and water arced across his shoes and pant legs. "Oops," she said.

His face remained impassive. He watched her step onto the deck of the *Mary Read*. "Dr. Nolan?" he called.

She turned in the doorway of the salon.

"Do you know that someone hacked into an Interpol database and downloaded my personnel file?"

"No, really?" she replied with surprise.

"Yes. But it was traced to the Liberian government."

"Bad Liberians," she quipped.

She glanced briefly at him once again. He appeared to be smiling to himself. *Guilty*, she guessed, was his verdict.

Ægir's Curse

The West Falmouth restaurant was a good place to avoid science groupies in Woods Hole, who seemed to accost Lindsey at every turn, requesting autographs, telling her of their "amazing discoveries," or inquiring after a job in her lab. It was not the best restaurant in the area, but the seafood was always fresh, the music not too loud or too dated, and there was a quiet back porch overlooking the bay. Halvorsen requested the table in the far corner.

Neither Nolan nor Halvorsen had much tolerance for small talk and had dispensed with most of it during the ride to the restaurant. This was his first trip to the United States, he explained, most of his international travel being to eastern Europe, the Middle East, or southeast Asia. She had never been to Oslo, she replied, but had traveled with Sara to Stockholm the year before.

A server returned to take the drink order.

"Club soda for me, please," she said.

"Heineken for me," he requested.

The server departed for the bar.

"How long have you been sober?" he asked frankly.

Her body tightened. The question confirmed her suspicions that Interpol had her under investigation. Reports about the car accident her freshman year, the other DWIs, the photos from the boat off of Montauk, that party in Provincetown, she was certain, were sitting in his briefcase or laptop somewhere.

"You obviously haven't studied my file close enough, or you'd know that," she snapped, pushing her chair from the table.

She gazed hotly across the tidal marsh, wondering if this meeting had just ended. Her hypocrisy irked her, as she remembered the Other Business that Sylvia Benson had done for her. Worse, she had nothing on him, nothing at all for leverage. He was a goddamn choir boy. She glanced over at him. He sat, unflappable and cool, studying the menu.

Finally he slid the menu under his plate. "Yes, I've read your file," he said matter-of-factly. "What impressed me most was your career of developing exceptional innovations that save lives."

His tactic was admirable: flattery. "Nice recovery," she replied sarcastically. "Now tell me why I'm here."

The inspector's engrossing story and an excellent flounder filet caused her irritation to wane, as he explained, between bites of clam strips, a case that he and his partner were working on.

An assortment of papers from an outbuilding at a Greenland monastery had been recovered. Most of the documents were fairly modern, records of land sales, marriage records, old newspapers and the like, the repository having served as an archival dumping ground for generations.

Last summer, however, a history teacher, a Mr. Jens Tryggvesen from Narsaq, had begun sifting through the papers in the hope of finding newspapers from the World War I era and had stumbled upon a wedding album. The album belonged to Harald and Karin Agard, married in April of 1911. The living relatives of the Agards had no knowledge of the album, nor any recollection of Harald and Karin, who would have been distant cousins. Tryggvesen found nothing exceptional as he leafed through the album, but then noticed a frayed edge near the back pages. Upon closer inspection he discovered that the frayed edge was from an old hide parchment tucked under the fabric of the back cover.

Halvorsen's English was perfect—he had earned a law degree and a master's degree in art history from Oxford, Lindsey remembered from his file. He lowered his voice as a server seated a young couple two tables over and they maneuvered a baby into a high chair. He pulled a cell phone from his pocket and leaned over the plates and condiments to display an image, prompting her to slide to the edge of her chair. His aftershave was some exotic blend that she had never smelled before. He studied the small screen once more before turning the phone in her direction.

It was an old map of Cape Cod, its outline drawn crudely in some black material, and certainly not to scale. The islands of Martha's Vineyard and Nantucket were too close together and too close to the coastline of Chatham, and the dots that represented the Elizabeth Islands were too numerous. The ragged promontory of land that was Woods Hole was amazingly accurate, however, suggesting that the cartographer had seen the area a few times at least. Two faint letters, a T and E, were visible in the corner.

"Can you enlarge it for me?" she asked.

"Yes, of course." He handed her the phone.

She studied the small screen for a moment longer. "This is clearly a hoax perpetrated by Tom and Eddie," she remarked facetiously, handing the phone back to Halvorsen. "When did you take this picture?'

Halvorsen ignored her dismissal and continued to lean forward. His voice lowered again. "I didn't. It's the only image that we have of it. The map was sent by Jens Tryggvesen to Professor Ragnar Ingvars of the University of Bergen to authenticate at a forensics lab."

She was familiar with forensic techniques, as she had double-majored in biochemistry and biomedical engineering at Hopkins prior to medical school. "And the results?"

"Professor Ingvars was a very thorough scholar. Two small samples were sent to two labs, one in Bonn, and the other in Zurich, in a blind test. Neither lab had any knowledge of what they were analyzing. Identical test results were returned. The medium was reindeer hide, the ink was made of ground-up ores. The map has been dated to the mid-1100s."

Her role in this was now becoming clear. While the prototype of the 5M imager was still in trial phases, she would be asked to test some sample of the hide, most likely to determine the molecular composition of the ink and corroborate the carbon dating. The imager's existence was no secret, as it had been featured in *Fortune* magazine a few months earlier. Sure, why not? Many small projects were in the queue anyway. What was one more? No doubt the inspector was telling her all of this to stress the importance of absolute secrecy. Secrecy was her middle name. The sample could be run one evening after everyone had left for the day. Though there were still some glitches in the software that Sylvia Benson was correcting, the results would be 97 percent accurate, that much she could promise. The results could be sent back to the inspector in Oslo in an encrypted format, if he preferred that level of security.

The server approached with the dessert menu, but the two of them declined. The young couple nearby was picking Cheerios off the floor that the baby had tossed over the tray.

"If these are replicable findings, which they appear to be, why hasn't Ingvars released this find to the scientific community?" she asked, baffled.

"Fake Vinland maps have surfaced before. As you said yourself, it has to be a hoax. Ingvars was a very cautious man and Norway's preeminent Viking authority, so the last thing he wanted was to retire under a cloud of doubt. He was waiting for more data."

"Was?" she asked hesitantly.

Halvorsen glanced over to the young couple with the baby, who were oblivious to their presence at the corner table. "Professor Ingvars was murdered, and the map has disappeared," he murmured. "The fingerprints of the suspect are on the windows and doorknob of your pirate ship, the *Anne Bonny*."

She sat back, momentarily stunned. "This person was on my boat? What about the *Mary Read* and *Green Monster*?"

"They were clean."

"And you did this when?" she continued, alarmed.

Halvorsen remained obstinately silent.

She eyed him doubtfully. No way with her new security system... and the deluxe package... could anyone breach the *Mary Read* or *Green Monster* where her family lived. It was possible that that cops could have climbed aboard the *Anne Bonny,* as it was a worthless, rotting hulk outside of the security perimeter. If anyone other than family members stepped onto the other boats, an alerting text message was immediately sent to her smartphone and the security company. The cop was lying, plain and simple.

Lindsey signaled to the waitress and grabbed for her purse. "Check please," she requested, perhaps too loudly. The pitch and quaver of her voice caused the young couple to momentarily stop their conversation and look protectively toward their baby.

"No, please, dinner was my idea," Halvorsen offered calmly, reaching for his wallet.

The time to argue was soon, but not in a restaurant and not over a forty dollar tab. "Fine. I'll wait outside," she replied caustically.

She started quickly for the blue sedan, but it was parked too close to the entryway of the restaurant, where a family waiting on the front bench would hear anything she said. Halvorsen found her behind the restaurant by the edge of the bay.

She fumed. "My children live on those boats! Why didn't you tell me immediately?"

"I tried the other day, but you were far from accommodating. Who is the woman on your boat, Dr. Nolan? How long have you known her?"

"No way... it's not her. She's practically afraid of her own shadow."

"What's her name?"

She silently smoldered.

"This is a murder investigation, Doctor. What's her name?"

She continued to glare. "Jessie."

"Jessie what?"

"I don't remember!"

"You have a woman living on your boat and you don't know her name? When you signed a lease, you never noticed her name?"

She paused, remembering the ad on the corkboard at the convenience store. "McCabe. That's it." She swayed nervously, from one foot to the other. "She didn't sign a lease. I just told her she could stay there until she finds a place in the village. She wants to live in the village, but she's waiting for the off-season when the rates drop."

"A stranger arrives on your doorstep and you simply put her up?" he asked in amazement.

"Yes, no. I mean ...." She remained silent for a moment. "I'm an idiot."

"Quite," he agreed.

Dave's Marina

In the marina parking lot, Lindsey bolted from the sedan but did not return directly to the *Mary Read.* Instead she flew in the direction of the bait and tackle store. She stomped up the steps, across the warped planks of the porch, and pushed through a screen door. A glass cabinet containing six-packs of beers were blurs in her peripheral vision. The thought of drinking herself into a state of oblivion no longer crossed her mind. Now she relied on two remaining stress-relievers. At the moment one was not an option, as he was at Fenway; however, the other was located behind the counter, next to the fishhooks, playing cards, and chewing tobacco.

The clerk, Sheila, jumped abruptly off a stool, spilling her Bud Lite next to the cash register. She nervously mopped up the beer from the counter.

"You look like you saw a ghost. You're so pale," Lindsey remarked. "Are you okay?"

"I, um, I was watching a scary show," Sheila stammered, wide-eyed.

Lindsey glanced skeptically at a portable black-and-white TV behind the counter. "Sheila, it's *The Simpsons*."

Sheila composed herself by chugging down the rest of the beer. "Um, it was a scary show before this one. What do you need?"

"Marlboro Lights, please."

"Don't do it, Lin. You've quit for a while now."

"Thirteen months, but who's counting. And a lighter, please."

"Do you want to talk?" Sheila asked with concern.

Both hands leaning on the counter, Lindsey stared into Sheila's freckled face. Sheila should be told, as her children, Max and Brianna, were in potential danger too, but Lindsey had promised secrecy to Halvorsen until more was known. He had tried to assuage her worries by saying that the suspect had likely moved on, but she knew better.

Sheila looked expectantly at Lindsey. "Really, are you okay?"

Lindsey had known Sheila and Dave for eight years and they had witnessed, without judgment or comment, the tempests in her life, drunk and sober. Danny, Maggie, Ava, Max and Brianna had been raised in a loose cooperative, the five children freely roaming between the apartment over the bait and tackle store and three houseboats that composed the Nolan-Jenkins domicile, being fed, watched over, and cared for by any combination of the four adults.

"Please put this on my tab." Lindsey stuffed the cigarettes and lighter into her skirt pocket. "I'm good, Sheila, no problems."

The screen door shut with a creak and bang, and Lindsey moved fleetly across the porch and parking lot. The blue sedan was gone. The *Anne Bonny* was dark. Running lights formed a sleek outline around the *Mary Read*. A string of hot chili pepper lights and a neon palm tree were alight on the *Green Monster*. The three boats floated quietly in the night. This marina was her cherished home. As she had climbed out of the inspector's sedan moments before, she had warned him, "No one, I swear it, no one's going to harm my children."

Woods Hole

The hot, humid air of the Cape sapped Sven Halvorsen. In his hotel room, he turned up the air conditioning to maximum, removed all of his clothes except his boxers, and pulled a water bottle from a mini-fridge. Waiting for his laptop to turn on, he mentally calculated the time in Oslo. His daughter and son-in-law would still be asleep.

After the death of Halvorsen's wife, his daughter, Anna, then in high school, had fallen into a chasm of depression. At a time when most teenage girls were dressing up for the boys, Anna would arrive at school in unkempt black attire, disinterested in all things, and retreat into headphones blaring the music of German metal bands. Mrs. Caspersen, Anna's chemistry teacher, was troubled by the girl's listlessness and apathy, and mentioned to the father at a parent-teacher conference that she was looking for a student helper after school to assist with the cleanup of the glassware. During that time, he'd been consumed by a search for two stolen Johan Christian Dahl paintings and oblivious to his daughter's declining condition, as he had largely left the raising of their daughter to his wife. The teacher, barely masking her annoyance with him, had said that the girl was coming to class smelling of marijuana and that she should not be home alone for so many hours before he returned from work. The after-school job might be a partial solution to fill in a void of lost hours, the teacher had said, adding stingingly that he needed to change his priorities.

A year or two later, his daughter was still working after school with Mrs. Caspersen and had become passionate about understanding everything about the nature of molecules. One evening she had sat with glue and scissors at the kitchen table. The assignment had been to create a poster on a famous living scientist. Halvorsen remembered Anna printing off a series of images from the computer and returning to the table with them. Having finished the dishes, he'd wandered over and looked at the spread of papers, which were of not one but two women. He'd never heard of either of them. They were Americans, Anna had explained, from Woods Hole, Massachusetts. "I'd put money on it, Papa, that these two will win a Nobel Prize someday."

Over the years, the names of Nolan and Kauni had arisen periodically, especially when Anna's interest in science grew and she set her sights on medical school. In Anna's second year of medical study, one email from her excitedly related that she had finally entered the clinical course where she learned how to use the BioCorp-Nolan electrode, which, she reminded him, Nolan had developed as an undergraduate. When he thought of the poster that Anna had created years earlier, he could remember the gorgeous partner, Kauni, but had no recollection of what Nolan looked like. When Anna's prediction finally came true, another email simply read, "Long overdue, Nolan and Kauni win the big one."

Halvorsen sipped from the water bottle and stared at the laptop. The current case was bizarre to the extreme. An alleged

Vinland map, which may actually be authentic, surfaces briefly and then disappears. The two individuals, Ingvars and Tryggvesen, who knew of the map's existence, were dead and missing, respectively. A curious and conspicuous spot on the twelfth-century map corresponded to the exact location of modern-day Woods Hole, a small village in the United States where his daughter had begged him to take her countless times. Stranger yet, the fingerprints of the murder suspect were on a futuristic doorknob on a boat belonging to his daughter's American science idol, Dr. Lindsey Nolan.

Dr. Nolan immediately understood the significance of the dot on the map, as she had asked him to expand the image on his cell phone screen and had stared at the image for a few seconds, taking a mental reckoning. The Vinland map was not enough for the thief and murderer. What was located at the black dot, at an inlet just to the north of the present-day village, had drawn this person there like a shark to chum.

Lindsey unwrapped the plastic from the cigarettes. She knocked a cigarette from the pack, put it to her lips, and searched her pockets for the lighter. She was glad to be rid of the cop and alone on the *Mary Read*. The yacht was refuge. When some victory or scandal caused the press to swarm the marina, she stocked it with provisions, motored through the marsh, across the Woods Hole Passage, and dropped anchor in a hidden cove off one of the uninhabited Elizabeth Islands until the news had lost its titillation.

The lighter stalled at the tip of a cigarette. Through the teachings of AA she had grown to understand her behavior very well; she was cursed with the most addictive of personalities. The lighter hesitated, her hand still shaking from the conversation with Halvorsen. This one cigarette would lead to a battle for weeks, months, possibly years, that she just might lose. She tossed the cigarette overboard, though she was too agitated to decide what to do with the entire pack. She placed them on a deck table and walked to the automatic doorknob that read the contours on her hand. The lock clicked open.

Halvorsen had provided her with few useful details about the case, maintaining a policeman's confidentiality. His words were a pathetic attempt to convince her that the police were close to apprehending the suspect. His voice was calm and smooth, as if to prove that he was in control of this mess, yet she was anything but soothed. Instead, each fragment of information triggered new surges of panic. She had been determined to say nothing further and had simply stared out the car window, holding back hot tears. By the time they had pulled into the parking lot, her panic had mutated into a seething resolve.

Adrian Arrano was the suspect's name, Jessie a possible accomplice. Halvorsen's partner, Ingrid, was in Boston, while he was working with police in Falmouth. Those facts were straightforward enough. But when had a team of forensics experts discovered fingerprints on the *Anne Bonny*? While she was in England? Did they get a warrant? Was any of this legal? How had the security perimeter been breached? Was there a glitch in the software? A brief power outage? Each question needed to be approached strategically and in isolation, and then the connections would be revealed. You can figure this out, she told herself, if you just stay focused, and very, very angry.

The door to her office on the *Mary Read* was never open, but that night she left it ajar and checked the clock obsessively. Her sole need was to see her children, hug them, and be assured that they were safe. As she waited for their return, she gave the three computers separate assignments, each searching through unique databases. Over a plastic floor protector, she scooted the wheeled office chair from screen to screen. Small epiphanies generated more questions, and new queries were typed into the keyboards. Around midnight, car doors slammed in the parking lot, and her family crossed the dock, the energy and excitement in their voices indicative of a Red Sox victory and too much cotton candy. She shut off the computers and closed the office door.

Ava drooped asleep over Rob's shoulder, and he placed her gently in her bed; they said prayers with Danny, including the nightly prayer for his deceased mother, Paola, and tucked him into bed; Maggie and Brian headed off to his apartment.

Lindsey followed Rob into the master stateroom.

He had noticed the cigarettes on the table outside, an ominous sign. "Are you smoking again?"

"No, but almost."

"Good, I'm glad." He stripped off his clothes, wanting to wash away the sticky grime of Fenway Park. "I need a shower."

She wiggled out of her skirt and blouse and followed him into the shower. Yes, there were better ways to cope with stress than smoking.

Before Halvorsen fell asleep, he composed an email message to Anna. It was brief and teasing. "I'm in the US, in Woods Hole. Guess who I had dinner with?" A vague ache for his wife—surprising him as he had not felt it in years—surfaced. It had been some time since he'd had dinner out with a woman, and though it was all business, Dr. Nolan's intelligence and volatility were stirring. Bearing bad news was a regular function of his job, and he had learned to deliver his lines with polite detachment. Her response to the news—rolling waves of anger, withdrawal, contempt, and mistrust—unsettled him in an unidentifiable way. And he had found in her an unexpected ally.

Something caused him to click open the Nolan file once more. It was not the financial records, awards, lawsuits, arrests, or discoveries that interested him. He searched for the folder of

Ægir's Curse

JPEGs. Most were images from newspaper articles and technology magazines. He clicked open a photograph of Nolan being presented with a Massachusetts state citation by Barney Frank and Ted Kennedy just months before Kennedy's death. No doubt she was a liberal Democrat, but it was not her politics that interested him at the moment. He closed the photograph. It was the Montauk Point image that he was searching for. Finally he found it.

Shot with a powerful telephoto lens, Nolan was sunbathing on the flybridge of the *Mary Read* with the arm of her dozing boyfriend, ex-Red Sox, Robert Jenkins, draped across her hips. These sad, puritanical Americans. The photo had gone viral within minutes of its posting by the New York tabloid. If she lived in Norway, she could sunbathe topless anytime without fear of scandal or monetary reprisal.

Chapter 8

Woods Hole

Sex in the cramped shower stall on her boat always required creative positions, and the next morning Lindsey's legs still ached. She struggled onto her bike seat, emitting a small groan.

"What hurts, Mommy?" Ava asked from her child's seat on the back of the bike.

"Mommy's good," Lindsey answered, feigning cheerfulness.

The bike ride into the village of Woods Hole only took a few minutes, across the marsh, down the Falmouth-Woods Hole bike path, through the parking lot of the Martha's Vineyard ferry, across the bascule bridge, and down Water Street. At the marine lab, she parked at a bike rack and unfastened Ava from her seat.

As on most Saturday mornings, Ava first wanted to play with the marine animals in a touch tank of the aquarium building. She dashed away from her mother and through the doors. The touch tank was at such a level that even the smallest of schoolchildren could reach it. Ava identified the animals aloud to her mother, fearlessly stroking all of them as she inched around the perimeter of the tank. Lindsey watched her daughter for a while, then wove between the circular tanks, stepping over PVC tubing on the floor, to where the scientists kept their research specimens. Her destination was the salt water tanks that held the sponges and corals. Over one of the tanks hung a sign, "Experiment in progress. Please don't touch. Thanks, Jessie McCabe."

The night before, Inspector Halvorsen had suggested that Jessie was a potential menace. Lindsey had googled the marine ecologist and found her Facebook page. Oddly, there were no new posts since Jessie had moved to Woods Hole. As far as Facebook was concerned, Jessie's life ended while she was a grad student at the University of Florida.

Jessica Eileen McCabe was born in and grew up in Toulossa, Florida, a tiny barrier island of three hundred and twenty inhabitants off the northwest coast of Florida. She attended Palm Grove High School, where she ran track and was a member of the Nature Conservation Club. After attending a community college on the mainland for two years, Jessie transferred to Florida State University, where she completed a BS in Environmental Science and an MS in Marine Ecology. Her PhD was completed at the University of Florida, though most of the time was spent, not in Gainesville, but at a marine lab on the coast near St. Augustine. It was during her years at the marine lab that she became an expert scuba diver and skilled at navigating small boats. Her publication record was typical of a new PhD—some referred abstracts, two papers coauthored with her dissertation advisor, and one in progress for which Jessie was first author. Overall, the young scientist had little experience and seemed a bit of a yokel. The suggestion that she was involved in international map theft and murder was ludicrous to the nth degree.

After Ava had squeezed and pestered every invertebrate in the touch tank, she announced that it was time for ice cream. Mother and daughter stopped in the ladies room to wash their hands, exited the building, and turned back up Water Street to buy popsicles. Halvorsen had told Lindsey that the only person who'd remembered seeing Arrano in the village was a clerk in a convenience store, and that was only the one time when he asked about chartering a dive boat.

But that was not true. She had seen him also.

Lindsey had been shocked the night before when she found Arrano's link on West Hampshire College's History Department web page. The departmental photograph was of the same flirtatious man, Lost Tourist, who'd invited her for coffee and called her Dr. Nymph. She had seen him at the store, and again at the seawall. Her shock was quickly replaced by a sickly dread. Knowing that Jessie was broke and needed money, she had recommended Captain McCabe and *Mermaid* to—an alleged murderer!

Ava could play on the swings at Taft Park, Lindsey promised, but they first needed to make one more stop. Climbing back on the bike, they pedaled along the seawall, turned onto Millfield Road, and passed the bell tower and its gardens. Sara's house was just a stone's throw from the bell tower. Lindsey parked her bike behind Sara's Land Rover and a large white motorcycle.

Through the French doors overlooking the pond, Sara spotted the two approaching her house. "It's open!" she called across the porch.

Ava tore around the house, pushed through the screen door, kicked off her shoes, scrambled across the hard wood expanse, and took a flying leap onto Sara's lap. She was greeted with the customary hair mussing and, "Hey, Curly!"

Lindsey removed her sneakers by the front door, respecting the Kauni household rule. An unfamiliar pair of woman's sandals, slightly smaller than Sara's shoe size, were lined up by the others. It had taken Sara some time to extract herself from the overbearing scientist from France, so it was surprising to see another woman in the picture so soon.

Ægir's Curse

As always, the house smelled like incense and marijuana. Remnants of a joint sat in an ashtray on the kitchen table, beside which Sara sat in her bathrobe. Across the table sat Derick Briggs, finishing up a stack of pancakes. Lindsey had met Derick only once, very briefly, at one of Sara's barbecues some summers ago. From first impressions, she thought him an arrogant know-it-all. She was in no mood for tedious small talk with a faint acquaintance.

"Hi, Derick," Lindsey said unenthusiastically.

There was a querulous edge to Lindsey's voice, so he replied cautiously. "Good morning, Lindsey. How are you doing, Ava?"

"Great!" Ava declared ebulliently. "I touched all of the animals in the touch tank!"

"Ava, can you run upstairs and wake up Zephyr?" Sara asked. "Tell him that he has soccer this morning."

"Sure." Ava slid off of Sara's lap.

"Ava, wait. I'll go with you," Derick said mischievously. "We'll pelt Zephyr with pillows."

"Yes!" squealed Ava.

Derick departed with Ava.

"I have two rowdy boys in the house," Sara remarked comically.

"How long is Derick staying?"

"Only until this afternoon. His summer rental becomes available today."

Lindsey recalled that Derick was a microbiologist who divided his time between his summer lab in Woods Hole and the Centers for Disease Control, CDC, in Atlanta. Over many summers she had seen the Ducati rumble down Water Street, the tall, dark man always in the same black leather vest with a patch across the back that read B.A.D.D.: Bikers Against Dumb Drivers. He and Sara had been neighbors in the same apartment building as grad students. During the summer he and Sara were inseparable, attending the same karate class and sampling bottles of wine together from local vineyards.

Lindsey reached for a mug, filled it at the coffeepot, and sat across the table from her assistant.

"So what's so important that you have to interrupt the nirvana of my Saturday morning?" Sara asked.

Lindsey leaned forward, her hands around the mug. "This is really important. I need to find Jessie. Have you seen her at all while I was in England?"

Sara leaned forward, her hands around her mug, imitating Lindsey. "This is really important. Yes, I've seen her. She's been hired for a dive charter for a few days. She's ecstatic to have some money coming in." She grinned widely.

"You're stoned," Lindsey remarked with a small laugh. "I can't talk to you."

"No, truly you can," Sara said, giggling and rocking back in her chair.

"Jessie hasn't been on the *Anne Bonny* for days, weeks, maybe, I don't know how long, and I don't even know where she is, or if she lives there anymore!" Lindsey exclaimed, her voice tinged by anguish.

Sara leaned forward again and said in a near whisper, "It's really alright. She's been living here."

Lindsey was momentarily silent. "Here?"

Sara paused for dramatic effect. "Here."

"She's a student!"

"She's a postdoc and an adult."

"And you're a cougar."

"Yes, and it's wonderful."

The conversation was going nowhere, Lindsey concluded with some exasperation, and Sara was right as usual. What Sara and Jessie were doing was none of her goddamn business. Turning toward the French doors, Lindsey looked at the empty slip at the seawall. "Did you see the person Jessie was chartering?"

"Yes. She's taken him on a few dives."

"Beard and mustache? Long brown hair? Named Adrian Arrano?" Lindsey asked urgently.

"Yo, Adrian!" Sara jested.

"This is not funny!"

"Lin, you're a buzzkill. This guy has a blond crew cut. He's a real preppy."

Lindsey felt her blood pressure return to normal and the panic and confusion subside.

"His name is Craig Russell," Sara added. "He's a photojournalist for *Quest* travel magazine."

Chapter 9

Woods Hole

Lindsey stood barefoot in the sand of Taft Park, pushing Ava in a swing. The rhythmic motion, like a pendulum in her undergraduate physics labs, had a soothing effect. She wished that she had Sara's ability to live in the moment, and Sara's ability to have one drink or one toke, and then be able to put it aside and move clearly through the rest of the day.

Even after years of sobriety, the concept of *one drink* was still alien. During a mental relapse, her imagination would stagger toward impending disaster, starting with a morning of breakfast beers, then a lunch of lunchtime beers, a liquid dinner with a "friend" who had the same proclivities, all capped off by a Glenlivet-fueled prowl through the Captain Kidd and clubs of the Cape. Her compulsivity in all things irked her. Though it should have been comforting to find that Jessie had been fine all along, diving with a travel writer and not a sociopathic murderer and thief, Lindsey still obsessed about the gaps in the Arrano case.

The night before, she had become so flustered in the sedan that she had forgotten to ask Halvorsen for an explanation of the sequence of events that led his team to Jessie and the *Anne Bonny*. Would he disclose this information to her? Perhaps the offer of a deal, an exchange of sorts, might get him to talk? Ava's head began to bob; the late night at Fenway, busy morning in the village, and pillow fight with Zephyr and Derick had tired her. Lindsey looked at the time on her smartphone. Later that day she'd have to call the rep at the security company about the breach. But now it was time for Ava's lunch and nap. Lindsey lifted her daughter from the swing. Rob and Dave were repairing a garage door on a space metal building that afternoon. They could watch Ava while she went to meet with Halvorsen. Before leaving the park, she called the cop's cell phone. He gladly agreed to the terms of the bargain.

At Sea

Two hours later, Lindsey's boat was tied up at the Falmouth Township marina. During their earlier phone conversation, Halvorsen had asked her what type of boat to look for. "Don't worry," she'd responded dryly, "you won't miss this one." The few hours left him with just enough time to finish up some paperwork in the office, grab a quick lunch, and pick up a pair of shorts and sandals at a local store.

Lindsey was right, he realized. The *Just for Today* was impossible to miss. It was a purple, glittery cigar boat with two massive outboards bolted to the transom.

He looked down at the boat from the dock. "Dazzling."

"American decadence at your most extreme. Leave it to Maggie to pick out the most ostentatious boat at the boat show."

Maggie, he recalled from his files, was the orphaned prostitute that had roomed with Nolan in the Newport drug and alcohol rehab, and had later been adopted by Lindsey Nolan and Robert Jenkins. The teenager was involved in a clinical trial for a new AIDS drug; both Nolan and Jenkins were volunteers, control participants in the study.

Lindsey reached up and offered a hand for support as he climbed down. "Find your sea legs, Inspector."

"Sven. Please call me Sven."

"Okay. I'm Lindsey." This last exchange was a ridiculous waste of words, she figured, as they obviously knew each other's names, but perhaps it indicated a truce of sorts.

As she uncoiled the lines from the cleats, he inspected the boat; it had absolutely no utilitarian purpose, except to burn obscene qualities of gasoline and shuttle tipsy tourists from one dockside bar to another. The aft deck consisted solely of comfortable nylon sofas surrounded by cup holders. Next to the instrument panel and pilot's seat, steps led down into a cabin. He ducked his head into the cool darkness to find a large v-shaped berth that extended to the bow. Float coats, coloring books, and crayons were stored in teak racks along the walls. The space was lit only by small portholes.

"Ava's hideaway," Lindsey explained. She stepped behind the steering wheel and slowly moved the throttle forward, and the *Just For Today,* a phrase that she and Maggie had seen on posters in rehab, eased from the dock with a low rumble of the engines. "Do you know how to drive a boat?"

"No."

"Well, you'd better learn fast." She left her position behind the wheel and climbed up to the bow to pull in the forward fenders. He scrambled to the vacated wheel and attempted to keep the boat in the center of the channel, but grossly overcompensated, causing the bow to veer toward the boats on either side.

She walked along the aft gunwales and pulled in the last fenders. "You're hopeless. Give me the wheel."

The *Just For Today* pointed directly at Martha's Vineyard, but they were not heading south. Clearing the marina and breakers, Lindsey veered westward. The dual outboards grumbled loudly and churned up the Vineyard Sound.

Ægir's Curse

For some minutes the two sat silently, as the engines left a foamy swath behind them. She would not press him for information immediately, as he seemed to be enjoying the wild ride, and for the moment she was content to be a tour boat captain. An Orioles ball cap was snuggly pulled onto her head to prevent it from skipping away on the breeze. His platinum hair was too short to be mussed by the wind, but without a hat he would fry in the intense sun. She tossed a tube of sunscreen at him, and a smile temporarily softened his angular face. He cleared salt off of his sunglasses with his shirttail, revealing eyes that were not the expected Nordic blue, but an uncommon golden brown. He held himself with a noble self-reliance, a man of Oslo's art set, now unsettled by turbulence. He firmly clasped an armrest.

Passing the Nobska Point lighthouse, the boat moved from the Vineyard Sound into the Woods Hole Passage. Restlessly, she searched the satellite radio and finally chose American honky-tonk. The day was unusually steamy, so she pulled her blouse over her head, dipped it in the icy water of a cooler, and draped it over her shoulders. Enough sightseeing, she decided. They had a deal and she was keeping her end of it, taking him on a survey of the coast in hopes of finding the black dot, the Viking inlet. When was he going to start talking and hold up his end? That was the agreement: a coastal survey in exchange for the specifics of the Arrano case.

"I also saw Arrano at the convenience store in the village. I feel horrible about it," she said to jump-start the conversation. "He asked me about McCabe Dive Adventures and I recommended it to him. Then I saw him later that day at the seawall, standing over *Mermaid*, Jessie's boat."

"When was this?" he asked, surprised.

"I don't know for sure, but it was before I went to England on June twentieth."

"What was he like?"

"A creep and a lech. Jessie no longer lives on the *Anne Bonny*. She's been staying at Sara Kauni's place in the village. Jessie's been chartering her boat to a person named Craig Russell who works for *Quest* magazine. Thankfully not Arrano! Jessie has not been off conspiring with Arrano, and she is not Arrano's accomplice!" she added insistently in Jessie's defense.

He listened intently, while wondering if her black bikini top was the same one that had been removed in the photograph from Montauk.

"Let's check on Mr. Russell." He pulled a cell phone from his pocket, accessed the Internet, and found *Quest*'s editorial page, which confirmed that Craig Russell was in fact an associate editor for the Boston-based magazine. He then called the number of his partner, Detective Ingrid Stevs. "Ingrid, can you check on a travel writer, Craig Russell, for me? Of *Quest* magazine." He exchanged some other brief comments with Ingrid in Norwegian, then returned the phone to his pocket. His gaze returned to Lindsey's ruby belly button stud and her skinny long legs. Her almond skin had no other piercings, tattoos, or blemishes of any sort.

When he did not say anything more, Lindsey picked up the thread of the conversation.

"Early in the summer, the Scandinavian Historical Society conference was held in Bergen, where Dr. Ingvars was a conference organizer," she said. "It was not a large conference as conferences go. Of eighty-three conference participants, fourteen were Americans. Three of them were from the east coast of the United States. If an American saw that map, they would have immediately recognized the outline of Cape Cod."

"You've been doing your homework, Doctor."

"I didn't get a lot of sleep last night."

"That makes two us."

The thermometer on the instrument panel read ninety-seven degrees. He pulled off his shirt and tried her method of soaking it in ice water from the cooler and slinging it over his shoulders, but it was no use. The American climate was simply intolerable.

"Then what happened?" she asked.

"Ingvars and Arrano probably had dinner together, as Ingvars's stomach contents showed that he had just eaten."

"So where did Arrano slip up?"

"In small but cumulative ways. We don't think that Ingvars's murder was premeditated. At dinner we believe that Ingvars could no longer contain his excitement about the map and showed it to his young colleague."

"I found on Arrano's web page that the two of them had published an article together three years ago, so there had to be some level of professional friendship and trust," she broke in.

"Yes. And possibly on impulse Ingvars showed Arrano the map, and Arrano made a snap decision that it was to be his. Arrano has no previous police record of any type. The toxicology report found the metabolites of sleeping pills in Ingvars's blood that were probably slipped into the professor's drink to make him sleepy."

"Were the pills made by an American drug manufacturer? Or made in Norway? Were any found in Ingvars' apartment?" she inquired.

"The pills were made in America, which was one reason why we began to look at the Americans. But they were not the cause of death. Ingvars was suffocated in his bed. Moreover, the apartment had been wiped clean. All homes are a mosaic of fingerprints, from the maid, deliveryman, kids, aunts, uncles, the whole domestic cadre of characters, and yet in many parts of the kitchen, bathroom, and bedroom, there were no prints at all."

Lindsey reached into the cooler, pulled out two water bottles, and extended one to him.

"Thanks." He continued, "Due to a stroke, the professor was semi-retired and working from his apartment. He was writing a book and still actively communicating with colleagues via email. His university office had been more or less vacated and has since been occupied by a visiting professor and his graduate students. When the police searched the apartment, the professor's laptop was gone."

"How did you find out about the map's existence?"

"Invoices from the two forensics labs were in a stack of bills in Ingvars's desk. He was a dinosaur who didn't pay his bills online. Even more curious was that he paid for those tests by personal checks."

"Which he should have paid for off of a grant, if he had one, but that would have alerted folks in the university budget office that he had found something," she remarked with perspicacity.

"Exactly. This made the police a bit curious about the significance of tiny leather fragments dating from the mid-twelfth century that Ingvars did not want university bookkeepers finding out about. When the detectives contacted the two forensic labs, the scientists of course remembered testing the samples, but had no knowledge of their source.

"Finally a detective found Ingvars's cell phone in his raincoat pocket, and there it was. That same image that I showed you last night. That image was sent to Ingvars from Jens Tryggvesen before the map was delivered to Ingvars for testing. When our graphics experts expanded the photo, they could see that a small fragment had been cut from the corner. We also found a handwritten letter from Tryggvesen to Ingvars describing how and where he found the map.

"Arrano's motive became clear; Ingvars had on his person an ancient map. That's when Ingrid and I were contacted, to see what we knew about such an item. Neither of us had any prior knowledge of its existence.

Ægir's Curse

"The murder coincided with the conference, so we began to investigate, among others, conference participants. A small group of Viking specialists had taken a side tour to Eric the Red's homestead, Brattahlid, in Qassiarsuk, Greenland. The group was mostly Germans and Poles, and one American, Arrano. All returned to Kangerlussuaq Airport and departed to their separate gates. Arrano, however, decided to postpone his flight at the last minute. A rental car charged to his credit card indicated that he stayed three additional days. A gas station attendant near Narsaq, Tryggvesen's hometown, remembered Arrano as he stopped to ask directions. We guess that he was trying to locate Jens Tryggvesen. It's unclear if the men met, as Tryggvesen has not turned up for questioning."

The *Just for Today* passed Woods Hole and Great Harbor and glided toward the peninsula of Penzance Point, where the summer mansions of New England's old money could be glimpsed behind their screens of scrub pines.

Sven continued, "According to Jocelyn, Arrano's wife, he obtained a travel grant and is conducting research at the University of Minnesota and in Iceland for the summer. However, when we checked with university administrators, they informed us that these grants were awarded to two other professors, not Arrano, and Immigration had no record of Arrano leaving the country to travel abroad. Jocelyn's been duped. The black dot on the map seemed like the logical place to start. Also, cell tower records showed that Arrano was sending emails, of a sexual nature, to one of his students from this area. The rest was old-fashioned police work. Photographs were shown around motels and marinas around the Woods Hole and Falmouth area. For some time we had no leads.

"Finally, an employee at a convenience store in Woods Hole recognized the man in the photograph who had been asking about dive charters a few weeks earlier. Arrano's inquiry prompted us to seek out *Mermaid,* which was found tethered at the seawall of Eel Pond. A small bag of trash was found on her deck that, when removed, was never missed by the owner. A water bottle from the trash bag had saliva from a female, while a coffee cup had saliva from a male—the same male saliva that was found on a teacup in the dishwasher of Professor Ingvars in Bergen, Norway, matched that on a coffee mug from the office of Dr. Arrano at West Hampshire College in the White Mountains. Our clever professor wiped down Ingvars's kitchen and stacked the dishes, but forgot to run the dishwasher."

At this point, Lindsey sucked in her breath, looking upset and bewildered.

"Through the marine lab's boat registry, *Mermaid* was traced to Jessica McCabe, a new researcher. The lab's personnel office had no local address for her, so an undercover police officer was asked to make inquiries. The officer wandered into her lab, explaining that he was a friend passing through town and hoped to find Jessie for dinner. His questions were readily answered by another scientist in the lab.

"Later that afternoon, the undercover officer approached me at my desk. At first I thought that I misheard the officer's explanation, the words perhaps lost in translation, so he repeated the information for me. 'McCabe is living with Dr. Lindsey Nolan on her houseboat, *Anne Bonny*.'"

Sven stopped, allowing Lindsey time to absorb the details. He remembered thanking the young officer for the fine investigative work and stepping outside into the salt-saturated air to reflect. Up to that moment the clues had revealed themselves with a quiet, logical expediency. Now a high-profile science celebrity was involved, one reputed to be troublesome at best. So far the inhabitants of Woods Hole were unaware of the murder investigation being conducted silently amidst the summer bustle; he'd like to keep it that way. Returning from his walk, he'd ordered a file compiled on Dr. Nolan.

Ægir's Curse

Sven continued aloud, "A search was conducted around the *Anne Bonny* and the marina. Arrano's saliva was found on a Coke can in the dumpster. The fingerprints that were found on trash from *Mermaid* and Arrano's West Hampshire office were also identified on the doorknob and windows of the *Anne Bonny*. Since he was not found at any local motels, we thought that he might be living with Jessie on the *Anne Bonny*, or on *Mermaid*. However, when the police returned to Eel Pond to put *Mermaid* under surveillance, she had swum away."

In her mind's eye, Lindsey visualized the stealthy investigation around the marina at midday, while she and Rob were at work and the children were at summer camps, or maybe when she had been abroad. The detectives, most likely dressed as sanitation or utility workers, could easily have rummaged around the dumpster and hopped quickly onto the *Anne Bonny*, where they found Arrano's fingerprints. But when was Arrano there?

What bad luck that the range of the new security cameras did not extend down the dock as far as the *Anne Bonny*! Again she asked herself, Was such a search legal? During the next meeting with her attorney, she'd inquire about this. And why did her security system fail? Her reservations about the cop lingered.

"Buzzards Bay," she announced, easing back on the throttle. "This is the site of the black dot. This would have been a good location for a settlement, as it's shielded from direct wave activity and currents from the Atlantic. Of course, this coastline has been radically altered by man's activities over the centuries, but maybe some early whaling maps could provide us with the profile of the original shoreline."

He studied the enclosure of water in front of him. The bay was landlocked on three sides and, even with an offshore breeze pushing up white caps, the waves that rolled in on the distant beaches were no more than knee height.

He stood suddenly and pointed over the port gunwale. "What's that?"

"I don't know." She moved the throttle from neutral and turned the boat.

A patch of water was rough and frothy. A ferocious energy flung red spray into the air.

"That's blood!" he exclaimed.

She nodded apprehensively.

"Not too close!"

"I need to see what it is." She squinted through the haze as she carefully brought the boat closer.

The stench in the hot air was gagging, and they quickly pressed towels over their noses. Floating in the water was a mass of black, white, and pink entrails, blood oozing outward in ribbons of red, surrounded and attacked by grey, torpedo-shaped monsters. They stood side by side, sating with nauseated fascination at the carnage. It was impossible to tell what type of whale it had been from the shredded remains. The sharks attacked again and again in an orgy of bloodlust.

"I'm calling the Coast Guard." She reached for the marine radio. "These sharks are too close to shore. The lifeguards on the beaches need to know about this."

"What are they?"

She turned to face him. His pupils were large discs of black, a sympathetic reaction to unexpected terror. His face was inches from hers, his breathing quick, a cosmopolitan taken far from his element.

"Great whites. There have been a record number of sightings this summer. Scientists think the change in ocean currents, due to global warming, is bringing schools of fish closer to shore, and the sharks are following them in. There's also been an increase in the local seal population that has been attracting them."

"Have you ever seen them before?"

Ægir's Curse

She nodded yes. "But never this close."

After an emergency response boat from Coast Guard Station Woods Hole arrived to monitor the feeding frenzy, the *Just for Today* rounded Penzance Point and returned to the Vineyard Sound. Off a quiet beach near Nobska Point, Lindsey dropped anchor in ten feet of water. Swimming relaxed her. The visibility in the water was excellent, and should a shark approach, she could quickly scramble to shore. Sven warned her not to swim, but she teased him from the dive ladder. "If Moby Dick appears, harpoon him, will you?" She hit the water with a splash.

Sven scanned the terrain around him. The American coastline had a rugged beauty, the alternating expanses of sand and rocky beaches reminiscent of a Norwegian seascape. The Norse would have felt a kinship with such a landscape. Only a few people sunbathed on the adjacent shoreline, as these were private beaches. Sailboats and Jet Skis skimmed across the water; as far as he could see, there were no black fins.

Out of nowhere, a memory resurfaced. He and his wife, Brigette, had taken Anna, then around five or six, to the aquarium. A shark bumped the plexiglass at the exact point where he had placed his hand. His hand jerked back suddenly, causing Brigette and Anna to burst into laughter and tease him for the rest of day. On this day, the sight of so many sharks in the red water had caused a sharp pain in his chest, and for a moment he had believed that he was experiencing a heart attack. A small consolation was that Lindsey Nolan had a medical degree, though he was unsure when she had last practiced medicine. She was a strong swimmer, he observed, her blonde hair fanning out to her waist. Eventually she returned to the boat.

"You know, speaking of Moby Dick," she said, squeezing water from her hair with a towel, "there was a dead whale in both *The Saga of Eric the Red* and *The Saga of the Greenlanders*. In the Greenlanders' saga, a beached whale helped sustain the struggling Vikings in Vinland. In Eric's saga, however, the beached whale caused sickness. What do you think? Is this whale a good or bad omen?"

He shook his head incredulously. "You read the sagas also last night?"

"No, of course not. I can't read Icelandic, but I can read wiki," she answered glibly. "There are many hypotheses that Vinland was further south than L'Anse Aux Meadows, and that L'Anse Aux Meadows was simply a staging area for more southerly expeditions. Also, Vinland was a place of mild winters, butternuts, and grapes, none of which are features of northern Newfoundland. Boulders with deeply carved holes, reputed to hold mooring spikes for Viking ships, have been found in Narragansett Bay and off of Sandwich Beach. And then there is the mysterious Newport Tower, whose builders have not been irrefutably identified. Wild grapes grow freely on the Cape. I've seen them myself, growing at the border between the marsh and scrub forest next to the marina."

"You've become quite the Viking authority," he remarked.

"I'm trying, Inspector. The Vinlanders should be considered our first immigrant group of European descent, though they didn't stay long. Freydis, Eric the Red's daughter, was a piece of work. I guess that she could be considered America's first mass murderer on record."

"That's an interesting way to think of Freydis. I never thought of her as an American. But yes, you Americans can adopt that charming person if you want her. She was your equal-opportunity murderer, equally happy to kill women as well as men. But she only murdered Icelanders, not any Greenlanders, as far as the sagas go."

Ægir's Curse

"And as they slept. Arrano's modus operandi. What was Freydis's motive?"

"They complained about her lasagna," he joked.

She laughed at his weird humor. "Good reason!"

Her laughter was contagious and he laughed heartily, which re-ignited her laughter in turn. It was the nervous, out of control laughter of a shared scare, blood and sharks in the water. When the laughter subsided, they stood face-to-face, still grinning. She was aware of studies on human pheromones, the inexplicit chemical secretions that underlie physical attraction: humans are subliminally attracted to those they are not closely related to, an evolutionary mechanism to increase genetic diversity and prevent inbreeding. Their respective bloodlines might only have crossed in olden times when his Norwegian ancestors pillaged northern Ireland, the origin of the Nolan family tree, somewhere around 800 AD. His attentive gaze, distinctly different from the passive observations of a detective at work, was arousing. His move would come eventually, and a decision would have to be made, of that she was certain.

Shockingly, he reached out at that exact moment. The warmth and strength of his hands on her bare hips was both stirring and disconcerting. Their heads bend forward, foreheads almost touching as his finger moved the belly button stud back and forth in a mesmerizing rhythm.

The cool solitude of the v-berth was just steps away. The cop was strong, intelligent, and confident, traits that excited her. But he was also a total stranger, she reminded herself. And it had taken so long to reestablish trust with Rob after her bad decision in Provincetown.

"I can't do this," she whispered.

"I lost myself," he said, flustered. "I'm so sorry."

A phone vibrated in his pocket.

"I have to answer this." Eager to escape the awkward moment, he released his hands from her.

She nodded and moved to a gunwale where, relieved, she watched the sway of seaweed in the shallows.

His brief conversation with Ingrid Stevs was in Norwegian. Then he rung off. He turned, grim-faced. "Craig Russell recently retired from *Quest* magazine and moved to Bar Harbor, Maine. Yesterday he celebrated his sixty-eighth birthday."

Chapter 10

Falmouth

Adrian Arrano had been unnerved by a freak encounter in a Falmouth pharmacy with his frat brother, Jud. Up to that point, his strategy for locating the Viking ruins at the black dot had been going perfectly, as well it should. He'd scrutinized all planned decisions again and again before executing them. There had been the day trip to the village of Woods Hole, and though he had not talked to the captain of McCabe Dive Adventures that day, despite his long wait at the seawall, he had seen that *Mermaid* was right for his purposes.

Upon returning home, Adrian had contacted the captain via the email address posted on the ad. He'd excitedly told his wife that he had been awarded a travel grant and took her out to dinner to celebrate. This was a huge coup for his career, he'd told her effusively, but he'd need to be at archives in Minnesota and Iceland for most of the summer. He'd miss her and call her frequently, he'd repeated solemnly throughout the meal. The great thing about cell phones was that his incoming phone number to his wife's cell phone would be the same whether he was in Minnesota, Iceland… or Massachusetts.

That same day Adrian had driven to his father's home and lifted up the garage door. The door had squealed, as it had not been opened in weeks, not since his father's move to the nursing home. Eventually the house and musty garage would have to be emptied out, but between his hectic schedule and his wife's, there was simply no time.

His father's compact car had been coated with a sheen of dust, and Adrian had brushed cobwebs away from the driver's side door. After a few turns of the key the car had coughed to life. On the front seat were his father's bowling ball case and a gym bag containing bowling shoes and a league shirt. After verifying there was still a half a tank of gas, he had turned off the engine and walked over to inspect the camping gear on the wooden shelves, including a Coleman stove that he and his father had used for camping along the Appalachian Trail and in Acadia National Park. The stove, lantern, sleeping bag, and tents all went in the trunk of the car.

If he could find a campsite in Woods Hole with a power outlet, he could set up the screen tent over a picnic table to use his laptop without bother of bugs or rain; yes, camping was the way to go, Adrian had decided happily. With money saved on lodging, there would be more to spend on boat charters.

Not long after, en route to his campsite, Adrian had been standing at a cash register in a Falmouth pharmacy, purchasing supplies, when he'd felt a slap on his shoulder. He'd turned with a gasp, recognizing his frat brother immediately. Jud had been two years ahead of him, a business major. Fatuous and boorish, he'd played Beer Pong at a sticky bar in the basement every night for the two years that they had both lived in the frat house. What Adrian particularly remembered was that Jud had been a sick bastard when it came to the rituals with the pledges, including him. Some pleasantries were exchanged, and Jud introduced his fat wife and equally grotesque children. The encounter ended with Jud pulling a business card out of his plaid shorts and urging Adrian, if he was ever interested in beachfront properties in the New Bedford area, to give him a call.

Ægir's Curse

Adrian had remained in the store and watched his frat brother pull out of the parking lot in his massive SUV, then he'd cursed his carelessness. He must not be recognized again! If a Viking scholar was known to be chartering a dive boat around the area, that would inevitably pique the interest of his colleagues, and possibly draw the press.

A barber shop, Adrian recalled, was just two doors down. He passed a magazine rack on the way back to the hair care aisle, where he picked up a box of hair dye, light summer blonde. On his way past the magazines once again, a photograph of the sand dunes near Provincetown on the cover of *Quest* magazine caught his eye. He thumbed through the various articles, hoping to find more information about the Woods Hole area, but it was not featured in that edition. He then scanned their editorial board and smiled devilishly. The name, Craig Russell, had a masculine, New England ring to it.

As Craig Russell, Adrian was having a wonderful summer on the Cape, especially without his wife in tow. He'd explored Woods Hole a few times by car, but found parking, even with a small car, a near impossibility, so on the days of the dive charters, he hopped a shuttle bus from the Big Bear campsite to a drop-off point in Woods Hole at the Martha's Vineyard Ferry. *Mermaid* was only a short walk from the ferry down Water Street. One morning he'd caught a glimpse of himself in a storefront window and was pleased. His appearance had morphed from swashbuckler to blond secret agent reminiscent of Daniel Craig's 007.

Mermaid's captain was a pro, able to drive the boat through the eye of a needle if need be. Each time he arrived for the charters, the tanks had air, the gas canisters were full, and a small refrigerator was stocked with sandwiches, sodas, and water bottles. His first meeting with Captain McCabe had been a delightful surprise. She was not a guy at all, but a chick with large chocolate eyes, dimples, and the trim body of a beach volleyball player. Best yet, she asked no questions about his business, but seemed content to take the boat to whatever location he pointed to on the charts. When he asked if he could pay with cash instead of a credit card, she contently said, "Cash works for me."

With the exception of running into the buffoon from his frat and a storm that postponed the charters for over a week, all was going exactly according to plan. The rain delay had given him time to wander the stacks of a local library in Falmouth and study early U. S. Geological Survey charts of the regional coastline. On another rainy afternoon, he passed the time watching movies at the Cape Cod Mall, then stopped at a dive shop to purchase a large, serrated dive knife.

At Sea

As far as customers went, Jessie McCabe found Craig Russell to be slightly atypical. Usually customers wanted her to suggest some scenic dive site, and she would motor them out to a reef, inspect the equipment, set out the dive flags, and then dive with them to ensure safe underwater procedures. Divers from the marine lab always had specific destinations in mind for the purposes of collecting specimens or recording data on any range of ecological parameters.

Craig, on the other hand, seemed unsure of how to approach his article. She hoped that his writing was better than his photography—which was pedestrian, judging from the angles and site selections he chose—or he would be unemployed before long. Perhaps he did not understand the assignment that his editor had given him? At times it seemed as if he were searching for something, but she wasn't sure that he even knew what it was.

Jessie couldn't imagine the form of his article. On the first day of the cruise, photographs were snapped of the Buzzards

Ægir's Curse

Bay shoreline, and then a few short dives were taken to obtain underwater shots—with nothing spectacular in view. The second day had been spent walking the beach and marshes of Quissett Inlet. He appeared to be looking for something amidst the tall grass, though she didn't ask for what; she was just happy to spend the day wandering the shoreline and collecting specimens and shells (while being paid for it!).

The third day, he asked her to conduct a side scan sonar survey of the bottom of Quissett Inlet. She explained that, if done correctly, a survey entailed a slow and monotonous zigzag back and forth from one end of the inlet to the other, which might eat up a day or more; but he insisted that was how he wanted to spend that day of the charter.

"Alright," she sighed. She backed off on the throttle and began the slow weave across the inlet.

By midmorning only a quarter of the small inlet had been surveyed. As Jessie suspected, the bottom consisted of soft undulating sand, clusters of rock, and patches of seaweed. *Mermaid*'s back-and-forth path was a mind-numbing activity, but, if nothing else, it gave her time to think.

Everything in her life felt tremorous. First, the excuse to her new boss about why she didn't want her name added to the lab's web page was pathetic. When she had told him that she didn't want competing labs to know what she was working on, he had remarked in exasperation, "Jessie, you study amoebocytes in sponges. You're not synthesizing some chemical to cure cancer." The truth, that she'd be too easy to google, was too suspicious an explanation. As long as she could keep her name off the web, Alan and Clayton wouldn't be able to find her.

Second, she continued to follow the news in Toulossa and had read that Mrs. Cuthbert, who lived in Alan's trailer park community, had suddenly and inexplicably died. That pleasant old widow had been in excellent shape, a disciplined walker and health nut.

Then she'd fallen for a woman! Her pastor had lectured over endless Sundays, over endless years, that such relationships were "wrong in the eyes of Jesus Christ." However, nothing about Sara felt wrong. Instead, it all felt very right.

Finally, the date on the side scan monitor caused her pulse to quicken. In two days she was supposed to attend a family gathering in Florida. Emails to her uf.edu account from Alan had become insistent and furious, while those from Clayton were groveling, written in elementary school sentences. Being at sea for a multi-day charter with Craig was a godsend. It left everything behind.

A convex rise in the sand appeared in the corner of *Mermaid*'s side scan monitor. The water at that site had a depth of forty-six feet.

"Here's something," she called to Craig, who was outside of the cabin photographing the shoreline.

He stepped back into the cabin and studied the screen for some time. "Looks fun. Let's dive on it," he replied casually.

Jessie would never get used to the water of the Cape. It was olive green and usually opaque, instead of the clear, teal blue of the Gulf of Mexico. Yet due to the stillness of the inlet that day, the visibility of the water was quite good. The wreck seemed to be a submerged boat or platform of some kind, and Craig had already swum down the length of it. Her exploration of the wreck could wait. In the tan and green marine landscape she searched for the usual inhabitants: periwinkles, slipper limpets, hermit crabs, starfish, tunicates, flounders. Sea lettuce, east coast kelp, and brown seaweed, attached to the grey rocks, undulated in the currents, and she was momentarily hypnotized by their movements. A yellow and blue spotfin butterflyfish darted directly in front of her mask, a fish carried north by the Gulf Stream from the tropics. She delighted in the rare sight and took it for an omen that her luck was going to change.

Jessie's attention returned to the mysterious wreck. The structure was about fifty feet in length and fifteen feet across. Both ends of the structure were tapered. At one end of the wreck, Craig had brushed away the sand to expose a beam of wood, and then carved off slivers with a dive knife. He placed the wood slivers in a small plastic bag taken from *Mermaid*'s galley. Why would a journalist want bits of old wood, she wondered. The beam where he worked was surprisingly intact, not porous and riddled with tunnels produced by the burrowing bivalve, *Teredo navalis*. This meant that the structure had been buried in the sand and silt of the cove for much of its existence. Perhaps it had been uncovered by the recent storms. Craig's rough brushing raised a cloud of particles, hiding him and one end of the wreck.

Since the visibility was obscured around him, Jessie swam to the opposite end where the water was clear. She slowly fanned away the sand. Oddly, the wood did not have the same solid appearance as the beam that Craig had exposed. Instead the beams were black and charred. The submerged structure was clearly a boat, as revealed by the longitudinal beams and perpendicular strakes. It was quite old, perhaps an alongshore whaler or inshore fishing boat, as New England had a rich maritime culture dating from the 1600s. Around midsection the charring stopped; the rest was the brown gray of unburned timber.

Fire onboard a boat was a sailor's worst nightmare, and Jessie envisioned what had happened—a panicked dash toward the safe end and a jump overboard. The survivors would have dragged themselves to shore to watch their goods, their profits, their livelihoods aflame, disappearing below the water with a sizzle and steam.

She checked the air volume in her tank. In a few more minutes they would need to ascend. She examined the crisscrossing planks of wood. A bent nail, brown and roughened with rust, poked from between two stakes, and she pried it loose. She tucked it into a pocket of her pink BC, a souvenir to be added to her shoebox in Sara's boathouse where she kept her sea treasures: sand dollars, starfish, skate egg cases, and mollusk shells found on her dives, or on walks along Stony Beach with Zephyr.

Jessie looked at the air gauge again and swam to the periphery of the cloud where Craig, nearly invisible in the suspended particles, still worked on a beam. Moving into his line of vision, she tapped on her dive watch and then pointed to the surface. He nodded and emerged from the cloud of particles. They needed one decompression stop during their ascent to avoid the paralytic effect of the bends. While hovering around twenty feet, she looked down at the wreck. A curious thing—the particle cloud where she had been diving was the gray-tan color of the sand and silt. But the large cloud that Craig had stirred up at the opposite end was a peculiar reddish black.

"Very cool wreck!" Jessie exclaimed excitedly, as she placed her air tank on a tank rack.

"Yeah, that was pretty cool," Craig agreed nonchalantly from the dive platform. He swished his regulator back and forth in the water. "I can't get this film off."

She peered over the transom. "What film?"

"This sticky film on my regulator."

"Don't worry about it. I'll soak everything in fresh water when we get back to shore. So," she asked, still intrigued, "what do you think the wreck was?" She placed her fins and mask in her dive locker.

He climbed into the boat. "It's probably a fishing boat."

"Why were you collecting bits of wood?" She reached for a water bottle.

He peeled off his wetsuit. "A friend of mine's an archaeologist. I thought that he might be able to date it for me. The wreck dive will add an interesting dimension to my article."

She took a long drink from a bottle. "The wreck was definitely old. I'm guessing that it's a Portuguese fishing boat."

"Probably," he concurred, looking with concern at his mask and fins.

"Or a coastal whaling boat. The whales used to be so plentiful in these waters that they'd hunt them right off shore. It was only when the whalers depleted these populations that they needed to build bigger ships and hunt the whales further out at sea. The ships became giant slaughter factories."

He coughed, and spit mucus into the water. He lifted his mask and fins and frowned. "This film is all over these too."

"Just put everything in your dive locker, and I'll take care of it when we get to shore. My last guess is that it's a Viking longboat."

He was silent for a moment. "That's preposterous," he finally mumbled. "I think the Portuguese whaling boat is more likely."

"Some scholars believe that Vinland was on Cape Cod."

"What's Vinland?"

She looked quizzically at him. For a journalist, this man was not well read. "The Viking settlement in the Americas."

"I thought that it was somewhere in Canada."

"That's L'Anse aux Meadows in Newfoundland."

"Whatever," he responded flatly.

"Do you want to continue with a side scan of the inlet?"

He looked at the side scan sonar, memorizing the coordinates of their present location. "No. Can I take some pictures of the Elizabeth Islands?"

"Sure." She turned on the engine, let it idle in neutral, and pulled up the anchors.

Craig leaned quickly over the gunwale and hacked up another gob of thick mucus into the green water of the inlet.

Chapter 11

Woods Hole

Derick Briggs pulled a cork from a bottle of wine and let it breathe, while Sara Kauni passed through the French doors and placed a tray of cheese and fruit on her porch table. She dropped into a lawn chair.

"I'm glad I followed your advice," she confessed.

"What advice?" he inquired.

"Not to use Lindsey's private investigator to check out Jessie's brother."

Derick shook his head in disgust. "I don't know what you were thinking. PIs are no better than bounty hunters. They operate outside of the law. Plus, you don't investigate the person you're dating!"

"I know ... I know," Sara admitted with embarrassment. "But the guy, whoever he is, did find out about that electronics company in Vermont and spared Lindsey and me tons of headaches."

Derick grimaced and poured wine into two glasses. "I don't like the sound of any of it. Lindsey shouldn't be associating with criminal elements." He handed her a wine glass.

Sara laughed absurdly. "I doubt if the PI is a criminal element."

"You know what I mean," he added sternly. "So what changed your mind?"

"The whole idea didn't sit right with me, and then Jessie told me why she had to leave Florida. She's not sure what's going on." Sara paused for effect. "But she thinks that Alan and a pastor, who own some Christian trailer park together, have some insurance scam going on."

Derick shook his head, reprovingly.

"I was afraid that Jessie was in trouble. Now I know that she's on the run, probably in hiding. She doesn't want to be incriminated in his business." Sara sniffed the wine, then took a sip. "Delicious. Where did you get this one?"

"It's from a family vineyard near Plymouth." He took a sip, held the wine in his mouth while considering the blend of flavors, and then swallowed. He frowned slightly. "It's too sweet for me. I like drier wines." He shook his head again. "The whole thing's incredible. The brother's not going to get away with that. Some insurance fraud unit has to be watching him."

"Alan's a crook. It's no small wonder Jessie doesn't say much about him. She's stuck between the proverbial rock and a hard place."

"It just occurred me. We're all using Woods Hole as an escape from our dysfunctional brothers. Here your brothers can't nag you to give them money. Jessie's hiding from Alan. And I'm avoiding my brother and his wife, and anything to do with the family business."

"Why don't you just move here permanently?" she asked.

"I need to stay around Atlanta while my grandmother's alive." Derick reached for some grapes. "Tomorrow's the anniversary of my father's death. His health was always so fragile, while my grandmother was, until recently, nearly indestructible. She's almost ninety-five. But smoking a pack a day has finally caught up with her."

"And brace yourself for this."

"What?"

"Jessie's supposed to be marrying Alan's best friend, Clayton, this summer! In fact, any day now."

"She's gay. Why did she agree to that?"

"That was the agreement. If they let her leave the island and go to college, that she'd return, marry Clayton, and work in the business with them."

"You're making this up."

"I'm not! Really!" she laughed.

"I can image the redneck wedding, since I've been to too many of them," he replied, smiling. "The groom, in a baby-blue tuxedo and his hair slicked over with Brill cream, sweltering at the altar in some backwoods church, while his bride-to-be is hiding from the whole circus fifty feet under the waters of Cape Cod."

"A baby-blue tuxedo," she said, giggling. "Is there a such thing?"

Sara's cell phone vibrated on the table. She put it to her ear and listened intently; Lindsey shouted her message over the boat engines. Sara sprang to her feet, her eyes filled with tears.

"I'm on my way!"

Sara was no longer laughing.

Lindsey slept but lightly in her stateroom on the *Mary Read*. Twice during the night she shuffled through the darkness to check on Ava and Danny. She found them sleeping soundly under summer blankets. Rob also slept deeply. Before falling to sleep he had mumbled from his side of the bed that this was a police matter and did not concern her.

His callousness about the whole situation was disturbing. "Jessie's a friend," Lindsey had remonstrated. "And Arrano's been to Dave's Marina. He might come back!"

"The marina's crawling with cops. If Arrano shows up, they'll nab him in seconds," Rob had grumbled, turning toward the wall.

Also upsetting was that Maggie had not returned home for another night. Was it three days or four since Lindsey had seen her? It was likely that Maggie was staying over at Brian's apartment, wanting to spend as much time with him before she left for her freshman year at college. But why wasn't she returning calls or texts?

Brian, a recovering addict, had met Maggie at a Narcotics Anonymous meeting nearly five years ago. Maggie had slumped angrily into a chair at her first NA meeting on the Cape, growling, "I'm Maggie and a drug addict." Glowering at the men across the table, she'd added, "And I'll fuckin' kill you if you come near me." Brian had been smitten, and he'd wandered by the marina for months, bearing gifts of chocolate and smoothies, before Maggie relented and went out him. Lacking any academic ambitions, he worked on the large trawlers owned by the marine lab that collected specimens for the scientists. He was a kind and faithful companion to Maggie and encouraged her regular attendance at NA meetings; for that Lindsey was grateful.

Five years earlier, Lindsey had worked with the director of a drug and alcohol rehab in Newport, Rhode Island, where she and Maggie were roommates, to obtain guardianship of the Arizona runaway. That first summer out of rehab, she and Maggie were inseparable. She employed Maggie in the lab during the day, much to the frustration of Sara, who found herself working beside two healing and, at times, cranky lab mates. They attended AA meetings after dinner and smoked endless cigarettes on the flybridge late into the summer evenings. It was Maggie who insisted on naming the houseboat the *Anne Bonny* and painted the pirate on the transom. Lindsey had been astounded—the girl was a natural artist.

Ægir's Curse

When the fall came, Maggie entered junior high school. At the galley table, Lindsey tutored the girl to catch her up on the years of neglected studies, encouraging her amidst her curses and tantrums about the tedium of the math and science. Lindsey, pregnant with Ava, and Maggie, trying to gain weight, ate big dinners together and discussed earth science, pre-algebra, and *Beowulf*. Over the intervening years they'd bickered incessantly and competed fiercely in everything, including their sobriety. By the grace of their Higher Powers, and by each one's determination not to relapse before the other, they had kept each other sober.

Lindsey checked her cell phone, but there was still no response from Maggie. After twisting under the sheets for another hour, she reached for the sleeping pills on the nightstand. As the sun was rising over the eastern horizon, just east of Nantucket Island, she finally drifted off to sleep.

Nearly all night, Sara stared into the darkness of a cabin on the *Mary Read*. Countless times she called the cell phone that she had recently bought for Jessie. Jessie was the last person in this century to own a cell phone, and Sara wondered if she had even made an effort to turn the device on.

It was still early in their relationship, so when Jessie's birthday had rolled around, Sara had struggled to find an appropriate gift. Birthdays, for some reason, resonated badly with Jessie. Sara had rejected the idea of jewelry, as that would imply a commitment and probably scare Jessie off. Then she'd considered silk lingerie, but Jessie only slept in the buff or, on cool nights, in sweats. Finally Sara settled on the functional and practical: a cell phone. Jessie had removed the flowered gift wrap and curiously turned the box over in her hands, offering a polite but hesitant thank you. Sara smiled as she remembered how next Zephyr had pulled his gift from his pocket and presented it: a necklace made from sea grass and shells. Jessie had loved it. After she tied the necklace around her neck, he'd challenged her to an arm-wrestling tournament. They'd promptly positioned themselves across the kitchen table, abandoning Sara on the sofa amidst wads of gift wrap.

The appearance of Jessie in Sara's life was an unexpected gift; she was the diametric opposite of her previous partner, Monique, who was only interested in borrowing money for real estate schemes. Also, Monique had no tolerance for children. The relationship had ended the millisecond she'd suggested that Zephyr attend a boarding school in upstate New York.

After their introduction on the *Mary Read,* that day when Jessie had emerged from the Atlantic, Sara had noticed *Mermaid* pull into Eel Pond as she was finishing her morning workout. *Mermaid* motored in and out of the pond all day, for Jessie had quickly found dive buddies. Though hardworking, Jessie seemed driven more by a simple curiosity regarding the natural world than career ambition. How many hours had Jessie and Zephyr sat on the stone seawall, pointing at tiny marine creatures flitting across the sandy bottom, while she'd paced the porch with her cell phone to her ear, bitching about noise-to-signal ratios to Lindsey? When Sara suggested that Jessie apply for tenure-track jobs after her postdoc, Jessie visibly quaked. Then she abruptly changed the subject, which was her singularly exasperating tactic of evasion.

Sara considered herself a woman with a wide skill set, but the seduction of Jessie had gone rather disastrously, as far as seductions go. When she'd interrupted Jessie's run that day, her plan had been to get high and have some laughs, then maybe lunch or dinner later on, and go from there. How was she to know that the marine biologist was an innocent in many ways—and that that would be so arousing?

Ægir's Curse

Then Jessie had dissed her on their walk from the bakery! That had been the last straw. She'd written Jessie off as unavailable and turned her mind to other matters.

Then, strangely, out of the blue, Jessie had appeared at her house.

It had been a night of torrential rain, and Sara had been lying on her living room sofa, her mind preoccupied with the spectrophotometer in the 5M imager. She'd spent hours on her back under the instrument that afternoon, and a long, hot bath was in order. Suddenly there was a shuffle of feet on the front porch and a knock at the door.

"Who is it, Mom?" Zephyr had asked, turning from the TV.

"I don't know, honey." She had rolled herself off the sofa and flipped on the porch light.

Jessie had pulled back the hood of her raincoat to identify herself. Seeing her pale face, Sara had unlocked the front door.

"What?"

"Can I come in for a sec?"

"Take off your wet shoes. No shoes in this house."

Jessie unlaced her soggy running shoes and hung her raincoat on a hook by the door. Then she stood unspeaking, facing Sara.

Sara waited. Jessie glanced at Zephyr, and then pointed toward the library across the hall. Sara nodded, and they stepped into the dark room.

Again, Sara waited. Frustrated, she finally asked, "What, Jessie?"

"I'd like to accept your offer, to stay in your spare room on the nights I do experiments," Jessie answered quickly.

Sara suppressed her surprise. "Okay. I'll go get you a key," she said. She turned to leave.

"Wait!" Jessie grabbed Sara's wrist.

Sara waited.

"Can I also stay Wednesdays?"

"Sure."

"Can I also stay …." Jessie choked on the rest of her words.

"What, Jessie?"

"Nothing."

"What!"

"I forgot."

Sara had lost all patience. "Let me show you the room."

Jessie nodded and followed Sara upstairs.

Derick jerked up and flung aside the sheets. He climbed out of bed and strode across the tiny studio apartment that he rented every summer from the widow of a famous oceanographer. The central air conditioning was too cold for his southern blood, and he opened a window. He drew in long, slow breaths of sea air. At Stony Beach across the road, waves slapped quietly against the sand. Insects sang amidst the reeds. Despite the calming nocturnal sounds, the nightmare still coiled amongst his thoughts.

At the phone call from Lindsey Nolan that afternoon, Sara had sprung from her chair, shattering the wine glasses and spilling the tray of cheese and fruit. "Something's come up! I need to go to Lindsey's immediately! I'll call you soon when I know more. Promise," she had cried.

What trouble had Lindsey gotten herself, and possibly Sara, into this time? It was annoying that Sara so revered her boss. True, the partnership with that arrogant know-it-all had changed Sara's station in life from that of a single mother struggling under student loan debt to an inventor of renown and wealth; but still, alcoholics, recovering or not, could not be trusted.

Equally disturbing was that that same nightmare that had terrorized his nights as a boy had resurfaced from dormancy after nearly four decades, and Lindsey was to blame for knocking it out of his subconscious.

He and his brother turned suddenly from the TV.

"Jared!" Derick said in a frightened, emphatic whisper. "She's in the house again!"

"Run as fast as you can and never stop!" Jared wailed.

The boys sprang to their feet and dashed up an endless winding staircase. Where were Papa and Grandma Katie? Though Derick was only seven and shorter than Jared, he was quicker. Jared's wheezes were close behind. The small boys scooted under their father's massive bed. Derick balled himself under the headboard, while Jared pressed against his little brother, shaking, as he was exposed to her grasp. The woman laughed shrilly. Tears squeezed from Derick's eyes and he willed himself to be a tiny, hard stone like those in the back creek. Somewhere in her taunting pursuit, her black shoes with the dagger heels had been lost; her bloody-toed feet paced by the foot of the bed. Jared whimpered as she gripped his ankle, her red talons sinking deep in his skin. Howling, Jared was pulled away while Derick tugged and tugged on his brother's wrist. But Jared was lost, and Derick was suddenly alone under the bed.

Derick forced himself to open his eyes. The hem of Jared's pajama pants quivered in front of the shimmering edge of her black garment. There was a sound of skin striking skin and Jared's cries. Suddenly she gasped, her lethal clench released.

"What the hell are you doing here?" screamed Grandma Katie from the hallway. She leaned over the balcony. "Clark!" she yelled.

His father struggled up the stairs, wheezing like Jared had. His face and shoulders drooped in confusion. "When did you return?" Clark asked the scowling woman.

Derick scooted from under the bed and wrapped himself around his grandmother's stout waist. He dared not look at the woman again—bony and tall in a black gown, wearing slicing stones around her wrists and red-clawed fingers—but he could smell her and it was horrible.

Derick stared out to the silent beach for some time. It was not a nightmare, he reminded himself. It was a memory. After that night he never saw his gin-sodden mother again.

Chapter 12

At Sea

Craig retreated to the berth with his laptop and sleeping bag, while by lantern light Jessie read the instruction manual to her new cell phone. Sara's gift had caused her dread. Every goddamn conversation with Alan and Clayton over the past decade involved a goddamn cell phone!

"We need to be able to contact you immediately, Jes, know where you are, what you're doing," one of them invariably said.

I bet you do, she had thought grimly. "I'm a broke student," she had said. "I can't afford it. If you want to buy it and pay for my data plan, then okay."

That had always silenced the tightwads. Her life would *not* be controlled by little beeps and buzzes; nor would she view the world through a screen of pixels. Of that, she was certain. Her life would be experienced firsthand.

Then Sara gives her, of all things, a cell phone for her birthday! All of the hints that she'd been dropping about that beautiful book on the shells of Cape Cod must have gone in one ear and out the other. Oh, Sara, *anything* but an all-controlling and invasive cell phone!

"Just to be on the safe side," Sara had said.

'The safe side of what!' Jessie had wanted to shout. 'I'm a marine biologist, not a policeman or brain surgeon who's on-call. The worst that might happen to me is that a heavy book might fall on my foot in the library.'

"The phone is The Latest and has all the bells and whistles," Sara had explained. Why did phones need bells and whistles that did gods-know-what? And it was ridiculously expensive. She'd felt uncomfortable accepting it, but Sara had insisted that she keep it. Eventually, Jessie had conceded that it might a good plan to have a cell phone onboard, should the batteries in the marine radio die. Also, she could take photos for Zephyr if any unusual creature was spotted while out at sea.

Sara had programmed her number and Zephyr's into the phone, so Jessie thought to text them about the intriguing wreck, but the directions were incomprehensible. The lantern flickered and dimmed as the batteries ran down. She put the instruction manual in her seabag, switched off the lantern, and slid into her sleeping bag for the night.

Hers was a restless, interrupted sleep on the aft deck of *Mermaid*, as Craig coughed throughout the night. Three times he awoke and stumbled to a gunwale to spit over the side.

Preparing breakfast the next morning, she cracked opened an energy drink, hoping it would wake her up. She placed two cereal bowls, plastic spoons, a cereal box and a milk carton on the galley table, as Craig struggled from his sleeping bag. Having untangled himself, he walked briskly by her and bent over the gunwale once again. Revolted by his gagging and hacking, Jessie glanced at the two bowls and suddenly placed hers back in the cabinet. She grabbed a banana and headed outside. "I'm going to check something on the radar," she said, escaping onto the roof.

"Whatever," he moaned.

Ægir's Curse

For some minutes, Jessie feigned checking the wires… like she had any idea what any of them did… and ate the banana. Convinced that the food had settled in her stomach and that she could converse with the runny-nosed, green-faced client, she climbed back down. Craig had spread a chart across the table and was honking into a napkin.

"Do you want me to take you to shore for a decongestant?" she asked from the safe distance of the deck.

"No, I'm fine," he responded curtly.

"Are you sure? It's not safe to dive with a respiratory tract infection."

"I said I'm fine," he muttered without looking up from the chart.

"We could go back to Quissett and dive on that fun wreck," she suggested to perk him up.

"I'm not sure."

Jessie entered the galley reluctantly, worried that his cold was infectious. She wordlessly returned the milk to the small fridge and placed the cereal back in a cupboard. She wondered if multi-day cruises were a good idea, especially on a small, confined boat such as *Mermaid*. Craig continued to study charts of the Elizabeth Islands and Buzzards Bay, as he had the evening before.

"How about we go to Cuttyhunk?" Craig finally proposed.

"Good plan," she replied, pleased to be getting underway. "I'll top off the gas tanks and get some more batteries there."

She stepped back outside. The sky was a cloudless blue. The morning was already warm, so she put on her shorty wetsuit rather than the blue one with the long sleeves. She poured gasoline through a small funnel into a larger gas reservoir.

"Can you show me how to send a text later on? I'm trying to learn how to use my new cell phone." She removed the funnel and screwed the lids on the tanks. Her hand rhythmically squeezed the bulb to force gas into the line.

"Sure," he answered. "Where's your phone? Let me have a look."

"Just a sec, I need to find it. It's in my bag somewhere." She returned to the helm, dropped into the captain's seat and turned the key to start the engine. The engine idled in neutral while she searched her seabag. "Here." She handed him the phone.

She exited the cabin, climbed along the gunwale, tugged up the anchor line at the bow, and wound the line around a cleat. She returned to the aft anchor and tugged on the anchor line. The anchor gave way for about a foot, and then stopped. She tugged again, but retrieved no more line. She bent over the transom. "I think we're stuck on something."

He placed the cell phone on the dive locker containing his equipment. "Let me try." He grasped the anchor line and yanked. Nothing. He repositioned his feet and jerked back with the entire weight of his body, but his hands slid and burned along the unyielding rope. "We're definitely stuck."

Jessie shut off the engine. "Let me check it out." She removed her dive equipment from the other dive locker while he handed her a tank off the rack. In minutes, pressing her mask against her face, she stepped off the dive platform and splashed into the waters off the small remote island.

Adrian dropped onto a dive locker in ecstatic relief at Jessie's absence. He had found it—a Viking wreck, he wanted to shout aloud. This and the map were conclusive evidence that Vinland was Cape Cod! And it was all Jessie wanted to talk about! She must not return to shore and mention this wreck to anyone. After all, the find was his. He was not about to share the credit with some no-name marine biologist! But how to shut her up?

Ægir's Curse

What with the coughing, he had been wide awake all night creating a thousand different scenarios, but none seemed just right. It was easy to rationalize helping an old, damaged man to die peacefully in his sleep. The man had had a stellar career, but it was time for the next generation to have their turn. Ragnarök! It had been bothersome not to have found Tryggvesen in the village of Narsaq. That was a loose end to tie up later.

The logistics of murder were an exhilarating problem-solving exercise, Adrian concluded. After the initial shock of seeing the map in Ingvars's apartment, he had surprised himself with his efficiency and detachment in carrying out the business. It seemed an out-of-body experience where, floating ghostlike above the room, he watched himself methodically drug the tea and smother the old man with a pillow. Perhaps it was more like watching himself star in a Hollywood movie, a murder mystery! But this was not a murder, he reminded himself; Ingvars's death was merely a mercy killing. Rubber gloves and disinfectant were located under the kitchen sink, and he'd carefully contemplated the old man's CD collection for the appropriate mood music. To Edvard Grieg's Opus 12, No. 1, the "Arietta", he had wiped down room after room before tiptoeing down the backstairs into the summer night.

Adrian leaned over the transom to see Jessie's bubbles ascend the anchor chain. Containing the young woman might not be as easy as the old man, but there was plenty of time to determine the best course of action, as this charter would last at least until the next day. Still, he wondered if he could perform this task with the same emotionless efficacy, for Jessie was young, healthy, and attractive. And she must have family and friends... she would be missed. He reached for her cell phone, as one's contact list was a catalogue of all important relationships in one's life.

Very odd, Adrian thought. Just two names listed. Sara and Zephyr. Sara, a friend? Sara Kauni, the hot Polynesian? No freaking way Jessie would know a Nobel laureate. Zephyr, a boyfriend? Five calls in her voicemail were all from Sara, but unfortunately he didn't have the PIN to access them. A text message, also from Sara, had been sent the night before.

Adrian broke into a sweat as he read the text. Before he turned off the phone and placed it back on the dive locker, he hit DELETE. But Sara's text was indelibly etched in his memory.

> 7:06 PM: URGENT. Get to shore ASAP. Make up any bullshit excuse. Engine trouble, whatever! Just get back here. Your client is not who he says he is. Just stay calm and get to shore. XO

Splashing at the dive platform awoke Adrian from his numb shock. "Your client is not who he says he is." What the hell did this mean? His time line to act had just changed.

Mermaid was tucked in a small cove. From the time the boat was moored off the island the evening before to this exact moment, the only onshore habitants they'd spotted were seabirds, horseshoe crabs, and rabbits. He scanned the island once again, and then the glistening horizon. The inlet was completely still. Jessie appeared inches under the surface and pulled a clump of seaweed from the propeller. He lifted a small pony tank from the tank rack.

Jessie's head broke the surface and she removed the regulator from her mouth to speak. "The anchor was stuck in an old fishing net, but I got it untangled. That was no small feat."

Adrian extended his hand over the transom, as if to help her onto the dive platform. She reached up to accept the assistance. At that second, his eyes watered and his head pounded... *the Viking jarl raised his battle axe over a cowering enemy. This enemy must die! She was trying to steal the treasure hoard.*

Ægir's Curse

A pony tank flew in a wide sweeping arc into Jessie's peripheral vision.

Impact. A crack of bone. Blackness. Jessie's head slammed into the motor.

Releasing the hand of his enemy, the Viking jarl let the limp body slide over the wooden strakes of the longship and into the water.

Adrian shook his head. It seemed that he had lost a few seconds of time. The headache, he supposed, had made his thoughts short-circuit. Then he remembered the cell phone.

"Your client is not who he says he is."

He smashed the phone with a dive tank and flung the bits into the inlet. With a boat hook, he nudged the bobbing body away from the transom. Throughout the charter he had been watching closely as Jessie started the engine, filled the gasoline tank, and stowed the equipment, so he could manage the boat on his own. He turned the key and the engine rumbled to life. The tide was already pulling her body deeper into the isolation of the inlet. It would be days before the corpse would be found, if ever.

He had assumed that Jessie was the only one who knew of Craig Russell, and at her death, Craig Russell would cease to exist. But if Sara, whoever she was, knew about him, what else did she know, and who had told her? Did Zephyr also know? This was now a colossal problem. In addition to Tryggvesen, he would eventually have to locate and deal with Sara and Zephyr.

Adrian's head throbbed from the excitement of locating the wreck and the sudden decision to prevent Jessie from sharing the find. If he could only find a quiet place to hide, plan his next move, and take a nap, maybe the headache would subside. Eventually he would have to return to land and distance himself from these events. How fortunate that he paid in cash, so nothing could link him to *Mermaid*! Captain McCabe would be presumed lost in a diving accident.

Chapter 13

Oslo, Norway

In her apartment on Madserud Alle, Dr. Anna Halvorsen had checked the US weather maps every day since her father told her that his next assignment would be at Cape Cod, Massachusetts. Before Sven left for the airport, she had asked about the painting that he was chasing to the States; but, as was his way, he had solemnly shaken his head and divulged nothing about the case.

Anna cursed the slowness of her laptop and added more creamer to her coffee as she waited for it to boot. She walked to the kitchen counter for butter and lefse and returned to the small table by the window. The laptop screen remained an unresponsive blue.

Her husband, Stefan, in his teal scrubs, entered the kitchen, his hair wet from his shower. He planted a kiss on the top of Anna's blonde head before he leaned on the windowsill and looked out across the road to Frogner Park. Every day he would single out different statuary in the Vigeland statue garden and offer his metaphysical interpretation of its meaning.

"You should have been a poet, not a physician," Anna remarked.

Ægir's Curse

Stefan smiled warmly and dropped into a chair. "But then I never would have met you. So, what is our international man of mystery doing in the United States today?" he asked, reaching for bowls of yogurt and granola.

"I haven't heard from him since his dinner with Dr. Lindsey Nolan. I'd love to know how she's tied up in an art theft. I'm trying to wiki her, but this computer is so slow." Wikipedia eventually appeared on the screen. "Finally."

The website described Nolan's educational background, inventions, patents, and corporate partnerships. The description was quite short, particularly in the personal section. Nolan had been married to a historian named Duncan McLeod for fifteen years; she had one daughter, Ava, and an adopted daughter, Maggie. There was nothing more.

"So what did Sven say about her?" Stefan asked.

"Absolutely nothing. He just whines about the horrible temperatures. You'd think that he was made of wax the way he complains about it. Let's see how miserable he'll be today."

Anna clicked on the bookmarks to find the link for the *Cape Cod Daily*, where she'd been checking the Cape's weather reports for the past few days. She stared wide-eyed at the computer screen.

"Well, how hot it is going to be?" Stefan asked. His wife continued to gaze at the screen. "Anna ...?"

"Very hot," Anna answered vaguely, turning the laptop in his direction.

Dave's Marina

Sunlight streamed through a porthole of the master stateroom, heating Lindsey's face. She squinted in disbelief at the clock, and then again at the portholes, circles of white light of late morning. The typical weekend morning sounds of cartoons, sports radio, the rumble of Jet Ski engines, and children jumping on the foot of her bed were disconcertingly absent. She went to the head to wash up, then dressed quickly. After grabbing her sunglasses, she stepped onto the aft deck of the *Mary Read*. To her left was the *Green Monster,* to the right the *Anne Bonny*. Men milled around the boat ramp. Dave glanced at her from the boat repair shed and then turned away without the usual wave or greeting.

What was that all about? Yesterday after the cruise with Halvorsen, she and Dave had chatted pleasantly at the gas pumps. He had asked her about her trip to the London Eye and Tower of London, then had added sadly that while she was abroad, he had spent much of the week in Barnstable, moving his parents into a long-term care facility.

Maggie must have returned earlier that morning; she sat with Sara at a table on the deck, coffee mugs between them. Otherwise there was no activity at all, only the quiet swish of water between the boat hulls.

Guardedly, Lindsey approached the table. "What the hell's going on here? Where are the children? Where's Rob?"

"How can you be such a fucking idiot?" Sara snapped.

"What are you talking about?" Lindsey snapped back.

Sara thrust her smartphone into Lindsey's face.

Appalled, Lindsey stared at the screen. She then studied Maggie's face, then Sara's, then Maggie's again. Maggie lit a cigarette, her hand shaking. Lindsey looked toward the marsh and beyond toward Nobska Point, struggling to recall the beach from the day before. Had there been sunbathers on the beach? Boats nearby? She hadn't paid much attention to the surroundings, engrossed in a conversation about Vinlanders, dead whales, and the Viking murderess, Freydis. She returned, still aghast, to the image on the screen.

The photo had clearly been taken from the shore, likely by a resident of one of the large beach houses who would have recognized the *Just for Today,* as every local knew that boat.

"Another maggot looking for a payoff. Not this time," Lindsey said, shaking her head furiously. "Maggie, I didn't do it! I promise you, I didn't do anything!"

Lindsey suddenly remembered the newspaper rack on the porch of the bait and tackle store. The image on the front page of the newspaper was identical to that of the website on the smartphone. She dashed across the parking lot, flew up the stairs, and yanked the entire stack of the *Cape Cod Daily* from the rack.

"Sheila!" she called hotly through the screen, "I'm buying the whole stack of these. Put them on my tab. Not guilty on this one!" She ran toward the dumpsters. "Dave," she shouted at the shed, "I didn't do this!"

At the green dumpster for paper recycling, she flung the stack of newspapers upward, catching one last glimpse of the image: she in her bikini, Sven's hands on her naked hips, their mouths only inches apart, hovering expectantly for a kiss. In a large red font the caption read, *More Boat Frolics for Laureate Nolan*.

Lindsey slumped despondently into a deck chair. "Maggie, I really messed up in P-town, and I told Rob that it would never happen again. And I mean it. Nothing happened on the boat yesterday. The officer made a play for me. I declined. He backed off. And that was it. It was over and done."

The three women remained silent around the table.

"I believe you, Lin," Maggie finally muttered. She reached across the table and Lindsey gratefully grabbed her hand. "You say shit that pisses me off all the time, but you've never lied to me." Maggie looked questioningly at Sara.

Sara was subdued. "I'm sorry for jumping to conclusions. Flies on—"

Lindsey broke in disgustedly, "Shit! I know the expression, Sara!"

"That's not what I was going to say!" Sara cried in defense.

"Just drop it." Lindsey knocked a cigarette from Maggie's pack and lit it. "Where are Rob and the kids?" she asked again.

"He took them camping," Sara answered.

"Where?" Lindsey inquired, smoking fiercely.

"Big Bear, I think."

"Zephyr, too?"

"Yes. He didn't want to be left here with me, all stressed out about Jessie."

"A campsite is a safe place for all of them right now," Lindsey concluded.

Maggie turned to Sara. "Don't worry about Jessie, Sara."

"How can you say that?" Sara blurted, blood vessels swelling on her forehead. "She's out at sea with a psycho! She has no clue who he fucking is!"

"But she has the BCs with C-trax," Maggie proclaimed.

Sara grabbed Maggie's shoulders. "What! How do you know this?"

"I gave her our BCs weeks ago. Jessie came by with these crap BCs that were so old and cracking that they were nearly nonfunctional. She's been borrowing ours until she can buy new ones."

"Oh my God! Thank God!" Sara gasped, hugging Maggie.

Lindsey jumped out of her chair and rushed to her office. "Open, goddamn it, open," she whispered to the door, her hand clutching the glass knob. Maggie and Sara followed quickly. The door opened and Lindsey dropped into a computer chair.

The C-trax device was still in its developmental phase, the design not ready to be sold to a manufacturer, but Lindsey and Sara knew the prototype worked because they had attached them to their children's BCs and life vests, where the GPS devices performed perfectly.

Lindsey's fingers flew across a keyboard. "Which one does she have?" she asked, swiveling in the chair.

Ægir's Curse

Maggie answered excitedly, "Two of them! The pink one and the black one!"

"Maggie, run to my bedroom and get my cell phone. I need to call Sven Halvorsen!"

"Got it!" Maggie hurried away.

Lindsey and Sara leaned toward the computer monitor while the C-trax software loaded. Finally they were able to activate the homing device in the pink BC, and a GPS chart of the Elizabeth Islands appeared on the monitor. "She's off Pasque Island, just offshore. They're probably diving."

"Where's he?" Sara asked anxiously.

Lindsey typed more commands into the keyboard to localize the C-trax device in the black BC. A different map appeared on the monitor. "Strange, they're not together. He's in the middle of Buzzards Bay."

"That means someone's with the boat and someone's in the water," Sara remarked somberly.

At Sea

Ping. Ping. The faint sound was clearly electrical in origin, so Adrian bent his head under the navigation panel to inspect the colored wires. No red indicator lights were flashing on any instruments to suggest that their power was running low. More puzzling was that he had not heard this sound before.

He slowed the boat and positioned the throttle in neutral to quiet the engine. The *ping* was not coming from anywhere in the cabin, so he stepped outside and moved toward the dive locker where he kept his gear. As he lifted the lid, the noise grew louder. The film that covered his dive equipment had dried overnight to a brown, flaky powder. As he tossed aside his fins and mask, the flakes lightly dusted his hands and arms. He rummaged deeper into the dive locker, the sound intensifying. At the bottom was the black BC.

Adrian inspected the vest, turning it over again and again, but there was nothing unusual about it except for the pinging. He lifted a Velcro flap, stuck his fingers in the pocket, and pulled out a plastic device that was slightly smaller than a pack of cigarettes. What the hell was this? And why had it been activated this morning of all mornings? The BCs were from that moody teenager at the marina, he recalled. Could she have placed the device in the pocket of the BC? Now this, like Sara's text, would nag at him. Whatever this device was, he did not want it anywhere near the boat. He heaved it out into the olive water.

Ping... splash.

Dave's Marina

Maggie returned to the office on the *Mary Read* and handed Lindsey her cell phone. "They've come back."

"Who's come back?" Lindsey asked anxiously.

"Rob and the kids."

Lindsey abruptly left the cabin and headed toward the parking lot. Rob bent into the backseat of a minivan to unstrap a sniffling Ava from her car seat.

"She won't stop crying. She wants her *mother*," Rob said caustically, handing her the child.

His emphasis on the word didn't escape her. Lindsey hugged her daughter while the girl's sucking thumb moved rhythmically against her neck. "Shh. Don't cry. We'll have a fun day with Maggie and Sara. We're going to take a boat ride." She looked toward the car to see Zephyr and Danny in the backseat bent over a handheld video game.

"I didn't do anything on that boat yesterday!" she whispered adamantly. "I promise you, I didn't. It's another scam artist trying to set me up!"

Ægir's Curse

"I'm so tired of this," he growled, deliberately avoiding her eyes.

"I didn't do anything, I swear it!" She paused. "We have been together for five years and I've been faithful to you."

"Danny and I are going to move in with my sister for a while."

She vigorously shook her head. "Don't do this. Moving him from this marina will kill him. Let him stay here with his sisters, his family."

"We're not a family as long as you are married to Duncan."

"We've had this conversation before, too many times. He won't divorce me until I pay his outrageous price. He's already getting a ridiculous cut of the BioCorp electrode and the keyless doorknob. Now he wants profits from the imager. It's extortion, blackmail!"

"Just pay it and be rid of him!"

"Mommy, I'm hungry," Ava interrupted, lifting her face from her mother's shoulder.

"You haven't had breakfast yet?" she asked, glaring at Rob.

"Daddy just woke us and we got in the car," Ava answered.

Danny's grave face was pressed against the window, while Zephyr was still mesmerized by the video game.

Lindsey gently placed Ava on her feet. "Sweetheart, go to the boat and ask Sara to get you some cereal. I'll be right there."

Ava crossed the parking lot and approached Sara and Maggie at the table.

"Get the boys fed soon. They must be hungry," Lindsey said. "We can talk later."

"There's nothing to talk about as long as Duncan's in the picture."

She scanned the marina, her gaze lingering on the door of the bait and tackle shop. Her heart suddenly convulsed. She had been in England during the same week that Dave had moved his parents! The security company rep had told her that her security system had been shut down manually at the control panel on the *Mary Read*... not coincidentally on the dates she and Dave had been away. Only she and Rob knew that password. She glanced around the marina once again. No one was in earshot of them. It was time to take a gamble.

She shifted on her feet, her fists shoved deep in her shorts' pockets. After a gloomy silence, she said cautiously, "Duncan's not really the issue here, is he?"

"What do you mean?" he asked, thrown off balance.

She whispered, "This is all about Tuesday mornings when I'm at work and Dave takes his father to dialysis, and you and Sheila have her quiet apartment to yourselves."

Rob's breath snagged in his chest, and his body rigid. He quickly searched the marina and located Dave at the opposite end of the dock near the gas pumps.

"Christ, Rob, he's your best friend."

He whispered frantically, "Sheila's always been a flirt. Things got out of control. And it was only a few times."

They stood locked in silence.

"Are you in love with her?" she asked tentatively, bracing herself for the answer.

"Yes," he stated firmly.

She felt blindsided, unable to piece words together. She finally turned toward the car, where Danny continued to watch from the car window.

"The boys are getting impatient. Go camping," she said, starting back toward the *Mary Read*.

"Lin ...?"

She halted.

"Do you think Dave knows?" he whispered.

"Probably not, or you'd be dead by now."

This was a problem of his making, so she walked away without further comment.

Chapter 14

At Sea

Sitting on a nylon bench of the *Just For Today*, Maggie sipped a soda and stared seaward. Sara glanced up from the laptop and mentioned that the pink BC had moved closer to the shoreline and was in less than five feet of water. It was too soon for the hurt and raw anger to settle in; Lindsey was just numb. Oblivious to the adult worries, Ava sat on her mother's knee, helping to steer the boat and singing along with a tune from *The Lion King* playing on a CD player.

Maggie had known about Rob and Sheila, Lindsey realized. This explained Maggie's protracted absences from home, more and more time spent at Brian's apartment. Her recent surliness toward Rob now made sense. Painfully, reluctantly, she allowed herself to remember ....

A few weeks earlier, Maggie had found Lindsey on the beach where she was watching Ava and a preschool friend playing with buckets and shovels.

Lindsey looked up from an Asimov novel. "Hey, Cowgirl," she had said in greeting, using the nickname from their days in rehab.

"You have a problem, Lin," Maggie had grumped, dropping onto the beach blanket.

"I have lots of problems," she'd commented wryly.

"Fuck it. Seriously."

"What?"

"Rob's banging Sheila!"

"I doubt it. We're old friends with Sheila and Dave." She'd added, "But why do you think this?"

"Do you remember last week when I had a new series of shots, and felt nauseous and sleepy the next day and stayed home from work?"

She'd nodded.

"A delivery truck came and Rob went into the store to help Sheila with the boxes."

"He always helps her move boxes when Dave's busy."

"After the truck left, Sheila put the closed sign on the door of the store, and they disappeared for a while. They came out onto the porch later, laughing. But he was not laughing when he saw me. He said, 'I didn't know you were around, I thought you were at work today.'"

"They could have been doing anything," she'd replied, unsettled. "Sheila's not his type. He thinks she's a bimbo."

"He's boning her. I can tell."

"Sorry, but I don't believe it," she had stated tersely. Dammit, she *knew* Rob was faithful! He'd just asked her to get off her birth control; he wanted them to have more children together. Maggie's suggestion was absurd, beyond absurd. Still, it wasn't like Maggie to mess things up between them, or make things up. This just didn't make sense.

Maggie had abruptly stood from the blanket. "Then I'm really sorry for you, because you're in total denial."

Ægir's Curse

Lindsey eased back on the throttle. "Maggie, can you drive for a minute? Sara, I need the laptop for a second."

Maggie dropped into the vacated captain's chair, and Ava climbed onto her knee.

Lindsey sat down next to Sara and pulled the computer onto her lap. She minimized the screen with the GPS image of Pasque Island and clicked into the software of her home security system. After a pushy reporter had camped out on the dock, even trespassed onto the deck of the *Mary Read* attempting to interview the children, a Boston security company had installed four cameras and a number of motion sensors around the houseboats. She typed in her security access code. Camera 3 recorded activities in the parking lot directly in front of the spaces where the family parked their cars. The front of the store and loading dock were visible in the left side of the frame. She pulled her cell phone out of her pocket, opened a calendar, and made a mental note of all Tuesdays in the past month.

She typed in the date of the Tuesday after Maggie's new drug treatment and forwarded through the footage. A delivery truck arrived at the loading dock at 10:47. On the porch Sheila flipped the red and white sign hanging on the door from *We're Open* to *Closed—Please return later*. Rob chatted briefly with the driver and, with a handcart, rolled boxes up a cement ramp and into a stockroom. After repeated trips up the ramp, Rob disappeared behind the metal door of the stockroom, and the truck departed at that same time. Lindsey fast-forwarded through the footage. Two boaters walked to the front porch, only to find the store closed. The cat, Tiger, crossed the porch twice looking for a handout of deli scraps. An hour later, Rob emerged from the front door of the store. His hair was wet and freshly combed. Sheila stepped out onto the porch after him, wearing a different shirt than earlier in the footage.

Lindsey checked another Tuesday, another one during the same month, and then a random Tuesday eight months earlier. She stared abjectly at the screen. Earlier that morning Rob had confessed that it was "only a few times." Sheila's odd behavior in the store the other night now made sense. The laptop screen blurred as her eyes teared; the lies stung worst of all.

"Prick," Sara whispered, reaching for Lindsey's hand.

"Yup."

Lindsey's blood now boiled. She blinked back the tears, struggling to maintain some semblance of composure in front of her daughters. She paced the deck, taking long sips from a water bottle. "I'm really sorry that I didn't believe you, Maggie." She kissed the top of the teenager's head. "You're right. I was in denial."

"Everything's so screwed up!" Maggie cried. "I don't want to go to college in the fall."

"Why? You've worked so hard to get to this point!" Lindsey said, astonished.

Maggie shrugged. "Maybe I can go somewhere local. Maybe go part-time?"

"You've been accepted to the Rhode Island School of Design, an excellent art school! The community college won't have all of the art courses you'll want to take," Lindsey pointed out.

"That's okay."

"You're not staying around because of what happened this morning? Thinking that I'm going to be alone?"

"Hell no," Maggie answered.

Maybe it was the new HIV medicine that had made Maggie so irritable recently. Or Rob's infidelity. Or both. Or... something else? "What's really going on?"

Maggie shrugged again, and then gazed out to sea.

"What, Maggie?" Lindsey persisted.

"I'm pregnant," Maggie muttered softly.

Ægir's Curse

"What?" Lindsey asked incredulously.
"I'm pregnant!"

Around noon, the *Just for Today* approached Pasque Island. Conversation had been sparse, each woman occupied by thoughts too personal too articulate. Maggie chain-smoked and said nothing. Earlier in the week she and Brian had watched the indicator of the pregnancy test change to a plus sign, which had caused him to pump his fist into the air and whoop, "Yes!" She had lumbered aimlessly to the window of his tiny apartment and stared outward in a daze. How the fuck had this happened? She always used birth control. Had the HIV-drug interfered with the action of her birth control pills?

Maggie's fury at Rob had not subsided and was expressed in every hot puff of smoke blown over the transom. She had felt queasy and traitorous telling Lindsey of the affair, as she and Rob were buddies in many activities—softball, tennis, ice-skating, and Jet Skiing. However, her loyalties were to Lindsey first. It was her unequivocal belief that her Higher Power had landed her in the same state, same rehab, even in the same room with Lindsey Nolan for some higher purpose.

Sara was determined that the events of the morning not dredge up memories of her father, a handsome seaplane pilot whose time was spent giving "flying lessons" to white women from the luxury hotels on her island. The worst of it was that every child on her small island looked just like her! They were certainly her half-brothers and sisters. The sole mission at hand was to find Jessie, she reminded herself. Her father was no more than an inconvenient memory from another lifetime.

She moved to the bow and pressed binoculars to her eyes. Gentle waves beat against a strand of beach that enclosed a tiny inlet. Scattered boulders speckled the shoreline. A stone fireplace, charred wood, and a pile of trash were partially covered by seasons of sand and seaweed.

A sudden swell knocked her forward onto her knees and she quickly grasped a railing. Maggie gripped an armrest, and Lindsey grabbed onto Ava's orange float coat.

"A big wave, Mommy!" Ava proclaimed with delight.

"Yes. That was very big."

Sara pulled herself to her feet, binoculars swaying from her wrist. She leaned over the railing and saw a shadow below. "That was no rogue wave," she replied nervously. "There's something under the boat."

"What is it?" Lindsey asked.

"I have no idea. It's too deep to see."

"We're getting out of here." Lindsey pushed the throttle forward. The depth sounder read thirty, then twenty, and finally ten feet of water, a depth where they could clearly see the bottom. A large shadow crossed the inlet in deeper water.

Sara climbed quickly back to the deck and checked the laptop. "The pink BC is here in this cove, but I don't see her anywhere. What if it's only the BC that's here, and she's still with him! I've got to find her!" She pulled off her clothes. Underneath she wore a flowered bikini. She climbed down a dive ladder.

"You can't go in that water," Lindsey warned her. "There's a very big fish out there."

"Jessie's somewhere on this island! She may be hurt!"

"At least let me get closer."

The boat eased slowly toward shore until the hull began to grind on the sand. Lindsey hit the engine kill switch, and the anchors splashed into the water.

Sara jumped off the dive ladder and strode through the water toward shore.

Ægir's Curse

"Omigod," Maggie screamed, her voice suddenly hoarse, "Sara, get the fuck out of the water!"

Sara looked quickly over her shoulder. "Fuck!" She dashed out of the water and doubled over on the beach, her lungs heaving.

Ava looked up. After a moment she expressed her concern. "Mommy, Maggie said that word again. And Sara said it too."

Then all were silent as a shark glided within inches of the dive ladder and veered off into the dark green depths.

Sara hurried along the beach searching for clues, but all she spotted were horseshoe and blue crab carapaces, fragments of shells, dried sea grass, and seaweed. A box of macaroni and cheese and beer cans at a fireplace were faded and crinkled by exposure to the sun and salt. Nothing indicated that Jessie or Arrano had been there. The beach ended at a trail, a narrow gap in the sea grass, and she stepped gingerly to avoid burrs as she climbed a dune. At the top of the rise, the island spread before her, undulating waves of grass, scrub trees, and poison ivy. Only a skeleton of a wooden cottage was present on the entire island. She returned to the beach, flicking a tick off of her leg, and started in a southerly direction toward the scattered boulders.

Ping.

"Did you just do something to the electronics?" Sara called to Lindsey.

"No. Why?"

"I thought I heard something." Sara ran toward the boulders. "I hear it again!" She rounded a boulder and stopped.

The body floated in a tidal pool, sea foam pink with blood. A scuba tank lodged between two rocks tethered the body to shore. Sara approached tentatively; a gash in the side of Jessie's head seeped blood. She pressed her ear against Jessie's chest. She collapsed to her knees, buried her face in her hands, and began to cry.

Chapter 15

At Sea

It was near the lat/long coordinates of the black BC that Detective Ingrid Stevs finally acknowledged Sven Halvorsen's existence, and only with a slicing glance of her steel blue eyes and a mutter in English, "Fokking idiot." He nodded in agreement, as all had gone badly for him that day.

A cell phone vibration that had awoken Sven that morning had been a text message, a rebuke from Anna that made no sense. He'd quickly logged onto the Internet and been mortified by the image. Throughout his career, discretion and professionalism had been paramount, which his record of service reflected. His impulsiveness yesterday on the boat had surprised even him, and now his reputation was irreparably tarnished.

When he arrived at the Falmouth police station that morning, the Americans treated him politely but with subtle reserve. Worse, sitting at his desk was his partner, her typically impassive face in a slow smolder. He was about to sit down when Ingrid stood abruptly and said in Norwegian, so that the Americans could not understand, "Do not yourself make comfortable, asshole. I got us a boat. If you are not able to handle this, then I will."

The *Zodiac* inflatable boat that Ingrid had acquired was at the same town dock where Lindsey had met him the day before. "This is not a police boat," Sven commented as he climbed over a black rubber buoyance tube, but Ingrid chose to ignore him and started the engine. As they motored out of the marina, he received a call from Lindsey; she explained that tracking devices were attached to Arrano's and McCabe's BCs. She was en route to Pasque Island to find McCabe at the location of the pink BC; she would leave it to the police to pick up Arrano. She gave Sven the GPS coordinates for the black BC, which seemed to be at a stationary point in Buzzards Bay, wished him good luck in capturing Arrano, and rung off.

Sven repeated the message to Ingrid, hoping that this might improve her mood. Since the BC's location remained fixed, he thought aloud, Arrano had probably dropped anchor and was diving. This meant that he and Ingrid could simply board the cruiser, arrest him, acquire the map, and be on a plane to Oslo by tomorrow morning at the latest. Ingrid's response was to scowl and open a backpack, remove a pistol, and attach its clip. They had not brought sidearms into the country; all was instantly clear to him. The pistols and boat had been provided by some authority who wanted the situation handled efficiently and quietly; without help, or interference, from the meddling Americans. *At all costs, the Vinland map must be restored to Viking hands.*

Maggie gave the emergency dispatchers *Just for Today*'s GPS coordinates from the depth sounder, while Lindsey splashed toward the beach and bent over Jessie. Jessie's head had been injured in two places; on the right side was a large gash, and on the left a hematoma was forming. If there was a neck or spinal injury, lifting her over a gunwale and onto the boat might cause further injury. A helicopter medical team would be required to get Jessie safely to an ER.

Jessie's breathing and heart rate were slow, but regular. It was a miracle that she was still alive, Lindsey realized. The inflated BC must have kept her upright in the water, and the tank had anchored her to shore; both had saved her. The wet suit had prevented hypothermia, but her extremities were chilled. Her parched lips indicated dehydration. Lindsey repositioned Jessie's legs and arms on the warm rocks and held her wounded head in her hands.

Sara paced nervously around the tide pool. "Do you think she'll be alright?"

"I hope so. The only injury seems to be to her head. It's an odd injury, being on two sides. Perhaps she was hit and then fell?"

The *ping ping* was grating. Lindsey reached into the pocket of the BC and removed the C-trax device. She unscrewed its plastic housing with her fingernail to deactivate the repetitive sound. A quick pain shot through her finger when she pushed the C-trax device back into the pocket. A fresh scrape ran down her finger. She probed the pocket to locate the sharp object. She studied it for a moment, then placed it in a small waterproof dive bag that she extracted from another pocket in the BC. It was a bent nail about two inches long.

A twenty-five-foot Defender Class response boat from Coast Guard Station Woods Hole and a Sikorsky Jayhawk helicopter out of Otis Air National Guard Base arrived within minutes of each other. The corpsmen from the Jayhawk unsnapped the patient from her BC and scuba tank and gently lifted her onto a stretcher. A cage holding the stretcher was winched into the gray metal interior, and the bay doors slammed. The white and orange helicopter rose and disappeared across the Vineyard Sound.

Maggie told the bosun's mate in the response boat about the shark that had been attracted by the blood oozing from the tide pool. The Coasties were skeptical, but started up the twin 225-horsepower engines and circled the inlet once to placate the teenager. Seeing nothing resembling a shark, they headed back to the beach, as they were more interested in assisting the two women in bikinis into the cigar boat.

"Any word on the blue and white cruiser?" Lindsey asked the on-scene commander.

"What cruiser?" he asked.

"This woman's boat's been stolen. It's a twenty-two-foot dive boat. Isn't there a search underway for the boat *Mermaid*?"

"This is the first I've heard of a stolen boat," the officer replied.

There was no sign of *Mermaid* amidst the sailboats and motorboats in Buzzards Bay. Ingrid Stevs pulled the binoculars away from her tanned face.

"Are you sure these are the right coordinates? I don't trust Dr. Nolan. She could be leading us on a wild goose chase while she goes after the map," Ingrid remarked tensely.

Sven's eyebrows rose at the suggestion. "I'm sure that's what she said." Still, he called Lindsey's cell phone to double-check.

Lindsey spoke loudly over the boat engines. "Correct, those are the coordinates. Jessie's been hurt, so a Coast Guard helicopter's taking her to the hospital. We're heading back in. Do you hear a pinging sound? The transponder pings when it's activated."

"Ingrid, turn off the engine," he ordered.

The cops listened intently, but the only sound was the wind and waves lapping against the inflatable's rubber buoyancy tube.

"Nothing," he replied in disappointment.

"And you don't see the BC anywhere?" Lindsey asked.

"No."

"It's possible that Arrano heard the transponder and removed it from the BC. That would mean that he's wanting the BC to dive again."

"I'll keep looking," Sven assured her. "Maybe I'll see you at the hospital later. Hopefully I can get some answers from Jessie."

"She was unconscious when I saw her. Her head's in pretty bad shape."

"We'll hope for the best."

"Why aren't there more patrol boats in the water?" Lindsey asked angrily. "The Coast Guard didn't know anything about this situation."

Sven looked over at Ingrid, who answered him with a deadly glare.

"I don't know," he replied cautiously.

Woods Hole

Despondent, Lindsey remained in bed the following morning. That afternoon the boys would be returning from the campsite, and a horrible conversation with Rob was inevitable.

After the P-town incident, Rob had been supercilious and suspicious of her every action for weeks. Admittedly, it had been boneheaded to go into a bedroom to "look at some paintings" with the two handsome artists that she had been dancing with. But, though tempted, she had done nothing with them. She'd put up with Rob's suspicions, only to find that he'd been having a play day with Sheila every Tuesday for over a year while she was at the lab, the children were at school, and Dave was at the dialysis clinic with his failing father. The hypocrisy sickened her.

She tried to invoke an important AA lesson... *you can't change people, places, and things.* People = Rob and Sheila. Place = the apartment over the bait store. Thing = the affair. The wisdom in this adage was obvious, but it did not diminish the ache of yesterday's revelations. Her only realm of control was over her own actions, and this day, through her actions, she would attempt to excise all of the negatives from her life.

Ava had slept in her bed, as she liked to do when Rob traveled to Red Sox alumni events. Did he travel alone to these gatherings, Lindsey now wondered bleakly. Ava was maneuvering fairy figurines over the sheets and, upon seeing her mother sit up, threw her tiny arms around her neck. Lindsey held her daughter, breathing in the scent of baby shampoo from the black curls, and for the moment nothing else was important. This was a gift from Higher Power to start her day. Ava fidgeted, remembering that it was a field trip day at summer camp, and sprang off the bed.

When the *Just for Today* had returned to the dock the day before, Lindsey had dropped Sara and Maggie onto the dock by the houseboats. Sara had rushed to the hospital. Maggie had departed for Brian's place, while Lindsey and Ava motored down to the gas pumps to refill the two engines. She had approached Dave with apprehension.

"A perfect afternoon in the world of baseball. The Yankees' pitchers had meltdowns. The Sox beat the Mariners by five, and ...." He had paused teasingly.

"And what?" Lindsey had said.

He had grinned.

"Dave... ?"

"And the Orioles hit a homer in the ninth to beat the Braves!" he had declared happily, grinning in anticipation of her delight.

Topping off the gas, he continued to chatter while she had smiled politely and tried to appear amused. In light of the circumstances, his banter was absurdly convivial. He was clueless about Jessie's injury, the murder investigation at his marina, and his wife's Tuesday morning activities. All was now clear. Rob and Sheila had been fucking on the *Green Monster*—their movements undetected by the deactivated security system while she and Dave were away and Maggie was at her job at the pizzeria. During which time, Arrano had left the fingerprints on the *Anne Bonny* which the forensics team had found.

Life at the marina was a closed chapter. Lindsey tore the sheets off the bed and stepped into the head. Transitions could be fun and exciting, she thought to cheer herself up, but all she felt was gloomy and bitchy. There was simply too much business to take care of that day. Like buy a house.

But who in their right mind bought a house in one day?

The evening before, as Ava dozed off to *Beauty and the Beast*, Lindsey had emailed the Realtor with the big hair who had sold Sara the house on Eel Pond, specifying her requirements: a dock, a water view, very secluded, and near or in the village of Woods Hole. It was of no importance if the counters were granite, or the appliances stainless steel. The house needed to be furnished in some form, and unoccupied. Flooring, window treatments, and wall colors were all irrelevancies that could be changed later. An immediate escape from the marina was the sole objective.

Lindsey packed Ava's lunchbox and backpack while Ava ate a bowl of cereal and talked exuberantly about her field trip to Plimoth Plantation to see pilgrims and Indians. Before locking up the *Mary Read,* she called in to Maggie, telling her to wake up for work, and was answered with the usual groan and obscenity.

Strapping Ava into the bike seat, she pedaled down the dock, across the marsh, and onto the Falmouth-Woods Hole bike trail. She veered off the trail and dropped off Ava at her summer camp, a small cottage in the woods surrounded by wood chips and play equipment.

The first stop at the marine lab was one she dreaded. Lindsey locked up her bike and set off for Jessie's lab building to explain to Jessie's boss why his postdoc might not be at work for a while. Returning to her building, she snuck into her lab by the back door to avoid any encounters with the graduate students who felt compelled to tell her of their weekend's antics. She then made a pot of coffee, grabbed a handful of Sara's trail mix, and turned on her computer.

An email confirmed that the Realtor would be picking her up at noon in front of the lab building. Lindsey called Sara at the hospital.

"Jessie's head has been shaved and stitched up," Sara reported.

"Any movements?" Lindsey inquired.

"No," Sara answered glumly.

"I'll stop by this afternoon, when Maggie gets home from work with the car."

"Derick's here with me. He can swing by and give you a lift on his motorcycle, if you need a ride earlier."

"I'll take a pass," Lindsey quickly replied.

"The doctor's here. Gotta go," Sara said, ringing off.

Lindsey removed the corroded nail from her pocket and walked to a laboratory bench. With a razor blade, she carved filings off the nail and let them drop into a mortar. She pressed the pestle into the mortar, grinding up the filings into a fine brown powder. She tapped the filings into a small plexiglass vial, then added a small quantity of organic solvent. She held her hand on the fingerprint-reading doorknob at the instrument room. The door swung open.

The prototype of the 5M imager sat in a back corner. It was not yet beautiful with the glistening covers and slick company logos that would be added by the highest bidder who would eventually manufacture the instrument. At present the imager was only functioning innards, mechanical and electrical blood and guts. She slid the vial into a port and clamped the lid shut. She typed a series of commands into a control console and pressed RUN. The sample would be ready in five-and-a-half hours.

She stood at the window and stared out to Eel Pond. She sipped her coffee in a simmering rage. If Sheila was cheating with Rob, was she also cheating with the stocky guy on the bass boat that she always flirted with? Lindsey turned toward her wall calendar. When was the last time she'd been to her gynecologist's office for a Pap smear? What if Rob had contracted some STD from Sheila, and now she had it? She suddenly felt filthy. Was there time to return home for another shower?

Chapter 16

Woods Hole

The Realtor's Volvo hesitated a bit in front her, Lindsey observed. She was standing on the curb of her laboratory building. The woman in the car was probably wondering if the thirty-something woman in a grey John Hopkins T-shirt and faded blue jeans was in the tax bracket for the property that she was about to show. Less than enthusiastically, Gladys McCarthy stepped out of the car and introduced herself.

The property was off of Quissett Avenue, Gladys explained to the new client, as they headed north out of the village. The water view was of Buzzards Bay rather than the Vineyard Sound. The Realtor asked Lindsey about her length of employment at the lab.

"Almost ten years," Lindsey replied flatly.

"Any major breakthroughs?" Gladys pressed.

The questions began to feel like an inquisition and Lindsey wondered if she should change Realtors. "I just build stuff," she replied vaguely, intending to keep the conversation on the house rather than her qualifications to buy it. "Who owns the house?"

"The owner, Eliza Bancroft, is deceased. She was the widow of the pharmaceutical executive Aaron Bancroft, and this was their summer home. There were no children, so the home is part of a larger estate in Boston that's being liquidated. Only a housekeeper occupies it now. We're here," the Realtor announced, lowering her car window.

"Already?" Lindsey glanced at her watch. The house was less than six minutes away.

Gladys swiped a card through a small barcode reader mounted into a stone wall, and two metal gates swung open. The proximity to the village and the security gates were already plusses. The old stone house was located some distance off the main road and was barely visible through a stand of trees. It had a wraparound porch and white balconies, and it was topped with a widow's walk. Across the lawns were two outbuildings: a gardener's cottage and a four-car garage with an apartment above for a chauffeur.

The women emerged from the car and climbed front porch steps that had been worn to troughs by countless footsteps. Cracked wicker chairs lined the front porch. The Realtor reached for the door, but it was opened before she touched the knob. An old woman looked down from the step and extended her hand. "Dr. Nolan, it is a pleasure," she said in a monotone. "I heard one of your lectures at the lab."

Upon finding that her client was a doctor of some renown, the Realtor perked up. "This is Mrs. Richardson, the housekeeper," she said cheerfully.

Mrs. Richardson was tall and bony and wore a cotton print dress in a style from the 1960s. Her inscrutable birdlike face continued to stare downward. "Come in," the old woman said, finally moving aside.

Everything in the house was of a bewildering scale, and as they moved from room to room, their footsteps and voices echoed ominously off dark wood walls. There were dramatic paintings, twisty banisters, and massive stairways throughout, the house having been designed by a man of substantial ego and eccentricity. The kitchen had industrial-size stoves, ovens, and walk-in refrigerators that had been used for elegant parties and galas. The library housed countless books and odd artifacts collected during the Bancrofts' excursions around the world. The home was more museum than domicile. A humid, salty breeze swept through the house and rounded the grand hallways; the house felt alive and breathing.

At the rear of the house, Lindsey paused at a large bay window. She opened the doors and stepped onto a back porch, her eyes traversing a large stone patio, a sloped lawn ending at a small beach, and a dock extending into the white-capped bay. Unfortunately the dock appeared too small to accommodate all of her boats, which meant either expanding the dock, building a boathouse, or mooring the *Mary Read* at a Falmouth marina.

The upstairs had the same cavernous, breathing atmosphere. The bedrooms were filled with four-poster or sleigh beds, large bureaus, and swaying lace curtains. At the back corner of the house, a circular turret overlooked the bay. It was empty except for an artist's easel, painting supplies, stacks of old newspaper, and boxes of rags. Some canvases leaned against the wall under a sheet.

"This was Eliza's studio. She often had models pose for her here," Mrs. Richardson explained.

Lindsey moved toward the canvases. "Mind if I have a look?"

"Please, be my guest," Mrs. Richardson remarked.

Gladys braced herself against the wall and prudishly averted her eyes.

Lindsey removed the sheet. "Wow!"

She'd anticipated pedestrian sunsets or seascapes, or perhaps some paintings of sailboats, not this. Lindsey studied one canvas, then another. "This is pornography," she pointed out.

"Mrs. Bancroft called it erotica," Mrs. Richardson stated loyally.

The models were in imaginative and sometimes extraordinary positions, half clad in historical or fantastical costumes. It all looked tremendously fun, and Lindsey felt her mood lighten. If these walls could speak ....

"Then erotica is it, Mrs. Richardson," she answered agreeably, returning the sheet to the canvases.

Mrs. Richardson's bedroom overlooked the front yard and circular driveway, a strategic sentry post that allowed one to scrutinize all visitors. A small bedside table was strewn with stationary, envelopes, and stamps. There was no sign of a computer, laptop, tablet, or printer anywhere in the house. The old woman had been sending out handwritten queries for employment.

Lindsey pointed to the woman's résumé on the table. "May I read this?"

"Of course," Mrs. Richardson replied.

Emily Richardson's résumé was less than a page in length, Lindsey noticed. "You have no references."

"They're all dead," the old woman said sadly.

"And you've only worked for one employer, the Bancrofts?"

"Correct. My father was their butler. I was born in the apartment over the garage. My family lived there over many summers."

Lindsey turned to Gladys. "Let's go have a look."

The garage housed a golf cart, an old pickup truck, and a snowplow. The back wall was lined with a substantial workbench for potential projects.

"What's included with this house?" Lindsey asked the Realtor.

"Everything on the property," she answered.

The studio apartment over the garage had wall-to-wall shag carpeting and wood paneling, suggesting a renovation in 1970s.

Ægir's Curse

It was one single room with a double bed, a small kitchenette, and a sitting area with a sofa and TV set with rabbit ears, also of seventies vintage. The bathroom was as dingy and unremarkable as the rest of the apartment.

The gardener's cottage across the lawn had much of the same late 1900s décor and furniture as the studio apartment, although it also had two airy bedrooms upstairs and a tiny attic.

Lindsey checked her watch. There were still many things to tend to in the lab before she pulled the metal sample from the 5M imager, picked up Ava from summer camp, and visited the hospital. Hopefully Maggie could watch Ava, since children weren't allowed in the ICU. She mentioned to the Gladys that she needed to return to the lab, so the three women followed a hedge of blue and pink hydrangeas to the driveway.

Lindsey turned to Mrs. Richardson. "As far as I see, this house's electrical system and HVAC seem to have been upgraded recently. The house is a classic and the view is spectacular. Why has it been on the market for so long?"

Mrs. Richardson glanced at the Realtor, and Gladys unsuccessfully tried to conceal a grimace.

Lindsey waited and, getting no response, started for the car.

"It's haunted," Mrs. Richardson confessed.

Lindsey stopped in her tracks and turned. "By who, or what?"

"By the Whaler," the old woman explained excitedly. "But only for two weeks in the fall. Andrew Stanton lost his wife in the Great Gale of 1815 and still looks for her. He lived in a small cottage on this property that no longer exists. This house was built over its foundation. A number of people over the years have reported seeing an apparition on the widow's walk the last two weeks in September."

"And does the Whaler abduct children or eat infants?" Lindsey inquired facetiously.

"Of course not, Doctor! Andrew's a benevolent ghost and is only waiting for his beloved, Rebecca, to be returned to him."

"Dr. Nolan, will you be wanting me to show you more listings?" the Realtor interrupted weakly. "I'm sure I have some more pamphlets in my trunk."

"No," Lindsey stated. "What are your plans, Mrs. Richardson?"

"I'll be seeking new employment upon sale of the house," the old woman choked out fearfully.

There was terror in Mrs. Richardson's face, Lindsey observed. She seemed of strong body and mind. But she was also quirky, ancient, and had no computer skills, and so was completely unemployable. Now Lindsey was saddened. "Do you cook?"

"I'm a superb cook, Doctor!" Mrs. Richardson stated unabashedly.

"I have two daughters. Ava is five and Maggie is eighteen." A terrible guilt overcame her for not mentioning Danny, but there was no way Rob would let the boy move with her. She could already hear Rob's furious words. "Danny's not your son! He's mine and Paola's!" Danny had the most to lose from the split, and she had felt horrible ever since seeing his distraught face through the car window. "Maggie's expecting a baby. So there will soon be four of us, five including Maggie's boyfriend, Brian, if he decides to move in here."

"The gardener's cottage might be suitable for a young couple," Mrs. Richardson offered excitedly.

Lindsey nodded. Between the turret of lust, the lovesick Whaler, and the spectacular view of the bay, the oddball beach house had piqued her interest. She turned to the Gladys. "If this house passes a home inspection, I'd like to purchase it immediately, and Mrs. Richardson, if you'd stay on as housekeeper and cook, I'd be delighted."

Ægir's Curse

Lindsey peered into her handbag and handed the Realtor two business cards. "Here's the contact information for my lawyer and my accountant. And if you can arrange for the home inspection tomorrow, and the closing to happen by the end of the week, I'll add a nice bonus onto your commission." She added wryly, "And I guess we'll also have to schedule a visit from the Ghostbusters."

Falmouth Hospital

Jessie heard noises outside the room, muffled and without meaning. Sometimes the noises made the whole room shake. The room had been dark for some time, though for how long she couldn't tell. She circled the room many times but there were no lights to be found. The blinds on one solitary window remained drawn. There was no door to enter or exit, but the room was sometimes occupied, most often by a pair of twins.

The girl twin wore a plaid summer dress, the boy matching plaid pants and a bow tie. The father asked for the boy to come to him, so he crossed the dark room. The girl remained seated on a stiff chair next to the mother. The mother was weeping and rarely spoke; often she coughed into a tissue that she pulled from a straw purse.

Then the floor of the doorless room became sand and the girl walked on it, her head bent downward. Occasionally she found a small shell in the sand and held it up for the mother and then dropped it into an old shoebox to admire later.

Sometime later a birthday party for the twins was held in the doorless room. The boy received a BB gun from the father, the girl a polished shell from Polynesia from an aunt. The girl kept the shell in her shorts pocket for two years before the brother in anger crushed it under his sneaker and the father called her a bad girl.

Derick Briggs, the biker, was waving a piece of dark chocolate under Jessie's nose when Lindsey entered the ICU room.

"What are you doing?" she asked him.

"I'm hoping that the odorants in the chocolate stimulate Jessie's medial temporal lobe memory centers to elicit consciousness," Derick answered matter-of-factly.

Lindsey pondered the response and gave him the once-over. He was in his typical attire, blue jeans, black T-shirt, and steel-toed boots. "That might work," she said, for Sara's benefit.

Sara's eyes drooped from fatigue and worry and she fell onto Lindsey's shoulder for a long embrace.

"Any news from the neurologist?" Lindsey asked.

"Nothing yet." Sara dropped dispiritedly into a chair at a small table covered with empty coffee cups and a magnetized travel chessboard.

Lindsey lingered at the bedside. Jessie's face was otherworldly and a ghastly white. Grey circles bordered her eyes. Her lips had the same grey cast. Lindsey turned toward the monitors. Jessie's blood pressure, particularly diastolic pressure, was quite low, and her heart rate was slower than normal, but rhythmic. Her blood oxygen level fell within the normal range.

"Why don't you go home and get some rest? I'll stay here for a while," Lindsey suggested.

"Alright. I'm exhausted," Sara said, standing. "Are you ready, Derick?"

"Yes." He brushed empty coffee cups into a trashcan and set the chess pieces back on the board in their starting positions. He asked in afterthought, "Do you play chess, Lindsey?"

"I was on the chess team in high school, but haven't played for years."

Ægir's Curse

He removed most of the pieces from the board and positioned the remaining red and black pieces into a perplexing strategic confrontation. "Then contemplate this," he said, daring her.

Sara hugged Lindsey one more time, while Derick retrieved his helmet from the windowsill. They departed.

Jessie no longer heard vague voices outside the doorless room, but something was still out there, moving silently. The twin girl was in the room, with a Haitian friend whom she had met on the playground, a girl who was shy, like her. For many afternoons, the twin was invited to swim in the friend's plastic swimming pool under a grapefruit tree. The friend's laughing mother spoke in a magical, musical language that she could not understand. The mother wore a flowered bikini and from afar the girl fell in love with her.

Then the room was a lagoon. Schoolchildren stood next to the girl, watching mermaids swirl and dance underwater. The girl was not sure if they were real mermaids or just pretty women breathing from air hoses. But it didn't matter, as they were enthralling. For all of her projects in art class thereafter she drew mermaids and doodled them on her lined paper in the classes that were boring.

Lindsey felt Jessie's temperature and checked the IV tubing taped at her wrist. Jessie's arms were flexed at the elbow, her legs extended. A large bandage covered her right parietal and temporal lobes. There could be memory impairment once—if—she came to. Bruises splotched the right side of her face. She lifted Jessie's eyelid and switched the bedside light on and off. The pupils were responsive, though eerily dilated. No flutter of the eyelids, no verbal responses, and no movement meant a disturbingly low rating on the Glasgow Coma Scale.

The church pew in the dark room was hard and a fly buzzed around, annoying the twin girl. She was in trouble again because she didn't want to go to church. The words of the pastor never made sense. Church was hot and her starchy dress chaffed, but she had learned to keep her thoughts to herself.

Jessie's nail was no mere nail, Lindsey thought, fingering it in her pocket. The imager had determined that the metal sample was a combination of iron oxides, trace magnesium, silicates, gravel, and sand, consistent with low-quality smelted iron. Its molecular fingerprint showed that it was bog iron from some Icelandic peat meadow forged during the medieval period. A search of the databases from a number of museums had revealed that the nail was identical in shape and length to those excavated from ship burial sites throughout Scandinavia. No one would be told this information, not Sven, not even Sara. This was Jessie's prize to announce to the world when she was ready. But was she aware of what she had found? What were Jessie's thoughts at this exact moment, sequestered in the silence of coma? And where had she found the nail? Had Arrano been with her? If yes, he would have immediately understood the significance of the find. And maybe Jessie had also.

The DJ at the dance in the doorless room had the music up too loud and it hurt the girl's ears. Her long dress was borrowed from her second cousin. She didn't particularly like the dress and it didn't fit right, but the mother could not extract enough money from the father to buy a new one. Dancing to the fast music was fun, though she hated slow dancing with Clayton and the other sweaty boys.

Ægir's Curse

A nurse entered to check the flow of the IV fluids and empty the catheter bag. Lindsey inquired about the EEG and CT reports, but the nurse said that the neurologist had left for the day.

The muffled voices returned and the room became a small, stifling living room. The air conditioning was broken again in the trailer. The father thought that he could fix anything with duct tape, but the air only became hotter. The father and brother drank too much beer and yelled at the mother. When they were like this, the mother escaped to her bedroom and the girl fled out the front door, hopped on her bike, and pedaled to the ocean. Beach walks always made her feel better. If the yelling was still bad when she returned, the sand dunes made a quiet place to sleep.

The twins resembled one another, but the boy was popular, even though he was sometimes loud and cruel. She was a nerd but had two friends from the track team. The boy always bullied her for her money from her part-time job. When she told her brother to get a job, her father grabbed for her wallet. She wished that the mother weren't in the hospital all the time, as she needed a woman to talk to.

Woods Hole

Once upon a time, during the dusk of summer, the children would have been jumping off the dock with squeals and splashes, or playing a kickball game in the parking lot, or lining the dock with their fishing poles and Styrofoam cups of night crawlers. Now the marina was ominously still. Both the *Anne Bonny* and *Mary Read* were silent; lights illuminated only the *Green Monster*.

On the dock, Danny gazed between his knees at the water below. At the appearance of Lindsey's Jeep, he sprang to his feet and ran toward the parking lot. His forceful hug knocked Lindsey against the car. She had difficulty breathing, his hug was so tight. His eyes were swollen and wet.

"I missed you so much. How was camping at Big Bear?" she asked, feigning cheerfulness.

"It sucked. Dad was mean and crabby the whole time, so Zephyr and I just stayed at the water park all day."

"Where's everyone?"

"Dad and Maggie had a big fight. She left and took Ava with her."

"Where'd they go? To Brian's?"

"I think so."

The marina was uncharacteristically dark and Lindsey realized why. In the apartment above the bait store, the windows were black. The bait store lights had been turned off before the normal closing time. Also closed prematurely was the boat repair shed.

Danny glanced fearfully over his shoulder toward the *Green Monster*. "And Dad and Dave got into a big fight," he whispered emphatically. "Then Dave went upstairs, packed up, and took Max and Brianna away. And Dad and Sheila were shouting at each other."

Lindsey pulled the ten-year-old into her for another hug. He had witnessed too much for one evening. She wondered about Danny's understanding of the tumult. "Do you know what caused all of this?"

He nodded, pained. "Max and Brianna told me. Dad and Sheila fell in love."

His direct words felt like undertow dislodging her footing. "I guess that's what happened," she admitted quietly.

She held firmly onto Danny's hand as they walked toward the *Green Monster*. "You sit out here for a minute while I talk to Rob. I'll be right out. Please wait for me here." Obediently the boy sat by a window on the aft deck and watched with trepidation as she entered the houseboat.

Wads of bloody tissues littered the galley table. Rob turned to her, his eyes glazed and deranged under a galley lamp. "I think Dave broke my nose." He paused. "Can you check to see if it's broken?" He tilted his head.

Their eyes locked momentarily, but there was no connection. It was the face of an unrecognizable and pathetic man. His eyes implored her to feel something, but all inside her was desolate and dark.

"Yes, it's broken," she stated emotionlessly. She started to the refrigerator for ice and then stopped herself, as he was no longer hers to tend to. "Call your AA sponsor and go to a meeting immediately."

At the hospital earlier that evening, while she'd been concentrating on the chess enigma, the Realtor had texted her that her offer on the Bancroft summer home had been accepted.

"I'm moving later in the week, so the marina is yours and Sheila's. Good luck with it," she said. The omission of where she was moving to was intentional. "Until you regain some tiny semblance of sanity, Danny's staying with me."

Oddly, there was no protest from Rob.

Chapter 17

Woods Hole

Mermaid was a perfectly constructed boat, Adrian concluded. The cruiser had been easy to maneuver up a narrow channel in a marsh and hide amidst tall grass in a shallow pond. When the tide went out every six hours, the boat lay tilted in the muck. Besides *Mermaid*, the only other boat in the secluded pond was a long-forgotten, rotting rowboat. Through the scrub pines, gray clapboard vacation cottages were visible, but during his time of hiding, none of the inhabitants had ventured into the marsh to bother him.

After days of ignoring his cell phone, Adrian finally decided to check his messages. The first was an arousing sext from his graduate student. He gloated and wondered if he shouldn't add another graduate student to his harem when he returned to campus in the fall. The second message, a voicemail from his wife, had the chilling effect of ice water to his libido. A female detective, a foreigner, had come by the house in the middle of last week, his wife explained. The detective had inquired after his whereabouts, asked if he had seen Professor Ingvars during the summer conference, and informed her of Ingvars's recent death.

Ægir's Curse

"Why would a detective be asking us about the death of your old professor?" his wife had wondered. "Please call," she had insisted. She missed him and she loved him. Blah, blah, blah.

If he could access the Norwegian newspapers, the *Bergen Tidende* or the *Aftenposten*, information about Ingvars's death might be revealed, but his laptop battery had died. During his long hours on *Mermaid*, he reviewed the precautions he'd taken in Ingvars's apartment. The apartment had been wiped down thoroughly, he was sure of it. The kitchen counter and sink had been meticulously scrubbed with soap. He had stacked the dishes and started the dishwasher. He *had* turned on the dishwasher, hadn't he? With this freaking headache, he couldn't think straight!

If he could access the local papers he might discover what was meant by Sara's text. What if the real Craig Russell had committed some crime, and they were looking for him to answer for it? Ridiculous, he told himself. His headache and cough had worsened, causing his thoughts to bounce between the rational and irrational.

Worse, he was having more of these bizarre blackouts. He had never had a blackout before this trip. And they were getting longer. At first he was aware of losing seconds, but now they stretched to minutes. He needed medicine fast. It would be impossible to drive safely back to New Hampshire if the blackouts continued. His wife would have to come and get him, which meant concocting some story about why he was on Cape Cod. Perhaps he could say that he was getting her a special nautical antique for her birthday? Or scouting out romantic B&Bs for their upcoming anniversary? He would think of something plausible. She would believe him. She always did.

Adrian rifled through Jessie's seabag, finding a brush, lip gloss with sunscreen, a toothbrush, toothpaste, and tampons, but no aspirin. It was urgent that he return to the campsite and get to a drugstore. His brown hair and beard were growing in.

In addition to medicine, he needed to purchase hair dye. The blond Craig Russell had to disappear and a new identity created.

As night fell over the pond, he slid his laptop into his backpack. Suddenly his eyes watered and his vision blurred. No!... another blackout!... *the Viking jarl climbed out of the longboat and waded through the muddy shallows. He was sure that he was being watched by the Skraelings crouched in the marsh grass. They dared not attack him. Blood and marrow from their last encounter still stuck to the blade of his battle-axe. A trail through the woods led to his camp. There he would celebrate the day's slaughter with berry wine and codfish, and his beloved, Freydis.*

A surfer girl in an old VW Westfalia picked up Adrian on Woods Hole Road and drove him as far as the entrance to the Big Bear Campground off the highway. Recharging his laptop at the power outlet in his campsite was the first order of business. He was ravenous and searched his cooler. The bread had gone moldy, which meant a dinner of peanut butter and jelly on saltine crackers. He dragged himself over to the camp store and bought aspirin and fresh fruit, just as the store was closing for the evening. Never could he recall a headache of such blinding intensity. Unfortunately the camp store did not have a decongestant. He would have to pick that up tomorrow at a drugstore.

Returning to the campsite, he gulped down four aspirin. He hoped that his hacking wouldn't wake the entire campground. In a bathhouse shower he struggled to scrape off the fine, sticky flakes of muck from the wreck dive that, days later, still adhered to his skin. Red dots had appeared on his arms and hands. After repeated scrubbings with a bar of soap, he returned to his campsite and bent into the tent, carrying the laptop with him.

Ægir's Curse

He zipped the door to keep out the bugs, except for a small opening for the extension cord to recharge the laptop. He slipped on a pair of clean jeans, warm socks, and a shirt. A rolled-up jacket would have to serve as a pillow. He cursed himself for leaving his sleeping bag on the boat. He curled himself into a ball on the cold nylon floor and prayed for a mild night and a deep sleep.

The desolation of the marina and his abandonment were intolerable. Rob gulped down another shot of island rum and, flashlight in hand, stormed off the *Green Monster* toward the storage shed. Reminders of loss assaulted him from every direction. The garage where he and Dave had worked on various projects together, while insulting the Yankees and lauding the Red Sox, was bolted closed. The training wheels on Ava's tiny pink bike had just been removed; he had promised to teach her to ride on two wheels. The Jet Skis that he had bought for Maggie and himself to race along the coastline floated silently in tandem next to the *Green Monster*.

Mercifully, the combination lock of the storage shed had been removed some time ago. In his present state, with his thoughts like scatter shot, recalling a series of numbers would have been impossible. Despite the shakes in his hand, the doorknob scanner read his prints, and the door swung open. His flashlight beam slashed the darkness, picking out a pup tent, sleeping bag, and lantern, which he carried to the minivan. He stealthily eyed the marina and, seeing it empty, walked behind the dumpsters and followed the beam from the flashlight down a narrow trail into a pine forest. A cooler had been hidden for weeks in a clump of scrub. He retrieved an unopened bottle of rum, stashed it in a backpack, and returned to the car.

Before turning the key in the ignition, he squeezed his eyes closed. As the last shovel of dirt had been tossed onto his wife's coffin that bitterly cold day, he had promised himself that he would be the best of fathers to Danny, a toddler at the time. He'd made the same promise upon cosigning with Lindsey Maggie's adoption papers; and again, upon seeing his newborn daughter, Ava, in the maternity ward of Falmouth Hospital. Rob's eyes remained shut, but the image of Danny's baseball glove and a plastic home plate on a shelf of the storage shed was seared to the back of his eyelids.

Since it was midweek, numerous campsites were available at the Big Bear Campground, so Rob chose an isolated one between the bathhouse and the forest. By lantern light he hammered the tent stakes as quietly as possible so as not to disturb other parents who were moving their children from the fire's glow into their tents or RVs for the night. As he should be doing at this hour—putting *his* children to bed, and then settling into bed with *his* woman! What nerve of that Norwegian bastard to show up at the marina, asking about Lindsey's whereabouts. Christ, where was she? He had returned from work to find the *Mary Read*'s slip empty. The *Just For Today* was also gone. His hammering of the tent stake intensified. It was a small consolation that the cop did not know Lindsey's whereabouts either. This meant he couldn't be screwing her.

Lindsey, he was sure, truly did love only him, and he loved only her. He did not love Sheila, as he had told Lindsey. His words had been meant to wound. And they had. She had left him. A terrible, terrible mistake had been made that he prayed was not irreparable. It was all because of that secret shared with Sheila. Years of harmless flirtations had escalated to kissing and fondling in the cold room, but then they had moved upstairs, and all had changed. Sheila could not enjoy sex unless she was buzzed, so she'd down a few beers before they got started. Despite knowing he'd been sober for twelve years and was a member of AA, one day she'd said, "You can have one with me, baby. I'll allow you to have *just one*."

It was not Tuesday morning, the single imported beer that he was permitted, or beer-breathed, sloppy Sheila that had become the obsession. The singular obsession was for Tuesday afternoons, when he would drive to a package store and cruise along the coastal road, sipping from a bottle of rum, vodka, whatever, the fluid warming his blood and rekindling in him the same invincibility of his rookie season. Then he would smoke cigars, chew breath mints, and arrive at practice where he had served as a batting coach for the Cape Cod Baseball League for the past few summers. When he returned home late on Tuesday evenings, his children would be long asleep. He would have been sober for hours. He would shower quietly. Lindsey might still be up, waiting up for him, expert and enthralling every time.

The single beer on Tuesday morning was just a trigger. Tuesday afternoons, not Sheila at all, possessed him. For an alcoholic cannot stop at *just one*.

The tent erected, Rob dimmed the lantern, readying himself to drink the rum in earnest. He decided to use the bathroom one last time before he became too drunk to walk straight. A sudden pain shot through his heel upon standing. A large blister had formed earlier that day. He was a professional athlete and knew better than to wear new cleats without bandaging up his feet first! He limped to the men's side of the bathhouse and relieved himself at a urinal. The soap dispenser was empty, so he walked along the empty shower stalls, pulling aside the curtains, searching for a bar of soap.

In the end stall, a tiny remnant of soap sat by the drain. He stepped out of his sandal and lifted his foot into a sink. The blister was already torn and seeping fluid. The soap slipped from his hand and into the sink. Retrieving it, he found the bar to be unusually slick, probably made with some expensive oil, and it contained tiny brown flakes that might be some exotic herbal ingredient. Yet like other ordinary soap, it stung on contact, and he winced as he gently rubbed it over the blister again and again to ensure that it was clean. Done washing, he dropped the bit of soap into a trashcan by the door, wiped his hands on his shorts, and set off for the campsite.

This would be his last binge, Rob promised himself. He'd sleep it off in the darkness of the tent, and tomorrow he'd call Lindsey at the lab, ask her to drive him to the rehab in Newport —as he had done for her five years before and which she would willingly do for him—and admit himself into a thirty-day inpatient program. In thirty days Lindsey and his children would be restored to him.

When funds from her bank account were wired to the Bancroft estate, the Bancroft family lawyer informed Lindsey that her family could move into the summer house at any time; the signing of the real estate transfer documents at that point were only a formality. This was welcome news. The move had been as effortless as untethering the lines of the *Mary Read* from a temporary mooring in Great Harbor and motoring over to the dock at the new house. Maggie followed in the *Just For Today*.

An absence of electricity on the dock meant that living on the *Mary Read,* even for the short-term, was not feasible. She backed the pickup truck to the dock's edge and shuttled belongings from houseboat to house. Her family was excited about the new home, despite the unsettling circumstances that spurred their sudden flight.

It was first necessary to create normalcy for the children. A swing set had been set up on the lawn next to the garage, although Danny and Ava seemed more content sliding down the winding banisters, climbing the ladders in the library, and exploring the large, drafty rooms. In the attic the children constructed a fort with sheets and old chairs. They had no encounters with the Whaler.

The artwork had been removed from the turret, so as not to encourage Maggie's interest in that genre of painting. Nor did Lindsey want to encourage Ava, who was at that age where she was attuned to noticing—and freely commenting on—differences in male and female anatomy.

Only at night were the strange creaks and rattles of the old house frightening, especially when winds blew off the bay. Danny and Ava slept with Lindsey, until she urged them to select rooms of their own, as she was exhausted from the strain of the past few days, compounded by the poking of little knees and elbows throughout the night.

Maggie appropriated the gardener's cottage and was rarely seen, except to sign for deliveries of furniture. Ava, too young to understand the reasons for the family's flight, simply considered the new house an indoor playground, as she had never lived in a house on land before. Danny, shaken by the events of the past days, clung closely to Lindsey and his sisters. He and Ava would prefer to share a bedroom, he told Lindsey, which seemed an adequate solution to her sleepless nights.

When voicemail messages appeared on her cell phone, Lindsey listened fearfully, expecting an incensed demand that Danny be brought back to the marina. Rob was the boy's biological father, she was not the biological mother, only a girlfriend, and no longer even that. Legally she had no leg to stand on. But to her relief and bafflement, the message never came.

The blackouts were increasingly troublesome. Adrian wandered over to the camp store to buy breakfast. The last thing he remembered was handing a clerk some dollar bills and stepping outside to pick up some firewood. When his sense of self-awareness returned some time later, he was seated on a bench next to the campground's miniature golf course. Fortunately, he had made no commotion; he found himself silently drinking coffee and eating a donut. The families winding their way through the golf course were more or less oblivious to his presence.

No way would he be able to drive to the Falmouth drugstore that day. He'd hop a bus later that morning. Nor could he drive himself home to New Hampshire. His wife would definitely have to come and get him, but with her bastard of a boss, it would be impossible for her to get off work on a weekday. The trip would have to wait until the weekend. Then he could get himself to his doctor first thing next week and get a prescription for whatever was ailing him. It had to be the sticky particles stirred up at the wreck, as the cough and headache had began immediately after the wreck dive. When he returned to Woods Hole with his team of underwater archeologists, they would have to take precautions. It still seemed unreal that he had both the map and the wreck! Within months he'd be as rich as a king.

Chapter 18

Boston

It was a wasted trip. Upon learning of Maggie's pregnancy, the physician in charge of the trial study of the new HIV drug immediately dropped her from the study. Unhappy as he was at losing a crucial participant, he was even more worried about possible legal ramifications. Lindsey, however, as a member of the non-infected control group, was given her shot, and her blood was drawn to assay her cytokines and lymphocytes.

As the physician bandaged up her arm, Lindsey listened to the commotion in the waiting room. Ava crawled underneath the chairs while Danny scolded her for taking off her sandals and socks. The children were tired and hungry, and likely to remain so. If Rob had been with them, it would have been his turn to pick the restaurant for their post-hospital visit dinner, and he would have chosen Italian, so each child could order something that he or she liked to eat. Instead, Maggie had decided on Thai food, as she was next in the queue behind Rob to choose. Maggie was the only one who liked Thai food.

Suddenly the querulous noises stopped. "Daddy!" Ava scooted from under the chairs and knocked a pile of magazines off a coffee table. Lindsey heard the muffled crash.

"Mr. Jenkins arrived earlier this afternoon for his shots," a nurse explained, "but he has a respiratory infection. He's to come back in a week."

Lindsey reluctantly left for the waiting room. Rob, on his knees, had pulled both Ava and Danny into his chest for a hug. He looked up at Maggie. "Hi, love." The teenager wordlessly retreated into the music of her iPod, ignoring him.

The room felt smothering to Lindsey. "Let's go outside. I need air," she said.

Rob grabbed his children's hands and led Ava and Danny along a maze of corridors, while Maggie and Lindsey lagged behind. Rob's gait had a slight limp to it. The family moved through a revolving door and onto a sidewalk that bustled with people in business suits leaving their offices on a warm summer evening.

"I need to talk to your mother for a minute," Rob informed Ava and Danny, releasing their hands. He reached toward Lindsey's arm to guide her out of the stream of pedestrians, but she jerked her arm away.

"Don't touch me! You've forfeited your right to ever touch me again."

His expression was fleetingly inscrutable and menacing, and she felt cornered and disoriented. His foot tapped nervously, a behavior she'd never noticed before. Abruptly he pulled a tissue from his pocket and blew his nose into it.

"I needed to get away from the marina for a while, so I've moved in with my AA sponsor, Leo," he said quietly. "I ended things with Sheila, permanently. It wasn't pretty." He paused. Lindsey said nothing. "I need time to sort things out. But Leo's is not the place for Dan. Can he stay with you? School starts in two weeks. This way he doesn't have to change schools, and he'll be close to his friends in the village."

All along she had thought it best that Danny remain with his sisters. "Yes. Of course," she replied with relief.

Ægir's Curse

Rob hacked violently into a tissue, causing passersby to increase their distance and quicken their step. His eyes were red and runny, still underlined with bruises. His nose had been reset and was covered with a large bandage. His general appearance was that of a defeated prizefighter.

"You sound and look terrible," she stated plainly.

"I caught a bad cold somewhere," he replied evasively. He paused. "Can I come over and have dinner with you and the kids occasionally?"

"No. I'm not ready for that yet. I'm still so furious with—"

"Lin, I'm so, so sorry," he cut in.

Maggie stepped up to them. "Can you two discuss this later? We're all starving. Rob, it's your night to pick."

"No, not tonight," Lindsey interrupted resolutely. There was something about him she could not put her finger on, something combustible and unstable. She turned to Rob. "You and I will talk another time, but not tonight." She herded the children quickly along the crowded Boston sidewalk, while his glare bored into the back of her head.

Woods Hole

The decongestant diminished the fire in Adrian's throat, but the aspirin didn't touch his headache. He caught a shuttle bus from the campground to the ferry stop in Woods Hole. Strong liquor would help take the edge off his assorted pains. He stopped in a liquor store and bought himself a bottle of scotch whiskey. Next to the liquor store was a shop that sold ice cream. A large milkshake would soothe his throat. Leaving the ice cream shop, milkshake in hand, he caught a glimpse of his reflection in the glass door. He smiled inwardly… god, he loved the new look!

Earlier that day he had purchased hair dye at a drugstore. Back at the campsite, he'd rubbed the dye through his hair and beard, which had grown in fast over the past few weeks, and walked, with a towel draped over his head, to the bathhouse. When he emerged from the shower stall, he preened in front of a mirror. The dark-haired swashbuckler had morphed first to blond spy, and now to a red-bearded Viking.

The sun of late afternoon was directly in Adrian's eyes as he moved across the street to Eel Pond. He pulled down the brim of his ball cap, as his eyes had become painfully sensitive to sunlight. He was tiring easily and decided to have his dinner of whiskey and milkshake at the seawall next to the bascule bridge. From there it was only a short walk back to the bus stop. It was doubtful that he'd be able to keep down any solid food that evening.

Across the pond at the marine lab, a reception was being held on a patio of one of the buildings. It was a semiformal affair, the men in blazers despite the afternoon heat, the women in dresses. Adrian discretely sipped whiskey from a paper bag and chased it down with milkshake. The fluids felt wonderful on his raw throat. Between the boats in the pond, he spotted Drs. Nolan and Kauni. The two women had broken off from the others at the reception and stood on the edge of the seawall. Their conversation was emphatic, both gesticulating wildly. Adrian couldn't decide which woman was lovelier. Nolan's hair was in a single long braid that dropped nearly to her waist. Her black cocktail dress was just snug enough. Kauni wore a strapless gown made of a bright tropical print.

It was disappointing that he and Nolan had been unable to connect. Just as well, he thought. All the changes in his appearance would have alarmed her. Beside, when he returned with his team of archeologists to excavate the wreck, they'd have plenty of time to spend together. Suddenly he felt his eyes burn and his vision blur. Shit! Another blackout... he willed himself to sit still at the seawall until it passed, to do nothing to draw attention to himself ...

Ægir's Curse

A flotilla of longboats rocked in the enclosed harbor. The rows of shields painted in shades of red and orange represented the warrior tribes from Greenland, Iceland, and the Faroes, that comprised his small army. His own warship floated alone at the entrance to the harbor, its bow a snarling gold dragon that shone in the light of the westering sun. At his bidding, his fleet of raiders would descend upon any Mainland port or monastery. But the Vinlanders' next attack was aimed at the Skraeling camp up the coast. For now, he permitted his warriors to rest and feast. The plentiful rabbit and deer on the peninsula simmered on spits. Casks of mead had been rolled from a storehouse.

That morning had been a particularly bloody one. The Skraelings had attacked in great numbers, just as the men were waking. Never before had the red people attacked so early, at daybreak. Even though their bows and arrows and wooden spears were no match for the Vinlanders' iron, his brother-in-law and cousin had been killed.

He sat alone, drinking mead from a horn. He was feeling ill. There had been too many skirmishes in the past few days, and old wounds were flaring up. His woman, Freydis, moved freely among the men. Her black-haired thrall was by her side, as usual. There were not enough thrall women for all of the warriors on Vinland. Last week the wife of a chieftain had died in childbirth. Another woman had been swept away in a rip current while casting nets. They must steal more women from the green island on their next voyage east.

When Adrian finally regained consciousness, the milkshake was warm and the party on the patio had dispersed.

Earlier in the day, before the reception, Lindsey had received an email. Rob was requesting a meeting to discuss the children. A meeting was inevitable, and it was better to get it over sooner than later, to promote the healing process. Besides, he was a kind father; the children missed him tremendously. His lies and infidelity still smarted, but she was trying to move on by spending time with the kids and at social gatherings. She had cooled down since their confrontation in Boston; it was possible that she could conduct herself rationally and calmly. She was a sane, sober woman, she reminded herself, who had five years of sobriety.

For some reason that only her Higher Power understood, the relationship needed a respite. She had done the right thing, she was sure, moving from the marina and buying the old beach house. She and Rob could reevaluate their feelings toward each other without being in each other's way. And there was still a glimmer of hope for them, since he had broken it off with Sheila. Many couples had problems with infidelity. Maybe this was another test from Higher Power that would bind them together with greater strength, commitment, and resolve for future years together. How many times had she cheated on Duncan when she was drinking? Countless! Half of the trysts she couldn't even remember. Was this payback time, so that she understood how it felt when the shoe was on the other foot?

Perhaps, when all was settled, Rob would move into the beach house with her, where the children had more space to run around. Perhaps they would even have more children together, the way he wanted. Being pregnant again wouldn't be so bad here—not with Emily Richardson to help. They could grow old together, contentedly seated side by side in the two Adirondack chairs by the sundial, watching their children and grandchildren splash delightedly in Buzzards Bay.

Rob's email said that he had moved back to the marina; he could not endure Leo's snoring. In her return email, she flat out refused to meet at the marina, but she changed her mind when Rob wrote that Sheila was out of the state for a few days, visiting her mother in New Jersey.

Ægir's Curse

Lindsey pulled into the marina at 7:20, having been delayed by the reception, and by a splinter in Ava's toe. "New rule. Pool shoes or sandals always on the dock," she had reproved, handing the tweezers back to Mrs. Richardson. "And while I'm gone, Mrs. Richardson is the boss."

There had been no time to change from the black cocktail dress and uncomfortable pumps, so Lindsey stepped awkwardly across the gravel parking lot. The marina was quiet, many of the slips empty. Sheila wasn't efficiently handling the business on her own. Dave never would have allowed trash to overflow the cans on the dock, or oil cans to be stacked next to the dumpster. Who was pumping the gas, repairing the boat engines, and managing the accounts for the store and slips? These were all tasks Dave had attended to meticulously and with good cheer, and which attracted boaters to his marina summer after summer. As far as she could tell, Sheila's skills were limited to making the deli sandwiches and stocking the shelves. But she clearly had other skills, Lindsey bitterly reminded herself.

Rob was smoking a cigar on the aft deck of the *Green Monster*, as she had seen him do a thousand times. The bandage had been removed and his nose appeared to be healing well, but the bruises under his eyes remained ghoulish and unnerving.

For the children's benefit, they needed to be cordial, because they had children to raise together. "The children can't wait to see you again. When will you call?" Lindsey asked in greeting.

"Soon," he answered guardedly.

She dropped her purse on the deck table. "Please call Danny. He's really confused."

"I scared the hell out of him that night, didn't I?" he asked, the regret plain in his voice.

"Yes. He's never seen you angry or violent." She paused. "What happened that night? You're always the calm, cool one."

"I don't know. "I just lost it." He stubbed out his cigar.

"Have you been working with Leo?"

"I fired him."

"You what? Leo's been your sponsor for twelve years!"

"I don't want to talk about Leo. Let's get a drink. It's too hot out here." He rose abruptly and disappeared inside.

She followed quickly, lecturing to his back. "Then find another sponsor! This is the time when we both need lots of meetings. We'll get through this. Really we will."

He turned from the refrigerator with a water bottle and a can of beer in each hand. "Which one do you want?"

She reached reflexively for the water bottle. "That's not funny!" It suddenly dawned on her. "That's beer! What are you doing with beer?"

He grinned insincerely. "Drinking it, like most people do." He cracked open the can. "I can handle beer. I just can't handle hard liquor. That's what did me in, the hard stuff."

"We're drunks. We're not allowed to have anything, beer included! Get to a meeting immediately. I'll take you there," she implored, her panic growing.

She grabbed his wrist before the beer could touch his mouth, and he stared at her clasped hand for a moment.

"Please. Let. Go," he said mockingly.

"Put down the beer," she demanded.

"Let go."

"Then put down the goddamn beer!"

He effortlessly pried her hand off of his wrist. He smiled savagely, chugged the beer, crushed the can, and tossed it over his shoulder, where it clanged across the counter. It suddenly occurred to her that he'd been drinking for a while—probably with Sheila.

Ægir's Curse

Lindsey had never seen Rob impaired and was overcome with fear. He had once told her that he was a mean drunk. That's what had gotten him thrown out of baseball during his rookie season and prematurely ended his career.

"You're insane, and I'm out of here," she cried, backing away. "Don't call the children and don't call me until you're sober again!"

"But our visit's not over yet," he answered tauntingly.

"Believe me, it is," she stated, heading for the door.

He grabbed her roughly. Despite his infected heel, he was swift. He lifted her off her feet and dragged her down a hallway and into a stateroom. She struggled to free herself, but his grip was strangling. He fell on top of her, pinning her face down into the mattress, briefly suffocating her. His hands fumbled at the hem of her dress, yanking it up over her hips. He tore at his zipper. His hands left her momentarily and she twisted to make an escape, but there was a fast jingling above her head, then the cold clasp of metal around her wrist. The other handcuff was attached to his own wrist, binding them together. In a rage she writhed under him, the metal cutting deep into her skin.

"Get it off!" she yelled.

"But it's one of your favorite toys."

"I mean it, you bastard! Get it off!"

He fumbled with his free hand under her panties. Her fight continued, but he was too strong and too quick and entered her easily. The sensation was completely familiar, but the man crushing into her a stranger.

"You came to talk, so let's talk," he growled into her hair.

"Get off me!"

"Say please …."

"You are drunk and sick …."

"Say it. Please …."

"Fuck off!"

He moved into her with greater force. "Say it! *Please*."

"Please," she hissed furiously through gritted teeth.

"After we talk."

"I'm not talking to a fucking drunk!"

"Then you'll listen to one," he said nastily. "You'll never insult me in public again."

"What the hell are you talking about!"

"In Boston! Not letting me come to dinner with my own children. Believe me, that will never happen again!"

"You were not insulted in public! That's bullshit. We were talking quietly. No one heard a thing we said."

"You disrespected me in front of my children!" he roared.

"Who's disrespecting who, you bastard? Stop this! You're breaking my wrist!"

"By the time I'm through with you, every bone in your body will be broken," he growled again.

Now she feared for her life. Would Sara take care of the children if he killed her? If she got out of this alive, she could never see him again.

"Rob, let me go," she pleaded. "Enough of this."

"We're not done. You were a crazy oversexed drunk." He laughed perversely. "Do you remember how crazy you were?"

"My wrist, I swear it's breaking ...." she whispered in agony.

"Shut up about your fucking wrist! I asked you a question. Do you remember it?"

She remained silent.

"Answer me!" he raged.

"Only some of it," she replied faintly.

"My favorite thing that you used to do was to fuck some boyfriend the night that Duncan was coming to visit you. Like the Jamaican. That used to make Duncan ballistic!" He laughed aloud.

"That's not funny, and it wasn't intentional." She wept into the bedspread.

Ægir's Curse

"What's not funny is that he'll never divorce you, so you'll never be my wife, and that *is* intentional. Fuck Duncan... fuck Duncan," he said, with each excruciating thrust.

She glanced at the nightstand with a glimmer of hope. If she could just slide herself a few inches.... With his next thrust she managed to move closer... it was almost within reach. One more painful thrust, one more slide. She grasped a baseball trophy on the nightstand and whipped it backward over her shoulder. There was a thud of metal against skin and bone. With a groan, he collapsed on her, compressing her into the mattress. He was silent, dead weight.

But silent for how long?

Struggling to crawl from underneath him, she stretched, still tethered to him, toward the edge of the bed. She prayed that the key to the handcuffs was in the nightstand drawer, where the keys and batteries to all of the sex toys were usually kept. Oh, thank you, God! Her quaking hand shook the key into the lock, and she was free. Before she fled, she turned briefly to look at the body sprawled across the twisted bedspread. It had been a direct hit to his forehead. A large contusion was beginning to form. Whoever that stranger was who had just assaulted her, he was still breathing. At any moment he might come to, and come after her! She dashed off the *Green Monster,* sick with horror at the transformation of the man she'd loved and lived with for five years.

Chapter 19

Woods Hole

The Jeep paused in front of the security gates of the beach house while Lindsey planned a discreet entry. If she snuck quietly through the patio door in the back, she might make it to the shower unseen by Mrs. Richardson. She sniffled into a tissue, then dug through her purse for the gate's swipe card. She glanced into the rearview mirror again. Thankfully Rob was not pursuing her. What to do next? Swipe the card to open the gates. Turn the wheel, press the gas pedal. Stay on the pavement! The security gates slammed behind the Jeep, and she drove slowly forward with a small sense of relief. If the madman was to come after her, he would have to climb the stone wall, and that would trigger the alarm system. By the time he stalked her through the forest, across the expansive lawn, and broke into the house, the police would be en route ....

She jammed on the brake. The blue sedan was parked in the circular driveway! She stared miserably at herself in the mirror. Her mascara had been carried away with the tears. Her hair was flying in a thousand frantic directions. Why bother primping? She was a wreck beyond repair. Maybe if she could talk to Sven briefly outside on the lawn, in the dark, he wouldn't notice her disarray. She eased her car in behind the sedan.

Ægir's Curse

All hope for a discreet entry vaporized as Mrs. Richardson and Sven, seated in the porch chairs, turned toward her car. Could this night get any worse? For a brief moment she thought to floor it around the driveway and flee back into the night. But Rob was out there somewhere, lurking somewhere, waiting. She turned off the ignition with a sense of futility. The old woman was happily conversing with the officer. Lemonade had been served in Mrs. Bancroft's best summer crystal, and Mrs. Richardson was in her best lace sweater. Shoes in hand, Lindsey reluctantly climbed the porch stairs, avoiding the cone of light over the front door. She had not seen Sven in person since the ride on the *Just for Today*.

He stood up and shook her hand. "Good evening, Doctor."

"Hello," she replied softly.

Mrs. Richardson remained anchored to her seat with no intention of leaving the elegant, sunburnt Norwegian. "Your meeting ran late," she stated with a prissy edge in her voice.

"Yes," Lindsey answered vaguely, unbalanced by the housekeeper's tone.

"I put the children to bed," the older woman added.

"Thank you so much. Is Maggie home?"

"Yes, and so is Brian."

"Mrs. Richardson told me of the fascinating history of this house. I can't believe that Greta Garbo was here twice. And Eugene O'Neill!" Sven declared, impressed.

"Really?" Lindsey replied with a pang of guilt. She had not taken the time to get to know her housekeeper, or anything else about her new home. "Mrs. Richardson, sometime soon you and I must share a pot of tea."

"Doctor, please walk with me, as I have to show you some documents. Mrs. Richardson," Sven said, extending his hand to the old woman, "it was a pleasure meeting you." He guided Lindsey by the elbow down the porch stairs.

"Thank you," she whispered as they passed by a hedge of hydrangeas.

"You had a bad night," he said with concern.

"Is it that obvious?"

"Yes. What happened?"

"I don't want to talk about it."

They strolled around the grounds, past the gardener's cottage where, Lindsey explained, Maggie and Brian lived, and then to a dock where she warned him about some splintery old planks that needed replacing. He listened patiently to her ramblings about any number of home improvement projects that she had in mind for the new property. There were lights over the workbench in the garage, she said, so they headed up a sloped lawn from the beach. She jerked at the garage doors, but they were locked.

She looked up at the black windows. "Maybe the apartment's open."

The studio apartment was dingier and more outdated than she remembered from her tour with the Realtor. A row of light switches was somewhere along the paneled wall; she groped in the darkness to find it. She lifted all five switches at once, and one light illuminated a circular table in the corner. Sven spread photographs across it while she opened a refrigerator, searching for water. The refrigerator was empty. In a cupboard was an old plastic cup, so she rinsed it at the sink and guzzled down two cups of water before joining him at the table.

"We believe this is Arrano," Sven said. "This man was captured on security cameras at the bus stop at the ferry, and a few minutes later at the MBL dock on the morning that he and Jessie left on that last charter."

The suspect was a young blond male, just as Sara had told her, with a backpack slung over his shoulder. "I never saw him when he looked like this. When I spoke with him he had long brown hair and a beard and mustache. So the professor's a chameleon, currently a blond one."

"It appears that way. I wanted to give you a heads-up, in case you see him as you go about your business in the village."

Sven studied Lindsey as she bent over the photographs. Her long hair, which she usually wore up or tied back in a ponytail, fell loose and wild. Her cheeks were flushed in distress; her large eyes were watery and exhausted. Standing so close to her, he detected a scent, a faint mixture of mint, cigarettes, sex, and fear. His view was drawn to her wrist, and she noticed him staring at it. He was a cop and knew that only one thing left a mark like that.

She returned to the sink for another cup of water and stared vacantly at the faded, crackling paint on the kitchen cupboards.

"These cupboards are really dreadful. And my friend's in a coma, my boyfriend's left me for another woman and started drinking again, and I can't locate my software engineer. If I can't find her to fix the software," she cried irrationally, "I'll never sell the design for my C-trax transponder and be able to divorce my husband."

"Is that all?" he asked lightly.

She laughed quietly. Then she wept. He smiled gently and held her for a while. Finally she pulled away, dried her tears, and poured herself another cup of water. Looking down, she noticed the torn hem of her dress; her mood darkened.

She crossed the room and gazed out over the black lawn to the sundial and the two Adirondack chairs. Fury was a rare emotion to her, and she felt ferocious. The assault on the *Green Monster* had been premeditated, as the handcuffs had been all too conveniently retrieved from underneath a pillow. A trap had been set for her, into which she had stupidly walked.

All along, these past months, while he was with Sheila, she had been a free woman. She could have enjoyed the two handsome artists in P-Town, and at the same time, too, if they were into that type of party. She could have shown this Norwegian cop red-hot American sex in the v-berth while some voyeur on Nobska beach snapped photos. The photos could have been published on the front page of the *Cape Cod Daily* and her response could have been a cavalier "So fucking what?" Opportunities had been missed. Her loathing of Rob intensified, palpable. Sven moved directly behind her, his enticing aftershave radiating off his warm skin. This singular moment would not be among those that she'd later regret.

She turned.

Sven lifted her sore wrist to his lips.

Time fast-forwarded ....

His mouth pressed on hers. He backed her quickly toward the bed while she yanked his shirt over his head. A magazine rack tipped over. Her hands worked skillfully on his belt and zipper, his nimble hands freed the buttons at the back of her dress. Fabric was torn. He pulled the dress off her shoulders and slid it down her body. She kicked the dress away and fell back onto the foot of the bed, waiting. He rushed her panties down her long legs, then fell between her knees at the edge of the bed....

None of this made sense. Her head, wrist, and lower back all throbbed. Sex held no fascination at the moment. You are a sane, sober woman, she reminded herself.

Lindsey pulled her wrist away from his lips and said decisively, "I need to see my children."

Falmouth

Events in the doorless room burst forth, like gas bubbles hot and hissing from a hydrothermal vent.

It was the best day of the girl's life. She was finally old enough to get a job at the dive shop, and she was able to purchase a used BC for only twenty-five dollars with her employee discount. The girl was getting smarter, cashing her paycheck in the next town and hiding a portion of it away for herself. The brother knew too many of the tellers at the bank in their small town.

The girl hated it when the brother's best friend tried to kiss her and put his hand on her breast.

The doorless room became a narrow road in a trailer park. Another trailer had caught on fire. This time an old man died. The girl didn't believe that it was started by his cigarette.

The girl met a new friend on a houseboat, but the friend was not shy like her. One morning she was invited into the friend's house for coffee, but she ended up falling asleep. The friend was a laughing mother who sometimes wore a flowered bikini and was beautiful. The girl fell in love with her and loved it when the friend kissed her and put her hand on the girl's breast.

The girl was alarmed! She was on a boat with a strange man off a flat green island. The man wanted to harm her. She paced the room for some time, figuring a way out. She stopped in front of the window. If she could open the blinds and get some light, she might be able to escape the doorless room and save the girl from harm.

Jessie opened her eyes.

Woods Hole

Sara swiveled in her lab chair. "You're late," she remarked.

Lindsey lumbered toward the coffeepot. "I'm so tired."

"What's going on?" Sara looked at her with genuine concern. "You don't look so good."

"I'm spent. There was too much drama last night. Ava and Dan were using one of the beds as a trampoline and the slats broke, which sent Mrs. Richardson into a tizzy. I should just get them a trampoline. Then Ava got a splinter in her foot when she was walking barefoot on the dock. And then the cop, Halvorsen, came over with these photos." She handed Sara the folder. Lindsey walked to the doorway and peered nervously down the hallway.

"Are you waiting for someone?" Sara asked, opening the folder.

"No," Lindsey replied, stepping back into the lab. She had hardly slept. Every creak and moan of the old house had jerked her awake throughout the night. "Is this the man you saw on Jessie's boat?"

Sara studied the photographs. "That's definitely him. Hey, Sylvia Benson called."

"Finally! Where was she?"

"Rome. She's interested in the C-trax software job."

"Good. We still need to figure out how to attach the transponder to the BC without it coming off so easily. I'm still pissed that Arrano tossed the prototype into Buzzards Bay. That unit wasn't cheap."

Sara's ringtone, the Pink Panther theme, sounded, and she reached across the desk for her cell phone. "Hello?" She listened intently and then sprang from her chair. "A nurse on the night shift noticed movement in Jessie's eyelids and legs. I'm out of here!"

For the rest of the morning, Sara's texts provided Lindsey with updates about Jessie's improving condition. She had not awakened fully, but she seemed to be out of the coma. When Sara arrived at the ICU, the room was empty, Jessie having been taken to another room for an EEG. Finally Jessie was wheeled back. The bruising had diminished. She looked peaceful, as if in a gentle sleep. The neurologist was pleased, because normal sleep waves were now predominant. Recent CT images showed that the hematoma and buildup of intracranial fluid had also decreased.

Ægir's Curse

Lindsey called Sylvia Benson, who said that she could get to the C-trax job by the end of the week. Next she called the accountant to discuss possible companies that might want to purchase the design for the C-trax technology. Small local companies run by entrepreneurial management teams had proven preferable to large corporations with unwieldy bureaucracies. This sale must be expeditious. She and the accountant batted around the pros and cons of a dive equipment manufacturer versus an electronics firm that specialized in GPS technologies. When the accountant, who followed emerging companies, said he would provide her with a list of potential partners in a few days, Lindsey's spirits lifted.

At Sea

The *Zodiac* paused at a narrow channel that was almost undetectable.

"If we go in," Sven worried aloud, "we'll never get out."

"Pretend you're on a safari," Ingrid said shortly.

Sven only wanted to pretend that he was submerged in a steaming Jacuzzi with strong jets aimed at his lower back, which throbbed from sitting on an unyielding wooden seat of an inflatable boat for nearly a week. The skin across his face was tight from sunburn, even though he'd slathered himself with sunscreen and worn a wide-brimmed hat. A dry martini would be wonderful as well, he fantasized, and the promise of excellent cuisine and a night at the Oslo-Filharmonien with an intelligent woman in a lovely gown.

Instead it had been another monotonous day of hugging the coast, searching every inlet and wetland for the cruiser. His companion an intelligent woman, true, but she was wearing camouflage shorts, a khaki ball cap, a gray tank top, and aviator sunglasses. The only consolation was that his partner was good-looking and, as the day got hotter, her humor became increasingly bawdy.

Ingrid ignored his protests and maneuvered the inflatable into the small channel, which meant driving not only into a stagnant pocket of humidity and heat devoid of sea breezes, but a voracious swarm of mosquitoes.

He was about to comment when she suddenly cut the engine and said, "Shh!"

They both rose silently, lifting their binoculars over a rim of sea grass. In the afternoon haze, floating in a few inches of muddy brown water, was a white and blue cruiser.

Seabirds rustled among the tall grass and insects chirped; otherwise there were no other signs of life around the hidden pond. They watched the boat for a while before Ingrid belted a holster around her waist, restarted the engine, and motored slowly forward.

"Shouldn't we should call for backup?" Sven whispered.

"We have our orders," she answered curtly. "Cover me when I climb into the boat."

He crouched, pistol in hand, and scanned the surrounding marsh and forest's edge as the inflatable eased forward until it was alongside the cruiser. Ingrid peered over a gunwale, expecting the suspect to spring from the cabin. The boat seemed abandoned, however, so she tied up to a cleat on the cruiser and climbed aboard.

"He's not here," she called out. "It's doubtful that he'd take off and leave the map on the boat, but let's have a look."

Sven followed her aboard.

"I'll search, you be lookout," she directed.

She moved to the v-berth first, slicing open the mattress and a plaid sleeping bag with a Swiss Army knife. The hull that formed the sloped walls of the berth was solid fiberglass with no wood paneling to hide a map behind. In the head, she pried off the wall mirror, only to find more solid fiberglass. There was a black comb next to the sink, and she pulled a small hair from it. "Look," she said, holding it out for Sven's inspection. The hair was less than an inch in length. Half of it was brown, the other half blond. "Arrano was definitely here."

The few cabinets in the galley were filled with canned food. A mini-refrigerator likewise contained only food, and behind it, only wires and plugs to an electrical panel and clumps of dust and sand. She maneuvered her head behind the instrument panel, only to find more wires.

The cabin was tiny, so the search did not take long. Another sleeping bag lay neatly folded on a bench seat in the galley. Again she sliced the panels of flannel and down lengthwise, but there was no map. A name on the corner of the sleeping bag read *Jessie McCabe, Bunk 5, Cherokee Cabin.* Jessie's seabag had been dumped onto the floor of the galley; Arrano had obviously been searching for something in her belongings. With a sigh, Ingrid stood up, stretched her back, then returned to her partner. "Nothing," she reported.

Sven dropped onto a diver locker, his lower back aflame, while Ingrid searched behind the gasoline canisters and dive tanks. She hesitated, then extended a pony tank toward him.

"Blood," she commented, pointing to a brown smudge on the tank. "I don't see any blood anywhere else. Do you?"

"No."

She opened the diver locker on the port side of the deck, which contained a long-sleeved blue wet suit designed for a woman, some extra straps for masks and fins, some weights for a weight belt, and a small bottle of anti-fogging solution.

She moved to the starboard locker, on which Sven was seated. "Up," she ordered.

He rose with a groan and turned to lift the lid. He removed a black BC. "This is why we didn't find the BC in Buzzards Bay. Lindsey said that the transponder should be in the pocket." He opened the Velcro flap to find the pocket empty. "She was right. Arrano tossed it into the sea."

"Lindsey, Lindsey, Lindsey. That's all I've heard the whole trip. She's much too young for you."

"And much too smart," he added humorously.

"That's the truth." She sifted through the gear in the starboard locker. "All of his equipment is here. All of hers is gone."

"He wouldn't have whacked her, put her in her dive gear, and then tossed her overboard. That makes no sense." Still carrying the BC, he looked down at the dive platform.

She moved next to him. "No blood there."

"Look there." He pointed to a dent in the engine casing. "He probably hit her while she was getting on or off the boat."

Ingrid nodded and walked through the boat one more time. "There's no map here."

He tossed the BC back into the open diver locker, causing a small poof of brown particles to rise into the air. "They were diving in muck." He frowned and wiped minute brown flakes from his hands onto his shorts.

The brown flakes stuck to her skin as well. "I have this stuff on me too," she said disgustedly, wiping her hands on her shirt. She halted.

"What, Ingrid?"

She walked quickly back to the v-berth and examined the shredded plaid sleeping bag. It was old and faded, having endured many trips in all kinds of weather.

Ingrid smiled slyly. "Dr. Arrano enjoys camping."

Chapter 20

Woods Hole

The jarl was dying. Though he was not an old man, years of battling men and the violent storms of Ægir's northern seas had knotted his limbs. He was now a dull blade who had once been a well-loved broad sword. He walked slowly through the village, searching for Freydis. It was almost their time to join the ancients. On a beach outside the village, his warriors solemnly erected his funeral ship. Dry kindling was stacked next to the ship. Two Skraeling scouts were reported in the area, watching his men from the scrub pines.

He climbed the many stairs of the timber fortress toward Freydis's room. In the doorway he stood for a moment admiring her, unnoticed. Her black-haired thrall was absent. Freydis sat alone, working at a table. Her bright red hair flowed like blood down her back. Her blue gown was of the finest quality wool that he had brought her from the continent. What a magnificent woman! But she was cursed with the wickedest of tempers. He was sure that it was Freydis who'd massacred the Icelanders while they slept. What had they done to anger her so? No one had dared accuse her of the crime, as she was his woman. He could not afford to lose any more men, to Freydis or to Skraelings. But he forgave her this, as he did all of her shortcomings.

"Freydis ..." he said tenderly, stepping into the room.

She turned slowly, her green eyes squinting at him. Suddenly they widened. "Adrian!" She jumped to her feet.

Who was Adrian? he wondered, somewhat confused. He didn't recall a warrior named Adrian in his army. Perhaps he was one of the new warriors that just arrived from the Shetlands? "No, Beloved. It's just me."

"You're not well," she exclaimed, backing away.

Clearly she had noticed the bleeding sores on his hands and arms. Fluid continued to stream from his eyes, and he had to blink frequently to clear his vision. True, he was far from the man he had been. This had to be disappointing to her.

"Sit down. Let me call an ambulance," she said, her voice shaking.

He stepped closer. "It's too late for healers, Beloved. It's time for the thralls to prepare you for the funeral. After I die tonight, you will meet with the Angel of Death." The old crone would drug her so she would feel no pain. The potions would make her thoughts float among the heavens, where she would talk to the sky gods and ancients. Warriors would rape her, sacrifice goats in her honor, and bathe her in blood. Then the throat of precious Freydis would be slit. He held out his arms to embrace her, but she sidestepped him. Freydis was often difficult like this.

"We must go," he insisted.

"Where are we going?" she asked nervously.

"We journey together aboard our burning ship to Other World, to Freyja's lovely meadow, Folkvangr," he explained reverently.

Freydis dashed for the door. He chased her down the hall. He caught her at the top of the stairs and grabbed at her gown. She lunged forward through the air, her red hair unfurled like a sail. How spectacular to watch Freydis take flight like a wind goddess! What a magnificent woman! And

Ægir's Curse

tonight they would lay side by side in death, rocking on Ægir's gentle waves while the flames of the funeral ship danced among the stars.

A Marsh

A spark hissed and sputtered along a black highway of fuse… across sand and transom… to red gas canisters. The flame dipped into the gasoline. *Blam!* The first explosion shook the marsh. The outboard engine, now nothing but scalding metal shards, rained into the sea grass. Glass sprayed outward, glistening briefly before it landed in the mud. A flock of birds burst from the marsh. The transom blew off en bloc, arced through the air, and crashed into a decaying rowboat. Insects abandoned their dizzying flights and darted into the reeds. An oily black cloud hung over the pond. Fox pups and a raccoon cowered in their burrows. For a moment the air hung still while the fire crept slowly across melting fiberglass toward the dive tanks.

Woods Hole

The Norwegian cops tied the *Zodiac* up at the marina, returned to their hotel rooms, showered, and had a meal of fish and chips at a local seafood restaurant. Sven picked up a bottle of California wine from a liquor store, and they returned to his motel room, where they searched the Internet. Four campgrounds were within a fifteen-mile radius of Woods Hole: Little Meadow, Big Bear, Piney Grove, and Pirate's Paradise. As Ingrid was finishing her glass of wine and leaving for her room, Sven's cell phone rang.

The remains of *Mermaid* had been located in a pond between Quissett and Sippewissett, a Falmouth detective informed him. A summer resident had reported the smell of fire wafting from a nearby marsh and heard a number of deafening explosions. The boat had been engulfed in flames when the resident arrived at the edge of the pond.

Fire investigators deduced that the fire had been started intentionally, as gasoline had been splashed throughout the compartments. What remained of the boat was a charred and melted heap of fiberglass. Any useful forensic evidence, the detective was sad to report, was probably destroyed. But what this meant, the detective continued on an up note, was that Arrano was still in the area, now covering his tracks.

"We are dealing with an adversary of some intelligence," added the detective, "as Arrano had the forethought to acquire a slow-burning fuse that allowed him ample time to escape the scene before the fire ignited." Another curious thing that the investigators had noticed was that the fuse material was a filament used primarily by miners and military units.

Derick Briggs had had a productive day of experiments in the lab with his undergraduate work-study student. It was wonderful to be in contact with students; he did not get that opportunity at the CDC. He preferred working with undergraduates, as they were still teachable and excited by the experimental process, and they had less attitude and ego than grad students. He closed up his lab around five o'clock and crossed the street to Sara's laboratory building to drop a few coins of thanks into the metal palms of Confucius. The coins, he knew, were taken by the children in the summer camps to buy candy up the road. He was looking forward to an evening ride down the coastal road on his Ducati when suddenly a red-haired man bolted down the stairs, slammed into his shoulder, and nearly knocked the helmet out of his hand.

"Where's the fire?" Derick angrily shouted. But there was no response; the man pushed through the front door and tore up Water Street.

Fire!

Derick's instincts went on high alert. Something felt terribly wrong. Sara's lab was directly upstairs, and Sara might still be there! He dashed up the stairwell, skipping steps as he ran. He stopped suddenly at the top landing, staring aghast at what lay before him. There was no blood around the woman's head, but she was so still... oh, God.... He wrapped her in his leather vest to keep her warm and called 911.

Chapter 21

Falmouth

Derick's cell phone vibrated and he pulled it from his leather vest. The text was from his brother, Jared, in Atlanta. His grandmother, Katie, was in the hospital again, the pulmonary specialists attempting once again to drain fluid from her lungs. Good luck, he thought sullenly. His grandmother had been smoking cigarettes since forever. And since she owned tobacco farms, she never had to purchase them, which only exacerbated her horrible addiction.

Derick fidgeted on the hard chair, flexing his throttle hand, which he feared was becoming arthritic; far too much time spent in hospitals this summer, not enough time taking motorcycle treks around the Cape. Jessie was in the ICU upstairs; now he sat in the ER watching over a woman he barely knew. Sara's boss was a walking catastrophe! What the hell had happened this afternoon?

Lindsey began to stir. An IV tugged painfully at her wrist, and she understood where she was. Derick's presence by the monitor, however, startled her.

"Derick?" she gasped.

"Can I get you anything?" Derick asked quietly, approaching her bed.

"It was Arrano. He's a redhead now! He's gone insane! He came to my lab and chased me ... he was ranting crazy stuff. I need to call Sven Halvorsen! Do you have my cell phone?"

"Shhh," Derick replied firmly. "All of this can wait. You just need to rest."

She nodded numbly. "Did you bring me here?"

"I found you in the stairwell and called for an ambulance."

"Thank you."

"Yeah. No problem."

"Will you sit by the door, in case Rob or Arrano comes by? Both are trying to kill me!"

"No one's trying to kill you," he said, baffled by the panic in her voice. "Everyone wants you to get better."

"You can't imagine what's happened to me in twenty-four hours. Please? Please watch the door for me!"

He crossed the room and placed a chair by the door. "If it will make you feel better."

"It does! Thank you!"

Derick glanced over his shoulder. She was weeping quietly into a pillow. Her wrist where the IV entered had the telltale marks of bondage. What had she been doing this afternoon? When he'd found her, her shirt had been torn down the back.

A weird recollection arose: his well-groomed father in pajamas and a silk robe seated by the door of his and Jared's bedroom, scanning the hallway for his mother, who might be prowling the night in a drunken fog. What goes around, comes around... with a surreal twist, Derick thought ironically. Now thirty years later, the ungroomed son sat, black chaps and heavy boots stretched outward, scanning a hallway to protect this alcoholic woman. From what demons, he wasn't sure.

Woods Hole

Adrian woke again. The fire in his head raged like a bonfire and he doubted that he would have the energy to make it to the bathhouse for a morning shower. Not only was the ground too hard to sleep upon without a sleeping bag, but twice he'd stumbled outside into the darkness to pass urine that felt like boiling water. He had managed to find a roll of paper towels to cough mucus into. Sometime during the night, the mucus had turned to blood. Cramps stabbed his abdomen. Nothing eased the pain in his head, nor would the cough relent.

To distract himself from the pain, he logged onto the Internet. He squinted at the glowing screen and struggled to read the last few days of local news. Someone had found the cruiser and lit it on fire! Probably some teenage punks getting high in the marsh. The entire back end had been blown away by the conflagration. To hell with it. When he returned to dive for the wreck, he'd charter a larger boat and hire a team of underwater archeologists. By that time, his manuscript on the rare map would have been published, and his funding sources would be bottomless. Thank God the map had not been in the boat.

He swallowed down another handful of aspirin, even though they would do no good. His thirst was so great that he longed to chug an entire bottle of water, but that would mean urinating scalding water, so he sipped slowly. The remaining loose end was Tryggvesen. Would the Greenlander have spoken to anyone, possibly to the police, about the map? Perhaps he could send Tryggvesen a collegial email saying that Ingvars had contacted him about some paper he was to review, gauge Tryggvesen's response, and go from there. Also, there was that person, Sara.

He moaned. A thousand details to sort out, and his brain was not functioning. Patience, he told himself. When the illness subsided, he could think rationally and calmly once again. He tugged another paper towel off the roll and half-retched into it.

The computer screen appeared hazy as his eyes drained and burned. He logged off and rolled over on his back, folding his hands into his armpits to keep himself from itching the infuriating scabs that had formed on his skin. To distract himself, he imagined the excitement of the press conference when he announced the map to the world. The news cameras and microphones would press anxiously toward him. There would be skeptics, of course, yet convincing them would be easy, for the samples would have been tested at the best forensics labs in the US. No doubt the scientists from the forensics labs in Zurich and Bonn would then step forward for a piece of the action and issue a statement proclaiming that they, too, had tested the samples. How to explain that? The story needed to be airtight. Could the map have been left to him by an anonymous Swiss or German donor on their deathbed? What? What? What?

If the map did not assuage the naysayers, the wreck would be irrefutable evidence of Vinland's existence on Cape Cod. The sunken ship, being in only forty or so feet of water in a protected inlet, was in an optimal location and with optimal conditions for an underwater archaeological excavation. Who could imagine what artifacts might be brought up? Ornate brooches, shields, swords, coins? These items, along with the wooden skeleton of the longboat itself, would be enough to build a Viking museum in the United States. He, of course, would be the museum's curator, a fitting job for the world's leading Viking authority. The opening gala would be a lavish affair with supermodels, senators, diplomats, and celebrities in tuxedos and gowns, clinking champagne glasses… *seated at his banquet table of course would be Freydis, and his fellow gods, Odin, Thor, Ægir, Freyja, Freyr, and that trickster, Loki, all toasting his wonderful achievements ….*

Ingrid Stevs and Sven Halvorsen checked the Pirate's Paradise campground first, but had no luck in locating a camper named Craig Russell, or anyone matching his description. The next closest campground to the Falmouth-Woods Hole area was Big Bear. They reached that campground just before noon, their car winding along a dirt road lined by tents, pop-up campers, and RVs. Five cars had New Hampshire license plates, so Sven recorded the numbers on a small pad of paper and called them into police headquarters.

They parked at a camp store, bought coffees and breakfast sandwiches, and sat outside at a picnic table. Neither of them was particularly talkative, as both had contracted the same sore throat and headache, which Sven blamed on dirty silverware at the diner. Though he had no clue why, Ingrid seemed fascinated with all things American and had insisted that they "eat what the locals eat"—breakfasts of eggs, bacon, and hash browns, and dinners of hamburgers and french fries at a local diner. The calories would come right off of her during her evening runs, but he felt every bite of oily American cuisine going right onto his waist. There was no mystery why Americans were as grotesquely obese as they were; he could not return soon enough to his normal diet of fish, bread, cheese, and wine.

About thirty minutes later, a Falmouth police officer called back and reported that New Hampshire plate GYU 4794 belonging to a gray Toyota Corolla was registered to a seventy-six-year-old man named Francis Thomas Arrano. Jocelyn Arrano had told Ingrid that she thought Adrian had signed a long-term lease with a rental car agency before heading to an archive in Minnesota, but Adrian had simply borrowed his father's car.

Ægir's Curse

Upon receiving this news, the two Interpol officers returned to the Grizzly Bear Loop, where they spotted the gray car in a campsite set off from the road. A screen tent was set up over a picnic table, and a smaller green tent was next to the forest. An orange extension cord ran from a power outlet and disappeared into a tiny opening between the tent flaps. There was no sign of activity, no embers in the fire pit.

Ingrid had overdone it a bit with her tourist disguise and was wearing a Celtics ball cap and a T-shirt that read *Cape Cod is for Lovers*, which Sven was sure she chose to poke fun at him. His was a preppy look: a white dress shirt with shirttails out, khaki shorts, and sandals. She parked in back of the Corolla, blocking the car should Arrano try to make a run for it.

She walked toward the green tent, preparing to act as an employee of the campground. "Mr. Russell, are you there?" she asked, standing near the flap of the tent. "Mr. Russell, wake up." She waited, and then whispered, "I don't think he's here."

"I'll check the bathhouse," Sven said.

Ingrid knelt cautiously in front of the zippered flaps, readying herself for the lunge of a knife or the swipe of a hard object. She lifted the zipper at the small opening where the extension cord entered the tent. Parting the flaps, she gasped and backed quickly away. The smell was appalling.

She pulled a tissue from her pocket—as she had been coughing all morning—and stuffed two clots of tissue up her nostrils. She would have to move very quickly to retrieve the laptop, backpack, and duffel bag. After several deep inhalations, she readied herself, held her breath, and ducked inside the tent.

Sven returned to find Ingrid in the screen tent, sifting quickly through the backpack and duffel bag. Their contents were spread across the picnic table.

"He's gone for the day," he concluded.

White-faced, she looked up at him. "Yes, but go see what he left behind."

He was puzzled and looked from her face to the opened tent. Ingrid was usually unflappable; seeing her so rattled made him feel uneasy in turn. He approached the tent slowly, kneeling as she had, and stared into the green space for some time. With his cell phone, he took a series of photos.

A pool of red slime, bloody paper towels, and what looked like human tissue, large scabs perhaps, littered the floor of the tent. Sven cringed every time he caught a whiff of the horrific stench. Ingrid duck fleetly back into the tent to return the repacked duffel bag and backpack to their original locations. She was particularly careful not to step into the pool of blood. Upon exiting, Ingrid walked briskly past him to the bathhouse, where she promptly tossed up her breakfast sandwich and coffee.

On the picnic table were a damp beach towel, a bathing suit, a men's shaving kit, a near-empty bottle of sunscreen, a guidebook to Cape Cod and the Islands, a flash drive, a tangle of keys, and a cell phone. But there was no map.

When Ingrid returned from the bathhouse, Sven said, "If we can't find the map here, we'll have to muddle through absurd amounts of paper work with the Americans. We might have to go to New Hampshire and search Arrano's house. Maybe even his father's house. We might take weeks to get back to Oslo." He checked the perimeter of the campsite, the cooler, and the propane stove. "It's doubtful Arrano would be so foolish as to leave a priceless treasure around a campsite, exposed to the elements."

Ingrid tossed him Arrano's car keys. "Stop whining."

Sven unlocked the driver's side door of the gray Corolla and searched the front and back seats. A bag with a scuffed-up bowling ball and a gym bag lay on the front passenger's seat. The glove compartment held receipts for car repairs dating back to the late 1990s, a pair of pliers, a pen light, and the Corolla owner's manual. The backseat was lined with bags of groceries, presumably to keep raccoons and skunks away from the tents. There was nothing under the seats except dried leaves, dust, and a few gum wrappers. The upholstery did not have any breaches in which a map could have been hidden.

He moved to the trunk. A car emergency kit contained tools, water, flares, matches, and a blanket. There was an iron car jack. He untwisted a large bolt that held the spare tire in place and lifted out the tire, but there was nothing in the wheel well. He peeled up a rubber mat that served as the liner for the trunk. A plastic bag lay underneath the mat, and he peered inside.

Sven beamed. "Ingrid, we'll be drinking wine in Oslo tomorrow night."

Their work here was done. The rest could be left to the local police.

Later, Sven called Lindsey to report that they had found Arrano's campsite.

"Arrano's certainly very sick, but we haven't located him yet," he explained. "A forensics team is at the campground now, trying to determine the nature of the illness."

Lindsey was too tired to think straight, and the ride home from the hospital had been harrowing, due to Maggie's texting while driving. She had meant to call Sven and tell him about Arrano; now it seemed the detectives had managed without her. Good. "Yes. He's extremely sick. He was covered with bleeding sores when I saw him. And he was delusional." Briefly, she described how he'd come after her in her office.

Sven's sense of triumph was abruptly quelled by this alarming news. "Lindsey, I need to interview you about your encounter with Arrano. But I am being called back to Oslo. I leave tomorrow. Can I come over now, or can we have dinner together?"

"No. Definitely no. I feel lousy. I'll tell you everything right now. The encounter was very brief. He came by my lab in a completely deranged state. He approached me, so I ran. He tripped me up as I was running toward the stairs. I don't remember anything after that. I woke up in the ER."

"I'm so sorry. Are you okay? Are you sure I can't come by?"

She was in no mood to elaborate. Every part of her felt broken. "I really need to be alone," she insisted.

"Perhaps a cup of coffee in the morning before my flight leaves?" Sven asked, hopefully.

"Yes, that's fine," she agreed tiredly, ringing off.

Sven placed his cell phone down on the hotel table and opened a local phone book. He called a local florist and requested that a bouquet of long-stemmed roses be sent to a specific address off of Quissett Avenue that same afternoon.

Chapter 22

Woods Hole

Lindsey sat in an Adirondack chair by the sundial and gazed out across the lawn to the bay beyond. Her mind drifted. The Percocets and chamomile tea had sedated her. She glanced down to the chamomile tea, imagining it instead a teacup filled to the brim with Glenlivet. Smooth scotch whiskey and Percocets would be a deliciously potent concoction to ensure numbness and amnesia. She lifted a pair of binoculars from her lap and scanned the perimeter of her property. No sign of Rob or Arrano creeping over her stone wall.

It was the middle of the afternoon and she was still in pajamas. She had a severe bone bruise on her hip and a sprained wrist; everything from head to toes throbbed. She blew her nose and studied the apartment over the garage. The space had real possibilities. If she bought a case of Glenlivet tomorrow, she could stash it there. Cases of Canadian ale could be chilled in the refrigerator. The lock to the door could be programmed so that only her handprint could open it. It would be her "private workspace," she would explain to Mrs. Richardson and the children. This time, she would drink in moderation. Besides, she was never violent when she drank... only amorous. No one would ever know that she was drinking again. Yes, the garage apartment would be the perfect hideaway to drink in earnest, and forget everything. She lifted the binoculars again.

That dinghy was way too close to her beach! Was it Rob, planning an attack? she wondered, panic-stricken. Thank God... it was just a teenage boy with a fishing pole. She squinted through the lens again. Or could it be Arrano in another disguise?

Lindsey lit another cigarette. It was some relief that the police had found Arrano's campsite, but where was Arrano? He could be lurking anywhere. Perhaps he was watching her at that very moment! If he had found her lab, he would certainly be able to find her house!

Mrs. Richardson bolted through the back door onto the patio, her hands a flutter of excitement. "Flowers have arrived! Two bouquets!" she called across the lawn in astonishment.

Lindsey rose with a moan, shuffled across the patio, and opened the screen door. She glanced down a long hallway to the front entryway. On a heavy mahogany table sat two bouquets, one of red roses and the other wildflowers. She returned wordlessly to her seat outside on the lawn, the old woman chasing after her.

"You're not going to read the cards?" the woman demanded, with no attempt to hide her perturbation.

"I will later," Lindsey mumbled. Besides, she already knew whom they were from. The roses were from Sven. The wildflowers... Rob always gave her wildflowers: on her birthday, on the birthdays of their children, and on her AA anniversaries. She anxiously searched her pocket for the lighter and cigarettes, and placed the binoculars securely in her lap. Mrs. Richardson walked away in a huff.

Lindsey despondently sipped the bland tea. Flowers from men meant an expectation that something would be given in return, a future obligation, a gift with strings attached. The thought of them made her vaguely queasy. Men, she decided, were terrifying, unpredictable creatures that she would have nothing further to do with. She lit another cigarette and blew the smoke toward the garage apartment. For now her sole intent was to plan a detection-proof relapse to obliterate any thoughts of violent men.

Falmouth

"Get these tubes out of me!" Jessie implored in a raspy, dry whisper. She raised her arm with difficulty, pointing toward her nose. "Get this stuff out of my nose!"

Sara rushed off to the nurses' station. A nurse returned with Sara and removed the oxygen tubes from Jessie's nose, but refused to detach the IV and catheter bag.

"I need to walk," Jessie urged.

Sara massaged Jessie's legs for a while, until Jessie was finally able to inch her legs over the side of the bed. Her arm around Jessie's waist and her other hand wheeling the IV and catheter, Sara shuffled Jessie down the hallway and back. The whole time Jessie remained silent, concentrating on keeping her balance.

Back in her room, she gasped, "I'm exhausted. That's enough." She moaned as she gingerly climbed back into bed.

Jessie turned briefly to Sara. "Where am I? Who are you?" She did not wait for an answer. When her head hit the pillow she was already asleep.

Elsewhere

By moonlight the jarl searched the marshlands. It was this marsh, he was sure of it, where the Icelandic chieftain had told him his funeral ship would be found. Perhaps the ship was still in the village where the final preparations were being made, the death banners being hung on the single mast and colorful shields hammered along the gunwales. Or the ship might be en route to the shore.

The jarl was stooped and broken from his wanderings. That rotting log was the perfect place to rest his weary head. He stretched his body amidst the tall grass and stared up at the heavens. His ears were pricked for the slightest sound. At any moment he would hear the throb of the warriors' drums and see the glow of torches winding down the dark trail from the camp. And he must remain on guard for the stealthy footsteps of Skraelings. His muddy fist grasped his faithful battle-axe.

Maybe the funeral was delayed by the disappearance of Freydis. A band of his fleetest warriors had been sent to seek her out. Perhaps her imminent encounter with the Angel of Death had frightened her. But Freydis was fearless; an old crone could not possibly scare her. Or maybe she didn't like the blue death gown, and wanted to wear a red one. With this temperamental woman, any number of things might create a ruckus in the warrior village. He smiled to himself with amused affection.

The jarl smacked at a mosquito on his arm. Old battle wounds had mysteriously opened, leaving islands of bloody sores along his hands and arms. He resembled the lepers on that storm-battered rock near the Faroes. Bugs had swarmed his wounds all day; the smoke from the torches would soon drive them away. But for now, he would just doze and wait: for the ship, for his beautiful Freydis, for the drums and torches to escort him to another world.

Chapter 23

Falmouth

The coffee from a hospital vending machine was watery and tasteless and Sven pushed the cup away with revulsion. Americans completely lacked the ability to make a decent cup of coffee. He glanced at Lindsey, who was having no trouble finishing hers. Her stomach must be cast iron, he figured. Her forehead was knitted in concern as she looked across the room at Jessie.

Jessie remained asleep. Sven checked his watch again. He left abruptly for the doorway to cough into a handkerchief.

"I hope I'm not infecting everyone in the hospital with this bug. Ingrid caught it too," Sven said apologetically to Lindsey. He checked his watch again. "I really have to get to the airport."

"I'll walk out with you." Lindsey stood with painful slowness. "I need to be getting to the lab."

"You're going back to work so soon?" he asked, surprised.

"There's way too much to do. I've already lost too much time."

A handsome couple entered the room, carrying balloons and an odd assortment of items that included Jessie's running shoes, a pint of her favorite ice cream, and a seashell necklace. Lindsey made introductions, though Sven recognized the woman immediately. It was Lindsey's lab partner, Sara Kauni. The man in motorcycle leathers was another colleague from the marine lab named Derick Briggs.

Sara tied the balloons to the metal bed frame and Derick slid a chessboard set from his backpack. Sven hacked into his handkerchief once again, then he and Lindsey departed for the parking lot.

"Here," Sven said, handing Lindsey a sheet of paper. "This is my contact information with my office, home, and cell phone numbers, and my condo address." He paused. "I know this is presumptuous of me to ask, but I was wondering why you moved so suddenly from the marina ... and the other night ..." His voice trailed off.

"Irreconcilable differences," she answered, offering no further explanation.

He nodded and held out his cell phone to her. "This is my hytte."

"Your what?" she asked.

He smiled. "A hytte is a summer cottage."

She stared at an image of a cabin on a pristine mountain lake. "Lovely."

"I'd love it if you would visit. I could show you Oslo and my hytte. Oslo has marvelous restaurants and theater. And you should bring your children." He flipped through the images on his phone. "This is my daughter, Anna, and her husband, Stefan. She just finished her residency in internal medicine. She and Stefan met in medical school."

Lindsey looked at an image of a young woman and man on cross-country skis.

"I can't return home without your autograph for Anna," he said. "She's your greatest fan."

Lindsey was taken back. "Really?"

"Really," he said with certainty. He bent into the front seat of the sedan for his briefcase and returned with a pad and pen.

Lindsey turned toward the hood of the car and inscribed a salutation on the pad, similar to the hundreds that she had penned that week in Stockholm.

He continued to scroll through the photos. His face became somber. "This is how we found Arrano's tent," he commented, holding the photo up to her again.

She frowned. "This is terrible. And they haven't found him yet?"

"No, he never returned to camp."

"Will you send me that JPEG?"

"Sure. I'll send it right now," he responded, forwarding the image to her email address. He checked his watch again. "I should already be on the road." He lifted her hand and pressed it to his lips. "I'd rather kiss your lovely face, but I don't want to get you sick."

She nodded tentatively. "Sven," she asked in afterthought, "what happened to the map?"

His face grew solemn again. "It wasn't found anywhere. It was presumably lost in the boat fire."

"What are you looking at?" Sara asked Derick, who was gazing out the window.

Derick's face was dark and troubled. "Lindsey talking to the cop."

"Is he proclaiming his undying love to her?" Sara asked kiddingly.

"Yes, actually. She seems reticent, but that's no surprise after the incident with Arrano."

Derick deciphered the messages in their body language. The cop had been trying to sell her on some idea, was showing her photos from his cell phone, and she was mildly receptive to his proposal. Then he asked her to write something for him, which she agreeably did. The man was clearly smitten with her, yet kissed her formally on the hand. It was a gallant gesture, but if he were leaving a lover, he should have left such a kiss on her mouth that she'd be thinking about it for days.

Then Lindsey asked the cop a final question. The question bothered him; his body tensed and his response was delayed. Whatever she had asked him, Derick concluded, the cop's answer was a lie.

Woods Hole

A confounding technical problem with the C-trax device made it impossible for Lindsey to stock the cabinets of the garage apartment as she'd intended during her lunch hour. Still, the idea of drowning herself in some variation of ethyl alcohol obsessed her. Before, she had been a boring whiskey and beer drunk; she reproved herself for such provincial tastes. This time she would drink everything... vodka, tequila, rum, bourbon, gin... and in every wonderfully numbing combination. Suddenly it occurred to her that it had been several minutes since she'd checked the hallway for possible invaders. She poked her head watchfully out the lab door.

Sara swiveled irately in her chair. "There's nothing in the fucking hallway! Stay in your fucking chair, or I'll tie you into it."

Lindsey shuddered and dropped into her seat. Even in jest, the thought of being restrained once again was horrifying.

With the exception of her ancient boss, Mort Somers, who was over seventy and had bones as frail as toothpicks, Lindsey was avoiding the men of the lab, even the ones she had conversed with on a daily basis for years. So far there had been no sign of either Rob or Arrano, but this would not lull her to drop her guard for even a nanosecond. Either of them could be waiting for some vulnerable moment to strike again. A number of times she wanted to go outside for a smoke, but decided that she'd be too exposed in the parking lot, so she remained in the lab all day, including lunchtime.

When she returned home that night, she'd go online to order night vision goggles. A gun might be a smart purchase as well. She had no background with guns; in fact, she'd never even held one. Should she buy a pistol, rifle, or semiautomatic assault rifle? Some research would be necessary before making such an important decision. She could spend every evening at the large bay window of the garage apartment, sipping martinis and peering out into the darkness with her night vision goggles. An assault weapon would be close by her side to blast the first thing that moved near her stone wall.

Now, if she could just get Duncan to divorce her, all ties with men would be severed. She reviewed the numbers from her accountant, who had found a company to purchase the C-trax design. A substantial profit from the sale would accrue to her and Sara. Sylvia Benson, Mort Somers, and the accountant would get percentages as well. Lindsey turned to her computer. She emailed Duncan to tell him that she had changed her mind and would pay his obscenely extortive price for his signature on the divorce papers. As she pushed SEND, there was a real sense that she might finally extricate herself from the mire that she'd gotten stuck in as an eighteen-year-old party girl and lush.

Two graduate students—females, thankfully—entered the lab and asked for her help in the electroplating room, so she worked with them for about an hour. When she returned to her desk and checked her email, there was an out-of-office reply that read that Duncan was still on vacation. Curiously, it was the same message she'd received a week before, and she wondered if his email had been changed to avoid communications with her.

Maybe, despite his lunacy and drunkenness, what Rob had said held a glimmer of truth? Duncan's refusal to sign the papers had as much to do with his neuroses, control issues, and bungling relationship with money as it was intended to drive a wedge between her and Rob. Duncan had succeeded in that. As far as she could recall, the sole source of tension between them had been her inability to get a divorce.

But this divorce was so close.... Really, it couldn't wait. She searched the online Yellow Pages in Fredericksburg, Virginia for her father-in-law's phone number. George would certainly have Duncan's most recent email address if it had been changed.

It had been years since she had spoken to George McLeod, though she always sent him humorous cards for his birthday and Christmas. George was everything that Duncan was not: strong, honest, and straightforward in all of his dealings with people. He was an exemplary police officer and captain of the Fredericksburg Police Force, though she guessed that he was retired by now. She located George's number and added it to the contact list on her cell phone. George was male, so she hesitated. After mulling it over, she put George in that rare category of men like Mort, her boss—an old man of integrity who was therefore no threat, unlike the 99.99 percent of the rest of them. She pressed the call button.

George's slow Virginia drawl drew a smile to her face, and he seemed pleased to hear from her as well. He was tying flies on the back porch of his house near the Blue Ridge Mountains. She jotted down Duncan's email address and, as she'd suspected, it had been changed. George proudly reported news of babies born to Duncan's older brothers, and yes, he confirmed, Duncan was still in Scotland, though not on vacation as far as he knew.

"And how are things with you, darlin'?" he asked.

"Just okay," she answered sadly. "Things didn't work out with Rob, so I moved out with the kids and bought a house of my own. It's the Addams family house with the Addams family housekeeper, but the kids and work are great and keep me sane."

"If I may ask, why do you want to reach Duncan?"

"Because I finally got the money together for the divorce," she proclaimed.

"Come again, honey?"

"I have the buy-out fee." George was silent on the other end of the phone. "Duncan said that you knew about it."

"It's news to me. And how long has it taken you to get this so-called buy-out fee together?"

"Five years."

"Let me get this straight. You've been wanting a divorce from Duncan for five years?"

"George, Duncan said you two had discussed this," she explained uneasily.

"Darlin', I'm going to make a phone call, and then call you back later. And have your calendar handy. It's time I come up for a visit and meet my grandchildren, even if they are yellow Yankees."

Panting, Jessie dropped onto a bench in Taft Park. One loop around Eel Pond had exhausted her, and she was only walking! At one time she'd been able to run for miles without tiring. Once, she even ran a half marathon and came in second place. Now she could barely walk one short loop! What the hell had happened to her? She readjusted the bandana that covered her head. She had always worn her hair short, as it was easy to manage when diving and quick to dry. Her hair was growing back fast, but she still had the equivalent of a crew cut and Frankenstein-like incision scars. And worse, that morning she had forgotten where she was. She'd wandered downstairs to see a handsome couple and a boy in a soccer uniform having breakfast together. She'd momentarily thought that the two adults were a married couple with their son. After a few seconds of nodding and smiling stupidly, she recalled that Sara was *her* girlfriend, the man was Derick, and the young boy, Zephyr. For seconds she had forgotten all of their names!

Yesterday afternoon a police officer had dropped by the house, requesting to interview her about 'the incident on the boat.'

What incident on what boat?

What the hell was the cop talking about! Sara had interjected that that was how her head had been injured.

Was the cop referring to *Mermaid*? After he left, Jessie had rushed out to Sara's deck to find slip sixteen empty. Perhaps the boat was tied up elsewhere? She frantically scanned the rest of Eel Pond.

"Where's *Mermaid*?" she had cried to Sara.

"Destroyed in a fire," Sara had answered softly. "Don't you remember anything about Adrian Arrano, Jes?" She'd pointed to Jessie's head. "The fucking asshole who did this to you!"

Jessie vacantly shook her head. After minutes of staring at the empty slip, she suggested, "Let's get high on the widow's walk."

"No, Jes," Sara had said firmly. "You shouldn't be smoking while you're healing. Especially if you're still having periods of amnesia."

Jessie had wordlessly walked away. Sara was starting to sound like her tyrannical father and brother. 'Jes, don't leave the house your own, in case you get lost... don't smoke weed... don't light candles or incense while I'm gone ... don't cook... I'll be back at noon to make you lunch... don't... don't... don't ...'

The children on the playground equipment occupied Jessie's thoughts for a while, until a cell phone vibrated in her pocket. She fumbled around, trying to recall how to use a touch screen. Sara must have telepathy.

"how r u feeling? what r u up to?"

Ægir's Curse

Jessie typed into her brand new... bigger than bigger... phone. "great. just watching tv."

"good. c u for dinner. b hungry. im cooking your favorite. ox"

Jessie looked at the time in a panic. Sara would be home in less than an hour! She stuffed the phone back in her pocket, determined to have nothing more to do with it.

A tennis ball bounced across the field next to the play equipment and Jessie turned on the bench. A playful Golden Retriever bounded after the ball. The dog was followed across the grass by its owner.

"Oh my God!" Jessie said aloud. She squinted into the sunlight of late afternoon. "It's Doug and Red."

Doug was the young firefighter who lived in the small house outside of Alan's and Pastor Reid's trailer community. Doug had helped put out the fire at Mr. Paoli's trailer. Where the old man had died. She always stopped to pet Doug's friendly dog during her evening runs. What were Doug and Red doing in Woods Hole, of all places? Taking a northern vacation to escape Florida's summer heat?

Jessie rose excitedly. Doug had asked her out once when she was home on spring break, years ago, when she still returned home during school breaks and holidays. Alan and Clayton would kill her if they knew that she was friends with Doug. She and Doug had gone out for a pizza and then to the movies. He hadn't make a pass at her; he was just a nice guy.

"Doug?" Jessie waved her arm over her head. "Red!" She clapped her hands. "Come, boy, come Red!"

That evening, in her anxiousness to see if her children were safe, Lindsey forgot to stop at a liquor store on her dash home from work. Earlier, Mrs. Richardson had left her a voice message that the trampoline had arrived, so after dinner, the two women wrestled a large circular net onto the wrought iron framework. Ava and Danny bounced on the trampoline for a while before bed, while Lindsey stealthily walked the perimeter of the property with her binoculars in hand. Had she a gun, she would have felt far more secure, but until she did her homework on firearms, that would have to wait. Fortunately, the security system was functioning properly and had not been breached or triggered throughout the day.

After putting Ava and Danny to bed, she returned to the patio and lifted her laptop gently onto her lap; her hip still ached. A new software program from the security company allowed her to view all angles of her property from the numerous hidden cameras. This way she would not have to walk out into the darkness alone to check the borders of her yard. Across the lawn, Maggie and Brian were goofing off on the new trampoline. First they were kissing, and finally they lay down in a tangled heap. She could not recall if she had ever had sex on a trampoline, but no matter... such behavior was in the past. There would be no sex again in this or the next few lifetimes. The only men going into her mouth, and she hoped it would be soon and in numbing, icy quantities, were Captain Morgan and Jose Cuervo.

She logged onto her email. Two new emails waited. "Oh my God," she blurted as she read the first one. She read it again and again to convince herself of its reality. Only one word would have meaning for the rest of the evening. Finally.

Another email from Rob requested a meeting. Her mood plummeted. She smoked two cigarettes while deciding on a response. "Only at a public place, only with your sister and the children present, and you must be sober," was her brief response. The message was clear; there was to be no replay of their last meeting.

To lift her spirits, she read the first email again, a reminder of Finally. The email from Duncan said that he was signing the divorce papers and paying all legal fees for an expedited divorce. He was requesting nothing of her in terms of monetary compensation. The divorce would be finalized within two weeks.

Thank you, George! Thank you, Higher Power!

Chapter 24

Woods Hole

George McLeod would be visiting Woods Hole at the best time of the year, when heat lingered late into the evenings, which permitted an after-dinner swim with the children, and the sidewalks in the village were no longer clogged with tourists and summer scientists, as they had departed for their homes and home universities. There were no lines for ice cream, and one could drive a car into the village and find parking once again. Summer lectures, receptions, seminars, and barbecues were in the past. The small village was restored to a handful of year-round residents. Late summer also held the promise of months of uninterrupted work, and Lindsey and Sara returned, at least until the next summer, to lives of grateful obscurity.

The temptation to drink still tormented her, but the plan to drink margaritas in the garage apartment, while acting as a sentry in her new night vision goggles, had to be postponed until George left. Should she also buy a flak jacket, she wondered while sipping a coffee at her desk. No, it was improbable that Rob or Arrano would attack her with a gun. And a flak jacket might be a bit extreme and frighten the children and Mrs. Richardson. The more she thought about it, the less ideal the garage apartment was for a guard post: it was not centrally located, and the large bay window would need to be knocked out.

But the attic could be converted into her home office, where she could monitor the security cameras via her laptop. And if the rickety widow's walk was rebuilt, she could mount a high-power rifle on a swiveling tripod to fend off intruders attacking from any direction. Yes, this was the perfect plan. She'd get Mrs. Richardson on these renovations immediately. Carpenters and electricians would need to be hired as soon as possible.

George would be arriving in a few days with his recent adoption from the SPCA, an old hound dog named Rusty. How wonderful to see George again! He could help her select the appropriate firearms and take her to a shooting range. Within weeks she'd become an expert marksman!

Lindsey's attention returned to the draft of a manuscript written by one of the engineering postdocs. She had a vague headache and a small cough. She'd had headaches and low-level fatigue for the past few days. It was a letdown effect of all the stressors of the past few weeks, she guessed.

Arrano's body had still not been located, and she worried incessantly that he might burst into the lab at any moment. She and Sara together might be able to defend themselves, particularly if he was weakened by some illness. And Sara knew karate. Still, as a precaution, Lindsey had prepared a syringe of neurotoxin to jab into Arrano's neck and tranquilize him until the police arrived. She checked again; the syringe was in close reach, in the top drawer of her desk.

Jessie trudged slowly up the stairs to Sara's widow's walk and dropped into a chaise lounge. She opened her laptop and stared blankly at an Excel spreadsheet created from experiments earlier that summer. Jessie tried to comprehend the spreadsheet on her laptop. Amoebocyte number?

Collagenase and trypsin? Huh? What the hell did any of this mean?

That episode at Taft Park had been so embarrassing!

Jessie hated to admit that Sara was right. Again! It was true that she shouldn't have gone outside on her own. Hopefully the man was a tourist that she would never see again. But that dog had looked just like Red ... in fact, identical. When she had called and clapped her hands, the dog had bolted right to her. When she'd knelt down to pet it, the dog had happily licked her face.

"Doug," she had effused when the owner approached. "Small world! How great to see you and Red!"

The man had paused. "I think you're mistaking me for someone else." Gesturing toward the dog, he'd said, "That's Casey."

Two mothers on the next bench had turned to watch.

Jessie had risen off her knees and briefly gnawed at a cuticle. "Oh. He really looks like Red."

"But he's Casey," the man had said warily, pulling a leash from his pocket. He'd quickly clipped the leash to the dog's collar and led him away, glancing over his shoulder twice as he departed.

Jessie had brushed the sand off her knees, looked askance at the two mothers nearby, and readjusted her bandana. The man and dog were already down the sidewalk.

What had happened to Doug and Red after the fire? She tried to recall. Christ! There were too many holes in her memory banks.

Some short-term memories were intact. She had suddenly recalled that Sara would be home at any time; she had hurried back to Sara's house. Fortunately Sara had never suspected that she had been out on her own that afternoon.

Jessie's attention returned briefly to her laptop, but the columns of numbers remained meaningless. No matter, she told herself. She had discovered the perfect solution to passing long hours alone in the house. She had found Sara's weed stash, hidden in the back of her underwear drawer. Woo hoo! Yes, it was a good time to sample the wares.

Jessie packed a small pipe with a bud of Hawaiian, flicked the lighter and inhaled deeply. She'd become expert at blowing smoke rings through the railings of the widow's walk. Her buzz was so pleasant... spreadsheets could wait. She clicked out of Excel and opened a website that streamed old comedies. All morning she had amused herself with reruns of *Mr. Ed* and *My Favorite Martian*. She took a few more drags. Hmm... how about this one? *I Dream of Jeannie*.

Only Marilyn Manson could soothe her nerves, Sara thought as she turned up the volume on her iPod and adjusted her headphones. She glanced across the lab to her partner, who was still a basket case from Arrano's attack and spending far too much time on military equipment websites. Lindsey's compulsive bouncing in and out of her chair to survey the hallway had been replaced with an equally annoying behavior ... a frequent opening and closing of her top desk drawer. What the fuck was so interesting about the contents of a desk drawer? Still, she shouldn't complain, as there was a small increase in Lindsey's productivity level; between the obsessive drawer checking, she was editing a post-doc's manuscript. To escape the constant squeaking of Lindsey's desk drawer, Sara headed to the electroplating room to work on her new proton electrode.

There was another reason Sara felt so pissy. It had taken forever to get out of the house that morning with so many bodies in the kitchen.

Jessie had returned home. During the day, she worked diligently on her research while convalescing on the chaise lounge on the widow's walk. Huge strides were being made on her amoebocyte-enzyme project, Jessie reported. In the evening, she and Jessie enjoyed the walks around Eel Pond or swims at Stony Beach. Yet when asked by the police about Craig Russell or any details of their dives, Jessie had no recall at all.

Derick had learned that his grant had been extended for another six months, so he wouldn't be returning to the CDC until winter. His summer lease having expired, he had moved into Sara's spare room. Zephyr was thrilled. He and Derick fought battles on the video game system and kicked a soccer ball around Taft Park. Now Sara had two boisterous boys in the house. All was working out well with her new tenant, with one exception. The Indian motorcycle project was not part of the agreement!

Sara had returned home from work to find that a delivery truck had backed across her lawn and was off-loading corroded motorcycle parts. Standing in front of the tool shed, Derick orchestrated the operation with the gravity and precision of a symphony conductor, his instructions to the movers precise and imperious.

With all of the commotion at her house, she was getting no fucking sleep! Last night had been all too typical....

As she was finally dropping off, Jessie's finger started to trace the tattoo on her lower back. Then Jessie fluttered kisses across the nape of her neck.

"I'm almost asleep," Sara had mumbled.

"I'm still horny."

"You drank too much wine at dinner."

"I love you," Jessie persisted.

"I love you too, but we made love twice tonight," Sara had protested into her pillow.

"I remember. My memory's not that bad," Jessie said, giggling. Her hand wandered across Sara's butt.

Metallic clang

Sara's body tightened. "What is Derick doing out there?"

"Forget about it. Concentrate on my hand."

Clang.

Sara sat up. "Why can't he hold onto his goddamn tools? He has to throw them onto the workbench instead of placing them quietly! I don't throw my tools around my lab!"

Bang of a door.

Sara rose abruptly and peered through the window. "Fuck! Now Zephyr's outside. I put him to bed hours ago!"

Raucous boyish laughter.

The Indian had to go!

Sara wandered from the electroplating room and poured herself another cup of coffee. Her colleague was marking up a postdoc's paper with a red pen.

"Why are engineers and scientists such terrible writers? The grammar is dreadful," Lindsey bitched.

Lindsey's new house had a large garage, Sara recalled. Two spaces were occupied by an old pickup truck and a golf cart, but the other spaces were vacant. That would be... an *ideal* site for the restoration of a vintage motorcycle!

Sara dropped her hand affectionately onto Lindsey's shoulder. "BFF, I have a favor to ask you ...."

The following Saturday, Lindsey watched Sara's Land Rover stop in front of her garage. George's old dog, Rusty, lumbered up to the vehicle, sniffed at each of the passengers as they emerged, and tiredly plopped down onto the cement. Zephyr, in his bathing suit, made a beeline for the beach, where Danny and Ava splashed in the water. George and Mrs. Richardson sat on the dock, fishing lines cast into the water.

Lindsey walked across the back porch while checking the time on her cell phone. She silently seethed. Rob had never responded to her email. When she'd called his sister, Rosalind, to ask about his whereabouts, she'd replied that she had not spoken to her brother in weeks. In fact, she was very concerned about him.

And that same morning, George had yelled at her, a first in all of the years that she had known him. "No Lindsey, I will not tell you what gun to buy or take you to a shooting range! You should not have at a gun at all! Guns should only be in the hands of law enforcement officers, no one else, especially not upset mothers with small children about! Your home security system is enough." He'd walked away before she could respond.

Lindsey bent to scratch Rusty behind his ear and approached the Range Rover. Derick had already moved into the garage and was assessing the potential workspace—tidy workbench, ancient but full set of tools, and numerous electrical outlets.

"Who's that on your dock?" Sara asked her.

"My father-in-law and Mrs. Richardson. They seem to have bonded," Lindsey replied.

"Let's swim!" Jessie tugged Sara toward the beach.

Derick stepped out of the garage. "Lindsey, this work area is perfect. There's more space and better lightning than Sara's shed. I really appreciate this."

Lindsey eyed him cautiously before she responded. Other than George, she would only permit a man on her property as a favor to Sara. Besides, she owed Derick. Had he not found her and called an ambulance that day, who knows what might have happened to her. And when she'd woken later that night at the hospital, well after midnight, he'd still been there, yawning, but sitting watchfully in the doorway.

"Let me show you the apartment above. When George leaves, you can use the sink if you need to wash up. There's also a refrigerator and bathroom."

Ægir's Curse

Derick followed Lindsey up the back stairs. She pointed to the keyless doorknob. "We need to get you access to this."

The apartment smelled of new carpeting, caulk, drywall, and paint. The new energy-efficient windows still lacked molding, and there were gaps in the kitchen counter where a new dishwasher and stove were to be installed. Rusty's dog bed occupied a corner, and an ashtray with George's pipe rested on a circular table. Nearby was sturdy suitcase from decades before rolling travel bags.

"Again, thank you," Derick remarked.

"Sure. Let's go in the house. I'll scan your handprint so you can access the garage and apartment doors. You'll also need a swipe card for the front gate."

The windows open, lace curtains luffed into the rooms of the old beach house, a breeze carrying the scent of salt water, dried wood, and hydrangeas. Lindsey and Derick climbed two sets of warped stairways and one more short set of steps to the attic. Carpenters' tools and ladders were propped against spackle and drywall. A large number of electrical outlets had been cut into the walls. Unopened cans of white paint lay in a corner. A new doorway had been cut through a wall and led outside to a new stairway rising to a widow's walk.

For security purposes, her first task had been to change the ancient brass doorknobs around the house to those of her keyless design, so a laptop and handprint scanner had been set up immediately upon moving in. All of the other office supplies and computers from the *Mary Read* remained in boxes. She eased herself down to the planked floor and placed a laptop across her knees.

Derick curiously poked his head outside. "Is it safe to go onto the widow's walk?"

"Yes," she answered, "but beware of the ghost."

"What ghost?"

"Andrew Stanton the Whaler," she explained wryly, "who supposedly appears in late September, mourning the death of his wife, Rebecca."

"I'll take my chances," he replied, amused.

For a few minutes the stomp of heavy motorcycle boots crisscrossed the roof, and dust floated downward from the rafters into her hair, which reminded her to have the carpenter put in a ceiling to prevent dust from getting into the computers.

Derick stepped back inside. "What a view! Is the only way to reach this room from the attic?"

"Yes, I did that intentionally. I had the stairs from the second-floor balcony torn down. I don't want the children to think that the widow's walk is a play area. It's a very long way down." Best not to mention its intended use, as a gunner's watchtower. She patted the planks near the scanner. "Sit down and place your hand here for a moment, and try not to move. Your background is in infectious diseases, correct?"

He sat with his hand on the scanner, and then answered with reserve. "Yes."

"I want to show you something." She pulled a cell phone from her pocket and clicked open the JPEG of Arrano's tent that Sven had sent her. "Notice the bits of tissue and bloody sputum. What causes such excessive cutaneous scabbing and bleeding of the respiratory tract? Poison or disease?"

His deep brown eyes widened briefly, and then his face became inscrutably blank. After a protracted silence he answered obliquely. "It's impossible to tell from this photo. A sample of blood and possibly cerebrospinal fluid would need to be assayed."

"I think disease. What disease would cause this?"

"As I said," he replied irritably, "only a test of the blood or CSF could determine that."

Ægir's Curse

On Sunday evening, George took the children night fishing on the *Just for Today* and did not return home until after ten, which meant that by the time the children had snacks and bathed, it was after midnight. "Some people have to wake up and go to work on Monday mornings," Lindsey grumbled angrily under her breath. And there was still no word from Rob; he didn't even return Danny's emphatic voicemails. Either he was back with Sheila and didn't care to admit it, or he was off on another bender, Lindsey concluded.

Nor had Sven emailed her with any information regarding Arrano or his mysterious illness. There was nothing in the obituaries of the *Cape Cod Daily* reporting Arrano's death. For all she knew, Arrano could still be freely wandering around Woods Hole, imagining himself a Viking lord! Sven's lack of communication proved he had just been humoring her by inviting her for theater, dining, and dancing in Oslo, and to his cottage on a pristine alpine lake. The fact of the matter, she bemoaned, was that she was getting old—nearing forty in a few years—and had lost her edge with the men. But no matter, she reminded herself; she was now a confirmed celibate. Still, it rankled.

As a result, Lindsey arrived at her lab on Monday morning in an elevated state of misandry. She scanned her list of emails, evaluating which had slipped through the spam filter and should be immediately deleted, which she needed to respond to, and which could wait. An email address that she hadn't seen before, from dbriggs with a CDC address, caught her eye.

What the hell did that haughty Southerner want? His standoffishness bordered on contempt. What scientist or medical professional would not want to discuss an unusual disease with another colleague? Instead he had dismissed her outright! Skeptical of his credentials, she had checked out his web page and found, to her amazement, that the man was an MD-PhD like herself. Most of his research focused on waterborne diseases in remote areas of Indonesia, and his publication record equaled her own. His unwillingness to discuss Arrano's disease state was baffling. She was indebted to him for taking her to the hospital, and she would allow him to work on his motorcycle in her garage, as she was a woman of her word, but she'd have nothing further to do with him.

Overcome by curiosity, she opened his email.

Lindsey, can we meet for lunch? It's really important. Your jpg took me by surprise. I need to explain. In person. I'd prefer that no one know about this. 12:30 at Taft Park? I'll bring lunch. You bring your cell phone with the image of Arrano's tent.

For some time Lindsey sat, considering the email. This would mean eating lunch outside of the protective enclave of the lab. It would be risky walking to Taft Park on her own, but she decided to chance it. Her email back simply said, "Okay." She slipped the neurotoxin-filled syringe into her sock under the leg of her jeans before leaving her lab building at 12:25. She reached the town park, unharmed. Derick had already arrived and was sitting on a park bench with his back to her. She rounded the bench and sat on the other side of his backpack, keeping a safe distance from him. An iPad was on his lap.

"You show me yours and I'll show you mine," he said dryly.

"What?" she answered, taken aback by the crass remark.

"Your JPEG of Arrano's tent."

She pulled the phone from her jeans, while he clicked on a JPEG and held out his iPad to her. Eyes wide, she scanned back and forth between the two images.

Derick's JPEG was also of the tent, but the sunlight was brighter, crossing the space in yellow beams of light. A time stamp read 2:11 p.m. The position of the empty water bottles, bloody tissues, and scabbing skin were identical in both images. However, there was a startling difference.

"I'm sorry for being so evasive on Saturday, but your photo completely took me by surprise. I needed time to think this through."

"And this one takes me by surprise!" she gasped, still staring at his iPad. "Where did you get this?"

"From a colleague at the CDC. And yours?"

"From Sven Halvorsen. The CDC is working on this case?"

"No, but a related group. Some emergency response specialists were brought in a few days ago at the request of the medical examiner. They're not from my unit, so I don't know most of them." He paused. "Their job is containment."

She asked nervously, "What's being contained?"

"We don't know yet."

"In my photo time-stamped 11:46 a.m., there's no duffel bag and backpack in the tent. In your photo at 2:11 they're present. Where did they come from? Does this mean Arrano was there?"

"Whoever moved the bags was wearing latex gloves, and some powder from them was found on the picnic table and car door handles." He reached into a bag for deli sandwiches. "Pardon my bad manners. I invited you to lunch and I'm not feeding you. Vegetarian or seafood salad wrap?"

"Vegetarian, thanks."

He pulled out two bottles of ice tea. "Ice tea or ice tea?"

"How about ice tea? So let me get this straight. Someone searches Arrano's duffel bag, backpack, and car, and then puts the bags back before the police arrive? Only a professional is going to be carrying latex gloves, not a petty thief looting a campground."

"Presumably."

"And what about his laptop?"

He viewed the images again. "I don't see a laptop in the photos."

"Neither do I, but what academic doesn't travel with a laptop? We go into withdrawal if we're without our computers for too long."

"You're right. So what probably happened was that someone in latex gloves searched the duffel bag, backpack, and car, put the bags back in the tent before the police arrived, and pinched his laptop."

"Who found Arrano's campsite?" she asked.

"I'm not sure."

"But Halvorsen took the photo when the duffel and backpack were missing. Was anyone with him?"

"The female cop, I think. And I'm hearing from my colleague that the Norwegians are being minimally cooperative. In fact, they're downright nonresponsive."

"Do you remember the name of the female cop?" she asked.

He shook his head. "No, I never knew it."

She searched her memory of conversations with Halvorsen. "I think it was Ingrid."

The two scientists sat wordlessly for a moment.

"Lindsey, you and I have been drawn into this in different ways, but we need to work together. I'm going to show you one more photo that must not go any further. This is why I wanted to meet in person and not send anything by email."

She nodded.

He clicked open another JPEG. It was a magnified blood smear; she immediately recognized the background of red biconcave discs, the erythrocytes, and some intermittent leucocytes that would normally be present. But also present were long rod-shaped cells, some type of *Bacillus* bacterium.

It had to be over ten years since she had taken a medical microbiology course, and she remembered little from it. "What is this microbe?"

"Something closely related to *Bacillus anthracis*."

"What!"

"But a strain we've never seen before. This bug came out of nowhere. This is what infected Arrano, not poison. It's not indigenous to the United States. Its genetic fingerprint is being analyzed as we speak."

"So this is Arrano's blood?"

"Yes. It was obtained from the puddle of blood in his tent."

"And Jessie's blood? Was it tested?" she asked, alarmed.

"Her blood was obtained from the hospital. It was completely clean, thankfully. It's urgent that we contact Halvorsen and his partner immediately, and anyone else who was associated with either Arrano or the campsite, directly or indirectly." He hesitated, dreading his next words, dreading her potential response. "I know I'm overstepping my bounds here, but Arrano was in your lab, and you and Halvorsen seemed… friendly." He withheld comment on her lovely picture on the front page of the *Cape Cod Daily*. "Could we test a sample of your blood?"

Her heart pounded in her chest. She leaned forward, her head in her hands, and shuffled her sneakers in the dirt. He was right; they needed to work together on this. He had confided in her about the bacterium in the blood smear, which he didn't have to do.

"You can test my blood."

The AA Big Book meeting at the Lutheran Church ended around 9:45 p.m. It was not a meeting that Lindsey N. typically attended, but she was hoping to find Patrick H., who was the treasurer and coffeemaker for that group. He was also a cop. Forty pounds overweight, the man had been relegated to desk duty, and she hoped that he might know something about the Arrano case. She tracked him down in the parking lot where he was chatting about the Boston Bruins with gray-haired men. Patrick H. visibly stiffened when she approached and asked to speak with him privately. He departed his group reluctantly; he had arrested her on a DUI years earlier when she was still drinking. What a temper she'd had that night!

"I'm wondering where you all are with the Arrano case," she asked.

He remained stubbornly silent. He was processing the paperwork on the case and was suspicious of her interest in the matter. Finally he replied. "This is a police investigation and not a civilian matter."

The conversation was going nowhere. A different tack was required. "Detective Halvorsen and his partner sent me a book on Norway's tourist destinations, and I want to send them a thank-you-note. Do you remember the last name of his partner?" she asked.

This was a harmless enough request, Patrick figured, and Halvorsen's partner had been the subject of numerous conversations around the coffee machine, so of course he remembered her name. The Norwegian woman was stunning in appearance and colder than ice water. If she'd uttered more than ten words to the American police officers all week, he'd be exaggerating.

"Ingrid Stevs."

Lindsey spelled out the last name. "S-T-E-V-E-S?"

"No, S-T-E-V-S."

Chapter 25

Woods Hole

Lindsey checked her watch numerous times throughout a talk in a small lecture hall. At any other time, the time-lapse photography of cell division and the visual details of the mitotic apparatus and proteins causing one cell to separate into two would have been fascinating, but she was too preoccupied by the file on Ingrid Stevs sent to her that morning by Sylvia Benson.

Stevs had worked for the Forsvarets Spesialkommando, or the Norwegian Special Forces, but had left the unit prematurely when a fall during an ice-climbing exercise shattered her hip. She had worked for Interpol for ten years, the past five years as the partner of Halvorsen. Like Halvorsen, Stevs had had an exemplary career. She was forty-two, had never married, and had no children. Her address in Oslo was on the peninsula of Bygdøy, just blocks from the museums housing the *Kon-Tiki*, *Fram*, and Viking ships.

Even more distracting was an email Lindsey had received the night before. It was from a Dr. Anna Halvorsen, who had come to the United States explicitly to see her. "It is urgent. Can we please meet tomorrow?" Lindsey had responded, "Of course. Ten o'clock?" Anna Halvorsen must have been waiting by her computer, as her return response had come scant seconds later. "Yes. Thank you!"

Lindsey checked her watch again. It was 9:54. It was clear that the lecture was not going to end on time, so she maneuvered down a row of seats and slipped out a back door.

Anna Halvorsen was already waiting in the lobby of Lindsey's laboratory building. It was the young woman from the photo that Sven had showed her, the one of his daughter and son-in-law on cross-country skis. She bore no resemblance to her father, with the exception of hair color. Her hair was cut in a short androgynous style, her ears had multiple piercings, and she wore a tank top, capri pants, and clogs.

Anna was excited and agitated at once, her blinking eyes behind thick glasses wet with tears. Lindsey offered to take her to breakfast at one of the restaurants up the road, but Anna declined, explaining that she had no appetite and just needed to talk. Lindsey tugged on her ball cap and sunglasses and steered her outside toward Waterfront Park, which faced the Woods Hole Passage and Elizabeth Islands. They found a bench at a far, quiet end of the park.

Anna searched a backpack for tissues. "Thank you so much for seeing me at such short notice. I've followed your career. Your work is amazing. I'm so honored to meet you ..." The nervous stream of words was interrupted by sniffles into a tissue.

"Thank you for your kind words. You're clearly upset. What's happened?"

"My father's dead! And no one's telling me anything!" Anna took a deep breath. "Something happened, I think here in the United States, that made him very sick."

Lindsey fell silent. "Anna, I can't begin ..." It was impossible to accurately articulate her feelings. Another piece to this whole incident felt horribly wrong. She pulled the hat further over her face and worriedly scanned the park. There was the usual line of tourists waiting to board the ecotourism boat. Children chased each other around the statue, while mothers with strollers chatted among themselves. But the blond man reading the newspaper on a bench at the opposite end of the park was way overdressed for a Woods Hole resident or tourist.

"Where are you staying?" Lindsey asked, standing abruptly.

"At a motel up the road."

"You're going to stay at my house, and we'll talk there," Lindsey urged.

"Would it be possible to first meet Dr. Kauni?" Anna asked timidly.

Lindsey and Anna stopped briefly by the lab to meet Sara, then collected Anna's belongings from the motel. "I only had four meetings with your father," Lindsey explained on the drive to her house. "A dinner, a boat ride, a visit at my house, and a meeting for coffee on the morning he flew back to Oslo. He was not feeling well that morning. He was coughing a lot and had a burning headache."

"My husband Stefan and I had dinner with him the night after he returned. He was still coughing and had the same headache. After that night we never saw him alive again."

"We're here," Lindsey announced, stopping at the stone wall. "My housekeeper will prepare us lunch." She checked her rearview mirror, but it did not appear as though they had been followed. She swiped her card and the gates swung open. A carpenter's van was parked at the front of the house, and as they emerged from the car, hammering was heard from the attic. They crossed the porch and entered the foyer.

"Mrs. Richardson?" Lindsey called. "Mrs. Richardson?" She turned toward Anna. "I know she's here somewhere, because the truck is in the garage. I never come home for lunch, so she's not expecting us. Let me show you to your room."

They climbed a wooden staircase to the second floor, and Lindsey selected a spare room in the back of the house with a balcony and a view of the bay. "The bathroom's down the hall on the left. You get comfortable, and I'll find Mrs. Richardson. I'll meet you in the kitchen in a few minutes."

Lindsey was growing hungrier by the minute, but she had been told by Mrs. Richardson in no uncertain terms, when that estimable lady had been establishing ground rules, that she was to stay out of the kitchen, and as far as she was concerned, that was just fine. She strode quickly across the back porch and lawn toward the garage apartment. She sprinted up the back steps, pleased that she had recovered enough to be able to, and knocked on the screen door.

"George?"

"Lindsey! Don't ..." he called excitedly.

"What?" She pushed through the door. "Oops."

Amused and impressed by the old couple's ardor, Lindsey returned to the beach house and conducted a quick survey of the refrigerator, as it was pretty obvious she would be preparing the lunch for her guest. Even she could manage cold cuts, cheeses, salad, and rolls. The murmur of the Ducati was heard in the circular driveway, and then heavy boots clomped across the porch.

"Come in, Derick!" she yelled into the hallway. "I'm in the kitchen. We're doing make-your-own sandwiches, so dig in."

"I missed breakfast," Derick replied. He stuffed a roll with cheese and meats. "There's a silver car down the road at the corner of your property."

"I think my guest is being followed," she whispered to him, glancing upward.

Just then, George strolled contentedly into the kitchen. A towel was slung around his neck, and he wore his bathing suit. "Derick, your Indian sure is lookin' pretty," he drawled. He turned to Lindsey, "And how are you, darlin'?"

"I'm fine, darlin', but not as good as you," she answered, mimicking him. "You've turned my garage apartment into the Love Shack."

"Darlin', I doubt that it's the first time it's been used for such purposes." He grinned at her, pulled a pickle off her plate, and popped it in his mouth.

She shrugged noncommittally. "No small wonder you haven't wanted to leave, you Romeo you."

"I had no idea that northern women were so hot. I'm going to marry Emily," George declared. "I asked her. She has superb taste in men. She said yes."

Lindsey hesitated. "But won't you take Emily back to Virginia? I'll never find a better housekeeper. The kids love her. I need her here. George, you two need to stay here!"

"There's no getting her off the Cape," he responded.

Lindsey exhaled in relief.

George's wife had died of leukemia thirty-seven years ago when Duncan was only three. He'd raised three sons on his own. Emily Richardson's husband had been a Coast Guard rescue diver who'd drowned in a hurricane when she was twenty-four. She had never remarried.

Lindsey put some sandwiches together and handed George the plate. "Here, take these to your bride-to-be. She must be hungry."

"She is. And very embarrassed," George said, laughing deeply. He gave Lindsey a kiss on the cheek and left.

A lunch hour was not sufficient time for Anna, Lindsey, and Derick to share their respective fragments of information, so Lindsey and Derick returned to their labs to work, agreeing to meet Anna back at the house for dinner. Anna was given a bathing suit and left to relax on the beach with George and Mrs. Richardson. By the time Lindsey returned home, having retrieved Danny and Ava from their camps, steaks were cooking on the grill. Anna was sunburnt and calmed, drinking champagne at a patio table with George, Mrs. Richardson, and Derick. The mood was celebratory, and talk focused on the upcoming wedding. Lindsey took no part in discussions of the exchange of vows, parquet dance floors, wedding invitations, or buffet selections, but inwardly, very privately, she rejoiced. Tomorrow her divorce would be finalized! The manacles of marriage would fall away for good. Unfortunately, her celebration with a large, chilled bottle of Dom Perignon Blanc would have to wait until all of her houseguests departed.

After dinner, Lindsey, Derick and Anna returned to the matter at hand. Anna knew nothing about her father's activities in the United States, knew nothing about what Sven and Ingrid had been seeking for Interpol. At their dinner in Oslo, Sven had described his impressions of America: the greasy food, obese citizens, wasteful cars and boats, ferocious sharks, and beautiful seascapes. Anna refrained from mentioning how frequently he had spoken of a certain scientist. She did say that he had complained of a debilitating headache; so bad, in fact, that he, a man who never missed work, was going to take some sick days.

When Anna called him the next day from work, there was no answer on his cell phone, so she had assumed he was sleeping. She hadn't been able to visit him until the following day, because of the activity in the ER. When she'd driven to his condo, there had been no response to her loud knocking, so she'd opened it with her key. The stench had stopped her in her tracks. She'd first seen Ingrid Stevs, sprawled on a living room couch, blood around her nose and mouth. Her father she'd found in the bedroom, with the same pattern of bleeding as Ingrid's. Strangest of all, his skin was blistered in a pattern that she, as a physician, had never seen before.

"What was Ingrid doing there? Did they live together?" Derick asked.

Ægir's Curse

"No, but they were inseparable," Anna responded. "She was a loner and workout addict. My father and she were very close. They had been friends since they were teenagers. They must have been taking care of each other while they were ill."

Distraught, Anna excused herself to go the bathroom, leaving Lindsey and Derick on the patio alone.

Derick said quietly, "Your blood is clean of the bacterium and everything is normal, except that your white blood cell count is elevated. Are you feeling okay?" He reached his hand toward her forehead, but she snapped her head backward and sprung to her feet, tipping over her chair.

"I was just going to feel your temperature," he said, surprised. "What did you think I was doing?"

She was embarrassed and flustered. "I—I don't want men touching me."

He lifted the tipped chair. "I'm a physician. I meant you no harm. Believe me, if you don't want me to touch you, then I won't touch you."

She dropped despondently into the seat and nervously fumbled for a cigarette. After a while she admitted, "That's a huge relief about my blood. I feel fine. Maggie, Rob and I are involved in a clinical trial for a new HIV drug. Perhaps that drug caused the rise in my white blood cells?"

He dreaded revisiting this topic, but it was important information that needed mentioning. "Or the antibiotics you received in the ER."

She nodded vaguely. "It sounds as if Sven and Ingrid died from the exact same thing as Arrano, if he is indeed dead. None of this makes sense. Jessie and Arrano are at sea for days together, but she doesn't contract it. I spend time with Sven when he's sick and visiting my home, but I don't contract it."

"You didn't contract it because your white blood cell count was high from the HIV drug, and you were given antibiotics.

Jessie went to the hospital and got an antibiotic in her IV, which is why she didn't contract it."

"Maybe it's not passed by human-to-human contact? Maybe it's only contracted by direct exposure to the pathogen. If that's the case, what is the source? Was the bacterium found at the campground?"

"Only in one small, isolated place: Arrano's blood in the tent. But the cops were wearing latex gloves, so they wouldn't have been exposed to it directly."

"Then all three of them had to be at another location where the pathogen was located."

Derick held up his hand to stop the conversation, as Anna had returned, with tissues. She settled herself again and resumed her narrative.

"When I was waiting for the paramedics in my father's condo, I became panicky. I took my father's laptops and put them in my car. I, I thought that they might contain documents related to my mother, or her death. I didn't want anyone from his office taking his personal documents. I have been questioned about the whereabouts of his laptop numerous times since then."

"You said laptops, plural?" Lindsey queried.

"Yes. I found two at his place. A PC and a Mac. The authorities were asking only about his PC. After I went with the bodies to the medical examiner's building, I returned to my hospital and put the laptops in my locker there, which was fortunate, since both my apartment and my car were broken into shortly afterwards. Someone is looking for something that my father had. Maybe he found something related to the death of my mother? I don't know!" Anna's agitation grew. "The police and medical examiner won't tell me anything! I don't how or why he died! "

"What happened to your mother?" Derick asked.

"She was a politician with very progressive views, a highly controversial individual. She died in a car accident when I was a teenager. Stefan and I went back and read the documents regarding her death. The events surrounding the accident were unclear. One witness reported seeing another car leave the scene, but then the witness disappeared, and the story just died." She paused, then admitted, "I lied to the police about the laptops. I'm obstructing a police investigation, but I don't care! My father must have found something, and someone is not playing by the rules!"

Lindsey shook her head and frowned. "I'm not sure that his death has to do with the death of your mother. The man Sven was searching for in the United States probably died of the same sickness as your father and Ingrid. He was an American, a history professor named Adrian Arrano."

"Lindsey's right," Derick agreed. "Probably at some location they were all exposed to the same pathogen, but we don't know where yet."

"What's the pathogen?" Anna asked.

"It's a bacterium related to anthrax, but its toxin is more virulent and fast-acting in the respiratory tract," he explained.

"Anthrax?" Anna's face scrunched in disbelief. "And you have no idea where it came from?"

"No clue," he stated. "We've never seen it before. It's completely new to the microbial record."

"Unbelievable. And what painting did this man steal?" Anna inquired.

"It wasn't a painting," he answered. "They were historical documents from your national archives."

Lindsey turned toward to Derick, but she held her tongue. Was this what the CDC and the police had been told by the Norwegians? Or was the whole story told to her by Sven Halvorsen about the Vinland map a ruse? Why would he go to all the trouble to seek her out, only to concoct a story for her? And what about the image of the map in his cell phone?

What was certain was that the nail found in Jessie's BC was made of twelfth-century Icelandic bog iron; that was definite, as she had tested it herself. She considered a number of scenarios, some plausible, some not.

"So what about the silver car I mentioned over lunch? The one that was parked down the road from Lindsey's gate at lunchtime?" Derick asked.

Anna answered nonchalantly. "A conservative group has been monitoring my family intermittently over the years. Any time there's political unrest, they believe us to be involved in some way. They can watch me all they want. I go to work, enjoy my friends, and love my husband. That is the cycle of my life. I was followed through Logan Airport, and the same car was in the parking lot of my hotel here." Anna turned to Lindsey. "I am so grateful for your hospitality. My father said a strange thing to me when I kissed him goodnight after dinner. He told me to contact you if anything happened to him, so that's why I'm here. He also requested that I bring you his laptops. "

"Where are they?" Derick and Lindsey asked in surprised unison.

"Upstairs, in my suitcase."

After Anna Halvorsen returned to Oslo, Lindsey was anxious for the carpenters to finish the work in her attic office. Once the electrical work and drywall were complete, she insisted on doing the painting herself, to speed up the renovation. The presence of George, however, and now Derick, forced her to postpone the wild, champagne-soaked party she'd planned to celebrate her divorce.

The two laptops were stashed under the floor planks and new carpeting. Anna had given Lindsey and Derick permission to access the data in the two laptops if they could. Sylvia

Benson had sent instructions on how to bypass computer passwords, and Lindsey was fixated on getting into them, particularly the white Mac—almost certainly Arrano's—which the Norwegian cops had lifted from the campsite before the American police arrived. But until her office was a clean, organized space, and an upgraded security system around the grounds was installed, the laptops remained under the attic planks. Their tantalizing nearness lured her up to the attic most evenings.

Apparently, they exerted a similar pull on Derick. She could hear his boots on the stairs.

Ava, dressed for bed in her pink pajamas, was sprawled on the carpet, coloring with her crayons and coloring book. She called out a happy greeting, "Derick, ciao!"

"Ciao, Bella," he answered in a mock Italian accent. He produced a Tootsie Roll Pop, which he handed down to the small girl.

Ava had taken to hanging around the garage, studying the photos of Ducatis, Moto Guzzis, and Benellis tacked to the wall, and learning words and funny rhymes in Italian. Lindsey was sure that Ava would be begging for an expensive Italian motorcycle the moment she turned sixteen. Derick's T-shirt was covered in motor oil, so he was as grungy as she was in an old shirt speckled with white paint.

Struggling to quit smoking, Lindsey had a sudden craving for sugar. "Do you have any more of those?"

"Only good girls get these. Right, Bella?"

"Right," Ava answered.

"Has your mother been good?" he asked coyly.

"Yes!" Ava said.

"Okay then." Derick reached into his back pocket and held out two pops toward Lindsey. "Which flavor?"

She reached forward. "Red."

He retracted his hand. "Red is not a flavor."

She gazed directly at him and extended an open palm. "Cherry."

He held her gaze for a moment longer and placed the lollipop in her hand.

"Thank you," she said.

"Prego." He wandered around the room, assessing the paint job. "You missed a spot," he said pointing.

"Because I was rushing," she sighed with exasperation. "Where?"

"Just kidding." He grinned brashly. He ignored her glower and stared down at the floor where Ava sat. Nights before, he had lifted the planks with a crowbar while she had held the two laptops. He was as anxious as she was to discover their contents.

"Everything should be set up by tomorrow night, and we can begin work," she said.

He nodded, noticing that peculiar look that was on her face again. There was something she was struggling to tell him.

"Honey, it's time for bed," she told Ava.

"Awww," Ava whined.

"Tomorrow is a busy day at camp with the end of the summer picnic. You need lots of sleep."

Grudgingly Ava picked up the crayons and coloring book.

Lindsey turned to Derick. "Can I talk to you before you leave tonight?"

"Sure. There's something I want to ask you also."

"I'll put Ava to bed, then I'll meet you downstairs."

So far, there was no reason to distrust the biker, Lindsey thought, as she crossed the open space between the house and the garage. If he were to open up the computers and see documents and correspondences about Vinland and Viking maps and she was somehow mentioned as knowing this, he would think her duplicitous and not collaborate further. Better she explain it first.

He was washing grease from his hands and changing into a clean T-shirt when she approached his work area. He started toward the Adirondack chairs, but she lingered in the garage.

"Are you coming?" he called to her.

"I'd rather talk here," she answered, not moving.

"There's no place to sit. I've been bent over the bike all night. My back is shot."

"How about we talk on the porch?" she suggested.

"What the hell is wrong with these chairs?" he protested. "They're closer."

"Fine," she replied tersely, walking across the lawn.

He positioned the chairs so that they were no longer side by side, but facing each other. He lit a candle to keep away the bugs.

She got right to the point. "Do you remember the other night when Anna asked you what painting Arrano had stolen?"

"Yes, of course."

She continued, "You said that he had stolen documents of some historic value from an archive."

"Correct. That's what my colleague from Emergency Response told me. He got that information from the police."

"But that's not what Sven and Ingrid were actually looking for. And you're not going to believe me when I tell you this."

"Try me."

"They were looking for a stolen map of Vinland."

"The Viking colony in North America?" he asked incredulously.

"Yes, that Vinland. Sven showed me a picture of it. The likeness to Cape Cod was amazing."

She summarized the trail of events for Derick, starting with the map's discovery in Greenland by a historian named

Tryggvesen, the results of the forensics tests in Europe as financed personally by Professor Ingvars, the murder of the professor, and finally Arrano's saliva found at the crime scene in Bergen and his fingerprints on the *Mermaid* and the *Anne Bonny*. The connection to the *Anne Bonny* was why she'd been contacted initially by Sven Halvorsen.

"This is so absurd that it's actually believable," he remarked.

"Oh, it gets better," she said ironically. "A large, conspicuous dot on the map is located in Buzzards Bay." She pointed to the water down the slope. "Arrano changes his appearance, and under the alias of Craig Russell charters *Mermaid* from Jessie."

"Jessie's a sweetheart and completely harmless. Why does he try to kill her?"

"Here's where we move from hard facts to pure speculation. I believe that they found a wreck, and he didn't want to share the publicity."

"What type of a wreck?"

"A Viking ship."

He laughed outright. "Your story was almost plausible to that point."

"The morning we found Jessie on Pasque Island, she had a nail in the pocket of her BC." She pulled it from her shorts pocket. "Here." She handed it to him. "I tested it in the imager that Sara and I have built. The nail was made in the twelfth century from Icelandic bog iron. If Arrano was willing to kill for a map, then he'd certainly be willing to kill for a Viking wreck. Consider announcing both the map and wreck to the world. He'd be famous beyond words."

Derick's face was knotted in thought as he gazed at the nail. "And only Jessie and Arrano know of this alleged wreck?"

"I guess. It's doubtful that Arrano would have announced anything until he had more information. If the Mac is his, then it's possible that Sven and Ingrid had read about it, but remember, they both returned to Oslo very sick and then died shortly thereafter. In their condition they probably wouldn't have had the time or energy to study the contents of Arrano's laptop. I'm also sensing that they, for some reason, were acting on their own. Anna said that the Norwegian authorities were asking only for the PC, which means that they probably had no knowledge of the Mac. I haven't had a chance to talk with Jessie about the wreck."

Derick scanned the bay. "This is extraordinary, if it's all true."

"All of this has been swirling around my brain for a while. I wanted to give you the background before we started sorting through the computers."

"Well, it sheds a whole different light on the events."

"What did you want to ask me?"

Derick answered carefully. "George has moved his things into the room next to Emily's, so I want to know if I can rent the garage apartment from you. I have number of reasons for this request. First, I'd be able to work on the Indian in all my spare time. Second, the relationship between Sara and Jessie is pretty tenuous right now, and they don't need a third party underfoot. And third, I can be an extra set of eyes around the place."

She considered his request. When she had moved from Baltimore eight years earlier—fleeing Duncan—her worldly belongings had been stuffed into an old Jeep. She still had the Jeep, but now she had three boats, a truck, a house, three children, a housekeeper, and a father-in-law living on the premises besides. Derick had shown no signs of violent or erratic behavior. What would be the harm in adding a biker/security guard to the whole domestic tumult?

"That's fine," she decided.

"I hope you don't mind if I have a roommate," he added. "Mrs. Richardson won't allow Rusty in her bedroom, so if you're okay with it, the hound dog will be living with me."

Chapter 26

Woods Hole

Sara angrily heaved her backpack into an office chair, the impact rolling it across the lab until it crashed into a trashcan.

"Fuck."

Lindsey turned from her computer. "Good morning to you, too."

"All Jessie wants to do is smoke weed and have sex!"

"And that's a bad thing?" Lindsey asked lightly.

Sara groaned in frustration. "I just don't feel like we're compatible anymore. I can't get anything done. And I can't think straight. She's just not the same as before the injury."

"Traumatic brain injuries can take a long time to heal. She sustained a lot of damage and she's lucky to be alive. It's not easy, but you need to be patient and give it some time."

"I know." Sara wheeled the chair back to her desk and prepared herself a cup of coffee. "I've suggested that she try acupuncture, but she just ignores me."

Lindsey's cell phone vibrated and she read the text. She stood. "I'll be back in a little while. My phone's on if you need me."

"What-fucking-ever," Sara mumbled.

In an odd coincidence, the text was from Jessie: "OMG! Can you meet me at the seawall now?"

"Be right there," Lindsey texted back. She pulled the nail from her desk drawer and left the lab. This was her opportunity to finally talk to Jessie alone.

Jessie was standing at slip sixteen. Lindsey crossed the parking lot watchfully, looking back and forth, until she reached the seawall. Jessie turned and threw her arms around her.

"What's that for?" Lindsey asked, surprised.

"This!" Jessie pointed down at the slip.

"Oh my God is right!"

"How can I thank you enough for this?"

Lindsey stood silently for a moment. "I didn't buy you this."

"Yeah, sure," Jessie replied, smirking in disbelief.

"I know nothing about this."

"Really?"

"Really."

The new cruiser glistening in the morning sun was nearly identical to Jessie's previous one, but it was the newest model. An outboard engine had been upgraded to 50 cc from the previous 40 cc engine. Jessie climbed down into the boat.

"Look." She handed Lindsey the paperwork. "I received this envelope in the lab mail this morning. It contained a boat registration form, two keys, and a note."

The boat registration was in Jessie McCabe's name and her address was listed as Sara Kauni's address on Millfield Street. A yellow Post-it note read, "I'm waiting for you in slip 16. Enjoy me! A fellow mermaid."

Jessie added, "Not many people know that I live with Sara. This has to be from someone who knows me pretty well. Climb down and check this out!"

Lindsey stepped gingerly into the boat.

"A new navigation system!" Jessie opened the dive lockers. "New BCs, fins, masks, regulators, and weight belts. New tanks. And a CD player. Bob Marley and Jimmy Buffett CDs! This is insane!"

"This *is* insane. The boat has to be from Sara."

"I doubt it. She knows nothing about boats. This person even filled up the gas tanks and primed the engine. This baby's good to go. Listen to the engine purr." Jessie turned the key and the engine started instantly. "Is that a beautiful sound or what? Check out the transom."

Lindsey bent over the back of the boat. The boat was named *Mermaid* like the other one, but the home port read Woods Hole, Mass., instead of St. Augustine, Fla. A mermaid with an uncanny resemblance to Jessie had been painted across the transom by an artist with substantial talent. "This is too strange. Even the mermaid looks like you."

"Yeah, I noticed that also. Weird."

"Someone went to a lot of trouble to make this boat perfect," Lindsey observed. "I have a little time before my next meeting. How about a spin around Great Harbor?"

"Yes!"

Mermaid was hastily untied from the cleats and backed out from between the other boats along the seawall. Once free of obstructions, the two women raised the fenders. Jessie maneuvered between the other boats in the pond, passed under the bascule bridge, and threw the throttle forward while still in the no-wake-zone.

"Let see how fast this baby can go!" Jessie was grinning like a lunatic and driving in zigzags and donuts in the water adjacent to the oceanographic institute. "Whoa, what a beast! How many knots do you think we're doing?"

"Fifteen at least," Lindsey shouted loudly over the engine. She was unprepared for the ride and had neither a ball cap nor sunglasses, and she was getting blown to bits by the sea wind.

Ægir's Curse

Jessie fumbled around, tightening the head scarf that protected her sutures and leaving the wheel unattended. The boat careened toward the stone wall of Waterfront Park.

"Watch what you're doing! We're going to crash," Lindsey yelled.

"That would be sick!" Jessie laughed wildly. She grabbed the wheel and veered the boat toward the Sound.

Lindsey watched apprehensively. Head injuries often manifested themselves in behavioral changes, and Jessie was a case study for this phenomenon. Since returning home from the hospital, Jessie's motor skills had seemed normal, and she had resumed swims and short runs. But she still had no recollection of the dives with Arrano, or the trauma he'd inflicted upon her. Either she was repressing the attack, or the memories were short-circuiting across damaged synapses, unable to rise to the surface of consciousness. The new Jessie was a gregarious, free-spirited hedonist.

It suddenly occurred to Lindsey that mysterious benefactresses bearing boats as gifts might be as dangerous as photographers on beaches, or Scandinavians in silver rental cars. "Slow down a little. I want to check out your boat."

"Alright."

Lindsey ducked her head under the instrument panel. No listening devices there. She then checked the cabinetry, stove, and refrigerator. Nothing under the mattress in the v-berth. Nothing in the tiny head, or in the dive lockers. Nor did the BCs have C-trax devices, which meant that the gift was not from Sara. Nothing behind the gas canisters, or as part of the engine. The boat seemed clean of surveillance devices.

Mermaid eased through the shallow waters of Devil's Foot Island. Lindsey returned to the seat next to Jessie. "Look." She held the rusty nail in her palm.

Jessie's tone was blasé. "Okay, it's an old nail."

"Have you ever seen this? Maybe when you were diving somewhere?"

"Nope. I've never seen it before."

"Do you remember any of your recent dive sites? Did you dive on any wrecks?"

Jessie paused. "I think that I dove on a Portuguese whaler, but I don't remember where it was."

Mermaid circled the tiny islands in Great Harbor before returning to Eel Pond about an hour later. The two women dropped the fenders before attempting to squeeze into the narrow slip. Jessie cut the engine and meticulously tied off the lines. No memory impairment there.

"I want you to promise me something," Lindsey urged.

The serious tone caused the biologist to pause and listen.

"That you won't dive until I put the C-trax devices in your BCs. Let me see how many you need." Lindsey opened the dive lockers and counted the BCs.

"That's not right!" Frowning, Jessie yanked the BCs from the dive lockers and dropped them in a heap on the deck. The two pinks ones she placed back in the left dive locker, while the two blue and black ones went into the right dive locker.

"Why did you do that?" Lindsey asked, puzzled.

Jessie shrugged. "I don't know. I always keep the female equipment on the port side, and male equipment starboard side. No reason, I just do that."

A Forest

Somewhere in the forest a gunshot rang out, and Rob jumped. He was terrified of the increasing blackouts; he was terrified of his drinking... he was terrified of everything. This illness had reduced to him to a trembling, sniveling child.

For two days he had sequestered himself in a dense pine forest to avoid the voicemails: admonishments from Leo ("Get your ass to a meeting!") and whines from Sheila ("Can we talk about this?") But the voicemail that he desperately needed to hear, from his beloved, was not forthcoming. He had broken her in unspeakable, unforgivable ways. She would never be his again. By hiding in the woods, he would not harm her or anyone else during his violent binges, or during the weird periods of lost time. The retreat also prevented circling liquor stores and a possible DUI. How could he be so insane when he drank? Violent thoughts never, ever crossed his mind when he was sober.

A cooler in the trunk of his car was stocked with hard liquor, beer, cereal, and milk. All of it was lukewarm; days ago the ice had melted. It was absolutely necessary that he drink right now, he rationalized, because the alcohol would kill the infection that had plagued him for nearly two weeks. Soon he would be feeling better and could go see Lindsey and his children, talk to Leo, go to a meeting and pick up a one-day chip.

Christ! How many one-day chips had he picked up in the past few weeks? It was beyond humiliating and embarrassing to slink into a meeting like a pathetic, beaten-down dog with his tail between his legs, to pick up yet another one-day chip. Only to return home that very night and get shit-faced! Why couldn't he piece together even a few days—he'd had twelve years of sobriety before this mess with Sheila!—like he had the first time he got sober in the Dominican Republic while courting Paola? It was said, time and again at meetings, that the disease of alcoholism progresses, even when one's sober. Truer words were never spoken. It was terrifying that he could not stop. He sipped from a bottle of rum and reclined the front seat of the car. A hazy veil of fluid suddenly covered his eyes and the forest beyond the windshield became a green blur. His temperature spiked. Hastily he fumbled the rum bottle into the cup holder so that it would not spill during the blackout. His eyes closed and his head dropped back against the head rest ...

When he was an old man reflecting on his life, this singular evening would be among the defining moments. Across a banquet table reserved for the Jenkins family, nine-year-olds Charlie, named after Lindsey's favorite uncle, and Rosalind, named after his favorite sister, were giggling uncontrollably. His beautiful wife, Lindsey, in an elegant evening gown, was trying to quiet them, but to no avail. Something was just too funny on YouTube, which they were watching on Charlie's smartphone. Lindsey gazed across the table at Rob and said quietly, "They're impossible. I give up." Rob grinned back her. It was too perfect an evening to concern himself with his incorrigible twins. Seated to his left, Ava was slyly glancing at her cell phone. No doubt it was some message from that roguish Zephyr Kauni. And on his right, his twenty-year-old, Dan, tugged at the collar of his tuxedo. His oldest son had not touched his salmon. Dan had grown up to have the same sensitive face of his Latina mother, Paola. She would have been weeping with pride at this moment; she adored her son and adored the game of baseball.

Suddenly Dan reached across the table toward Lindsey, nearly knocking over his glass of champagne. She held his hand firmly.

"What do I say again?" he asked her with panic in his voice.

"Just say thank you and that you're tremendously honored, if you don't want to say more," she answered, squeezing his hand.

Dan muttered quietly, "I'm going to wet himself."

The twins burst into hysterical laughter. Anything involving bodily excretions was hugely amusing to the nine-year-olds.

Rob smiled reassuringly. Dan could stand at the home plate of Fenway with ice water in his veins and whack balls over the Green Monster wall at Fenway Park in front of thirty *thousand frenzied fans, but he turned to mush at the sight of a reporter's camera or microphone.*

"You'll be great," Lindsey whispered.

"And now, the reason why we're celebrating tonight ..." said the man at the podium.

A hush fell over the room, and suddenly all eyes were on their table. Dan swiped his forehead with the back of this hand.

"The American League East's Most Valuable Player is proudly awarded to Daniel Jenkins ..."

Rob awoke from his blackout, crying, though he remembered none it. Anyway, it was only a dream. What he knew for certain was that he was an alcoholic, and that alcoholics die alone.

Chapter 27

Otis Air Force Base

Finally the mysterious Containment Team and the CDC were recruiting her help, Lindsey thought, as a guard at waved her car through a security checkpoint. She had offered her laboratory expertise to Derick on the bench in Taft Park that day, but he had been adamant that the pathogen be handled in accordance with the policies and procedures of Containment, and only by their personnel. At the time, Derick's dismissal of her offer had annoyed her.

But then Dr. Randall Hunter from the team had left her an urgent voicemail that morning, saying that it was extremely important and they must meet immediately—that same day. Certainly Hunter knew of her previous biochemical and microbial work at Hopkins with her mentor, Anne Davids, and their flurry of famous publications on bacterial and invertebrate neurotoxins—for which she had received a MacArthur Award. He must have recognized her potential value as they assessed the pathogenesis of the bacterium and determined its source. She was glad to help in any way possible.

Hunter had instructed her to drive to Building 26, which was located at the far end of the base. It was a plain grey-green building made of corrugated sheet metal, with an array of old tires, barrels, and nebulous gray boxes piled up outside. Despite the drab exterior, the brand new air-conditioning units and elaborate filtration systems that sat on the roof hinted at a state-of the-art sterile research laboratory—set up rapidly to study the pathogen in Arrano's blood.

She was met at the door by Hunter, a paunchy man of fifty-something. He was dressed in a light blue seersucker suit with a plastic security badge clipped to his pocket. As he led her to a conference room, he chatted pleasantly about the antique stores along Route 28 and the gifts he was bringing home to his wife. In the conference room he politely pulled out her chair, thus dictating where she was to sit. Already present around the table were, as introduced by Hunter, "Dr. Ness from Applied Research, Dr. Gunther from Emergency Response, and Lieutenant Johnson from Base Security. I'm from Central Admin, the paper pusher of the group," he admitted wryly. "Dr. Blane, the medical examiner, planned to attend," he added, "but she was suddenly called away to a homicide."

Hunter sat himself in front of a thick blue folder and a laptop. A sudden uneasiness, caused by the unyieldingly grim faces, overtook her.

"Dr. Nolan," Hunter said, "you're already aware of the putative death of Dr. Arrano and the deaths of Detectives Halvorsen and Stevs by the same pathogen, some cousin of *Bacillus anthracis*, whose DNA is 98 percent homologous with the unknown strain. This strain is highly adaptable and forms highly resistant spores. The bacterium appears to infect the body either through the inhalation or via cutaneous wounds. Its symptoms are identical to pulmonary anthrax exposure. In short, this is anthrax on steroids."

"Meaning that it's one hundred percent fatal if an antibiotic is not administered in time," she replied.

"Correct."

"Does the strain release the same three-protein exotoxin that shuts down the enzymatic machinery inside the cell, or does it cause cell lysis?" she asked.

"It uses both mechanisms of action."

"And it primarily targets cells of the respiratory and immune systems?" she added.

"Yes," Hunter replied. "But it also produces bleeding sores in the skin."

"So you want me to analyze the exotoxin's protein subunits in my 5M imager to determine the three-dimensional structures and amino acid sequences, right?"

The men looked curiously at one another.

"Why no, Doctor," Hunter answered, taken aback. "Drs. Ness and Gunther have already done the molecular analysis." He paused, searching for the precise words. "We are facing a potential epidemic here on the Cape and we are attempting to contain the pathogen with the utmost safety to the public and our employees before it spreads. We are counting on your discretion and cooperation in this matter. The last thing we need is widespread panic." He hesitated for a moment, and then stated matter-of-factly, "You're here to identify a body."

"I thought that you hadn't found Arrano," she said, confused.

"We haven't. But there are a number of other bodies."

"Bodies... I don't underst—"

"Please come this way," Hunter insisted, standing up from the table.

Hunter led her to a plate glass window that looked into a sterile, white laboratory. For the moment the room was devoid of activity. Moments later two bulky white forms, Drs. Ness and Gunther in hazmat suits, rolled four bodies on gurneys from a back room and positioned them in a line in front of window. Ness pulled down the sheets of two brown women.

"Have you ever had contact with them?" Hunter asked.

Ægir's Curse

Lindsey shook her head, horrified at the number of corpses in front of her. "No. Why would I? Who are they?"

The two women, possibly in their mid-twenties or early thirties, bore a close resemblance to one another and had the appearance of the indigenous people of Central and South America.

"They are sisters, Claudia Gustava and Rosita Rojas. Both were chambermaids at the hotel where Detectives Halvorsen and Stevs were staying and were assigned to their floor. Their gem of a boss was having the two women clean bathrooms without protective gloves," Hunter remarked bitterly. "He told us that he was trying to save money for the hotel chain. These women would have had no recourse to issue a complaint, as they were in the country illegally and were being paid under the table."

Lindsey put her palms to her forehead. "Halvorsen and Stevs brought the pathogen from the source to the hotel! Did you find it in their rooms?"

"Nowhere. The women must have cleaned the tubs thoroughly and washed it down the drains. Luis Gustava, Claudia's husband, remembers his wife complaining about cleaning a difficult brown ring from a bathtub and calling the Norwegians filthy foreigners."

Ness pulled down the sheet of a third woman of about twenty. She was tattooed and tan. "This is Kira Wesley, a student at the University of Alabama. She was spending the summer traveling up the East Coast to surf and visit friends. The pathogen was found in the form of brown flakes on the passenger's seat of her van. We believe that she might have met up with Arrano somewhere and given him a ride."

Derick rushed into the room, his hair wild and his motorcycle leathers covered in road dust.

She lashed out at him. "When did you know all of this?"

Before he could answer, Hunter interrupted. "Dr. Briggs is not working on this case. He was just informed. When the fourth body came in."

She regretted her outburst and looked apologetically at him. His eyes had a strange, glassy look. Before she could speak, he enclosed her hand in both of his hands and pressed it to his lips, an unnerving, unprofessional gesture, especially as carried out in front of a supervisor. "Lindsey, I'm so—"

"This man," Hunter interrupted again, "was found in his car in the woods in Mashpee early this morning by two deer-hunters. It's still unclear what killed him, the pathogen, or a lethal blood alcohol level. Probably both."

At the mention of alcohol, she was hit by a wave of dread. Perhaps it was a close AA friend who'd had a slip? She looked questioningly through the glass at Ness and Gunther, and felt Derick's hand slip firmly around her waist. Was the necrosis so grotesque that he wanted to support her as she viewed the corpse? Hunter sadly nodded to Ness behind the glass, and Ness pulled back the sheet.

Woods Hole

The cause of death entered on Robert Jenkins's death certificate read "Respiratory Complications." Dr. Tracy Blane, the medical examiner, ordered that his body be cremated immediately. Rob's mother demanded that the ashes of her only son be buried next to his father in the neighborhood cemetery in south Boston, despite Rosalind's protestations that her brother should be buried on Cape Cod with his wife, Paola. Lindsey, as she was not related by blood, was relegated to second-class citizenship in his mother's estimation and smartly stayed out of the feud. Besides, the ornery old bitch would win this battle, as she did all of them.

Ægir's Curse

The funeral service was a public and chaotic event. Numerous Red Sox players showed up to pay their respects; even some New York Yankees were momentarily permitted into the city. Also in the pews were Rob's friends from the AA community on Cape Cod. Dave and Sheila were, not surprisingly, absent. In the end it was a standing-room-only event. Lindsey was grateful for the warm condolences of friends, and even more thankful for the large attendance that let her family hide in the obscurity of the crowds.

During the days before the funeral, the Nolan household was silent and lugubrious, the expressions of grief by the children as unique as their fingerprints. Danny was weepy and clingy, vociferating his fears that he would be sent to a horrible workhouse like in *Oliver Twist*. Maggie was murderous in her mourning, muttering, "Sheila is a dead woman. When I see her, I'll kill her." Ava, like Danny, was teary, but did not fully understand the permanence of death and at times reveled in the relatives' attention and gifts. Lindsey was anchored down by a numbing guilt, replaying a thousand scenarios that might have prevented Rob from taking up with Sheila and drinking. If she had been a better lover, parent, friend, would this have happened? If she had not moved... had she not taken Danny. She asked herself a thousand if-I-hads and if-I-had-nots. None of which could ever be answered.

After the funeral Lindsey could not get out of her black dress and black high heels fast enough. The dress she tossed into the back of a closet, next to the black cocktail dress with the torn hem. Why was she even keeping that cocktail dress, she wondered. The sight of both dresses made her ill. She stood at the end of her dock and flicked a cigarette butt out into the bay. Black was the most accurate word to describe the past few weeks.

Black, black, and more black.

She could not shake the black mood and the daily mental relapses; the "dry drunks" persisted. Eddies swirled around the pilings of the dock and she sadly realized that even when the tide was out, the water would still be too deep to toss herself in and successfully kill herself on the jagged rocks. What bad luck! At best, she might break a leg, but then she'd be unable to guard the perimeter of her yard every evening. Rusty escorted her on her nightly walks, lumbering next to her, dripping drool on her sneakers and lifting his leg on every passing tree. With a broken leg or spinal injury, it would be difficult to go to work and support what was now a large family of two couples—Maggie and Brian, George and Emily—and two small children. Plus a slobbering hound dog.

Everyone else had changed out of their stifling black church clothes as well. Derick, with a wheelbarrow, was moving mulch toward Emily Richardson's vegetable garden. George weeded, and Danny sat alone, lost in thought, on the trampoline. Ava shot down a sliding board and ran across the lawn toward the trampoline. She scampered up its small ladder and crawled through an opening in the safety net. Danny suddenly strode menacingly to Ava, lifted her, and heaved her out the opening. Her skinny body flew through the air and she landed flat on her back in the grass. For a moment there was no sound as the stunned girl stared at the blue sky above. Then she let out an ear-splitting wail.

Derick turned suddenly and watched Lindsey dash toward the trampoline. He too found himself moving reflexively toward the children, but stopped himself. These were not his children to console or discipline. Lindsey bent over Ava, whispering something to the girl. Ava rose from her splayed position in the grass, threw her arms around Lindsey, and whimpered into her neck. George rose stiffly off his knees in the vegetable garden and wandered over, asking what had just happened. Lindsey explained the incident and asked him to watch Ava for a while.

Lindsey turned furiously, her fists clenched, and glared at Danny, who stood motionless in the center of the trampoline. Derick watched in a sweat. His mother's response would have been swift, brutal, excessive, and executed with precision amidst a tornado of alcoholic fumes. Still Lindsey continued to glare at Danny, as if unsure of what to do next. Finally her fists relaxed and she motioned him off the trampoline. They walked to the end of the dock, where they talked for a while, then they climbed the slope back to the house. She disappeared into the house and returned with her purse. She and Danny climbed into the pickup truck and disappeared.

An hour later, they returned. The two of them carried a new Shop-Vac, broom, and dustpan into the house and down into the basement. So, Derick figured, Dan's punishment would be to clean out the basement. Lindsey and Danny returned to the truck and dragged large sheets of plywood across the driveway and into the basement. Now Derick was unsure what Danny would be doing. He wandered over and offered to help, but he was quickly dismissed.

"Thank you, Derick, but Danny has a job to do on his own," she said in a polite but no-nonsense tone.

Bewildered, Danny looked up at Derick.

"Right, Dan?" she added sternly, to draw his attention back to her.

"Yes," Danny answered in a subdued voice.

Finally all the supplies were transferred from the truck into the basement. What she did next unnerved Derick most of all. She wandered into the garage and grabbed some tools off the workbench, returned to the house, and installed one of her handprint-reading doorknobs on the basement door. It was programmed to allow only her and Danny entry into the dank, dark basement.

Chapter 28

Woods Hole

Rusty sniffed Lindsey out on the widow's walk. "Shame, shame on me," she said to the redbone coonhound while scratching behind his droopy ears. Danny's behavior was shocking for a number of reasons. Terrifying was the prospect that the boy might have inherited his father's alcoholic and violent tendencies. Danny had never shown anything but good humor and affection for Ava, and everyone else for that matter. Where had this outburst of temper come from? Even he didn't know. He was unraveled by his actions and had sobbed about it on the dock, fearing that Ava would never speak to or play him again.

The shove, she realized, was a cry for help.

She might have been more cognizant of the boy's sorrow over his absentee father, and more proactive in getting Rob to meetings, or to a doctor, if she had known more about the pathogen spread by Arrano. But clarity was muddled by anger, and she had been sulking around in a cloud of self-absorption and self-pity, planning grandiose drinking binges and arming herself against a battalion of demons who would never climb her stone wall. She had been there in body, but emotionally she had neglected her mourning children. Danny's outburst was a wake-up call. If she could not save the father, she might be able to save the son. And herself.

Leaning on the railing of the widow's walk, she stared outward toward the forests and marsh. Anthrax was usually associated with dirt. Somewhere out there, it's cousin, a killer bacterium, a sleeping plague had been awoken. It was obvious that Hunter and the containment team wanted her nowhere near the investigation. She would find it on her own, and as quick as possible. She walked down the stairs to the attic office and erased her whiteboard of electrochemical formulae and computations. She replaced the numerical scrawl with a time line of the Arrano case. The chronology of events included the dates when Arrano and Jessie went to sea, when Jessie was attacked, when the boat caught fire, and when Halvorsen, Stevs, Gustava, Rojas, Wesley, and Rob each had died.

Six horrific deaths in total... seven if Arrano's body could ever be found.

These victims were more than names on a whiteboard. They were real people, with loves, dreams, and aspirations. The two Latina women, Gustava and Rojas, were seeking a better life in America and working their best at whatever job they could find. It was clear these women had contracted the pathogen in the hotel bathrooms. The pathogen was brought there by Halvorsen and Stevs. The free-spirited Wesley, who was taking the surfing road trip of a lifetime, contracted it in the van with Arrano. Rob, her wonderful partner of five years, father, brother, son, baseball player—she needed to remember the good—had most likely contracted the pathogen at the Big Bear campground, through some contact with the Arrano or via the bathhouse they had both used. Water, contaminated water, had been the vector for Gustava and Rojas; it might have been that way for Rob. If only the physician in Boston running the clinical trial had given Rob the HIV drug that day, the one that seemed to boost the immune system, he might still be alive!

But where was the singular place where Arrano, Halvorsen, and Stevs all contracted the pathogen? If not campground, where? That cursed place had to be found and quarantined to prevent other deaths.

Later that night, she and Derick searched the Arrano and Halvorsen laptops, but they only served to reveal aspects of the men's respective personalities. As they'd suspected, Arrano's computer was the small white Mac. Arrano's emails showed that he had both a devoted wife and a devoted girlfriend—a student. The emails also revealed which campus committees he served on, which courses his advisees should take in the upcoming semester, and the content of his course syllabi. PowerPoints for his history courses were well conceived and interesting. His list of manuscripts was adequate for an assistant professor, though he appeared to have had a recent lag in his publication rate, which would have been a red flag for the promotion and tenure committee. He was first author on most publications. All in all, Arrano seemed to a fairly competent professor who was willing to work with his students (in all sorts of ways). They agreed that, if he had somehow survived, Arrano would probably not receive tenure unless his publication record improved, and definitely not if the college administration found out about the student sex partner.

Most telling was an outline for a book sketched out the evening before he attempted to murder Jessie, written while they were out at sea. The working title was *Discovering Vinland in Massachusetts*. Chapter 1 was to describe his boyhood years and that seminal experience of visiting Dighton Rock and staring in wonderment at the mysterious inscriptions carved into the rock. Chapter 2 was to describe Arrano's determination to learn runic and various modern Scandinavian languages. His formal undergraduate and graduate education in Scandinavian studies and his early career were to be summarized in chapter

3. Chapter 4 would detail an amazing revelation, the finding of a shipwreck of great significance.

The location and nature of the wreck were unclear, though there was mention of a wood sample that he had carved off the wreck with his dive knife. Lindsey urged Derick to check with his CDC colleagues to see if a wood sample had been recovered during the search of the campground. If yes, could she have a small piece of it to date in the 5M imager?

What they concluded from Arrano's laptop was that behind an easygoing, collegial facade was a scholar of huge ego and lethal ambition.

In the wake of Rob's death, Emily Richardson and George McLeod thought it best to postpone their wedding for a few weeks; but as September approached, Lindsey insisted that the couple no longer wait. Plus, this would be a happy distraction for the children. And so it proved to be. The ceremony was conducted by Emily's pastor of many years from the Episcopal church in Woods Hole. Her father long dead, Emily was given away by the withered Bancroft family attorney.

Rows of chairs on the bride's side of the aisle were occupied by a spinster sister, some cousins, women from Emily's Bible study group, and various neighbors from the Woods Hole community. Sara, Jessie, Zephyr, and Derick watched from the back row. Rusty, in a black velvet tie, sat in the grass next to Derick, held to good behavior by the bacon-flavored treats in his roommate's tuxedo pocket.

Seated on the groom's side of the aisle were George's sons, Ian and Hamish, both police officers, and his youngest son, Duncan, who had flown in from Scotland. Thankfully, Snail-brain, the girlfriend who had urged Duncan to deplete the BioCorp accounts, did not attend. Also in attendance were fellow retirees and former officers from the Fredericksburg police force, who had rented two large vans and drove up en masse to attend their captain's wedding. The Nolan brood sat amidst the police force of northern Virginia.

Only a few scattered clouds drifted over the bay, and the water was warm; the family had gone swimming off the beach that morning while tables were set up on the patio. It was not a day to be sitting in a silver gown on a folding chair on the beach, Lindsey silently pouted. If she could only snap her fingers and make the wedding party, gown, and insufferable high-heeled shoes disappear, she could be swimming in twenty steps or less. Or perhaps she could be up on the lawn with the autistic boy, Trevor Forte, and his jar and collecting net, chasing butterflies around the sundial. That too would remove her from the droning words of the pastor. Everything about weddings and marriages made her nauseous. But, she reminded herself, George and Emily were nearly seventy—old enough to know better, very compatible, and in love, so their marriage might actually work.

Her gaze moved toward the dock where the new *Mermaid* was tied next to *Anne Bonny*. The cruiser was a beauty, and it was still a mystery as to who had delivered it in the dawn hours to slip sixteen, but its arrival had salvaged the relationship of Sara and Jessie. Jessie was no longer milling around the house getting high, but out on the reefs again collecting sponges with her dive buddies. But the dive charter business, Sara had ordered, was closed for good.

To reach the wedding, *Mermaid* had motored around Penzance Point and across Buzzards Bay to the Nolan dock. Zephyr had jumped off the boat before it was tied up and bolted off in search of Danny. Like Bond girls, Sara and Jessie had emerged from the boat, laughing and windblown in their gowns.

At any large event, something was invariably overlooked, and Lindsey now realized what it was: a blockade to keep children off the dock. Hopefully, the trampoline and swing set would keep the smaller children near the house. The older boys would inevitably congregate in the living room at the Xbox. She searched nervously for Trevor and found that he had curled himself into a ball and fallen asleep next to the sundial. Still, for the rest of the afternoon, the dock would be under her continuous surveillance. Please, she prayed to Higher Power, let nothing mar this happy occasion.

George and Emily kissed to a sudden clapping of hands, whoops, and a few Rebel Yells, then made their way along the aisle, slowed by the outreached hands and hugs. They climbed onto the backseat of a golf cart that had been decorated with colorful streamers by Danny, Maggie, and Brian, and were driven up to the patio, where a band was playing their first number, "This Will Be," a song made famous decades before by Natalie Cole.

Lindsey's shoes were already pinching, so she removed them for the walk up the slope. Luckily, Duncan was immersed in conversation with his brothers and passed by without noticing her. She lingered behind the wedding party, hoping to have a quiet moment to herself, but Sara and Jessie remained on the beach, shooting selfies with Sara's smartphone.

Sara smiled devilishly. "Can we borrow your hand to open up the *Anne Bonny*?"

"You're going to smoke weed in my clean and sober boat," Lindsey quipped.

Jessie giggled. "I think I left some of my stuff in there."

"Right," replied Lindsey, believing none of it.

Sara was filming the scenery as the three women walked down the dock to the *Anne Bonny*. Lindsey held her hand on the keyless doorknob and the door swung open.

"Are you making a film for YouTube? You might call it Gorgeous Gay Girls in Gowns," Lindsey remarked kiddingly.

Sara and Jessie burst into laughter and promptly closed the door. Lindsey walked up the hill to join the reception.

Emily Richardson's years of planning lavish parties with Eliza Bancroft was evident. A parquet dance floor covered the brick patio and was encircled by tables draped in white linen. The flower arrangements were simple and elegant, the buffet tables covered with a vast selection of steak, seafood, and vegetarian selections. Bartenders were serving champagne and beer, nonalcoholic sparkling cider, and soft drinks. No hard liquor.

From her place at the end of the receiving line, Lindsey noticed that Maggie, Brian, and the children had already found a table together and were well into their meals. Duncan and the police force of northern Virginia had congregated around the bar, and Emily's friends had filled their plates and occupied tables by the band. Mrs. Forte was by the hydrangeas, imploring Trevor to get a plate of food, but he was searching for insects between the leaves and ignored her every word. Exasperated, she eventually left him to join her friends at the buffet. Derick was in the garage with two police officers, who were admiring the motorcycles.

"I have you to thank for this happiness!" George said to Lindsey in greeting. He lifted her off the ground in a bear hug. George, a giant redhead, was still a head turner, particularly in that classic black tuxedo.

"I'm so happy for the two of you," Lindsey replied. She turned to Emily. "You are beautiful." The older woman glowed. Her hair had been dyed a tasteful silver blonde. Her eyebrows had been made more delicate, and she had put on just the right amount of makeup. The appearance of George in her life had taken years off the woman's looks.

Ægir's Curse

The best man called to George from the dance floor. "Dance! We need a dance!" Applause erupted from the tables.

"Excuse us, darlin." George took his new bride by the hand and escorted her to the center of the parquet floor.

The dance floor filled up fast. Many of the police officers were widowed or divorced and quickly located women from Emily's Bible study group of similar status. Lindsey was the last through the food line and, as she approached the table, Ava departed for the swing set, leaving her mother to hold her sandals. Danny and Zephyr, in an excited conversation about a video game, disappeared into the house. Maggie and Brian left for the dance floor and immediately put all of the other dancers to shame. Lindsey glimpsed the dock through the twirling dancers.

She gasped, dropped her plate on a table, and scurried toward the golf cart. Derick noticed her, jogged out of the garage, and hopped into the passenger's seat. They sped down a sandy path toward the water.

Trevor Forte stood precariously close to the edge of the dock. His head quivered uncontrollably. Again and again he lifted the jar of insects to his face to ensure that his insects were safe behind the glass. Lindsey and Derick approached slowly, so as not to surprise him.

"Trevor, we need to leave the dock and go back to the party," Lindsey cautioned. "The dock's not safe."

The boy's face was pale. "Fire Boat," he said, pointing. "Fire Boat."

She looked at Derick and then back to the boy. "What do you mean?"

"Fire Boat. Fire comes off it." He made sweeping gestures with his arms. "It's hot."

"This boat?" she asked, pointing.

"Yes. Fire Boat."

"Where did you see the fire boat?" she asked.

"In the place with dragonflies."
"Did somebody make the fire?"
"Two."
"Two people made the fire?"
"Yes."
"Boys or girls?"
"A boy and a girl."
"Big or little boy and girl?"
"Big."

"Was his hair this color?" she, asked pointing to Derick's black hair, "or this color?" pointing to her own.

The boy pointed twice toward her blonde head. "Boy this color, but little hairs. Girl this color with big hairs."

"Trevor, did you really see them make the fire?" she asked again.

"With long grass."

"Trevor, let's get you some food. Are you hungry?"

"Yes." He continued to stare at the boat. "Fire Boat has big sound that hurts my ears."

The Fire Boat that Trevor had pointed to was Jessie's blue and white cruiser, *Mermaid.*

Trevor refused to ride in the golf cart back to the reception, so he walked back with Derick, while Lindsey returned the golf cart to the garage. Mrs. Forte walked Trevor along the buffet table, but there was nothing there he would eat. He shouted aloud for macaroni and cheese, so Mrs. Forte found her purse on the back of a chair and hugged her friends in good-bye. Lindsey escorted the Fortes to their car.

"Trevor was pointing to one of the boats and called it a fire boat. What did he mean by that?" Lindsey asked the boy's mother.

"There was a boat that burned in the marsh behind our house during the summer," Mrs. Forte explained. "Trevor frequently collects bugs in the marsh. He was troubled for days by the burning boat."

After the Fortes departed, Lindsey headed into the house and climbed the stairs to her bedroom in the turret. The high heels she kicked off, fearing she might break an ankle if she decided to dance later. She slipped into a pair of low pumps and glanced at herself in a full-length mirror. Her gown now dragged on the ground, and she'd look even punier amidst the tall police officers, but at least she'd be comfortable. She passed the living room where Danny, Zephyr, and Hamish's sons were mesmerized by battling aliens in a video game.

The band was playing a raucous version of "Staying Alive," and Lindsey watched from the porch. Mrs. Richardson's sister was spinning in the arms of a handsome, silver-haired Hispanic officer. One of the volunteers from the marine lab gift shop and an officer with a large beer gut were particularly graceful dancers. Sara and Jessie gyrated wildly on the dance floor. Jessie had removed her head scarf and twirled it in a circle above her head. Sara broke off to weave among the dancing couples, recording them with her smartphone, and nearly collided into stacks of clean plates and glasses on the buffet table.

A large hand suddenly squeezed Lindsey's butt. She didn't need to turn around; the cloying aftershave was all too familiar.

"Hi, Duncan," she said tonelessly.

"You're still a killer, Lin. That dress is amazing. How about we slip upstairs for a quickie?"

She turned to face him, and he pressed a long, unwanted kiss on her mouth. He smelled like champagne, a lot of it. His stare slithered down her body. "Well?"

"No," she said firmly.

"Hey, it was worth a try. I'm sorry to hear about Rob," he commented, staring unabashedly at her breasts.

"No, you aren't."

"You're right. I hated that son of a bitch. He stole you from me."

"We were broken long before Rob."

"You bring out the worst in me," he said casually. He looked to the swing set, toward Ava, whom he had never met before this event. "Ava's adorable."

"Thank you."

Duncan's eyes were suddenly moist. "Why didn't we have children together, Lin? Maybe things would have been different for us."

"Because I'm a drunk and a workaholic, and you're a porn addict, and we're both basket cases."

"You're right. Do you want to dance?"

"If it will stop this mindless chatter."

For weeks Lindsey had been working with her AA sponsor on her phobia of men, so she was no longer completely terrified of interacting with them, especially as most were policemen. The flatter shoes allowed for injury-free dancing with Duncan, George, Ian, Hamish, and a few police officers whose names she would never remember. The sun was setting on the other side of Buzzards Bay, and a caterer walked among the tables lighting tea candles. George and Emily had changed into their travel clothes, said their good-byes, and left for a hotel in Boston; the next day they were catching a cruise ship to Bermuda. Small girls in party dresses had tired from the swings and trampoline, so they lined themselves on a sofa in the library to watch a DVD of *Toy Story*. After setting up the movie, Lindsey returned to an outside table where Sara and Jessie had settled down to eat. They were still giggly and giddy.

"Lin, we posted our video. It's gone viral and we're famous!" Sara sputtered with laughter.

"You two are so lit," Lindsey remarked. "Jes, I'm taking your boat keys. You two can sleep here tonight."

"Sweet," Jessie declared gleefully, "then I can have more champagne!"

A vocalist from the band announced the last dance of the evening, and police officers and their new lady friends shuffled out to the dance floor. Maggie and Brian slow danced as if they were asleep in each other's arms. The selection was a syrupy love song, Alicia Keys's, "Fallin."

Lindsey watched in dread as both brothers, Duncan and a recently divorced Hamish, zeroed in on her from differing directions.

Sara laughed uncontrollably at Lindsey's predicament. "You're a dog in heat!"

"That's not funny!" Lindsey blurted.

"Is it going to be Bachelor Number One or Bachelor Number Two?" Sara continued, goading her.

Lindsey felt a warm hand on her bare shoulder, but it was not a familiar touch.

"Bachelor Number Three," Derick said. "This dance is mine."

The reception ended when the bar closed around nine o'clock; the officers headed back to their block of hotel rooms for a night of cigars, poker, and whiskey. George and Emily had truly enjoyed themselves. Overall, the wedding had been a success.

Derick headed to the garage apartment and changed back into his jeans and T-shirt. He circled the Indian motorcycle and glanced across the lawn. The caterers had packed up the tables and chairs into their vans, but the parquet floor would be removed the next day, as well as the grills, after they cooled down. Her bare feet up on a railing, Lindsey sat on the back porch, smoking one of Maggie's cigarettes. The windows of her house were all dark. The children had quickly dropped off to sleep, Zephyr tucked into a sleeping bag on the floor of the children's room. Sara and Jessie had staggered up to a guest room.

His attention returned to the Indian. Nothing more could be done on the rear brake until the part from eBay arrived. Still, he could never get enough of just admiring the bike and envisioning its evolution from a nondescript metal framework to an aerodynamically unified work of art. Motorcycles were no mere instruments of transportation, but mechanized sculptures that moved the rider through space and time in a heightened state of reality. The act of riding itself was a sensual experience that combined at once the rider's emotional and psychological state with the ever-changing visual scenery; the scent of leather, gasoline, oil, and plants along the roadside; and the tactile sensations of one's hands on the throttle and vibration under the boots.

He glanced to the porch once again. Lindsey's silver gown was lovely. He liked the feel of her while dancing ... sleek and silky. Could she have known that that gown was the same exact hue as a 1947 Triumph Grand Prix and complemented her hair and skin perfectly? There was no better color for her. His mercifully brief conversation with her loutish ex-husband had been underwhelming, and he realized that she'd been ensnared by inferiors. Lindsey, an Aprilia, had been riding in the dirt with lowbrow Harleys. An Aprilia needed to ride with a Moto Guzzi, an Agusta, a BMW, or perhaps a Ducati.

Chapter 29

Woods Hole

A loud crash caused Lindsey to jump out of bed. She quickly stepped into the hallway.

"She fell out of bed and hit her head. I need ice!" Sara said urgently. Lindsey dashed to the kitchen and returned to the guest room to find a dazed Jessie sitting up in bed, holding her head.

"Where did she hurt herself?" Lindsey asked.

"Luckily, on the side opposite the stitches." Sara wiggled onto the bed to press an ice pack against Jessie's head.

"Jes, we should go to the hospital and get it x-rayed," Lindsey suggested.

"No more hospitals," Jessie groaned. "I'm still drunk. I just need some sleep."

"Really, Jes, we should get it checked out," Sara urged insistently.

"I just want to be left the fuck alone!" Jessie shouted.

Sara froze. Profanity from Jessie was unusual.

Jessie snatched the ice pack from Sara's hand, rolled onto the other side of the bed, and turned her back to the two women with a "Fuck off."

The next morning, shouts of caterers pulling up the parquet floor, a rattle of grills being carted away, and the children eating pancakes in the kitchen did not rouse Jessie and Sara; nor did the commotion in the foyer when Rosalind came by midmorning to take the children to a carnival in the town square.

As the car doors slammed shut, Lindsey realized that she had a rare moment to herself. She changed into a bikini, grabbed a beach blanket from the closet, and walked down to the beach. It was one of the last warm days of the year, so she swam laps between her jetty and her neighbor's. Swimming was cathartic and seemed to dissipate, if only temporarily, her muddy emotions about forgiveness and loss. At the party, she'd overheard someone saying that Dave had moved back to the marina with Brianna and Max and reopened his business. Sheila had fled somewhere west. Lindsey still felt blindsided. How could Dave not be feeling the same thing, as he had lost both his mate and his best friend? She returned to the blanket to find it occupied by Rusty, still wearing his bow tie from the night before.

Sometime after noon, Jessie and Sara wandered down to the beach to find Lindsey asleep on a blanket, her arm slung across Rusty.

Sara gave Lindsey's foot a nudge.

Lindsey woke up slowly and brushed sand off her belly and legs.

"So you've finally wised up and found that dogs are preferable to men," Sara said.

Lindsey squinted up at the two women. Sara's face was dour and Jessie's a sickly white. Sara's gown was torn, and Jessie's corsage hung like a dead weed. Derick stood silently behind them, his hands in his pockets.

"How do you feel, Jes?" Lindsey asked.

"Like crap."

"Do you want me to make you something to eat? Something bland and easy on the stomach?"

"I just want to go home," Jessie wailed. "Sara doesn't know how to drive the boat. Will you take us back to Woods Hole?"

"Sure. Let me get my stuff."

Lindsey rose from the blanket, returned to the house, pulled on a T-shirt and shorts over her bathing suit, and grabbed a ball cap, sunglasses, and her cell phone. When she returned to the dock and climbed down into *Mermaid*, the engine was already idling in neutral.

"Text me when you get to the village, and I'll pick you up," Derick told Lindsey.

"Okay. My Jeep keys are on the key rack in the kitchen."

Jessie sat on one of the dive lockers, her head in her hands. Sara was silent in the passenger's seat. The tension between the two women was palpable.

Derick untied lines and pushed the boat away from the dock with his booted foot. Compared to the *Just for Today*, the cruiser was light and easy to manage. Lindsey pushed the throttle forward and turned the wheel, and the small boat cut through the surf in a southerly direction. Large beach homes of Quissett lay on the port side, and off starboard the bay was speckled with the white sails of day sailors.

"Stop!" Jessie suddenly cried.

Lindsey pulled the throttle back. Jessie sprung to her feet and vomited over a gunwale. She choked and coughed, and got sick again.

"I, I remember now!" Jessie said, sobbing. "I remember everything... Craig reached to help me into the boat... he swung a pony tank ..."

Sara draped her arm across Jessie's quaking shoulders.

"Then he put a gun to my head ..."

"Arrano had a gun?" Sara interrupted quickly.

"Alan, Alan put a gun to my head. He and Clayton didn't know how to drive a boat, so they made me ..."

Sara and Lindsey looked at each other, perplexed.

"Alan was furious that Doug and Red wandered by the trailer after the fire. Red was sniffing around the debris."

"In Florida, Jes?" Sara asked.

Jessie nodded. "They must have stolen Red from the yard... when Doug was at work... I didn't know what was in the tarp... they wouldn't tell me... they just ordered me to drive up the boat up the river ..." Jessie cried uncontrollably for some time.

"What, Jes? What happened?" Sara asked.

"Those sickos dumped Red's body by the gators!" Jessie wailed. "I, I never returned home after that, not even when my mother was dying."

Jessie wept into Sara's shoulder.

"It's okay, everything's okay now," Sara whispered.

"I never said goodbye to her ..."

"She would understand."

"I'm a coward in everything ..."

"Everything's okay now," Sara soothed.

"I didn't mean what I said last night."

"I know," Sara said gently.

Jessie leaned over the gunwale again, but only dry-heaved. "I think I got it all out of me. I'm so sorry."

Lindsey handed Jessie a water bottle.

"My head's throbbing," Jessie moaned.

"We really overdid it last night," Sara admitted guiltily.

"Did we ever." Jessie struggled to slow her breathing. "I've been here. Sara, we've been here. Haven't we?"

"Not with me. Maybe on a dive?" Sara wondered.

"Yeah, maybe." Jessie slumped onto a dive locker and sipped from the bottle. "Lin, this is where I dove on the Portuguese fishing boat that I told you about."

Ægir's Curse

Lindsey's heart still pounded from Jessie's revelations. She had wanted to ask a stream of questions on *Mermaid*, but Jessie had staggered, green and queasy, to the berth, collapsed onto the mattress, and lain there with her forearm draped across her eyes for the remainder of the trip to Eel Pond. Now Lindsey was waiting on Sara's front porch step, and Sara was upstairs, persuading Jessie to talk to a psychotherapist to unravel these traumas, Lindsey fervently hoped.

Then there was Jessie's mention of the Portuguese wreck. Portuguese? Or was it something else ... like a Viking wreck? Lindsey's mind raced, pondering the far-reaching, historical implications. On the way home, Jessie had mumbled that she'd be willing to dive on it—later, when she felt better. If a slice of the wood could be obtained, it could be tested in the imager. If the date and source of the wood matched that of the nail, then Jessie would have found herself an astonishing wreck!

Lindsey heard a rising noise and turned to look up Millfield Street. It wasn't the rumble of her old Jeep, but the low hum of the Ducati. Her blood pressure skyrocketed and her mouth went dry. No way would she would ride on that thing! Impossible! She would simply tell him that she'd decided to walk. Her house was only a few miles up the road.

Derick stopped the motorcycle in front of Sara's house and slung his leg over the seat. He removed a spare helmet from a luggage carrier and slipped off his leather jacket. He held the jacket up for her. She remained frozen on the front step.

"Put the jacket on. It will cut the wind."

She stared in mild panic at the motorcycle, avoiding his unquestioning eyes.

"I can't! I've never been on a motorcycle," she admitted. "They scare the hell out of me. My Uncle Charlie was killed on one."

He considered her words for a moment. "I'm really sorry about that. I didn't know, or I would have brought a car, but I also need to get you home. I'll drive really slowly and carefully, and I'll never ask you to ride on it again."

She stood transfixed, barely breathing.

"Lindsey, I have to get you home."

"Okay. Never again, and really slow," she conceded. "Promise?"

"I promise."

She approached apprehensively, slipped on the jacket, and then the helmet. He climbed on first and held the bike still while she climbed on the back.

He spoke over his shoulder. "Keep your feet on the pegs at all times so you don't touch the exhaust pipe. Sit straight even when the bike leans. And don't fidget."

"I won't fidget because I'm paralyzed with terror!"

"You're going to love this. I can see it now. You'll be pestering me for rides all the time. Here we go. Hold on tight."

As promised, Derick motored slowly up Quissett Road while her hands were clenched in a death grip on his belt. Once at the beach house, he stopped the motorcycle in front of the garage and she climbed off. She draped his leather jacket across the workbench and unstrapped the helmet. She was in a confusion of emotions... revulsion and sadness from Jessie's story... and from that goddamn Ducati ride exhilaration and arousal! The kids would not be home for hours, so she imagined herself slipping on a pair of jeans and hoodie, and if Derick was agreeable, going for a long ride down the beach road. But she was determined not to ask him for another ride; better to deny him the smug satisfaction of being right.

"I hope that wasn't too bad," he said, pushing the motorcycle into the garage.

"No, it wasn't. Do you want to start on Halvorsen's laptop tonight?" she asked to change the subject.

"Definitely."

She could still feel that warm wind in her face and vibration between ...

"Gotta go," she said, turning suddenly. She headed rapidly for the beach, stripping off her T-shirt and shorts on the way. She couldn't get into that cool water fast enough.

Chapter 30

A Marsh

Trevor Forte wound down a narrow trail toward the marsh, his father's small binoculars that they used at Patriots' games swaying off his wrist. Despite the frightening Fire Boat that the police had towed out of the muddy pond, this marsh was still his favorite because of all its animals. Here he had watched raccoons, ospreys, and even a red fox and her kits visit the pirate. He knew what a pirate looked like because he had seen the Pirates of the Caribbean movies with his cousin at the Cape Cod Mall, where he got to have an extra-large popcorn with butter. And after he had cleaned his bedroom, his mother ordered him *Treasure Island* from Netflix. This Halloween he needed to remind his mother that he was going to be a pirate.

Trevor could keep a secret, and he told no one that a pirate was in the marsh, because that person might tell Captain Barbossa and the fearsome crew of the *Black Pearl* where the treasure was hidden. He lifted the binoculars to his eyes, but saw no ghost ships searching the coast for the pirate. All he saw were small sailboats.

In his tall rubber boots, he continued deep into the marsh, his eyes to the ground, searching for a large X marking the spot where treasure might be buried. It was difficult finding treasure without a treasure map, he thought, discouraged. At the place where the tall grass met with the lapping water, he found the log where the pirate had died.

Trevor approached the log fearfully and scrunched up his face at the gagging smell. Holding his nose, he examined the pirate carefully while shooing away flies. Every time he saw the pirate, he looked different. Today rib bones, licked white by the fox pups, poked through a large tear in his shirt. His other clothes were wretched and shredded, almost entirely buried by sand and clumps of seaweed. An arm had been dragged away by a fat raccoon, and the leg bones swept out to sea during the last storm surge. Trevor wanted his pirate costume to have a long black coat and wide black belt, not normal clothes like this pirate. Plus, most pirates wore a big hat like Jack Sparrow's, and an eye patch. This pirate didn't have a hat or eye patch, but Trevor was certain that he was a pirate because his head looked just like the black pirate flag, and fiddler crabs climbed in and out of his eye holes, just like in the movies.

Woods Hole

Lindsey erased another red question mark on the time line and added a new fact to the whiteboard in her attic office: *H & S on Mermaid in marsh*.

The *Mermaid* had been burned intentionally by arsonists who'd attached a slow-burning fuse to the gas canisters, which had allowed them ample time to flee. The fuse had to be Trevor's "long grass", and it's presence had been the most mysterious component of the case. But if the two blonds spotted by Trevor Forte on Jessie's boat were Sven Halvorsen and Ingrid Stevs, it made sense. Sven's background and training were almost exclusively academic, but Ingrid had worked for the Special Forces and would have been trained in demolitions.

Lindsey swiveled her office chair toward Derick, who was lying on his back with his hands behind his head, resting on the new carpeting. "But why would they burn the boat?"

"To cover their tracks?" he ventured. "It was easier to destroy it than answer to the local police when the boat was found and their prints were all over it."

"Up to that point, the police were searching motels and B&Bs, but something on the boat led them to the campground the very next day. *Mermaid* and the campground appear to be the two common locations that Arrano, Halvorsen, and Stevs all visited, but only minute traces of bacterium were found at the campground. So maybe they all got infected on the boat. But where did the boat come in contact with the bacterium?" She handed him her laptop. "Here's Stevs' file."

He placed the laptop on his knees. "Where did you get this?"

"A friend."

"Who?"

"A friend."

"A private detective?"

"A friend."

He scowled slightly and reviewed the folder on Stevs' personnel files and photographs. "I think I've seen her somewhere before."

"Maybe she was around the village."

"If I'd seen her, I wouldn't have forgotten it. This woman's pretty unforgettable. She seems familiar in some way."

Stevs' military record consisted of a steady progression of promotions and commendations, terminating with that unfortunate climbing injury that ended her employment with Special Forces. For about a year, she appeared to have been unemployed while undergoing a number of surgeries; then she was hired by Interpol and assigned to a unit supervised by Sven Halvorsen. The two cops traveled extensively together, their passport records indicating trips to different directions of the compass.

"What's in Greenland?" he asked.

"I don't know. Why?"

"Nine trips to Greenland together in the past five years? Business or pleasure, I wonder."

"Who knows. Here's Halvorsen's wife," she replied, directing the black PC toward him. Unlike Arrano's new Mac, Halvorsen's laptop was a heavy old model.

Brigette Halvorsen was lecturing at a podium in what looked like a huge convention center. Signs and banners at the rally were in Norwegian, so their meaning was lost on the two Americans. The politician was dressed in a dark tailored dress. From her stance, she appeared aggressive and no-nonsense. Lindsey clicked through a number of photos from other political rallies, marches, and community events. Photographs of family gatherings and vacations showed the woman's more frivolous and gentle side. She had dark hair and eyes, and an engaging, confident smile.

"Anna bears no resemblance to her mother or father," she commented.

"Find me a photo of Anna as adult."

She clicked through the JPEGs from the family folder.

"Here's one."

Derick climbed into a chair next to her and placed the laptops side by side. "Huh! Compare these two photographs. Anna looks a lot like Ingrid Stevs."

"You're right!"

"That's why I thought that Stevs looked familiar. Because I was seeing Anna in her face!"

"How old do you think Anna is? About twenty-five?"

"Yes, about."

"What was happening in Stevs' career twenty-five years ago?"

He returned to her folder. "She would have been eighteen. She didn't join the military until two years later. There's no information on her before the military, just her birthdate and city of birth. I'd guess that if your career aspiration is the Special Forces, having a child is not going to factor well into your plans. What was Halvorsen doing at the time?"

She searched the laptop for Halvorsen's résumé. "He was twenty-four and a law student at Oxford. He was married to Brigette by then, so I guess we'll never know if Halvorsen was the biological father or not, and it's not important. But at some point around that time, perhaps Sven and Brigette adopted Anna, and Stevs joined the military. Maybe Stevs stayed in touch with the Halvorsens to watch her daughter grow up from afar? Later when she has the hip injury, Sven works to get her a job at Interpol?"

"Your guess is as good as mine," he replied with a shrug.

She accessed Sven's email. "Of course the emails are in Norwegian," she remarked with frustration. "I'll have to cut and paste these into a translator program, which is going to take forever."

He arose from the chair and stood in front of the whiteboard. "Tell me the dates when you had meetings with Halvorsen." He lifted a dry erase marker from the table.

"I believe that he showed up at the marina here," she pointed, "and I was pretty rude and turned him away. Maybe that was a Tuesday. Then he reappeared on that Friday and we went to dinner in West Falmouth, where he told me about the map and Arrano's prints on my boat. The next day, we went out on my boat so I could show him Buzzards Bay. On Sunday morning, a photo of our boat ride appears in the *Cape Cod Daily,* and my world falls apart," she muttered sadly.

He pondered her remark for a moment. "That photo was a catalyst for positive change in your life," he said decisively. "You gained the truth about your boyfriend, even if it wasn't the truth that you wanted. You purchased a beautiful house. You reconnected with George and found a great housekeeper. You divorced Duncan. And you gained a comrade sleuth and a hound dog."

She nodded and looked at Rusty, dozing on the carpet. "You're right. And Sara's right… I should stick to dogs, who are unconditionally loving and faithful. I'm going to forget about men forever."

He smiled at her in a way that demanded a reality check.

She grimaced at him. "Everything still aches. Rob's death, demented Arrano in my lab, the fall. A cop at an AA meeting told me that they finally called off the search for Arrano. They don't have the manpower to sustain it. There's been no sign of him, and no more cases of the disease. The presumption is that Arrano wandered into the woods and died." She paused momentarily. "What if the coyotes got him, and the sickness is spreading through the wild animal populations?"

"If that were the case, rangers would be reporting a rise in animal deaths.

She nodded. "The whole summer still seems nightmarish and surreal. Especially Rob, and how he wanted me to have a baby while he was drinking and … you know, with Sheila. That's what I just can't get over. I was about to tell him yes."

Derick's face darkened. "And it will hurt for a while. But broken hearts heal with time. Believe me, they do. My fiancée, Isabel, ran off and married my brother, Jared. I was lost for a very long time. Then one day I wasn't, and I had the capacity to trust women again." He paused. "But it still makes for really miserable family gatherings."

"How could she do that? What does your brother have that you don't?"

"Vast amounts of money, charm, and good looks. Hers was a choice between an itinerant microbiologist or a suave CEO. It was entirely my fault. I had wanderlust and was more interested in traipsing around Irian Jaya collecting bacteria than being at home with her. She got tired of waiting and fell in love with my brother. Today she's the trophy wife from hell and Jared's colossal headache; so, in retrospect, I got the better end of the deal." He had surprised himself, as he rarely divulged personal information, so he quickly deflected the conversation back to the time line. "And after that Sunday?"

"The week was a blur, because I was busy moving from the marina. I can't remember what day of the week Halvorsen visited the house. Maybe the following weekend? I just can't remember. I'm repressing so many events of that week."

He wrote down these new events on the time line. "And how many times did you meet Stevs?"

"I never did. Halvorsen mentioned that she was working out of Boston. He called her there from my boat on Saturday."

"And I'm betting that the newspaper photo prods her to come to Woods Hole to get her partner in line. She rents a boat and she and Halvorsen search for Arrano on their own."

"Why rent?" Lindsey asked with surprise. "Weren't they working with the police that week?"

"No. They went off on their own, which made the police uneasy." He stared at the time line. "So they're searching for Arrano for this segment of time, roughly a week. Then they find the boat here," he continued, pointing. "They're unwittingly infected with the pathogen, and they light the boat on fire. Then they search the campground the next day. Then after that they leave for Oslo. Which raises the question ... *why didn't they stay on to search Arrano's office or his home for the map?*"

"Sven told me it was destroyed in the boat fire," she said.

A dark cast moved across Derick's face again, and he frowned at the implausibility. "No historian's going to take a priceless map out to sea. It was never on that boat."

She concluded grimly, "Then they must have found it at the campsite."

Chapter 31

Woods Hole

"Peer-review is an important process," Sara explained to the graduate student, "and only serves to improve the manuscript. Let's review the referees' comments and see where their criticisms lie."

In a snit the student plopped down in the chair next to her and griped, "They're idiots."

Lindsey entered the lab in a joyful spirit. The old Jeep had not started that morning, so she'd had a glorious three-mile ride down Quissett Avenue on the back of the Ducati. At five o'clock she would have a perfect ride home with muscular, broad shoulders in her face and a small, tight butt between her thighs.

While her computer booted, Lindsey headed to the coffee machine, still daydreaming. She had had sex in countless places and certainly in every position imaginable and anatomically possible, but not leaning against, bent over, or straddling a motorcycle. While stirring sugar and cream into her coffee, she fantasized about various positions that would be fun, possibly with Derick, notwithstanding the fact that he was not remotely interested in her.

She opened her computer. An IM soon appeared.

Cobainlust: Print out a hard copy of this attchmt then it's disappearing 4good.

Scibabe: Doing it now.

Lindsey opened the attachment, hit Print, and moved to a printer across the lab. Sara continued to review some circuit diagrams and mathematical equations with the pouting graduate student. Lindsey peered curiously over their shoulders. The student's errors were obvious, but she was not going to do his homework for him, or he would never learn on his own. He was typical of their current students, all of them from the entitled I-want-it now generation, for whom patiently contemplating a mathematical series and appreciating the beauty and nuance of numbers was becoming a lost art.

She returned to the printer. The document spooling from it was quite long and had been translated into English, indicating that Benson knew of a Norwegian-English language software program that could be used to translate Halvorsen's emails.

Lindsey scanned the document, astonished. Sylvia Benson must have installed an ear in Interpol's computer system that triggered off any correspondences with the words Halvorsen or Stevs. A spike in email traffic among upper-level Interpol bureaucracy appeared just after the photo appeared in the *Cape Cod Daily*. Another spike of e-activity occurred predictably upon the deaths of Halvorsen and Stevs.

Of particular interest was a message sent by Halvorsen's direct superior to the Oslo bureau chief regarding Halvorsen's last performance review. She read this section twice to commit it to memory. Instead of his typical yearly rating of Exceptional, the year before Halvorsen had received a mere Excellent. The rationale for the lower rating was his failure to recover three artifacts that year, which included a Fabergé egg stolen from the home of a Norwegian ambassador to Russia, some obscure works from Harald Sohlberg, and a tenth-century gold brooch found at an archeological site in Iceland. Lindsey had a very bad feeling about this. She stuffed the papers in her backpack; these would be best kept in her office at home. From the year before, another artifact remained unaccounted for—a ninth-century Norse sword from an evacuated burial ship in northern Ireland.

En Route

Derick read the text message and was not surprised at Jared's news. His grandmother had been declining for some months. Within a few minutes of returning to the garage apartment after work, he changed into heavy leathers for highway travel. His bike luggage was strapped on the passenger's seat where Lindsey's lithe, warm body had just been pressing against his. How much fun was it to feel her spread legs jiggle against his, to quickly swerve around potholes to make her gasp and grab onto him? He motored through the front gates of the beach house. Instead of heading northwest toward Logan Airport, he headed east toward Marstons Mills. Thirty-five minutes later, he pulled into an airfield, parked the bike in a corner of hangar 2, unsnapped the luggage, and climbed up the stairway of his brother's Bombardier Learjet 85.

A humorless man in a pin-striped suit, Jared's assistant, outstretched his hand. "Dr. Briggs, sir, it's nice to see you."

"Good to see you also, Davis." Derick shook the man's hand and dropped his luggage onto a seat. "How is she?" He tossed his jacket over the luggage.

Davis glanced disapprovingly at the heap of motorcycle gear. "Not well. She has a few days at the most." He stiffly carried the luggage and jacket to a closet.

Freddie, Jared's pudgy cook, rushed down the aisle of the plane. "Baby bro!" He embraced Derick affectionately. Derick asked after Freddie's family, causing the man to proudly enumerate the recent activities and achievements of his children.

"The doctor might be hungry," Davis interrupted irritably.

"I have a steak for you that you can cut with a spoon. Do you want it cooked the usual way?" Freddie asked.

Derick's stomach rumbled. "Yes, please. With Cajun spices that inflict pain."

"You got it." Freddie paused. "So good to see you, mon." The cook departed for the galley.

The plane approached the runway. The Briggs Tobacco corporate logo assaulted Derick from every direction: from the leather seats, cocktail napkins, ashtrays, and carpeting. He sunk sullenly into his seat. Davis approached with a stack of business magazines, none of which were remotely interesting to Derick, though Jared would have pored over every one of them, searching for some cunning advantage over his competitors.

"This one, sir, might be of particular interest to you," Davis said, his tone dripping with innuendo.

It was *Business Technology and Innovation* with a picture of a prototype of the 5M Imager on the cover with a smaller inset photograph of Lindsey and Sara.

"Yes, thank you," Derick replied politely.

His blood ran cold. The meaning of the gesture was not lost on him. Davis, no doubt at the request of Jared's prying wife, had been investigating his living arrangements.

Woods Hole

Sylvia Benson's translation software accelerated the conversion of the emails from Norwegian to English, and Lindsey leaned anxiously toward the screen of her home computer. The two officers' emails to one another were professional, but familiar as one would expect of longtime partners. His language was exact, reserved, and proper, while hers was earthy and laced with obscenities. They appeared to be from different social classes, but were equals in intellect. Their email exchange did not reveal anything that Halvorsen had not already told her at dinner and on the boat. Their mission in the United States was straightforward. They were to find Arrano and work with the US government to extradite him to Bergen for a trial and return the "stolen article," as the map was referred to in the emails, to officials in Oslo. At least the second part of their mission had been accomplished, if Derick was right about their finding the map at the campsite.

Among Halvorsen's emails were the e-tickets for the two officers' departure home. His return ticket was dated for the afternoon she had met him at the hospital for coffee. Lindsey studied the timeline on the whiteboard to confirm this. He had returned home on a nonstop flight from Boston to Oslo on Scandinavian Airlines.

"Hmm ... odd," she said aloud.

Stevs had left the day before, on the same day that they found Arrano's campsite, on an Air Iceland flight that had stopped at Narsarsuaq Airport in Greenland. Her connecting flight from Narsarsuaq to Oslo left only one hour later. Lindsey scooted her chair to her laptop and located the SAS airline website to check the flight histories.

There was a nonstop flight from Logan Airport in Boston to Gardermoen Airport in Oslo on the day that Stevs traveled home. So, why would one make an unnecessary stopover in Greenland, and only for an hour, especially if one was feeling ill, when she could have taken a direct flight to Oslo?

Lindsey nervously clicked her pen. Answer: To talk to someone in person, if they feared surveillance of their phones or Internet activity. Or to deliver something. Or both. Her pulse quickened. There was a reason why the police had so aggressively questioned Anna, and why her car and apartment had been ransacked. She leaned back in her chair and stared up at the ceiling. "Shit."

Halvorsen and Stevs never delivered the map to authorities in Oslo.

Suddenly she remembered Derick's question.

"What's in Greenland?" he had asked.

"I don't know. What?"

"Nine trips to Greenland together in the past five years? Business or pleasure, I wonder."

She reached for a legal pad and made a list of all references to Greenland.

1. The map was made in Greenland in the mid-1100s
2. The map was located in a Greenlandic monastery
3. The map was found by a Greenlander named Tryggvesen
4. Tryggvesen gives the map to Ingvars to date
5. Arrano goes to Narsaq to find Tryggvesen
6. Fate of Tryggvesen unknown

She typed Jens Tryggvesen into a search engine. The few hits revealed him to be a rather big fish in the small pond of Narsaq. His personal web page was linked to the senior high school where he taught both honors European and American history. Photographs showed him with his students at a history conference in Iceland and at an academic quiz show where his students had won a second-place trophy. Projects that his honors students researched were distributed between the topics of World War I and the Norse in the North Atlantic and North America.

The man was in his fifties, and in all photographs he was wearing the same fleece jacket and felt alpine walking hat. His face was pleasant and smiling; his body was stocky and fit.

Ægir's Curse

Lindsey breathed a sigh of relief. Arrano had not weighted Tryggvesen's body with rocks and sent him to the bottom of a desolate fjord, for his web page had been updated just the week before. Jens Tryggvesen appeared to be happy and alive somewhere in Narsaq, Greenland.

Buried many layers deep in Tryggvesen's website was a link to the Narsaq Historical Society. The site had a translation feature that allowed it be to read in either Danish or English. She clicked on the British flag, and the Danish text turned to English. Tryggvesen was jointly serving as treasurer and acquisitions coordinator. Acquisition of what? The society's newsletter described a number of events that included upcoming lectures on the archaeology of Eric the Red's farm Brattahlid, the evolution of stave churches, and Viking art from the late Oseberg period. A vigorous fund-raising campaign was underway to bring over an administrator-historian from Parks Canada to give a talk on L'Anse aux Meadows.

From what she could tell, the historical society was composed of a bunch of Viking groupies. At the bottom on the home page was a photograph from what might have been a holiday party, as some of the members were wearing festive party hats, some with Viking horns. Tryggvesen was among the society members, most of them middle-aged or elderly individuals, standing along a stage of a church or town hall. He appeared to be enjoying life and was smiling broadly. Lindsey's eyes suddenly locked onto two singular faces. In the midst of these individuals were Sven Halvorsen and Ingrid Stevs.

Chapter 32

Buzzards Bay

Mermaid arrived at Lindsey's dock on a Saturday morning when the white caps on the bay temporarily abated and a bright sun promised good visibility. The cool air portended the coming of fall, yet the maples and oaks around the grounds showed no tints of red and orange.

George and Emily had prepared for a day on the beach and sat side by side in beach chairs, sharing sections of the *Boston Globe*. Rusty had appropriated their beach blanket. Ava and Danny were visiting their kindly Aunt Rosalind. Maggie was having morning sickness and wanted to be left alone, so Brian had volunteered to help his brother build a deck in Hyannis.

The batteries of two underwater towing machines, sea scooters, had been charged in the garage the night before, and they were loaded into a golf cart with rest of the dive gear. At the last minute Lindsey tossed a dive knife into the equipment to carve wood samples off the wreck. She drove the golf cart to the dock, then lugged the scuba equipment onto *Mermaid*.

"You ladies be careful out there!" George called over the edge of his newspaper. "Call me if you need me!"

"We will," Lindsey yelled back. "Like we're ten-year-olds," she whispered to Jessie, climbing onto the idling boat. She stowed the dive equipment next to the gasoline containers in the back, while Jessie waited in the captain's chair and Bob Marley sang "No Woman No Cry." Lindsey unwound the lines from the cleats, pushed the boat from the dock, and returned to the passenger's seat.

"Are you sure you didn't buy me this boat?" Jessie asked.

"No, I really didn't. Did you ask Sara?"

"She's swears that she didn't either."

"So strange ...." Lindsey said with shrug.

With *Mermaid*'s upgraded outboard engine it took only ten minutes to get to Quissett Harbor. Jessie was an able, cautious captain, Lindsey observed. The hedonistic Jessie had vanished after her drunken tumble from bed knocked loose that flurry of terrible memories. Jessie switched on the side scan sonar and started the slow zigzag to image the sandy bottom while outside Lindsey wrestled on her wet suit and slid new high-vis C-trax devices into the pockets of the BCs. Another C-trax was duct-taped to a sea scooter. While Jessie slowly wove back and forth across the inlet, Lindsey cautiously eyed the water. *Mermaid* was not far from where she and Halvorsen had spotted the great whites feasting on the whale. And that shark off of Pasque Island was a monster.

"Found it," Jessie announced.

Jessie entered the water first and held onto the two sea scooters while Lindsey climbed down the dive ladder. She dropped into the water and reached down to ensure that the dive knife was strapped securely to her leg. Her heart pounded. That night she would run the wood sample in the lab; by tomorrow morning, the origin and date of the wreck would be certain!

"I can't wait to try this sea scooter!" Jessie exclaimed. "I sold a ton of these in the dive shop, but never had a chance to use one." She floated a scooter over toward Lindsey. "Ready?" she asked, moving the regulator toward her mouth.

"Ready, girlfriend," Lindsey answered excitedly.

The two divers aimed their sea scooters downward at the wreck. Just as Jessie had described, the old boat was about fifty feet in length and tapered at both ends. Most of it was covered with sand, but some wooden strakes and beams poked through. The wreck was very old. Lindsey pulled a small camera from her BC pocket and shot pictures of it from above. Jessie seemed more interested in testing the maneuverability of the underwater towing machine; she cruised in large circles above the wreck. Lindsey's attention returned to the wreck. The next order of business was the wood sample for the imager. She descended a bit farther and hovered a few yards above the wreck. Strange ... the strakes underneath her were blackened as if by a fire. It was uncertain she'd get good results from sampling burnt wood, so she motored toward the opposite end, where the wood was not charred. There ... perfect ... an unburned beam popped from the sand. She headed downward and reached down her leg for her dive knife.

Suddenly she felt it. Something violently jerked her foot! Her body was being yanked away from the bottom! A shark? A great white? She turned in a panic, dropping her dive knife into the sand.

She exhaled in relief. Thank God, it was only Jessie, who for some reason had tugged her off the wreck. Yards above the wreck, Jessie finally released her.

Lindsey faced her and gestured a puzzled "What?"

Jessie shook her head frantically in the negative and pointed upward. Her eyes were wide and emphatic behind her mask. She was putting her hands around her throat and making a coughing motion.

What the hell was she trying to say? Lindsey wondered. Air was bubbling from Jessie's regulator and she seemed to be breathing just fine. Still Lindsey took a deep inhale, and offered Jessie her regulator. Jessie shook her head again and motioned that her regulator was operating fine. Once again she pointed toward the surface, but Lindsey pointed down at her knife and started down to retrieve it. Jessie quickly grabbed her arm, restraining her, and again pointed urgently toward the surface.

How goddamn frustrating not to be able to talk to Jessie and find out what had spooked her! She should build a dive helmet with speakers or something, so she and Jessie could converse while underwater. Only one small slice of wood was needed for the imager, she wanted to explain. It would only take a second to nick off one tiny piece. But Jessie persisted and pointed adamantly at the surface. Lindsey nodded reluctantly.

They aimed their sea scooters upward and followed their bubbles to the surface. Their heads popped from water and they pulled the regulators from their mouths.

"I just remembered when I saw you on the wreck!" Jessie blurted. "I suddenly remembered everything about the wreck dive with Arrano! I swam over the charred end, but he stirred up this sticky muck at the wooden end, and it got all over his equipment. It must have also gotten into his regulator, because he came up coughing, and the next day he had a respiratory tract infection!"

"Sticky muck! Clogged regulator!" Lindsey choked out. "Let's get the hell out of here! I'll explain in the boat!"

Lindsey and Jessie swam quickly to *Mermaid* and climbed aboard.

"That boat is toxic! It's carrying some horrible disease ... a plague from God-knows-where," Lindsey cried.

"What plague?"

"There's a pathogen on that wreck that infected Arrano, made him delusional and probably killed him." She was under strict orders from Hunter not to discuss other casualties: Halvorsen, Stevs, Rojas, Gustava, Wesley, and, her stomach twisting, Robert Jenkins. "That muck you described. The wreck needs to be quarantined!"

The two women pulled off their dive gear in shocked silent. Lindsey noticed that Jessie neatly stowed her equipment in the female diver locker. She recalled Jessie's early comments about keeping the male and female dive equipment in separate port and starboard dive lockers. Jessie's neat arrangement of the dive equipment had kept her equipment from being contaminated by the deadly muck that had contaminated Arrano's gear. Jessie's fastidiousness, and the antibiotics in the IV bag at the hospital, had saved her life.

"I have good news for you." Lindsey reached into her dive bag for Jessie's nail, which she had been meaning to return when the timing was right. "This nail is yours." She handed it to Jessie. "Did you remember if you pulled it off of this wreck?"

"Yes. But what about it? It's just a nail."

"It's not *just* a nail! Never, ever lose this! It was in the pocket of your BC when we found you on Pasque Island. I tested it in the imager. It was made in Iceland in the mid-twelfth century. It's low-grade bog iron. What's down there is no Portuguese fishing boat. May I congratulate you, my very famous friend?" Lindsey said, smiling broadly.

"Oh... my... God ...."

"Yup. You've discovered the first Norse wreck in North America."

Chapter 33

Woods Hole

Sleep was impossible. Around midnight, Lindsey finally gave up trying. She tugged a hoodie over her head and stepped onto a balcony off the turret. Though hers was the smallest bedroom in the house, fitting only an old four-poster bed and a dresser, its view faced directly westward to the wide expanse of the bay. She sat tensely on the edge of an old wooden chaise, too agitated to stretch out her legs and relax under the stars.

She shuddered, recalling the dive earlier in the day. Jessie's grabbing of her fin and yanking her away from the muck had scared her at the time, but the plague risk terrified her. She gazed out to Buzzards Bay. Out in those waters was a Viking wreck. Vikings had walked these same shores, maybe across her own beach!

She returned to the turret, but she was still too rattled to sleep. She walked the long hallway, peeked in at the children, and held her hand on the doorknob to her office. The knob clicked quietly in the darkness and then the door swung open. Flipping on the office light, she climbed the short staircase and added new—and hugely significant—facts to the time line on the whiteboard.

Jessie and Arrano find wreck in Quissett Harbor
Jessie retrieves nail
Arrano infected by pathogen located on wreck
Halvorsen and Stevs contact pathogen from Arrano's dive equipment on Mermaid.
Stevs delivers Vinland map to Greenland.

The last addition to the time line she wrote in giant red letters.

CAPE COD IS VINLAND!

"I am a Vinlander," she said in realization. "And Jessie McCabe's life is forever changed."

Longing to talk to Derick, she pulled her cell phone from the hoodie pocket. Would he even believe these extraordinary events? Or would he laugh at her? She'd become accustomed—looked forward—to their nightly sleuthing and banter. He would need to contact the CDC immediately to cordon off the wreck. But it was well after midnight. And this information should only be discussed in person. And he was grieving for his dying grandmother. The wreck had been submerged for nine centuries. All of this could wait a few more days.

She returned to a desk holding the laptops. Something undefinable nagged at her about Halvorsen's old PC. What was it? It held some other vital information—some clue, but what was it? She paced the room, feeling increasingly edgy. A cigarette would calm her, so would a no holds barred fuck. Derick was probably wild in bed—not happening, she quickly reminded herself. Fuck! She dropped in frustration into her chair, pressed the *on* button on Halvorsen's computer and typed in the password bypass code.

When she typed a Search command into the PC, no emails revealed any correspondence with Tryggvesen, though this wasn't surprising. If Halvorsen and Stevs were corresponding with Tryggvesen, they certainly would not have been using an Interpol email address or laptop. It would be impossible to find their personal e-accounts, particularly if they were sending messages from cyber cafes.

And her time with Halvorsen's PC was running out!

A few days earlier, a postcard of the Sagrada Familia cathedral in Barcelona, allegedly from Anna Halvorsen, had been sent via snail mail to her office at the marine lab. The postcard read that two of Sven's friends would be coming by soon for his computer. Skeptical that the postcard really was from Anna, Lindsey took a chance and called Anna's home in Oslo. Anna answered and seemed pleasantly surprised to hear from her. Their conversation was friendly, short, and superficial, as both women assumed that the call was being monitored. Anna confirmed that she and Stefan had been vacationing in Spain and that she had sent the postcard. Nothing was said about visitors coming to Lindsey's residence; instead Anna chatted casually about nightclubs and good restaurants along the Barcelona beachfront.

Lindsey logged off and closed the lid of the PC. By all indications, Stevs had handed off the map to someone in Greenland. If she had given it to her friend Tryggvesen, it should eventually come to light as part of his research. But why not return the map to the authorities? And was there a connection between the Vinland map and the other items that Halvorsen and Stevs had reported "not finding"? She reread the document from Sylvia Benson. The missing items were a jeweled egg, some lesser Sohlberg paintings, a tenth-century Icelandic brooch, and a Norse sword from Ireland.

Lindsey opened a desk drawer and pulled out a curled photograph that marked a turning point in her life. When lost, confused, fatigued, or lonely, all of which she had felt over the past weeks, this singular photograph of her and her mentor, Professor Anne Davids from Johns Hopkins, grounded her.

Anne was the bedrock in her early career. One of the postdocs in the Davids lab had taken the photo the first summer that she worked for the professor. It had been taken a week or so after her drunken car accident coming out of Camden Yards. In the photo, both the professor and she were in white lab coats. Professor Davids had a lab notebook folded into her arms; Lindsey was blowing a pink bubble, her arm affectionately slung over her teacher's round shoulders. Despite her cocky posturing, inside was a shattered girl whom this teacher—despite the gravest reservations—had taken a chance on....

That fucking accident changed everything! All of her roommates badly injured and she barely had a scratch! Her family disowning her. Being penniless and homeless, although another student named Duncan McLeod offered to let her live in his apartment over the summer. In her pocket a job advertisement for a part-time salesclerk at a locksmith's shop ....

On the laboratory bench behind them in the photograph was a half dissected oscilloscope. In her aimlessness that summer, she had decided, in addition to running her experiments on invertebrate neurotoxins, to disassemble and examine the inner workings of the laboratory instruments. If she could just keep busy, incessantly busy ... tinker, tinker, tinker ... at the lab and at the lock shop, it would keep her away from the apartment and the booze.

Machines were the only things in her broken and chaotic world that worked logically and predictably. Only machines made sense. Over the years, her appreciation and fascination with machines only grew. Their beauty and development, like living organisms, was a function of evolution, driven by human forces. She slid the cherished photo back into the drawer and, gnawing on a pencil, stared at the two laptops in front of her.

Arrano's white Mac was a relatively new model; she thought: Evolved.

Sven's black PC, on the other hand, appeared to be of some primitive design, constructed of metal that could probably deflect bullets. She decided: Less Evolved.

Once before she had dissected her own Mac, studied its internal components, and so understood how it was an elegantly designed machine. Tinker, tinker, tinker. She threw the chewed up pencil onto the desk and walked across the room. From a toolbox, she pulled out screwdrivers and needle-nose pliers. In her itchy restlessness, she decided to examine the circuits and chips of Sven's PC.

Around two o'clock in the morning, Lindsey's cell phone vibrated. It was a text from Jessie. "I can't sleep. Can we talk tomorrow?"

Lindsey texted her back. "Bfast @ my place when u wake up?"

Jessie responded instantly. "Wake up? Who can sleep?"

Georgia

Derick stared into the darkness. A small guest cottage down by the river's edge was a retreat from the ceaseless bickering of Jared and Isabel in the main house. At that moment, Katharine "Katie" Briggs was dying peacefully in her sleep as a morphine drip slowly counted down the final moments of a long and astounding life. She would be laid to rest next to Clint, her husband and business partner of fifty-eight years, in the mausoleum at the edge of the estate. At the respective ages of sixteen and seventeen years old, she and Clint had fled her parched farm when she found out that she was pregnant. Katie's father was a brutal man, and the teenagers knew that no good would come to them if they remained in Mississippi. The night train they stole onto terminated in a nameless freight yard in Georgia. Seventy years later, Katie and Clint's tiny tobacco business had grown into a main supplier to the cigarette kings in Virginia and South Asia. The family-run enterprise was later managed by her son, Clark, and then by her eldest grandson, Jared. Derick, her youngest grandson, was only interested in riding a dirt bike around the farm and tagging along after the veterinarian on his rounds to vaccinate the animals. In fact, Derick shunned the family business, ashamed that the family's wealth was built on the peddling of an addictive and debilitating product. To assuage the guilt, Derick chose a career in medical research.

Katie had had a few lucid moments with Derick earlier that day. The thing that impressed him most about his grandmother was her generosity. She had bought the impoverished school district new computers, funded the college educations of his best friend in high school and the children of the cook, Freddie, built a hospital and school in Haiti, provided funds for a marine sanctuary in the Florida Keys, among many other good deeds. Each project was funded by an anonymous patron(ess), as Katie hated publicity and fanfare. She just wanted the job done right. Her most recent project had been a small one; she had replaced a small dive boat for a marine biologist whose boat had been stolen and set on fire.

It was her wish, Katie rasped from behind the oxygen mask, that Derick manage her portion of the estate for philanthropic purposes. The prospect was staggering, and he got a headache just thinking about it. His entire undergraduate and graduate education had been devoted to coursework in immunology and microbiology, and he had intentionally avoided anything remotely related to accounting, business, and economics. Time dealing with his own finances was kept to a bare minimum so as not to detract from the more interesting aspects of life, like motorcycles and microbes.

Derick's thoughts floundered. Where to start with setting up the Katharine Briggs Foundation for ... Education? Biomedical Research? International Aid? Endowment for the Arts? Perhaps

Ægir's Curse

Lindsey could help him with this, as she had acquired a business acumen over the years, sadly out of an instinct for sheer survival. What kind of a family discards an eighteen old girl? Sara had told him recently about Lindsey's car crash as a college freshman. All of the roommates had drunk too much at an Orioles game; but Lindsey was the one who got behind the wheel.

Derick's cell phone buzzed and he sat up quickly, hoping it was her. But it was Davis, informing him of Katie's passing. Instead of the large and highly publicized funeral fit for a queen that Jared had hoped for, Katie had ordered her attorney and Davis that the funeral be held quietly with only family members and her closest personal friends in attendance. For this Derick was grateful. As it was to be a small gathering on the estate, he could be back in Woods Hole by the next day.

After the call, Derick checked his phone again, but there was still no text or voicemail from Lindsey. True, she was an alcoholic, like his viper of a mother, but there the similarly ended. How had he been so wrong? A sudden compulsion to send her a lengthy message overtook him and he started to type, but he reminded himself that she was on the mend, grieving a lost lover, too recently divorced, and therefore off-limits. He placed the cell phone back on the nightstand, fell back into the pillows, and listened to the river swish through the tree roots until sunlight sifted through the windows.

Woods Hole

Jessie picked at an omelette that Emily McLeod had prepared for breakfast. Lindsey doused hers with hot salsa and Tabasco sauce, devoured it in minutes, and then followed it down with a jalapeño bagel.

"I came to the marine lab for two reasons: to escape Alan and Clayton and their murderous scam; and to find a job as a lab technician," Jessie explained.

"You're too educated to be a lab technician," Lindsey protested.

"But that's what I'm truly suited to do. Or maybe I could work on a trawler collecting animals?" she wondered aloud. "Or go to the Caribbean and work at a resort teaching tourists how to scuba dive?" She paused. "But I couldn't leave Sara. Maybe I could work at a local dive shop."

Lindsey was baffled. "You just spent four years of your life getting advanced degrees, and now you're throwing in the towel? What are you afraid of?"

"Everything! I can't announce that wreck to the press! Alan and Clayton would find me, blackmail me, kidnap me!"

"Your fame will make it too dangerous for them to go after you—they'd stir up way too much trouble for themselves. But if they do bother you, you tell us, and you go to the police. They know how to deal with blackmailers." And, she thought to herself, Sara and I are not without resources.

"And I'm terrified to speak in public! I was a terrible graduate teaching assistant. The absolute worst. You should see my evaluations on Rate My Professor.com. One student wrote that I was unintentionally funny. That's how inept I am! I feel nauseous and sweaty when I have to speak in front of people. I *can't* announce the wreck to the press—if in fact it does turn out to be a Viking wreck. I'd have a panic attack. I'd wet my pants!"

"I doubt it. I'm sure you'd do fine. Do you understand the implications of this wreck? This would bring you instant job security. You'd have your pick of any university in the world to work at."

"I know," Jessie whimpered. "And I'm so tired of being broke. But I just can't. How about you announce it for me?"

Ægir's Curse

Lindsey shook her head. "I didn't find it. This is your claim and your achievement. Public speaking just takes practice. First practice in front of small groups and get comfortable with that. Then you'll be more comfortable with a larger audience. And relay your information like a story. Long before there were Kindles, books, papyrus, and stone tablets, there was only the spoken word. The human brain is captivated by a good story told by a good storyteller."

Jessie was silent for a long interval, pondering this. "What should I do?"

"Not be afraid of your own success. Embrace it."

At the Marston Mills airfield on Cape Cod, Derick pushed the starter of his Ducati, stuck all at once by a sense of purpose that had been missing for years. He listened to the murmur of the engine and breathed in the wonderful smell of leather, metal, and motor oil. He closed the visor of his helmet and tightened the chin strap. The air in the hangar was chilly, the temperature having dropped drastically during his week in Atlanta. He zipped the jacket snugly around his neck; at the speed he'd be traveling, the temperature on the road would be at least fifteen degrees cooler. The family jet was in the hangar, refueling for the trip back to Georgia. With his grandmother gone, there had been no reason to stay in Atlanta, none at all. Many scientists had year-round labs at the marine lab. He could conduct his experiments for the CDC in Woods Hole.

During the flight back to Massachusetts, he had written out a series of instructions for Davis. His few personal belongings and furniture from his condo in Atlanta, with the exception of his bike gear, computer, and books, were to be given to an aid organization. A Realtor was to sell his condo; his season tickets to the Atlanta Falcons games were to be given to Freddie's family.

He tightened the straps on his gloves and clicked the bike into first gear. He eased out the clutch and pulled down the throttle, and the Ducati cruised out of the hangar. His business was now entirely in Woods Hole. He pulled down on the throttle; the motor roared as he raced across the tarmac.

At the breakfast table, Lindsey announced that she was going to New York City for a few days. "Some interesting investment opportunities, and it's quite important that I leave this morning." Emily and George McLeod were handed an address of a small family-owned hotel in Greenwich Village where she would be staying, along with the times and places of the children's afterschool activities. Her cell phone would always be on if she was needed, and she would call each night to check in, she assured them.

There was a restrained urgency and determination in her voice that made Derick take notice. Warily, he sipped his coffee. Her financial consultants and accountant were in Boston. Never before, did he recall, had she ever mentioned friends or colleagues in New York City.

After breakfast, she waited at the front gate to put Danny and Ava on the school bus before her drive to the Amtrak Station in Providence. Derick was leaning against the Jeep as she approached with her rolling suitcase.

"How about I go with you?" he suggested. "We would have fun. You could do what you need to do during the day, and we could go to jazz clubs at night."

The offer was tremendously tempting. She glanced down at his distracting black leather chaps... also tremendously tempting. Finally she said, "I'll definitely take a rain check on that, but I just need some personal time for a few days."

Personal time! Bullshit! This was a compulsive, workaholic woman who had probably never taken a personal day in her entire life, and now she was taking three days in a row! Had she possibly met someone online? Was she going to meet him in New York? Stop, he told himself; this line of thought would make him insane. But there it was: the time of standing on the sidelines was over.

"Alright. Just be safe." He pressed her against the car and gave her a long kiss on the mouth. Then, without comment, he released her and walked toward the garage.

Lindsey stared after him, completely rattled. That marvelous kiss was going to distract her for days.

Chapter 34

Woods Hole

The old beach house shook and rattled from slashes of the sleet and wind of an autumn nor'easter, but down in the basement Lindsey heard nothing except the commentator for an Orioles-Red Sox game and Danny's excited chatter about a baseball camp that he might attend in the spring. The boy struggled in reading and math and would probably never be a strong student, but he was dexterous and had his father's extraordinary eye-hand coordination. Together he and Lindsey had cleaned the floor, covered it with cheap carpet from a remnant sale, installed banks of fluorescent lights in the ceiling and space heaters in the walls, and then set up worktables around the room. In the middle of the large basement, they'd bolted large sheets of plywood to sawhorses. Danny had painted the plywood blue to represent the water, and green and brown for the land masses of Woods Hole, the Elizabeth Islands, Martha's Vineyard, and Nantucket.

The Beloved Places diorama was emerging in astonishing detail. It depicted Dave's Marina with accurate replicas of the three houseboats, Shark Rock offshore, Eel Pond, and the surrounding village of Woods Hole, including Zephyr's house, the bascule bridge, Taft Park, and Stony Beach. Up the road in Quissett was their home. On the widow's walk were the reunited ghosts, Andrew and Rebecca Stanton, and Rusty, the hound dog. Plastic baseball players were placed at all of the locations that Danny and Rob had loved to go together.

That afternoon Danny was hanging biplanes from the pipes in the ceiling, so a SPAD, a Fokker, and a Sopwith Camel circled the skies over Woods Hole. Upstairs, on a TV in the living room, Darth Vader conspired with the cloaked Emperor Palpatine, while Ava and Derick watched transfixed. From the kitchen across the hallway wafted the scent of Emily's spaghetti sauce.

Lindsey checked her watch. It was 2:52. She held the ladder while Danny fastened another airplane, a Curtis Jenny, with fishing line to the basement ceiling.

Anna Halvorsen had sent a second postcard to Lindsey's laboratory, this one from the Van Gogh Museum in Amsterdam. It was scribed in the same neat handwriting as the first one, and it stated that two men would be arriving at the Nolan home in Quissett to pick up her father's laptop. Their arrival was slated for three o'clock this very afternoon.

Lindsey checked the time at three, 3:08, and again at 3:23, and wondered if the men had been confused by the different time zones. She walked upstairs and into the living room to see Luke Skywalker and the Rebel Forces climbing into their attack aircraft.

At 3:48 a buzz at the security panel in the foyer announced the guests' arrival at the stone wall. The words that came through the speaker were spoken in a Danish accent. The speaker blamed his tardiness on an accident that had closed one lane of the highway outside of Plymouth. Emily pushed the access key on the security panel, and a compact rental car moved through the opened wrought iron security gate toward the circular driveway.

Two men hurried from the car, their faces hidden by the hoods of their raincoats. They dashed up the steps to the porch, where they peeled off their wet gear and draped them over the wicker chairs before striking the brass door knocker. Emily McLeod shooed Lindsey and Derick aside in the hallway and proceeded to answer the door, as it always had been and continued to be her job to greet all guests.

The two men in the entryway had friendly, inquisitive faces, not at all like the "men in black" Lindsey had been dreading. With solemn formality, Emily introduced Mr. Jens Tryggvesen; then his companion, a large Inuit, introduced himself to Drs. Nolan and Briggs simply as Joe. The guests were guided into the dining room, while Emily scurried to the kitchen for cookies and hot chocolate.

Tryggvesen was a talker and monopolized the conversation, as teachers often do. He spoke about his recent meetings with Anna in Oslo, the upcoming projects of the Narsaq Historical Society, and with sadness about the disturbing deaths of Sven and Ingrid, longtime members of the Society. On occasion Lindsey interjected a comment or question, while both Joe and Derick remained watchful and silent.

"May we see the laptop?" Tryggvesen finally asked, a quavering excitement in his voice.

"Yes, of course," she replied.

Derick rose from the table. "I'll get it."

"Anna gave you permission to read the contents of the computer. Did you find anything interesting?" Tryggvesen inquired, his eyebrows raised.

"Only emails from coworkers that were all bureaucratic in nature, and some family photographs," she answered.

Tryggvesen and Joe stared keenly as Derick placed the laptop on the table. Joe impatiently unzipped the carrying case. He flipped open the lid and waited for the computer to boot. Then his fingers fluttered adroitly over the keypad.

"Should I have found anything interesting?" she asked, as if an afterthought.

Ægir's Curse

Joe, silent to this point, let forth a deep guffaw. "Who's the Norse god of the sea, Dr. Nolan?"

The Inuit's outburst startled her. "Wait. I knew this once." She sighed, shaking her head. "It's not coming. I just don't remember."

Derick looked at her in disbelief. How did she not know this? Library books on everything related to the Vikings were stacked all over the turret.

"Ægir," Derick answered.

"You're right, Derick. I remember it now," she agreed.

Joe leaned across the table and rotated the laptop to face her. "Type it into the computer."

She typed AEGIR, and then looked questioningly at Joe.

"Now hit ENTER," Joe added.

She pressed the ENTER key. The four of them sat silently for a moment, searching one another's faces while the storm jostled the trees outside.

A nearly imperceptible hum emanated from the laptop, followed by three quiet clicks. A lock disengaged. A narrow panel identical in dimension to the laptop slid outward from behind the screen. Recessed into a shallow panel in the lid was a transparent plastic envelope that contained an old hide map. It was the map in the photo from Sven's cell phone.

"No way!" Lindsey whispered incredulously. Derick shook his head at the irony. For weeks, hunched over the laptops in the attic office, the two of them had speculated on a thousand different fates for the missing Vinland map, and the entire time it had been hidden in Sven's old laptop, just inches in front of them. Lindsey reached out apprehensively and pried the map from its snug fit in the panel. The four of them gazed silently at it for some time.

"So, our Interpol officer has a smuggler's laptop," she said humorously.

"True, but he was only returning the map to the people of Greenland, where the map originated and belongs," Tryggvesen countered in Sven's defense.

She searched the man's face for any trace of subterfuge. Was he the ringleader of a smuggling ring, or a historian? "But it's a Vinland map, Mr. Tryggvesen. Shouldn't it stay here in Vinland with us Vinlanders?" she suggested kiddingly.

He laughed heartily at her humor. "If we hadn't intercepted it, this map might have ended up in Norway or Sweden in a private collection of some corporate magnate or high-level government bureaucrat, and the public would never see it, or be able to appreciate this important artifact. It will be housed with the other Greenlandic artifacts that the historical society has acquired for the museum. And you must visit our museum in Narsaq sometime."

"And what about the Norse brooch and sword that Sven and Ingrid supposedly never found?" she asked cautiously.

Tryggvesen turned white. How had she had found out about the other items that Halvorsen and Stevs had not returned to the authorities? "Those were returned to their rightful owners. Their only intent was to return artifacts to their countrymen, I can assure you of that. There was no profit motive involved in any of this," he explained in an annoyed, defensive tone.

"And why did Ingrid Stevs stop in Greenland?" she persisted.

"Originally she was to deliver the map, but she realized that she was being followed. So she stopped to tell Joe where the laptop was to be picked up later, and to let him know the access codes. Where invaluable artifacts are concerned, we communicate verbally whenever possible. However, we had no idea that Ingrid and Sven were so sick, and that the laptop would end up with Anna and eventually in the United States."

"So Anna had no idea that Sven's laptop contained the map?" Derick asked.

"Of course not," Tryggvesen answered firmly. "Sven would never have involved her in his business, though he did instruct her to bring it to you for safekeeping. I'm assuming that he thought that a small seaside village in the United States seemed an ideal place to temporarily hide a map while his and Anna's properties were searched. Your home, he had to know, has a substantial security system."

"Ingrid Stevs was Anna's mother, wasn't she?" Derick said.

Tryggvesen's jovial face became serious once again. Beads of sweat appeared on his brow. Joe glanced curiously up from the map, his eyes on Tryggvesen. Silence suffused the room.

Eventually he spoke. "Yes. Ingrid got pregnant shortly before she was to begin military service. She and Sven were student members in the historical society at the time. Sven and Brigette adopted the baby, as they were unable to have children of their own." Tryggvesen looked down at his hands for a moment, then continued.

"Anna and I met for the first time a few weeks ago, when I told her that her father had left some important information for me in his laptop, and I needed their help retrieving the laptop from you. In our first meeting, she and her husband were skeptical and told me only that they'd think about it. I didn't hear back from her, and I feared that she thought me an agent from the right wing. She was clearly hostile to anything related to them. To prove that I was not associated with them, I showed her links to our Society's website and my years of professional correspondences with her father. That's when she agreed to meet with me again and write the postcards to you so that the Society could obtain the laptop."

"Who is Anna's father?" Derick asked.

Tryggvesen shifted in his chair, in obvious discomfort. "I am."

Epilogue

Woods Hole, Two Summers Later

The marine lab was abuzz about the upcoming speakers at the Friday Night Lecture Series. Well before eight o'clock, a large crowd had slowly squeezed up the front steps and into the auditorium. Lindsey had arrived a bit late and had to sidestep along a back wall; all of the seats were filled and the press had blockaded the aisles with cameras. A palpable electricity crackled in the air. This was a big night at the lab, as the two speakers were Woods Holes' own.

The lights dimmed, and a black-haired woman stood in front of a podium and waited for the audience to settle themselves. With affection and humor, Sara Kauni introduced the speakers. The first speaker from Atlanta had received an undergraduate degree from Vanderbilt, a PhD in infectious diseases from Cornell, and a medical degree from Harvard; the second speaker, a native of Florida, had a BS and MS in ecology from Florida State University and a PhD from the University of Florida.

Lindsey had trouble seeing the speakers, who sat in metal folding chairs in the shadow along the side of the stage. The first speaker, Dr. Briggs, rose from a chair and moved toward the podium. An electron microscope image of a rod-shaped microorganism appeared on a large screen behind him.

"During the medieval period, waves of plague spread across Europe, the Middle East, and Asia," he explained, "some causing massive mortalities, like the Black Death, while other plague outbreaks were smaller and isolated, and not well understood or well documented. The bacterium on the screen, a variant of *Bacillus anthracis*, had a brief and virulent history in medieval Europe before disappearing from the microbial record. The strain was presumed extinct until a minute population of the bacterium—which had been lying dormant, encapsulated in water-resistant spores—were stirred out of the sand by some scuba divers."

Dr. Briggs was intentionally oblique about the wreck where the spores had been discovered, as that was to be the subject of the second part of the evening's lecture. Instead, he focused on the unusual molecular properties of the bacterium's capsule that allowed it to remain sequestered in the sand for so many centuries, and its ability to penetrate the cells of the human host and launch a devastating enzymatic assault on the host's respiratory and immune systems. The later part of his lecture described the extensive precautions taken by the dive team from the CDC to remove and destroy the pathogen before the wreck itself could be safely excavated. Concluding his part of the presentation, he moved from the podium and whispered some words of encouragement to the second speaker, who tentatively rose from the shadows.

Cameras from the press flashed in unison, catching the second speaker in a nimbus of light. The young woman fidgeted momentarily, struggling with the remote. Her words stumbled a bit at first, but she eventually calmed and hit her stride once PowerPoint images of the wreck site appeared on the screen. Flashing a red laser pointer at the images on the screen, she circled the stage and told a story of a destitute marine biologist who had moved to Woods Hole and started up a small dive business.

The wreck found in Buzzards Bay by a side scan sonar survey was not one of the sleek, stealthy Viking raiders that attacked cities in the narrow rivers of Europe, but a knarr, a rugged transoceanic merchant vessel. The craft had been originally constructed in Norway, as revealed by the dendrochronology of the Norwegian oak beams that comprised the ship's hull. It had been repaired a number of times in different ports of the North Atlantic, as revealed by the metallurgy of the iron nails from bogs in Iceland and Ireland. Until somebody builds a time machine, the speaker remarked, they would never know how many trips to Vinland the knarr had made, or how the fire onboard originated. The knarr, along with the artifacts found on it—coins, axes, and cutlery—would eventually be on display at the Vinland Museum that was still under construction in Falmouth, funded by the Katharine Briggs Trust.

At times during the lecture, the entire auditorium collectively stopped breathing, awaiting the next revelation. This was not a dry lecture, but a riveting story of scientific and historical discovery. The speaker, Dr. McCabe, was unpolished but funny and self-effacing. The lecture ended in uproarious applause.

Jessie offered a small, tentative curtsey, while Derick gave a nod of his head and seemed to want the whole business to be over with. Sara motioned the two speakers back to the podium and wrapped her arms around their waists, standing between them. Then, over the heads of the audience, Derick spotted Lindsey in the back, and suddenly decided to pass on the reception afterwards.

Lindsey leaned against a wall, deep in thought. Jessie's story was only a fragment of a greater saga. There was no mention of a cruelly ambitious professor, or two Interpol officers who believed that native artifacts should be returned to their native peoples, or two chambermaids trying to eke out a living in a foreign land, or a surfer girl in pursuit of the perfect wave, or a loving father who could not get sober, or a high school teacher who, while caring for a wife dying of MS, had a brief affair with a beautiful teenager that produced a daughter. Or an eighteen-year-old alcoholic who worked in a locksmith's shop to earn grocery money, who seventeen years later would be tinkering with a computer in the middle of the night, only to discover a curious locking mechanism, activate it, and hear three quiet clicks.

Nor was there a mention of an Internet search that located a Mr. Jones, an art restoration and replication expert, who for three days worked with a client, Ms. Smith, in a paint-spattered basement studio in Greenwich Village to duplicate an old hide map.

Just up the road from the auditorium, the original map lay undisturbed, at least for the moment, in a safety deposit box in a bank on Water Street; for a Vinland map should remain in the hands of Vinlanders.

The End

Ægir's Curse

An excerpt from *The Bends*, the third novel in the Woods Hole Thrillers series.

Three years after *Ægir's Curse*, a most sinister and elusive killers is on the loose at Maggie's art college ....

The *Jack Rackham* floated silently in a shadow of a cliff. The mural on its transom was painted in graphic and gruesome detail. Bright splashes of color depicted the pirate, Calico Jack, dangling off a gibbet in Port Royale, Jamaica. In the background amidst the palmettos was a small prison. From its windows two women gazed at the decaying body of their captain. The blonde pirate, Anne Bonny, had a look of smug contempt, while Mary Read's face was wracked with despair.

The jagged spire of rock that loomed over the trawler bore no tropical trees or lush vegetation. The only inhabitants of the pinnacle were seabirds that nestled along the narrow ledges, and below the surface, invertebrates clung precariously to a slick rock wall. The seclusion of the island was what attracted the artist of the pirate mural to this destination. The art student, Maggie May-Nolan, loved secluded places.

The unseasonably warm October evening permitted a rare late season dive. Thirty feet below the gentle swells, Maggie and her dive partner, Lily Tate, hung off the rock wall. Beyond the cones of light from their dive helmets all was an impenetrable black. Maggie held an underwater camera over a patch of coral, positioning it for a perfect shot, while Lily waved a piece of fried chicken in front of a crevice. Odorants from the soggy chicken washed into the crack, rousing the lobster within. The crustacean inched forward from its hiding place, the temptation too great to ignore. Two lobsters already writhed in Lily's mesh dive bag. If she could capture a third, it was time for a seafood feast on the *Jack Rackham*. The lobster's antennae poked curiously outward; then the chelipeds emerged: the pincher and crusher claws; next came the quivering antennules, and finally the cephalothorax. "Just a little further," whispered Lily. She moved the chicken teasingly out of grasp, coaxing the animal out of the crack. The net crept silently behind the lobster's tail, the telson. *Swoosh...* the furious lobster flailed and twisted in the net.

"Dinner time!" Lily declared triumphantly into a speaker inside her dive helmet.

From within her helmet, Maggie said, "Just one more shot." Her camera paused over an orange coral. The tentacles swayed, searching for suspended food particles in the slow current. In a sudden blast of light the pulsating tentacles were forever frozen in a digitized form. Back at the art college, images from the dive camera would be translated into bursts of color on canvas. The marine invertebrates and underwater landscapes by the emerging young artist were attracting attention at local art exhibitions and auctions. The canvases were large and vibrant and resembled, said a Cape Cod art critic, the paintings of Gloria O'Keefe.

Maggie tucked the camera into her dive bag. "I'm so hungry."

"You're always hungry. How can you eat all the time and never gain a pound? That's why I hate you," Lily proclaimed cheerfully. She glanced down to the net to insure that no lobsters had escaped.

Ægir's Curse

As usual, Maggie didn't comment. She seldom did. Besides, Lily was happy to do the talking for the both of them. Maggie's opinions were expressed by a nod or shake of the head, and moods shown by the speed and direction at which cigarette smoke was ejected from her lungs. Fast smoke directed at the sky meant anger or vexation, while a languorous stream directed down toward her feet expressed ennui or contentment.

"Did you hear that?" Maggie asked suddenly.

"Yeah," Lily responded warily. "It sounds like a motorboat."

"Dim your head lamp. Who the hell would be out here at this time of night?"

"Whoever it is, I hope they don't spot the *Jack Rackham*! What if they're pirates, and steal the boat? And kidnap Kyle!"

"Kyle's too old to kidnap, but we'd still be screwed. We'd have to hold onto the rocks until Lindsey motors out to get us, which would mean for hours—"

"By then our legs might be chewed off by sharks!" Lily interrupted anxiously.

"And Lindsey would bitch and moan for the next few eternities about us diving at night." Maggie stopped to listen. "That boat is definitely getting closer. Hug the wall and turn off your light completely."

Lily shut off her helmet's lamp. "Hold my hand, so we don't lose each other in the dark," she said, her voice quavering.

The two divers hovered in the blackness, staring upward. The air tanks and helmets scraped quietly against the rock wall, and bubbles trickled from their regulators in the cool silence. They strained to slow their breathing, lest the bubbles reveal their presence.

The motorboat approached and then stopped directly above them. Lily's grip tightened on Maggie's glove. The engine idled. The boat was silhouetted against a clear, moonlit sky. It appeared to be a rigid hull inflatable with a small outboard engine. It was unusual for such a small boat to be so far out at sea, thought Maggie.

Clink ... clink... clink ...

"Weird," Maggie whispered, "it sounds like hammering."

Clink... clink ...

"I hope they're not tethering their boat to the rock! Let's swim to the other side of the rock, where the *Jack Rackham* is, and make a run for it!"

"*Jack* can't outrun a snail." Maggie paused, listening. "The hammering's stopped."

The two divers hung in black silence. Suddenly they heard it—a large splash.

An oblong object drifted toward them. They gasped into their speakers and their locked hands tightened. The boat revved its engine and sped away. The object continued to drop, teetering back and forth in descent.

"I'm gonna turn on my head lamp," Maggie whispered nervously.

"Me too," Lily whispered back.

"Oh my—my—God!" Maggie stuttered.

A body, shrouded in white linen and rope, was visible only for an instant, before it disappeared into the blackness.

About The Author:
Leah Devlin

Leah Devlin is a marine biologist who grew up in the Washington, DC area. She has undergraduate degrees in English Literature, Biology, and Environmental Science, a MS in Zoology and a PhD in Neurophysiology.

In addition to being a writer of novels, Leah Devlin is a biology professor with research specializations in biological exploration in the Arctic in the early nineteenth century and neuromuscular control in marine invertebrates.

The Bottom Dwellers, Ægir's Curse and *The Bends* comprise a trilogy of mystery-thrillers centered on the scientific village of Woods Hole, Massachusetts, where Leah was a scientist at the Marine Biological Laboratory for over ten summers. The novels center around the brilliant yet disturbed Nobel Laureate, Lindsey Nolan, her colleagues and family.

Leah's second series of thrillers, the Chesapeake Tugboat Murders, are set in the fictional village of River Glen in the upper Chesapeake Bay. The first novel in this series, *The Vital Spark,* a modern pirate yarn, has just been completed. The second novel in this series, *Spider*, is underway.

Leah enjoys outdoor adventures of all kinds: motorcycle journeys along winding back roads, boating, diving, rock-climbing, skiing, and long-distance trekking. When not traveling, she divides her time between Philadelphia and her boat on the Chesapeake.

IF YOU ENJOYED THIS BOOK
Please write a review.
This is important to the author and helps to get the word out to others
Visit

PENMORE PRESS
www.penmorepress.com

All Penmore Press books are available directly through our website, amazon.com, Barnes and Noble and Nook, Sony Reader, Apple iTunes, Kobo books and via leading bookshops across the United States, Canada, the UK, Australia and Europe.

THE BOTTOM DWELLERS

BY

LEAH DEVLIN

Bioengineer and Party Girl...

Lindsey Nolan has it all: inventions paying large dividends, a dream job in the scientific village of Woods Hole, Massachusetts, and a stable of eager playmates. But when Lindsey wakes up in rehab with no memory of how she got there, her world is turned upside down. Her roommate, an HIV-positive teenage prostitute named Maggie, is the most volatile patient on the ward. The facility is plagued by disturbing thefts. And another theft unfolds when her competitor, an engineer named Karen Battersby, discovers and steals Lindsey's astonishing new invention from her Woods Hole lab. Lindsey and Maggie must face the consequences of past transgressions if they hope to deal with present perils and ascend from the desolate world of the Bottom Dwellers.

PENMORE PRESS
www.penmorepress.com

Force 12 in German Bight
by
James Boschert

Considering that oil and gas have been flowing from under the North Sea for the best part of half a century, it is perhaps surprising that more writers have not taken the uncompromising conditions that are experienced in this area – which extends from the north of Scotland to the coasts of Norway and Germany – for the setting of a novel. James Boschert's latest redresses the balance.

The book takes its title from the name of an area regularly referred to in the legendary BBC Shipping Forecast, one which experiences some of the worst weather conditions around the British Isles. It is a fast-paced story which smacks of authenticity in every line. A world of hard men, hard liquor, hard drugs and cold-blooded murder. The reality of the setting and the characters, ex-military men from both sides of the Atlantic, crooked wheeler-dealers, and Danish detectives, male and female, are all in on the action.

This is not story telling akin to a latter day Bulldog Drummond, nor a James Bond, but simply a snortingly good yarn which will jangle the nerve ends, fill your nose with the smell of salt and diesel oil, your ears with the deafening sound of machinery aboard a monster pipe-dredging ship and, above all, make you remember never to underestimate the power of the sea.

–Roger Paine, former Commander, Royal Navy.

PENMORE PRESS
www.penmorepress.com

WILDFIRE IN THE DESERT

BY

BRUNO JAMBOR

Action Adventure, Crime, Mystery,
Southwest History

Highly entertaining, well researched and original:

A Navy veteran returns home to his ancestral land to escape the pace of modern life. His nephew begs him to hide the drugs he is transporting to escape his pursuers.

An astronomer trying to find a replacement for his estranged wife finds solace in his work with the stars.

Police and the drug cartel try to recover the missing shipment, regardless of consequences, ready to sacrifice any opponent.

The antagonists crisscross the desert of Southern Arizona in a chess game where the loser will be eliminated.

Unexpected help comes from a famous missionary who blazed new paths through the same desert three centuries ago.

The climactic resolution will captivate readers of this thriller with deep spiritual undertones.

PENMORE PRESS
www.penmorepress.com

A Gathering of Vultures

Donald Michael Platt

Murder, mutilation, and carrion... in paradise?

"There shall the vultures also be gathered, every one with her mate." -ISAIAH 34:15

Professional ballroom dancers Terri and Rick Hamilton aspire to be world champions. Unfortunately, Terri's recurring back and health problems place that goal well out of reach. They travel to Terri's birthplace, Florianópolis, on the scenic island of Santa Catarina off the coast of Brazil to vacation and visit their best friends and mentors.

Along the picturesque beaches, dead penguins and eviscerated bodies wash up on the shores of paradise, and Antarctic blasts play counterpoint to the tropical storms that rock the island. The scenic wonder is home not only to urubús, a unique sub-species of the black vulture, but also to a clique of mysterious women who offer Terri perfect health and the promise of fame—at a terrible price.

Praise for "A Gathering of Vultures

PENMORE PRESS
www.penmorepress.com

Penmore Press
Challenging, Intriguing, Adventurous, Historical and Imaginative

www.penmorepress.com

Lightning Source UK Ltd.
Milton Keynes UK
UKOW06f0357100616

276022UK00019B/413/P